MW01125105

ANGELS & PATRIOTS

ANGELS & PATRIOTS
BOOK ONE

SONS OF LIBERTY
LEXINGTON AND CONCORD
BUNKER HILL

SALINA B BAKER

Inquiries should be addressed to the Publisher
Culper Press
Austin, Texas

First Printing 2017

This is a work of fiction. However, some characters, dialogue, events, and places are real and some are products of the author's imagination.

Due to the adult content and themes, this book is not intended for persons under the age of 18.

ISBN: 978-0-9987558-0-9

Library of Congress Control Number: 2017958287

Printed in the United States of America

*This book is dedicated in memoriam to
Dr. Joseph Warren and Major John Pitcairn.*

"Our country is in danger, but not to be despaired of. Our enemies are numerous and powerful –but we have many friends. Determine to be free and Heaven and Earth will aid the resolution. On you depend the fortunes of America. You are to decide the important question, on which rest the happiness and liberty of millions yet unborn. Act worthy of yourselves."

—Dr. Joseph Warren

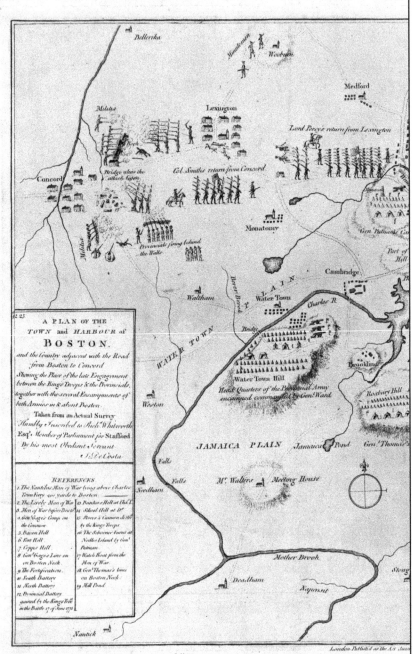

Billerika

Woburn

Medford

Militia

Lexington

Lord Percy's return from Lexington

Concord

Bridge where the attack began

Col. Smiths return from Concord

Militia

Provincials firing behind the Walls

Monatomy

Gen'l Putnams Ca

Part of Hill

Cambridge

Beaver Brook

Waltham

PLAIN

Charles R.

Water Town

WATER TOWN

Bridge

Brooklin

Weston

Water Town Hill
Head Quarters of the Provincial Army
encamped commanded by Gen'l Want

Roxbury Hill

JAMAICA PLAIN

Jamaica Pond

Gen'l Thomas's

Falls

Mr. Walters

Meeting House

Falls

Needham

Deadham

Mother Brook

Napenset

Stough

Nantick

A PLAN OF THE
TOWN and HARBOUR of
BOSTON.

and the Country adjacent with the Road
from Boston to Concord
Shewing the Place of the late Engagement
between the Kings Troops & the Provincials,
together with the several Encampments of
both Armies in & about Boston.

Taken from an Actual Survey
Humbly Inscribed to Rich'd Whitworth
Esq'r Member of Parliament for Stafford
By his most Obedient Servant
J. De Costa.

REFERENCES
1. The Nautilus Man of War lying above Charles
   Town Ferry 400 yards to Boston.
2. The Lively Man of War
3. Men of War before Boston
4. Gen'l Gages Camp on
   the Common
5. Beacon Hill
6. Fort Hill
7. Copps Hill
8. Gen'l Gages Line on
   on Boston Neck
9. The Fortification
10. South Battery
11. North Battery
12. Provincial Battery
    gained by the Kings Troops
    in the Battle 17 of June 1775
13. Bunkers Hill at Cha. T.
14. School Hill at D'o
15. Stores & Cannon destroy'd
    by the Kings Troops
16. The Schooner burnt at
    Noddles Island by Gen'l
    Putnam
17. Watch Boat from the
    Men of War.
18. Gen'l Thomas's lines
    on Boston Neck
19. Mill Pond

London Publish'd as the Act direc

7: 2447

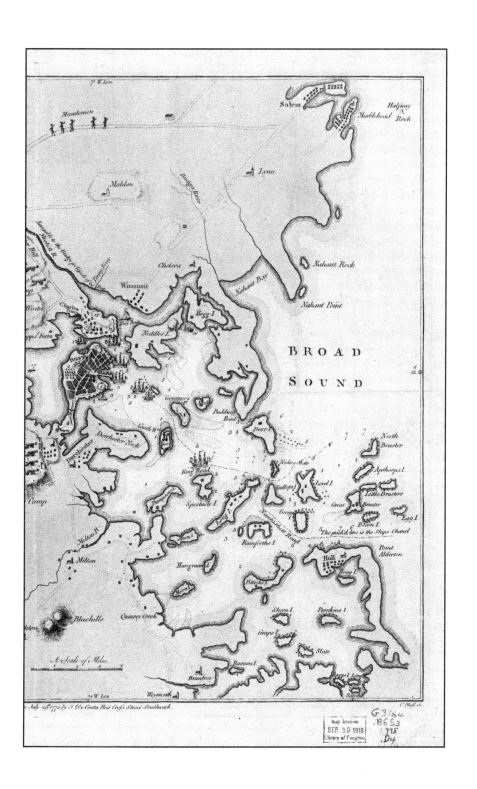

Minutemen

Salem

Halfway
Rock

Marblehead

7¼ W. Lon.

Maldon

Lynn

Bridge River

Chelsea

Winusimit

Nahant Rock

Nahant Bay

Nahant Point

Winter

Charles

Epps's Point

Hogg I.

Neddles I.

B R O A D

S O U N D

Georges's

Padding
Point

Castle W.

Dorchester Neck

Deer

North
Bruster

King Road

Nixes Mate

Apthorps I.

Gallops I.

Lovel I.

Little Brusters

Camp

Dorchester

Milton R.

Tompsons

Spectacle I.

Green I.

Great

Bruster

Egg I.

Bacon I.

Rainsford's I.

Nantasket Road

The prick'd line is the Ships Chanel

Point
Alderton

Milton

Hangman I.

Hull

Hogg I.

Meads I.

Bluehills

Quincey Creek

Shern I.

Pankius I.

Grape

Slate

A Scale of Miles.

Braintree

Racoon I.

Spesay I. Lower

7¼ W. Lon.

Weymouth

C. Hall Sc.

July 20.1775. by J. De Costa Red Cross Street Southwark.

ONE

WEXFORD, IRELAND

MAY 1169

"Get below decks!" Colm Bohannon shouted.

His younger brother, Michael, ignored the order and stubbornly exchanged fire with the Norman soldiers, who stood on the docks and shot flaming arrows at the men aboard the cog *LE' Eithne*. With Michael open to enemy fire, the other six men under Colm's command hesitated to take the order.

Under a waning crescent moon, the Norman lord, Robert Fitzstephen, watched and listened to the Irish die in the water and on board the cogs in the harbor. Fitzstephen's army cut down the Irish soldiers who'd stormed the docks to defend their town and their comrades.

Colm knew his brother was destined to die in an act of defiance. An arrow pierced Michael's left shoulder and knocked him backward. He refused to give in to the pain, and reloaded his bow. A flaming arrow struck him in the heart. His shirt and curly black hair caught fire. He collapsed and hit the cog's railing, causing his spine to snap with a dull crack. His limp body fell overboard and splashed into the dark water.

"MICHAEL!" Patrick Cullen was frantic. He ran to the cog railing and looked into the water. "MICHAEL!"

Brandon O'Flynn ran to the railing beside Patrick and looked over. Horror stained his blue eyes as they searched for Michael's body in the water.

Colm had tried to reach his brother in time, but failed. Enraged, he knew he couldn't let Michael's death render him unable to protect his

1

SALINA B BAKER

other men. He jerked Brandon and Patrick away from the railing, "Get below decks, now!"

Seamus Cullen hooked an arm around Patrick's neck and shouted over the din of screaming men and burning cogs. "Obey Colm's order!"

Patrick struggled with his older brother. "Stop it, Seamus!"

"Everyone but Liam's out of arrows!" Seamus shouted.

"THEY KILLED MICHAEL!" Patrick screamed. He tried to twist his head out of the crook of Seamus' elbow.

Ian Keogh pinned down Patrick's flailing arms and helped Seamus drag Patrick out of harm's way.

Liam Kavangh returned arrow fire and covered Brandon O'Flynn and Fergus Driscoll until they could get below decks. A Norman arrow pierced Liam's right eye and embedded in his brain. He dropped dead on the deck.

Fergus Driscoll, Colm's second in command, returned topside with a handful of javelins. He and Colm made their last stand with the cog's only remaining weapons. There was a loud whoosh when the timbers of the LE' Eithne caught fire. In less than a minute, the burning cog was at the bottom of the harbor. Colm Bohannon and his men were sucked into the water's netherworld.

An ethereal rain of silver crystals spiraled down from the starry night sky and gathered on the streets of Wexford and drifted against buildings. They wet the Irish and Norman soldiers' hair and clothing. They soaked the docks and splashed into the black waters to extinguish the flames.

The blood-rinsed waters of the harbor brightened with silver light—green, purple, yellow, red, and blue flashed within the light.

The soldiers on both sides of the conflict feared they were witnessing the rapture. Some fled the docks in terror. Others dropped to their knees in reverence.

The lights went out. Gossamer draped reapers arrived to escort the souls of the dead to their final destination. With their souls gone, the bodies of Colm Bohannon and his men became vessels for the spirits of eight angels, who were trying to slow the relentless pursuit of demons God had created to kill them for their disobedience.

They had been running from the demons since the time of the Flood of Noah. Some of the angels had created what God had forbidden—the Nephilim—children of human women. Three angels copulated. Five angels tried to stop them. In God's court, they were all found guilty and were banished from Heaven.

2

The angels' commanding archangel was desperate to protect his tiring brotherhood. He hoped taking vessels belonging to the children of man would confuse the demons and slow their pursuit. It did for 145 years.

By 1314, the demons' leader realized what the angels had done. He and his army of demonic spirits went to Scotland to the scene of the Battle of Bannockburn where the Scottish king, Robert the Bruce, clashed with the English king, Edward II.

There were many human vessels to be had as the soldiers died on the battlefield. The demon leader possessed the body of an English knight, Sir Henry de Bohun, a man Robert the Bruce killed in the battle. Wearing their new vessels, Henry and his army continued their ruthless pursuit.

By 1575, the archangel saw that his angels were tiring again, but now, they were killing demon-possessed *living* humans in their desperate attempt to survive. The angels left Ireland for England, in hopes of escaping Great Britain. On April 27, 1584, the archangel, who was now known by his human name, Colm Bohannon, and his angels left England on a ship bound for North America.

It would take Henry two hundred years to find them.

TWO

BURKES GARDEN, VIRGINIA

DECEMBER 1774

Jeremiah Killam relaxed his aim and lowered his musket when he realized it was Colm Bohannon emerging from the dense white oak and hickory forest. Flung over Colm's left shoulder was a doe carcass; its head flopped with each step and left bloody smears on his bearskin coat and in his long wavy brown hair. A long rifle rested against his right shoulder.

Despite the seeds of Manifest Destiny that came across the Atlantic with the first colonists, King George III had issued the Proclamation of 1763, restricting settlement of Great Britain's thirteen colonies to east of the summit line of the Appalachian Mountains. For nearly two centuries, Colm and his brotherhood had been living west of the Proclamation Line in a valley, now called Burkes Garden, Virginia. After their ship arrived in Roanoke Island in July 1584, the brotherhood of angels wandered for six months before they found this sanctuary.

Jeremiah put his musket aside and said, "Liam and Seamus have been lookin' for you."

Colm laid the deer on the blood-stained skinning table in front of Jeremiah's one room cabin. He enjoyed the hunt, but he had no inclination for dressing out game. "Did they say why?"

"They didn't say so don't start worrin' about 'em." Jeremiah slid his skinning knife from the pocket on the thigh of his breeches. He poised the knife over the deer then reconsidered. "Wait a minute. Mkwa brought whiskey, yesterday."

He went inside the cabin and returned with an uncorked jug. He swigged the whiskey then handed the jug to Colm. He set about skinning the doe and said, "Did I tell you what the Continental Congress is askin' us ta do after it met last September in Philadelphia?"

"What's the Continental Congress?" Colm took a swig from the jug.

"Men representin' the colonies called a meetin' in response ta the Brits passin' the Intolerable Acts ta punish Massachusetts for the Boston Tea Party. The patriots dumped 340 crates of tea inta Boston Harbor ta protest the taxes Britain levied on tea. Anyway, they're askin' us ta boycott British goods. War's comin', Colm."

Colm considered Jeremiah with his grizzly beard, disheveled dark-blond hair, deerskin clothing, and unwashed body. He was as tough as any mountain man, but in Colm's opinion, Jeremiah had three important divergent qualities—he could read and write, and had an appealing forty-year-old face under the beard. He was the equivalent of the town crier. Without Jeremiah, those who lived in Burkes Garden would have little knowledge of what was happening in the outside world.

"Why do ya say that?"

Jeremiah began to remove the doe's hooves by slicing the leg off at the knee joint. "The British military's been occupyin' Boston all these years. Now, they've replaced the Royal Governor of Massachusetts, Thomas Hutchinson, with General Thomas Gage. From what I hear, Gage pulled his garrisons from other places like New York, Philadelphia, and Halifax, and formed a British naval presence in Boston. Then, he angered folks by confiscatin' provincial gun powder from some place in Massachusetts."

The angels had not participated in the French and Indian War because Colm had not perceived the war as a demonic threat to his brotherhood or the children of man. But what Jeremiah was describing had the potential to become a full-scale war on the thirteen colonies, and a danger to their sanctuary in Burkes Garden.

Colm thought, *I wonder if Henry suspects we're here, and he's fanning the flames of war to smoke us out of hiding.*

There was a sudden explosion of raucous laughter. Michael Bohannon, Patrick Cullen, and Brandon O'Flynn burst out of the forest and stumbled across the clearing in front of the cabin.

Jeremiah paused and looked up. It was times like these, when the boys were happy and rowdy that he marveled over how much Michael and Patrick looked alike with their medium statures, curly black hair, and feminine facial features.

Michael reached for the whiskey jug.

"Don't," Jeremiah warned.

Michael sneered at Jeremiah, snatched the jug, and raised it to his lips.

"I warned you," Jeremiah growled. He stabbed the tip of his skinning knife into Michael's up turned elbow then jerked the jug from Michael's hand.

"Why'd you do that?" Patrick asked Jeremiah. "He ain't hurtin' nothin'."

Michael looked at his elbow. Blood wet the small tear in the elbow of his bearskin coat. He shrugged and let his arm drop to his side.

Brandon stumbled backward then lurched forward. "That's it, Jeremiah. We're having a go right now!" He weaved an unsteady circle around Jeremiah with upraised fists.

Jeremiah chuckled and said, "One jab, and you're gonna fall forward."

"He's gonna throw up before that," Michael snorted with laughter.

Colm crossed his arms over his chest. The boys were drunk, and it wasn't yet nine o'clock in the morning. He suspected they'd been in the woods most of the night acting like fools and terrorizing the superstitious Shawnee with their drunken noise.

Brandon stopped circling, stumbled, and threw up, which elicited more laughter from Michael and Patrick.

"I told ya!" Michael gloated.

Colm smiled and shook his head. Michael, Patrick, and Brandon occupied twenty-one-year-old vessels, which meant they often displayed twenty-one-year-old behavior.

Boots crunching on the crust of frozen snow announced the arrival of Ian Keogh, Seamus Cullen, and Liam Kavangh. The angels entered the clearing and took note of the situation.

Ian raised an eyebrow when he saw the vomit clinging to Brandon's brown hair.

Brandon swiped at the long dirty locks but only managed to smear vomit onto his cheek.

Michael shoved an elbow into Patrick's side. The boys didn't look at each other, but they snickered.

Seamus threw a disapproving glance at his younger brother, Patrick.

Michael blurted out, "Colm, can me and Patrick and Brandon go to Massachusetts to fight the British?"

Colm narrowed his eyes at Jeremiah. "Did ya fill their heads with this?"

"It wasn't just Jeremiah," Michael said. "The word's all over Garden and Brushy Mountain. I even heard it from Mkwa, Jeremiah's Shawnee woman."

"Leave Mkwa outta this," Jeremiah growled.

"So, ya *did* put this in their heads," Colm said.

"We *need* to go," Patrick said. "Liam thinks Henry suspects we're here and—" Patrick burped. His gray eyes watered. He swallowed the disgusting bile in his throat.

Colm knew that Liam's opinion echoed his own thoughts about Henry.

Twenty years ago, Colm had admitted to Jeremiah why the angels were in Burkes Garden. Jeremiah had listened to Colm's biblical tale without comment. He just glanced up at the sky and said, "Seems like God wou'd know where you're hidin'. Ain't he omnipotent?"

"Aye, but he's not hunting us, Henry is," Colm had replied.

Colm regarded the angels who waited quietly for their archangel to speak, before he said, "If we *do* go to Massachusetts, we go together."

"Fergus is already gone," Seamus announced.

Ian and Liam exchanged glances. Michael, Patrick, and Brandon sobered in surprise.

All eyes shifted to Colm.

Colm tightened his jaw. Silver light flashed in his green eyes.

Seamus stroked his neatly trimmed beard. "Fergus got the notion in his head that he wanted to be a general in a human army. He got impatient waitin' for you to come back from huntin'. He left for Boston this mornin' before daybreak."

Fergus' lofty goal was not a laughing matter. If what they had just spoken of was true, the children of man could be facing a war that would be far worse than they could ever imagine.

Colm considered the possible consequences. He glanced at Ian and Liam. Both angels were solitary wanderers. Ian often left Burkes Garden for months at a time. Liam usually stayed on Garden Mountain, but he, too, strayed for long periods of time.

However, as long as Colm could sense their spirits, he knew they were safe. He kept his fear of losing spiritual contact with Fergus to himself so as not to upset the brotherhood.

The angels left Burkes Garden the next morning bound for Boston.

THREE

YORKTOWN, VIRGINIA

JANUARY 1775

Fergus Driscoll rode on horseback from Burkes Garden to Yorktown, Virginia. The winter snows were merciful outside of Burkes Garden, and the three-week journey was tolerable for both horse and rider. The fortyish looking rider with boyish dimpled cheeks, blue eyes, and blond hair wore dirty travel-worn homespun and deerskin clothing.

In Yorktown, Fergus spoke with a man in the taproom of the Cat and Wheel Tavern, where the conversation and atmosphere was decidedly rebel leaning. The man had a pitcher of flip—an American beverage. Flip was two-thirds strong beer sweetened with molasses and rum topped by a red-hot iron loggerhead that made it foam. It had a burnt, bitter taste and packed a punch.

"The name's Linus Ames." He offered his fat hand to Fergus.

"Fergus Driscoll."

The men shook hands.

Fergus learned that Linus was a widowed forty-two-year old merchant from Salem, Massachusetts.

"My clipper is often in Yorktown delivering goods, therefore, I am often in this tavern," Linus slurred. "I've never seen you. Where are you from?"

Fergus took a long draw from his tankard of rum. To speak of Burkes Garden would endanger his brotherhood. He had not anticipated that being a stranger would invoke so many questions. He now understood why Colm kept a tight rein on his men when it concerned conversing with the children of man. Angels were incapable of lying. Colm, however, had refined the art of remaining silent or brief about his answer when the question didn't suit him.

Fergus took his cue from that, and said, "Virginia."

Linus' fat cheeks quivered with laughter. "This *is* Virginia!"

Fergus frowned.

"Alright, tell me where you are going."

"I'm going to Boston to join the rebel army."

Linus narrowed his eyes and snorted. "Army? You must mean militia."

Fergus did not know the term, but assumed it had to be military-related. He remained silent.

"I know a man who is a member of the Boston militia," Linus said. "His name is William Dawes. He is a tanner." Linus lowered his voice and stepped in closer to Fergus. "He is also a member of the Massachusetts Sons of Liberty."

Fergus didn't know who the Sons of Liberty were, but decided not to speak unless he was asked a direct question.

"Dawes and his father provide temporary safe havens for colonial rebels. I assume that may be of interest to you." Linus took another generous gulp of the flip and spoke freely to the stranger.

He leaned in closer to Fergus. "I must warn you. If you arrive at Dawes' house unexpectedly with no prior introduction, he will be suspicious of you. One does not simply stride into Boston and expect the Sons of Liberty to welcome you without question."

Fergus had no such intentions.

"Spend some money on proper clothing and clean yourself up," Linus advised. "That will not make Dawes less suspicious, but it will provide you with a bit of self-esteem." He eyed Fergus. "You seem unsure of yourself."

Self-esteem was a human trait Fergus didn't understand. He drained his tankard of rum and motioned for the barkeep to bring another. He guessed he would learn what self-esteem was when he bought his new suit of clothes.

❧

The tailor in Yorktown was expensive. Fergus was forced to sell his horse to pay for the finery. He packed his new clothes in a small second-hand leather trunk and purchased a ticket on a schooner bound for Boston.

On the night of January 25, 1775, an apprehensive Fergus stood on William Dawes' doorstep. The new clothes had not provided the self-esteem

9

Linus Ames had promised. He reminded himself why he was there—to become a general in a human army. He made a fist and raised his hand. The door swung open before he could knock. He took a startled step backward.

"Why have you been standing on my doorstep?" William Dawes asked. He shoved the nose of a pistol into Fergus' chest.

Fergus glanced at the pistol.

William Dawes quickly inspected Fergus' fitted dark blue coat, gray silk silver-buttoned waistcoat over a fine white linen shirt, neatly bowed cravat, gray breeches, white silk stockings, and silver-buckled shoes.

"Answer me," William growled. He pressed the muzzle harder against Fergus' chest.

Fergus heard women talking inside the house.

Twenty-nine-year-old William Dawes glanced over his shoulder at his wife, Mehitable, and her female guests, who were engaged in Sunday night Bible study. He stepped outside and closed the door behind him.

"I will not ask you again," William threatened. "What do you want?"

"I want to join the Boston militia. I met a man in Yorktown who said he knew you and that you belonged to the militia here."

William stared at the stranger for a moment. The man's blue eyes were bright and his forehead was smooth, which indicated, to William, there was no underlying deceit. "What is your name?"

"Fergus Driscoll. You *are* William Dawes, aren't you?"

"Yes, I am," He lowered the pistol and set the sear. "I cannot invite you inside and discuss such matters at the moment. However, if you have an inclination to speak of this further, I will be at the Green Dragon Tavern on Union Street tomorrow night."

Fergus offered William a small dimpled smile and nodded. Fergus turned and walked away.

William watched him leave. A sudden chill urged him to join his wife's Bible study group.

The waning gibbous moon did little to illuminate Fergus' way through the sleeping neighborhoods of Boston. The cold arms of a freezing January night gripped him. He realized that he was hungry and exhausted, and he had no idea where he was going to sleep in this unfamiliar town.

As he skirted the southern edge of Boston Common, a small group of rowdy drunken British soldiers stumbled toward him. Fergus thought it would be wise to avoid the soldiers so he went through an alley.

10

Near Faneuil Hall, he saw the warm candlelit windows of an inn. A gust of wind caught the wooden sign that hung over the door and rocked it back and forth. Fergus looked up at the swaying sign and contemplated what he had done.

Although Colm disapproved when any of the angels ventured out of Burkes Garden alone, it was not forbidden. Fergus knew that despite Colm's leniency, he had disobeyed his archangel by leaving his brotherhood to align with the children of man. The punishment for disobedience was a price Fergus was willing to pay.

FOUR

CHARLES TOWN, SOUTH CAROLINA

Ian Keogh separated from his brotherhood after they left Burkes Garden. He followed deer trails and trekked the desolate country eastward across the Appalachian Mountains. When he smelled the salt air of the Atlantic Ocean, he knew he was entering Charles Town, South Carolina.

He had discovered Charles Town for the first time in November 1730, on one of his solitary journeys. Ian was one of the three angels who had created the Nephilim. He had spent the past six hundred years looking for a way to fulfill the human-like lust he'd learned millenniums ago from the Grigori angels, whom his archangel once shepherded. There had to be a way in which he could fulfill his lust and avoid committing the atrocity again.

As he walked the sparse streets on that warm November day more than forty-four years ago, he came upon a churchyard adjoined to a meetinghouse. The mere idea of human suffering and death made his angelic spirit ache.

Ian entered the churchyard, wandered among the graves, and stopped here and there to read the inscriptions on the gravestones.

He heard a feminine voice say, "You appear as a man, but I sense that you are not a man."

Ian looked around. A young couple with tear-stained cheeks stood beside a small grave. He was certain they had not spoken to him.

"Look down," the feminine voice said.

He was standing on a grave. There was a skull with wings carved across the top of the slate gravestone. The epitaph read:

Sidonie Roux Denning
Wife of Asa
Daughter of Lucille and Charles
Died October 7 1730 Aged
33 yrs 16 days

The human body Ian had possessed also died at age thirty-three.

"They laid you to rest only a month ago," he said.

"If I was at rest would I still be here?"

Where's her energy? he thought.

"Look at the meetinghouse."

Her spiritual energy radiated a hologram of her physical form against the backdrop of the sandstone meetinghouse wall.

"Are you Sidonie?"

"Yes, and you are an angel of God. Say your human name."

"Ian Keogh."

"You are beautiful."

"Your spiritual energy should not be on Earth," Ian said. "Why have you not gone to Heaven or Hell?"

"I do not know."

"Did you hide from your reaper?"

"I saw no reaper."

"All human souls are reaped," Ian said. "Unless…an angel didn't feel the struggle your soul endured as your body died."

"Can you help me?" Sidonie asked.

Ian's unseen silver wings rustled in distress. "It's too late to help you."

"Why?"

"An angel must guide a soul to its egress when the body dies. Then, we summon a reaper to take the soul to its final destination."

"How do you decide where a soul goes?"

"God decides. We're his messengers, but that message is relayed only at the moment of death. If I call your reaper now, I will not be able to tell it where you should dwell. You may end up in Hell."

"Do you know God?" she asked.

"Yes."

"Perhaps you can ask him where I should go."

Ian did not intend to tell this lost soul that he was banished from Heaven, and God would never grant him an audience. He left her to face the fate of an Earthbound existence. He had a desire to fulfill, and she was a distraction.

Twenty-one years passed before Ian thought of Sidonie Roux Denning again. He returned to Charles Town to look for her. She was there—a decaying soul dismally haunting the churchyard and the meetinghouse. Her parents were buried beside her body. Only death relieved the grief of losing their daughter to smallpox.

Ian approached her drifting soul and asked, "Do you remember me?"

She neither saw nor heard him.

"Your energy is almost gone. You're dying. I didn't know that was possible," he said.

A bell tolled. A group of young men carrying a bier, on which a coffin rested, entered the churchyard. A minister and a small group of mourners followed them. Ian had seen this ritual before, but he did not understand the purpose. He watched the mourners gather around as the men placed the bier over an empty grave.

The man bearing the pall draped the coffin in blue velvet. Tears wet the man's cheeks, and he said, "Be with God, my daughter."

The woman's grieving mother held the cause of her daughter's death in her arms. The infant mewled and waved her tiny fists. Strands of the new grandmother's black hair came loose from beneath her bonnet. Her pale blue eyes shed tears that soaked her face.

Ian knew who she was and why her daughter died. *The mother looks like Sidonie once looked*, Ian thought. *Perhaps the dead daughter does as well. I wonder if a woman who dies in childbirth can conceive an angel's child if her body is resurrected?*

The men lowered the coffin into the ground and shoveled dirt into the open grave. The dead woman's family sobbed. A sorrowful wind swept through the churchyard and blew dead leaves from the walkways and ruffled the mourners' clothing.

When the mourners were gone, Ian silently unfurled his silver wings. They showered the churchyard with silver crystals. The crystals gathered on gravestones and drifted against the meetinghouse sandstone walls. He summoned the essence of his angelic spirit—his glimmering red aura.

He gathered Sidonie's dying soul beneath his wings and infused it with the red light of his aura. Ian doused his light and released her soul. Charged with his spiritual essence, her luminescent soul flashed like a firefly on a summer's night. Ian's wings fluttered and with ethereal delicacy, they furled into obscurity. He walked to the new grave and looked down.

An angelic spirit can resurrect a dead human body if that spirit takes sanctuary within it. Can a human soul infused with an angel's spirit do the same? Ian wondered.

The shovel used to bury the woman was propped against the meetinghouse wall. When night fell, Ian used the shovel to exhume the dead woman. He pulled her from her coffin and laid her on the ground at his feet.

"I gave you the ability to possess her body," Ian said to Sidonie's soul. "Take it."

Sidonie's glimmering soul wavered above the woman's body, and then the luminescence went out.

Ian carried the woman's body inside the meetinghouse. Representations of angels, etched in the stained glass windows, wore halos above their heads of flowing hair. White gowns draped the angels' bodies, and their small wings looked as if they belonged to birds instead of the sons of God.

A painting, depicting a male image with long curly brown hair and the same bird-like unfurled wings, hung on the wall behind the pulpit. The male wore a breastplate, carried the scales, and brandished a sword as he trampled Lucifer under his sandaled feet. It was the human portrayal of the archangel, Michael.

An angel's spirit was the whole of their existence, and that was something no painting or likeness could depict. Ian supposed his human image was disappointing in contrast to the splendor the children of man bestowed on angels. He had no idea how wrong he was.

He laid the dead woman on the floor in front of the altar and removed her clothing. Sidonie's soul woke when the moon disappeared below the horizon. Ian straddled the naked body her soul possessed. She sighed. He undressed, and then he lay beside her until he could no longer control his lust.

Sidonie did not remember any of those things.

She had no choice but to take work as a kitchen maid when Ian had resurrected her soul and given her another body. Now, she worked in the house next door to the home where she lived with her parents before her body died in 1730. Twenty-four years after the resurrection of her soul, her body had not aged just as Ian's human vessel had not aged because of the eternal energy of an angel's spirit.

Mr. Emory Boddington, Sidonie's employer, knew the man who visited her once or twice a year was an angel. The first time Ian came to visit, Emory entered Sidonie's small bedroom, uninvited and under the pretense he heard strange noises. He saw Ian unfurl his wings and radiate silver and red light as Ian had an orgasm inside Sidonie. What he saw frightened him. He spoke of it to no one, and he did not interfere with Ian's visits.

Ian's visits often left Sidonie feeling lonely and melancholy. She concealed her feelings because she knew Ian did not understand those physical sensations. He never asked her how she felt, what she wanted, or what she needed. He never told her he loved her because an angel's definition of love did not exist in terms of the spoken word or action. It simply was.

Ian's arrival in January surprised her. Winters were harsh on Garden Mountain, and he did not travel during those months. Tonight, his erotically tender lips kissed the back of her neck and made her forget how lonely she would be when he was gone.

She was reminded of that loneliness when he suddenly stopped kissing her, and said, "I'm going to Boston from here. We think Fergus is already on his way there. If war breaks out, Colm wants us fighting with the patriots."

Sidonie turned to look at him and sighed. She had been expecting this for years, but now that the time was here, she was uneasy. The angels fought wars for centuries against the demons that pursued them. This time the angels would be fighting an evil that was also humanistic. She thought it was an evil they would not understand.

"We think the demons' leader, Henry, has stirred up dissent between the British and the colonists in order to draw us out of hiding," Ian said. "If that's true, we have to fight."

She studied Ian's delicate facial features, flawless complexion, and pale blue eyes. *You are so beautiful,* she thought.

"I won't return," he said as if it was an ordinary thing to tell someone.

"You have come to tell me goodbye forever?"

"Yes. If we defeat the demons, we'll leave our human vessels. If the demons win, we're all dead."

She fought off tears. She knew the consequences the angels faced, but to hear him say those things was agony.

Ian resumed kissing her neck and luxuriating in her scent of sweet magnolia.

She pulled away from him and said, "Stop for a moment."

He raised his head, confused. She never told him to stop doing anything.

A lock of his long black hair came loose from its ponytail at the nape of his neck. She swept it away from his face with one dainty forefinger and said, "If you intend to never come back to me, I want you to end my life."

"No," Ian said.

"You resurrected my soul for your pleasure."

"I resurrected your soul to keep you from dying," Ian whispered.

"If you never return, it will be the same as dying."

"What are you saying?"

Tears wet her cheeks.

He never saw her cry. He didn't understand what she was trying to tell him, but he understood tears. The sight of them aroused anguish in his angelic spirit. His wings rustled in distress. He pulled her into his arms.

She laid her head on his chest.

"Did I cause your tears?" he asked.

She nodded into his chest.

"How do I soothe you?"

She looked up into his beautiful face. "Take me with you."

"Why?"

Oh Ian, she thought. *I love you as I would love a human man, and I know you cannot return that kind of love.*

She said, "So I will not suffer without you."

Now, he understood the source of her tears, and that he had the ability to alleviate her dismay. If found out, Ian's archangel would put a stop to it.

FIVE

BOSTON, MASSACHUSETTS

Tensions between the loyalists and the patriots were mounting through-out the colonies, but they were most acute in Massachusetts Bay Colony. For years, the patriots had been planning self-governing strategies and electing men to appointments of leadership and delegation during their formal meetings. The first Provincial Congress of Massachusetts was one such meeting. It was held in the Salem courthouse in October 1774. Three members of the patriotic group the Sons of Liberty—John Hancock, Dr. Joseph Warren, and Samuel Adams—were among the delegates.

Colm, Seamus, and Liam sat drinking rum in the Green Dragon Tavern on Union Street, where the Sons of Liberty often met. They learned from the tavern keeper that the men in the tavern who wore red coats were officers in the British army under the command of the Royal Governor of Massachusetts, General Thomas Gage.

When the angels were not in battle mode, Colm tried not to control what his men did with their leisure time. But he was certain they *should* be in battle mode, which in his opinion, made Fergus a deserter.

I suppose, until we are truly fighting again, the men shou'd decide if Fergus' actions are harmful to us, Colm thought.

"I have been studying faces," Liam said to Colm. His blue eyes darted through the crowded tavern. "The men in this tavern look tense and suspicious."

"Ya mean suspicious of us?"

"No. The tension seems to be between the soldiers in the red coats and everyone else. Our bigger concern is that we do not know if demons are here or if the demon leader still possesses the vessel of Henry du Bohun."

"Liam's concern is worrisome," Seamus said. "We're at a disadvantage."

Colm drained his tankard. "I think Henry might have taken a living human vessel, maybe a British general. He'll possess someone with a high military rank, if he is indeed trying to start a war."

"That's possible?" Seamus asked, surprised. "Ain't no livin' human can contain our spirits. How're they containin' a powerful demon like Henry?"

"Henry is not a son of God as we are," Liam reminded Seamus. "He is not a spirit. He was created from God's wrath."

Seamus was on his fourth tankard of rum. He snorted and said, "That ain't no explanation."

The tavern door swung open and two men entered. One man, judging by his dress, was of high social status. A man sitting at the table nearest the fireplace stood to greet the newcomers.

The angels overheard their conversation. Liam took note of their faces.

"Are they here, Samuel?" one of the men asked.

"Yes, they are, John."

"Good. Are we discussing matters of public safety today?"

Samuel nodded, and a smile played across his lips. "I do not think you need to ask how I condone matters of safety overall."

"I disagree with the rowdy mob mentality among your Sons of Liberty," another man interjected.

"I realize that, John," Samuel said. "Perhaps, someday, I shall be able to convince you to join us. We are, after all, cousins with similar views."

Satisfied that the newcomers were not demons, Liam continued his vigilant watch.

Michael, Patrick, and Brandon bounded through the tavern door in a flurry of laughter and talking.

A sailor leaving the tavern collided with Michael. He shoved Michael and said, "Watch where you're going, you filthy swain."

Michael seized the lapels on the sailor's coat and yelled, "Fucker!" He tightened his grip and dragged the man sideways until he was able to shove him against the wall.

All eyes turned to look at the young man and the sailor.

Brandon and Patrick snickered.

Seamus and Liam started to get to their feet. Colm stopped them with a flash of his green eyes. If he didn't allow Michael to release some of his frustration, he would be too hard to handle.

"Take your hands off me," the sailor warned between clinched teeth. He snaked his hand into the pocket of his coat. Just as he withdrew a knife, Michael knocked his head hard against the wall. The knife dropped from the dazed sailor's hand and skittered across the floor.

Colm said to Seamus, "Go ahead and get Michael off that man. Get ya brother and Brandon away from the door."

Seamus took the order. He nodded at Liam. Both angels got up from the table and approached the boys.

"Let go of him," Seamus ordered Michael.

Michael didn't look at Seamus when he asked, "Are ya going to make me?"

"Don't test me, boy."

All the men in the tavern were on their feet. The four British officers in attendance let their hands fall to the hilt of their sabers.

Colm didn't want to interfere unless absolutely necessary. They were going to have to fall back into rank and file to prepare for the inevitable fight that lay ahead. Fergus Driscoll was his second in command, but with Fergus gone, that command went to Seamus. Colm needed Seamus to establish his authority.

The sailor in Michael's grip regained his senses. He punched Michael in the jaw, then shoved him. "I told you ta take your hands off me!"

Michael staggered backward. Patrick and Brandon jumped the sailor and knocked him to the floor. Patrick shoved his hands into the sailor's chest and pinned him down. Brandon threw his knees on either side of the sailor's flaying legs and tightened his thighs until he had control.

Liam restrained Michael before he could retaliate.

The British officers drew their sabers and ran at Patrick and Brandon.

If the soldiers were only human, their sabers wouldn't kill Patrick and Brandon, but they would severely injure the angels' vessels. Colm jumped up and threw himself between the soldiers and his angels.

The British officers came to a halt and shouted, "Move!"

Liam had Michael sufficiently restrained. Seamus darted at Patrick and Brandon. He got a handful of Patrick's curly black hair, jerked it, and growled, "Stop it!"

Patrick let go of the sailor and groped at Seamus' hands.

Without Patrick's restraint, the sailor sat up and rammed his head into Brandon's stomach. All the air went out of Brandon's lungs. He grunted and fell backward. The sailor got to his feet and ran out of the tavern.

Colm faced the four somewhat hesitant British soldiers as his men calmed themselves.

The basement door opened with an exaggerated groan in the silent tavern. A man stepped through the door, followed by three other men, one of whom was Fergus Driscoll.

Fergus saw Colm and stopped walking.

The angels looked at one another with mild surprise.

Fergus assessed the situation. Colm and the brotherhood had followed him to Boston for good reason. And Michael was misbehaving, as usual.

The other angels cast their eyes at Colm and then at Fergus.

A man with Fergus said, "I gather you are acquainted?"

"Yes, Dr. Warren, we are," Fergus said. His eyes remained on Colm.

The first man, who had emerged from the basement, impatiently asked the men of apparent high social status, "Shall we convene?" He attempted to walk to the tavern's basement door, but a British officer stopped him.

"Mr. Revere."

Paul Revere turned to face the officer. "Captain Langdon."

Captain Langdon favored Colm with a sneer, swept his arm outward, and asked Paul, "Are you, Dr. Warren and Mr. Dawes, acquainted with this— swain?"

William Dawes, the third man with Fergus, looked at Colm. "We are not."

A second British officer, Captain Anthony Farrington, snapped at William. "Captain Langdon was not addressing you! Let Mr. Revere speak for himself."

The three men standing near the fireplace moved toward Dawes and Revere. Samuel said, "Captain Farrington, may I …"

"You may not, Mr. Adams." Captain Farrington pointed his saber at the two men with Samuel Adams. "John Hancock and John Adams, you will also stand down."

"We do not know that man," Paul said, irritated. "However, our new acquaintance appears to know him."

Captain Langdon decided to leave well enough alone. Governor Thomas Gage's policy of leniency did not condone antagonizing Americans. However, Langdon was of the opinion that they needed antagonizing. He said to Captain Farrington, "We are wasting our time. Let's go."

When the captains left the tavern, William Dawes, Paul Revere, Dr. Joseph Warren, Samuel Adams, John Hancock, and John Adams took the stairs to the basement.

Colm waited until they were out of sight before he asked Fergus, "What are ya doing?"

"I've joined the Boston militia and offered my services as a patriot."

Michael and Patrick snickered.

Colm's jaw tightened. His eyes didn't leave his second in command's face.

Fergus shook off his archangel's intimidating stare. "You know as well as I do that a war is looming."

"Those men aren't soldiers."

"There is no American army, either; at least not yet."

"Fergus, are you coming?" William Dawes called from the basement doorway.

"Yes, William," Fergus turned and took a step toward the basement door.

"Dr. Warren wants you to bring your friend," William said.

Fergus walked to the basement door without a word. Colm's choice to come with him was out of his hands. Fergus brushed past William and walked down the steps. Fergus knew Colm had made the choice to join the patriots when he heard William say from the top of the steps, "It is good of you to join us."

"Seamus, take them back to the inn and stay there until I return," Colm said before he entered the basement door. "I don't want any of ya exposed to this until I understand what's happening between Fergus and these men."

Colm heard the angels' wings rustle. The brotherhood was uneasy. "Take the order," Colm said. He watched them leave the tavern. Then, he entered the basement.

William offered his hand to Colm, and said, "I am William Dawes."

Colm considered William's plumpish face, and saw loyalty and discretion in his eyes. He shook William's hand.

Paul frowned, but he stepped forward and said to Colm, "I am Paul Revere. And you are…?"

When Colm didn't respond, Paul said, "Relax, sir. Fergus has told us nothing of you or your comrades. It is clear to me that he served under your command. We are not the enemy."

Colm's green eyes flashed.

Paul brushed off the odd feeling he experienced and continued, "We have taken your friend, Fergus, into our group at face value. There must be an element of trust between us to begin an association—if that is what we are doing." He narrowed his eyes at Colm. "That *is* what we are doing, is it not?"

Dr. Warren remained silent and scrutinized the tall silent stranger.

With an edge of conceit, John Hancock introduced himself to Colm, and then said, "This is Samuel Adams and his cousin, John Adams. We are patriots and have nothing to hide."

"We aren't here to extract secrets from patriots," Colm said as he met John Hancock's stare.

"Then pray tell us, why *are* you here?" John Adams asked.

Colm carefully considered his response. Finally, he said, "My men and I are here to determine if we need to fulfill a mission."

"You and your men?" John Adams asked. "Are you in command of a militia company?"

"No."

"I see that what has brought you and your men to Boston is a matter you take very seriously."

"I am still waiting for you to identify yourself," a skeptical Paul said.

"And if I don't, what of Fergus?" Colm asked. "He's come in earnest to be of service to ya cause."

"You are clearly a military man. I venture to say that Fergus is guilty of desertion and other crimes," Paul said. "Will you punish him if we turn our backs on his offer?"

"That is none of ya business."

Colm glanced at Joseph Warren before he said, "My name is Colm Bohannon, but ya won't believe me when I tell ya who I am or why I'm here."

"We are listening," John Adams said.

"Not today."

"Suppose Fergus has a mind to tell us anyway?" Paul challenged.

"I said not today." Colm threw another glance Joseph Warren's way, and then left the basement without looking at Fergus.

SIX

LONDON, ENGLAND

General Sir Henry Hereford was educated at Eton College. He obtained his first British military commission as an ensign in the 1st Foot Guards in August 1759. While studying abroad in Florence, Italy and Geneva, Switzerland, his regiment sailed without him from the Isle of Wight to the continent to fight in the Seven Years' War.

A year later, he participated at the Battle of Minden, a major battle that prevented a French invasion of Hanover, Germany. After the battle, Henry purchased a captaincy in the 85th Regiment of Foot. By 1762, he had risen to lieutenant colonel. He served as a Member of Parliament from 1772 until he was promoted to major general in 1774—a respected thirty-nine-year-old bachelor.

Unbeknownst to his countrymen, he was possessed by the most powerful demon God had unleashed upon his banished angels. It surrounded itself with minions masquerading as military officers, politicians, soldiers, sailors, and common folk.

Yet with all that power to wield, Henry still did not know the exact location of the banished angels. At one time, as Henry de Bohun, he suspected they were hiding in a place sparsely populated, if populated at all, by the children of man. His lower demons had searched the globe for Colm and his men. They scoured the corners of the Earth from the jungles of the Amazon, to the royal courts of China, to the frozen tundra of the Artic.

Then, thirty years ago, a demon possessing a Shawnee Indian reported spotting Colm Bohannon in the Appalachian Mountains of North America. The demon was unable to pinpoint the location, claiming it had no idea where his possessed Shawnee was actually hunting. However, this apparent blunder was the single named sighting in two hundred years.

Henry clung to the report. He was certain that the archangel would not sit idly by while the colonial children of man were in the clutches of a war demons had a hand in creating. So, Henry caused dissent between the American colonists and the British Crown, until war was at hand. Colm Bohannon would show himself if he was indeed in the Appalachian Mountains.

On this cold January morning in 1775, Henry was at his home in Mayfair, a fashionable and wealthy residential district in the West End of London. His aide-de-camp, Captain Robert Percy, was with him, making final arrangements for Henry's trip to the American colonies.

Robert was not possessed by one of Henry's minions. He had been assigned to General Hereford after the general's previous aide-de-camp mysteriously disappeared. There was not a single clue to indicate what may have happened. The matter had been dismissed summarily; therefore, Robert had no reason to believe that the general may have had a hand in it.

In fact, Robert was pleased with his new assignment. It brought with it a promotion to captain, and an escape from the recent death of his twenty-four-year-old wife, Ann. Her death, from a seizure in November 1774, made Robert a thirty-four-year old widower.

"Mr. Smith has the carriage packed and ready for departure," Robert said to Henry. "We sail tomorrow morning. The colonies are at the apex of turmoil. I understand your desire to be there if there is a rebellion."

You understand nothing about my desire or what I will do to fulfill it, Henry thought. He intended on killing Robert Percy as soon as they arrived in Boston. His second in command was there, awaiting a permanent dead human vessel. Henry looked forward to watching "Robert Percy" commit atrocities. It was a sport Henry played often and with skill.

Ten years ago, the demon leader possessed the British Prime Minister while he issued decrees unpopular with the colonists such as the Sugar Act, the Currency Act, and the Stamp Act. The demon left the Prime Minister's body before it began to rot and stink of the evil within. The King dismissed the Prime Minister in 1765.

The demon once again returned to possess the new Prime Minister. In March 1766, the possessed Prime Minister passed the Declaratory Act, which asserted that the British Parliament had the right to legislate for the American colonies in all cases.

Six years later, Sir Henry Hereford became a Member of Parliament. The demon leader was delighted to possess Henry's handsome rugged vessel.

In March 1774, the British Parliament passed a series of four acts they called the Coercive Acts, which were meant to restore order in Massachusetts and punish Bostonians for their Tea Party. A fifth act, the Quebec Act, allowed Catholics the freedom to worship in Canada. The acts infuriated the colonial patriots. They viewed the acts as a violation of their rights and referred to them as the Intolerable Acts.

Indeed, Captain Robert Percy understood nothing about General Sir Henry Hereford's desire to destroy Colm Bohannon and his brotherhood.

SEVEN

BURKES GARDEN, VIRGINIA

Snow fell all night. The morning sun's weak rays tried and failed to glisten on the pure white landscape. Mkwa removed Jeremiah's hand from between her legs and got out of the rickety bed. It was a miracle the bed was standing. It was a miracle *she* was standing. Jeremiah's drunken sex had seemed to go on for hours.

She gathered her scattered clothing and dressed quickly in rough linen leggings, bearskin leggings, a buckskin dress, and a bearskin coat. She slipped her feet into doe skin moccasins then crossed the small cabin to the fireplace to stoke the fire and stir the pot that contained leftovers from last night's supper.

Mkwa spoke English well because Jeremiah was a patient teacher. He was teaching her to read from the book his mother had used to teach her sons to read.

And Jeremiah had given her a child. Her flows had not come for two months. After ten years with Jeremiah and thirty years of watching another summer come and go, she thought she couldn't bear a child. She had no intention of telling him she was pregnant. He was leaving her today. She was terrified that she would never see him again. He was possibly going to war, and worse, he was going to be among white women. Mkwa had no idea what those women looked like or what they did to bewitch men.

Jeremiah grunted and rolled out from the rickety bed. Bleary-eyed and dizzy, he stumbled over his bearskin coat and fell with a grunt.

Mkwa watched Jeremiah struggle to his feet and sway. With great effort he focused on her face. "Damn it woman, git over here and help me dress. I'm freezin' ta death!"

She lowered her head to hide the smirk on her lips, and went to do as he commanded. He swayed and stumbled while she dressed his muscular body. For love of their creator—The Great Spirit, Our Grandmother—he tempted her carnal desire.

"Eat," she said when he was dressed.

"I cain't." He stumbled outside and threw up.

Mkwa filled a bowl with stew.

Jeremiah stumbled back inside, took the bowl she offered him, and sat on the dirt floor beside her with a plop. "I told Colm I'd meet 'im in Boston by the end of the month. If I don't leave this mornin', I ain't gonna git there in time."

"Who's stoppin' you?"

"I'm gonna miss you, woman."

She covered her trembling lips with her fingertips.

He set his bowl aside and tried to take her in his arms.

She resisted and asked, "Why are you willin' to die for them?"

Jeremiah attempted to memorize her flawless brown face, long shiny black hair, and eyes so dark they seemed like doors to another universe. God help him if he never saw her again. Aside from her, the angels were the only family he had.

"Do you really gotta ask that?" he asked.

She swallowed her tears and shook her head. "Finish eatin'. It's time to git you goin' on your journey."

"Mkwa, I know you ain't had your time in two months."

Her stomach lurched. She couldn't tell him that she was terrified of white women as much as a war with an enemy she couldn't picture. The two things were the same. She couldn't speak. *Don't tell me you'll return to take care of us.*

He saw the wetness in her eyes. He shouldn't have told her he knew she was with child because it made no difference. He was leaving her to bear her burden alone. Nausea rumbled in his stomach. He ran outside into the pristine white snow and vomited.

❧

The brotherhood was lodging at the Greystoke Inn in Boston where Fergus was already staying. The afternoon after their first encounter with the Sons of Liberty, they gathered outside the inn to ensure they were not overheard. The angels' exhaled gossamer wisps of frost as they spoke.

Colm asked, "Do we let the patriots fight for a cause that may be a demonic illusion? Can we become their allies without telling them who we are?"

"Their fight isn't an illusion. Their freedoms are still at stake," Fergus said.

Michael laughed. "Two months ago, ya didn't know what a patriot was. Now, ya know everything about them?"

"Shut your mouth," Fergus warned.

Michael tempted Fergus by saying, "Ya're an idiot."

"Cain you control your mouth for the time bein'?" Patrick asked Michael.

Michael shrugged.

Seamus said, "That don't mean we gotta tell them who we really are."

"I agree," Brandon said. "There's nothing to gain by telling them. We're just patriots, same as them."

"They're gonna see things ain't right with us," Patrick countered. "They're smart men."

Liam shook his head. "It is more than that. The sum of the tension I felt in the tavern is beyond our comprehension."

"We still don't know for sure if Henry's poking the colonists," Michael suggested. "Aren't we going too fast?"

"Maybe," Colm said. However, if they waited for certainty, it could be too late to suit the patriots with the proper armaments. Colm was unsure if there were such weapons, but he knew many of the patriots were deeply religious Christians born of Puritan roots. They were raised to believe in angels and demons and God's wrath. *How would they react if they actually saw those things at work?*

Colm looked at the faces of the loyal angels whose intentions were never heinous. Despite the lustful transgressions Ian, Seamus, and Michael had committed, they were honorable and trustworthy. He didn't want to engage in allied warfare with human men whose characters were anything less. An important reason, in his opinion, the brotherhood should proclaim itself.

There was another pressing matter. "Fergus, ya need to be punished for desertion and revealing ya name to men ya don't know."

Fergus looked at Colm.

"I was going to ask the men for a vote on ya fate, but I've changed my mind. Build trust with the patriots and show them ya strengths. I'm releasing ya from my command."

The angels rustled their wings in distress. With Fergus no longer under Colm's command, their brotherhood would be incomplete.

Fergus had not considered that, in order to achieve his aspiration, he would have to yield to someone's command other than Colm's.

"Can ya arrange a meeting with the men we met in the tavern?" Colm asked Fergus. "I want it to take place as soon as Ian and Jeremiah join us."

"Most of them will be gone before that. Samuel Adams, John Adams, Dr. Joseph Warren, and John Hancock are leaving soon to attend an important meeting in Cambridge. They referred to the meeting as the Provincial Congress."

"Then arrange for just the two of us to meet with them before they leave. I think they'll be more apt to respond to what we got to tell them if they feel they're in control."

"You mean without us overawin' them," Seamus said.

"Aye."

❧

Three days later, on Monday, January 30, Colm and Fergus met Samuel Adams, John Adams, John Hancock, Paul Revere, William Dawes, and Dr. Joseph Warren in the basement of the Green Dragon Tavern.

John Hancock disguised his disquiet by saying, "Get on with it, Mr. Bohannon."

The basement door swung open. Twenty-three-year-old Dr. Samuel Prescott descended the steps. When he saw the strangers in the basement, he stopped.

John Hancock motioned for Samuel to join them. "You have arrived from Concord just in time."

Samuel remained where he was and asked, "In time for what?"

"Shut the basement door," Paul barked. "And get down here."

Samuel Adams repeated what John Hancock had said. "Get on with it, Mr. Bohannon."

The disruption caused by Samuel Prescott's arrival gave Colm time to decide how to begin. He asked, "What are ya opinions on angels?"

"We are not here for a sermon," Samuel Adams said. "We are here to discuss who you and your men are, and your patriotic intentions."

"Answer me," Colm insisted.

Paul took a step toward Colm. "Did you not understand what Samuel said?"

Fergus slid his right hand inside his coat and gripped the hilt of his dagger.

John Adams said, "I would be more than happy to discuss my opinions concerning angels if my cousin wishes to withdraw from the conversation. I can see that you have a point to this Mr. Bohannon, and I am curious enough to play your game."

Joseph Warren saw Colm's jaw tighten.

Ya know this isn't a game, Colm thought.

"I no longer cling to the doctrines of my Puritan ancestors," John Adams said. "I have turned to the more liberal views of the Unitarian Church. But that is not what you have asked Mr. Bohannon. The Puritan minister, Cotton Mather, claimed to have had an angel sighting, yet he and his father had denounced such sightings. They believed they were mischief or a transformation of Satan. Why would the Good Angels of God make themselves visible to man?"

"That, Mr. Adams, isn't an opinion," Colm pointed out.

Dr. Joseph Warren watched Fergus. Fergus did not look at Colm when he spoke. He listened with intensity, and constantly gauged the tension in the room. In contrast to Colm, with his long curly brown hair and pleasant thin face, Fergus was exceedingly handsome. Colm wore homespun. Fergus was dressed like a gentleman.

"No, it is not," John Adams agreed. "Rather it is an old-fashioned opinion that angels have no function except to look over mankind while we sow our own fate with no real guidance from God. That opinion has changed in recent years. There has been a shift in the religious world view. I believe there is the miraculous intercession of a heavenly messenger as we search more actively and optimistically for our ultimate destination in the house of the Lord."

William said, "My wife and I believe that if an angel comes to us after we have prayed, and tells us we shall be among the saved, then it will be so if we listen to the word of God."

"What I found unbelievable about Cotton Mather's sighting was the description of his angel," John Adams noted.

"Well, here is my opinion," Samuel Adams snickered. "Mather was in his cups. He claimed the angel had the features of a man. Angels do not have a gender unless they have possessed some poor hapless slob."

"I have read Mather's description," Paul said with assurance. "The angel wore white and shining garments and a long robe. That seems to be the view most agree with in these times—an angel with a shining face wearing a splendid tiara with wings on his shoulders."

31

"It is what our churches depict in the beauty of their stained-glass windows," William added.

"This is absurd," John Hancock spat.

"If they did walk among us, what do you think they would look like?" William asked Colm.

Colm had no physical form before he took his thirty-two-year-old vessel; therefore, he had no idea what *he* looked like. That concept was difficult for all of the angels. No matter how many times they saw their own reflection, they couldn't connect what they saw to who they were.

Colm said, "What they look like isn't important."

Joseph noted that neither Colm nor Fergus fidgeted. They did not appear to be hatching a lie. He detected uneasiness in their demeanor.

Joseph knew what Colm was about to say was going to sound unbelievable because what Joseph suddenly saw was unbelievable. Moreover, it appeared that he was the only man in the basement who could see it.

"Paul and William, may I have a private word with you outside?" Joseph asked.

Paul gave Joseph a suspicious look. "Why?"

Joseph did not bother to answer. He and William exited through the exterior basement door. Paul shot a doubtful look at Colm, and then followed the others outside.

Samuel Prescott and Samuel Adams walked to the basement window and peered through the small, blistered glass panes.

Paul's voice rose above the others. "Do you know what you are saying, Joseph? They cannot…" The sound of his voice abruptly ceased.

Joseph, Paul, and William returned to the basement. William shut the door and threw the bolt latch. He climbed the stairs to the interior basement door and locked it.

The angels rustled their wings. It was one of several ways they comforted themselves. Most of those habits revealed their celestial being. Therefore, they were often deprived of self-comforting. A human who could hear their wings rustle was extraordinary.

Joseph heard the rustling. He looked at Colm and Fergus as if they had reinforced everything he had just said to Paul and William.

Colm made eye contact with Joseph.

John Hancock's foreboding intensified. "I have had enough of this." He turned to mount the steps.

"No, John…wait," Joseph implored.

John complied.

"What Joseph told Paul and me is so fanciful, that I cannot grasp it," William said. Yet, he felt calm, and strangely soothed.

Samuel Adams frowned and asked, "What did Joseph tell you?"

Fergus willed his eyes to stay focused on whoever was speaking.

Joseph and Colm made eye contact again.

Joseph said, "Mr. Bohannon, if what I am about to say is true, I expect you to demonstrate integrity and tell the truth."

"I will."

"You and your men are angels of God."

John Hancock erupted. "That cannot be, Joseph! You have been led astray!"

Fergus tightened his hand around the hilt of the dagger inside his coat.

"Dr. Warren speaks the truth," Colm said. "We're banished angels. Some of us disobeyed God and created the Nephilim—children of angels and human women. God, in his fury, summoned the Flood of Noah to kill the Nephilim, and he created an army of demons to kill us. The demon who leads them will never stop chasing us until we're dead."

Samuel Prescott turned to flee the basement. Paul seized his arm and said, "No, Samuel!"

"You cannot believe this!" Samuel shouted. He jerked his arm away from Paul's grasp. "War may be upon us, and now we have been cursed by the workings of Satan. This is too much!"

"We aren't doing the work of Satan," Fergus objected.

"What does your sin against God have to do with us?" John asked.

Colm said, "Angels can't sin. Only the children of man can sin."

Samuel Adams challenged Colm. "Prove your claim, sir."

"We can't unless ya truly believe angels are representations of God's work; and even then, I'm not sure ya will be able to see our proof."

"You had better find a way to prove yourselves," John Hancock said indignantly.

"Joseph, they have bewitched you!" Samuel Prescott shouted.

Fergus allowed himself to look at Colm. They conjured memories from a time before three of their brotherhood learned to feel lust; before they were afraid of God's demons; before they took human vessels and the names they had now. They listened to hear the beatific melody of Heaven. It was a tune so ancient that no living thing could recreate the tones and chords.

Without a sound, Colm and Fergus unfurled their divine silver wings. Silver crystals showered upon the patriots' faces and wet their hair. The delicate crystals gathered on the floor and drifted into the corners of the basement.

Colm's imperial wings touched the ceiling, and the delicate plumes brushed Fergus' widespread wings. Together, their wings filled the basement from wall to wall and floor to ceiling.

The patriots drew in a breath and fell to their knees.

Colm evoked his spiritual essence. The basement was washed in the light of his green aura, and something God had bestowed to the archangels—golden radiance. It was part of Colm's primordial being, as ancient as the heavenly music he and Fergus heard. It was his destructive power. The green light and the gold radiance swirled and glided like a flock of birds coming home to roost at sunset.

The purple aura God had granted to the angels entrusted to an archangel's second in command, shined intensely from Fergus' angelic spirit.

The angels furled their wings into obscurity. The dazzling light that constituted a celestial being's essence faded. The silver crystals remained.

"Get to ya feet," Colm said softly. "We aren't to be revered."

The men rose. William ran a hand over his brown hair. He stared at the silver crystals in his palm.

"We offer ourselves to ya cause for freedom," Colm said. "If Henry has provoked the colonies into war to draw us out of hiding, ya must know what ya are up against. It isn't just England's power. It's also a demonic army. Ya have to be prepared for the horrors of war, and the horrors of God's wrath."

John Hancock was trembling. "We cannot prepare our fellow patriots for this. You must have proof that this demon is indeed provoking us. And even if we do have proof, we cannot convince the masses that Satan is behind this revolution."

"Ya aren't listening!" Colm said. "Satan has nothing to do with this! These are God's demons!"

John Adams gathered his wits and said, "Mr. Bohannon, we shall take your council under serious advisement when you find your demon and not before."

Fergus was astonished by the patriots' response.

Colm warned, "We aren't in control! Henry and his demons are. Ya must be prepared to fight them on the same ground as the British army!"

Human skepticism impregnated the basement of the Green Dragon Tavern. There was nothing else Colm could do to convince these unsuspecting men that the threat to them, their families, and their country was not only twofold, but also unknown.

๛

The HMS *Invincible* sailed into Boston Harbor on Tuesday, January 31. She was a seventy-four-gun, third-rate ship of the line of the Royal Navy. General Henry Hereford had commissioned her specifically for his journey across the Atlantic Ocean to Boston. She slipped through the icy winter waters accompanied by the pink and orange globe of the rising sun.

Lieutenant Edward Anson escorted Henry and his aide-de-camp, Captain Robert Percy, above decks just as the ship docked. Lieutenant Anson's responsibility was to see that General Hereford was disembarked and taken to his place of quarter: the home of the Royal Governor of Massachusetts, General Thomas Gage. Henry was looking forward to meeting General Gage, whose reputation preceded him. Gage was drawing criticism for his cautious approach with the colonists.

The 15,000 residents of Boston were beginning their day as Henry's coach rolled through the streets. The city was a small peninsula, only 789 acres wide. It consisted of five hills: Mount Vernon, Beacon Hill, Pemberton Hill, Copp's Hill, and Fort Hill.

These backcountry people have taken great stock in their places of worship, Robert thought, observing the many beautiful churches they passed along their route. He glanced at Henry. Goose bumps rose on Robert's arms. *I must remember to ask the Gages where they worship.*

The Gage's lived in Province House located on Beacon Hill. Although the Gage's brought their own personal servants to Boston, slaves and servants were already part of the household. An elderly black man, Squire, was one of the slaves to whom the Gage's had taken a special liking. They regarded him with the fondness of a family member.

The carriage drew up to Province House. Squire awaited their arrival. He placed a wooden step below the coach door, and then shouted at two sullen adolescent black boys to unload the luggage from the rear of the coach.

Thomas Gage stood on the portico, accompanied by his forty-year-old wife, Margaret.

Robert noticed the faces of many children framed in various windows. Curtains parted then closed as a child was shooed from a window only to reappear in another. Robert found children to be little more than an aggravation, but at that moment, he felt alarm for their safety. He wondered about

35

the source of his unexplained discomfort. Perhaps it was a manifestation of being in an unfamiliar place among people whose loyalty to King George III was questionable.

Henry knew his aide-de-camp was uncomfortable. The demon general smelled fear like a beautiful maiden inhaling the scent of a red rose she had received from a suitor.

"Welcome to Boston," Thomas Gage said, reaching to shake Henry's hand.

Henry reciprocated. "It is an honor to meet you, General Gage." His yellow-green eyes moved to Margaret Gage's face, then traveled the length of her body to the tips of her shoes as he bowed. He had heard that she was considered a beautiful and desirable woman, and what he saw proved that claim to be true.

She was tall and thin with an ample bust line. Her mass of brown hair was piled in seductive curls on the top of her head. Henry imagined running his fingers through those curls.

He wondered what the much older, droopy-eyed, and pot-bellied Thomas Gage had done to win her hand in marriage. Henry surmised their marriage was a union of mutually social benefit as most marriages were. Still, the idea that a comely woman like Margaret Gage could gaze upon her husband's dogged-face with pleasure, while he fucked her, was amusing.

"Mrs. Gage," Henry said with a sweeping smile and a slight bow. "It is a pleasure to meet you."

Margaret tried to be courteous. Instead, she narrowed her eyes and took an unconscious step back.

Henry smirked at her.

Lieutenant Edward Anson was already acquainted with the Gages. He knew very well that Mrs. Gage was a cultured and educated woman. Rude behavior toward an important guest like General Hereford was unthinkable, yet that was what she was doing.

Robert introduced himself. "I am Captain Robert Percy, at your service, General Gage."

Thomas offered Captain Percy an indifferent acknowledgment. He did not like the way the general was looking at Margaret. He was sure he detected lust in the general's strange eyes when he spoke to her. That would explain Margaret's less than hospitable welcome.

However, Thomas could not afford to be anything less than the doting host. *Perhaps, I will speak to Margaret about this later,* he thought, knowing that he would never cajole her for rebuffing a flirtation.

"Please, be my guest," Thomas said. He stood aside so Henry, Robert, and Edward could pass through the door ahead of him.

Margaret led the men to the dining room where the breakfast table was set.

Squire entered the dining room. He pulled a chair out from the dining table, and without looking at Henry, motioned to the chair and said, "Please, sir."

"What is your name?" Henry asked.

The last thing in Heaven and on Earth Squire wanted to do was look into the general's unnatural yellow-green eyes, which would be tantamount to looking into the eyes of Lucifer. But Lucifer had not sent this demon. This demon was spawned from an atrocity committed by angels. Squire knew his Bible and the word of God well.

Henry saw the old man quiver. He licked his lips, smiled and said, "Look at me and speak your name."

Sweat beaded on Squire's forehead.

Margaret bit her tongue to keep from ordering the general to leave Squire alone. Instead, she said, "Squire, please go to the kitchen and assist Wenona with the serving plates. I am sure our guests know how to seat themselves."

The old slave's brown eyes looked at Margaret with loving relief. He nearly threw himself through the door to the kitchen.

General Gage motioned to several pitchers in the middle of the large dining room table. "Gentlemen, please have some cider or rum."

Wenona and two Pokanoket women brought plates, meat pies, muffins, and pastries into the dining room. Squire was notably absent. When the women had breakfast set on the table, the guests served themselves before the Gages.

"General Hereford, Mrs. Gage has planned a party to acquaint you with the officers assigned to Massachusetts. I hope that is agreeable."

"Anything Mrs. Gage does is agreeable with me," Henry sniggered.

Margaret remained silent and studied General Hereford with discretion. His dark hair was ponytailed and quaffed in two neat rows of curls at his temples. His jawline was strong. Stubble was visible on his cheeks, chin, and upper lip although, unknown to her, he had shaved only hours before. His voice was gruff. She would have thought him exceedingly handsome and masculine if not for his unnerving yellow-green eyes.

Lieutenant Edward Anson quietly ate his breakfast. He hoped that he would be relieved of his duty to General Hereford and sent back to the HMS *Invincible*.

EIGHT

BOSTON, MASSACHUSETTS
FEBRUARY 1775

Ian and Sidonie stood on Long Wharf under the steel gray sky of a Massachusetts February afternoon with no plan and no direction for the future. Forty-five years after their first spiritual encounter, they were virtual strangers who neither belonged on Earth nor belonged together.

Sidonie saw Ian do something she should have anticipated. He looked for orange eyes in every face among the shifting throng of British redcoats, sailors, dockworkers, fishermen, peddlers, and civilians.

"Demons?" she whispered.

"I see none." He afforded her a glance but remained vigilant. "Come. Seamus is supposed to meet us."

She was separated from him as they walked the crowded Long Wharf toward Faneuil Hall. Ian was nearly out of sight when she saw a man with a full beard wearing a narrow brimmed black hat. The man looked Ian's human age. He clapped a hand on Ian's shoulder, and then pulled Ian into a brief embrace.

"I've brought Sidonie," Ian said to Seamus Cullen.

Ian realized he could no longer smell Sidonie's scent of sweet magnolia. "Seamus, I've lost her," he said calmly.

"I cain see that. What're you doin' bringin' her here?"

"She cried."

As one of the three fools who had been lustful, Seamus understood the smell that drove a man to distraction, but Ian's actions were unacceptable. Sidonie's body should be buried and her soul escorted to its destiny.

38

"Summon a reaper," Seamus said.

Ian's eyes searched Long Wharf and found Sidonie. He pointed and said, "She's there."

British soldiers had taken notice of her.

"Summon a reaper," Seamus growled.

Ian quickly glared at Seamus and said, "No."

A tall young redcoat moved in so close to Sidonie that his saber scabbard parted the folds of her skirt. She looked at his face and took a step back without moving her eyes. A soldier standing behind her wrapped his arms around her waist.

Ian pushed his way through the crowd toward Sidonie. His red aura, which was normally invisible to humans, but visible to demons, shimmered brightly. It announced his whereabouts to demons if they were on or around the wharf.

Seamus grumbled under his breath and followed Ian. His purple aura was no less visible.

Ian barged through the circle of British soldiers who surrounded Sidonie and took her hand. He turned to lead her out of her predicament when the steel blade of a saber slipped across the lapel of Ian's coat. Its sharp tip came to rest under his cleft chin.

"You are not thinking about taking her with you, are you, Yankee?" the tall young soldier smirked.

Ian's eyes traced the saber to its hilt, which was gripped in the soldier's white-gloved hand.

"I wager he is fucking his sister," the soldier who had Sidonie by the waist said. He smiled at the thought, and then took her by the chin. "Look at them, James. They look alike!"

James, the young soldier holding the saber, pressed the saber's tip harder under Ian's chin. "Is Charles right? Are you fucking your sister?"

Ian narrowed his eyes at his captor in reply.

Seamus reached the soldiers surrounding Sidonie. He saw no orange eyes among them.

"I wager I can make him squirm," Charles said. He moved his hand from her chin and squeezed her breasts. "She feels nice and ripe. Does that fire your jealousy, Yankee?"

The people, who gathered to watch, murmured among themselves. A British soldier was molesting an American. The act reminded them of what had started the Boston Massacre.

Sidonie's eyes remained on the soldier holding the saber to Ian's chin.

Ian reached up and batted away the saber, and then tugged on Sidonie's hand.

Charles tightened his arm around Sidonie's waist and pulled her so close to his body that she felt his erection through the skirts that draped her buttocks. He continued to squeeze her breasts. "Answer me, Yankee!"

James flipped the tip of the saber back up under Ian's chin. "You had better answer Charles or I'm going to shove my saber through your chin and out the back of your head. Your brains will be smeared all over the blade." He exhaled a throaty laugh. "Then, we are going to kill your filthy swain friend with the hat."

Ian glanced at Seamus. He heard Seamus' wings rustle.

Sidonie said, "He does not—"

"—quiet, woman, or I'll shove my bloody saber up your cunt after I kill your incestuous brother!"

Rage slammed Ian. He struggled to keep his silver wings furled when he seized the saber's blade and jerked the weapon from James' white-gloved hand. Blood flowed from Ian's sliced palm and spattered the stunned soldiers when Ian flipped the saber and pressed the blade against James' stomach.

"Tell the man touching Sidonie to let go of her," Ian said to James. "Or I'll shove this saber through your body and sever your spine."

Ian's red aura flickered with rage, and James saw it. His eyes watered, and snot ran from his nose and rolled down his lips and chin. A thick white glob dropped onto the saber blade.

Charles let go of Sidonie.

Ian noted Seamus' position among the humans. Seamus was beside Sidonie, and he was uncompromised. Ian flung the saber over James' head into the waters of Boston Harbor.

Ian and Sidonie clasped hands without looking at one another.

Seamus pulled a flintlock pistol from his coat pocket and released the sear. "Walk," he said.

When they reached Faneuil Hall, Seamus set the sear on his pistol and stashed the weapon in his coat pocket. Ian stopped and looked for orange eyes in the gathering darkness.

"Colm's expecting us. We're lodgin' at the Greystoke Inn," Seamus said.

Ian had not considered what his responsibilities toward Sidonie's well-being entailed. Providing shelter for others was a strategy innate to Colm, and taught to the angels who served as seconds to archangels—Fergus Driscoll and Seamus Cullen.

Sidonie sacrificed sustenance, knowing Ian would be incapable of providing food. But starving was better than never seeing his beautiful face again, or experiencing the storm of his silver crystals as they showered from his wings when he had an orgasm, or feeling the powerful softness of his hands pulling her close to his body.

Ian tightened his bleeding hand around Sidonie's delicately boned fingers. His physical body was weary, and he longed to lay down with her.

"She's staying with me," Ian said to Seamus.

"No, she ain't. Colm'll send her back to Charles Town without another thought."

"I have money."

"That don't matter. Like I asked you before, what were you thinkin' bringin' her here? And don't say she cried."

"She was going to suffer if I left her behind," Ian said. He hugged her close. He suddenly had an erection.

"You've always been the best of us at comfortin' humans, but this ain't right," Seamus said.

They walked to the Greystoke Inn through the quiet night of British-occupied Boston.

࿂

With Ian's return, Colm wanted to take the next steps toward an alliance with the patriots. For now, Colm's actions were stalled because John Adams, John Hancock, Dr. Joseph Warren, Samuel Adams, and Fergus, were in Cambridge attending the adjournment of the second Provincial Congress of Massachusetts. The agenda was set to address their entitlement to freedom, and relief from tyranny.

They had asked for action from General Thomas Gage to concert some adequate remedy to prevent the abuse of civilians by the military and provide for public safety. The Congress' messages were printed in the Boston newspapers. Gage's exasperated response was that no one, except avowed enemies of the Crown, was in danger. Therefore, nothing was to be done.

The patriots not only held congressional meetings in an effort to prepare for what lay ahead, they also wrote missives speaking of the freedom they believed in. The loyalists had plenty to say in response. These missives were published in various newspapers in the Boston area and usually under a Latin pen name. Although John Adams was not a member of the Sons of Liberty (he disapproved of their thug-like tactics), he and his much older cousin, Samuel Adams, were particularly active with a quill.

The patriots' meetings gave Colm time to assess the angels' new surroundings and take steps to draw out Henry, if indeed, he was in Boston.

On a late and snowy afternoon in the first week of February, the angels gathered around the fire pit behind the Greystoke Inn. A few inn guests drifted across the backyard, but none regarded the angel men with suspicion or curiosity.

From the kitchen window, the innkeeper's daughter, Jane Greystoke, watched Brandon O'Flynn, who was among the men around the fire pit. He was tall, and his blue eyes captivated her seventeen-year-old desire. She had been watching him since he and his friends had checked into the inn. She forced a neutral expression on her face and walked outside to offer refreshment to them.

"Sir? Rum or ale?" Jane asked Brandon.

"Rum," Brandon said. He avoided looking at her.

"I cannot pour your rum without a cup to pour it in."

Brandon looked at the cup in his hand, and then held it out to Jane.

She studied his high forehead and broad chest. The pitcher of rum in her hand remained poised to pour.

Brandon had no practical experience with women. He tried to brush away the discomfort he felt under Jane's scrutiny, and in doing so, their eyes met.

"Are you gonna pour the rum?" he asked her.

Michael elbowed Patrick and in a loud whisper said, "Do ya think he's gonna kiss her?"

"Be quiet," Patrick hissed.

Michael's comment embarrassed Jane. She poured Brandon's rum, and then quickly offered refreshment to the others. When Michael's cup was the only one left to fill, she returned to Brandon and said, "I will not serve your rude friend without his apology for suggesting that I would allow you, or any other man, to kiss me."

Brandon saw the smirk on Michael's pouty lips. He had no idea what he was supposed to say to Michael or the girl. He looked to Ian for guidance, but Ian merely raised an eyebrow.

Jane frowned and returned to the kitchen.

"Why do you gotta be uncouth?" Brandon asked Michael.

Michael shrugged. "If ya weren't scared of girls, I wouldn't have to say anything."

"Shut ya mouth, Michael," Colm said. "It's time to kill ya habit of belittling others. We're facing a serious war, and I'm not standing for it anymore."

"I was just…"

Colm killed Michael's excuse with a terse look. *His cockiness is going to get him killed*, Colm thought. *How do I get him to stop?*

"Jeremiah should be here in the next few days," Colm said. "When he gets here, I'll send him to find weapons. In the meantime, Patrick, find out what ya can about the Boston militia and the Sons of Liberty. Michael and Brandon, walk every inch of Boston so ya can understand our surroundings. Ian, ya are going to get us a place to live."

"I don't know how to do that," Ian protested.

Colm flashed his eyes at Ian.

Ian backed down.

"Liam," Colm said, "ya are the best of us to write a missive to draw Henry's attention. Deliver it to John Adams. John can get it published in the local newspapers. If Henry's here, he'll read the newspapers. I want him to know we're here, and we aren't afraid."

Liam nodded.

"Seamus," Colm continued, "go to Long Wharf and ask about ships that've arrived from England in the past month with British officers on board. See if ya can find out where the officers are quartered."

"What about Fergus?" Seamus asked.

"He's not under my command anymore."

"I mean, where's he gonna live?"

"He's on his own."

"That don't seem right," Patrick said. "He's one of us, and you're just lettin' him fend for himself?"

"What do ya suggest we do, Patrick?" Colm asked.

Patrick studied the toes of his boots and shrugged.

"He belongs with us," Brandon said.

"Aye, he does," Colm agreed. "Why don't ya ask him what he wants to do when he gets back from Cambridge?"

"I intended on talking to Fergus," Liam said. "I do not think it has really come upon him that he will not be fighting with us. I do not think he has had time to feel separated from us."

43

Michael rolled his eyes. "That's horseshit!"

"I agree with Michael," Ian said. "Fergus left Burkes Garden without looking back. He doesn't care."

Colm knew letting Fergus go was hard on all of them. "Go to bed," he said. "We'll get started at dawn."

The angels took the order.

Ian remained and stared into the fire pit. The dying flames looked like demonic eyes that dared him to tell Colm that Sidonie was lodged at the inn.

"Ian, go to bed," Colm said.

Ian looked at Colm's somber face.

"Colm, I…"

Colm tightened his jaw.

Ian dropped his gaze to the snow-covered ground. He was sharing a room with Liam and Seamus, and he had not spent one night with Sidonie since they arrived in Boston for fear that Liam would notice his absence. Tonight, Ian could hear her crying in her room. He had not alleviated her suffering, and he had disobeyed his archangel. Colm had never spoken the order, but Ian knew what he was doing was considered disobedient.

Colm waited silently for Ian to go to bed.

Sometime after midnight, when the white sheet of clouds was pulled back to reveal the moon, Ian left his room and went to Sidonie. She lay on her side curled into a tight naked ball and burrowed deep beneath the pile of blankets on her bed.

Her skin was cold when Ian slipped his bare body against hers. He touched her cheek and traced the wetness to her linen pillowcase. His erection brushed her soft belly. He rolled her onto her back. She spread her thin tight legs and wrapped her arms around his back. Her fingers pressed against the hard muscles there.

Ian kissed her forehead, tear-stained cheeks, and then her lips. Her fingers moved to untie the ribbon that held his long straight black hair in a ponytail at the nape of his neck. His hair draped over her face. She pushed it back so she could return his hungry kisses. He eased his erection inside her. His red aura burst forth warm and strong, and he moaned. His wings unfurled and showered her with his lust.

అ

When the sun struggled to cast its golden rays upon the town of Boston, Ian and Sidonie woke warm, naked, and wet from the silver crystals of an angel's orgasm. But Ian was incapable of basking in the beautiful luxury of a morning countless humans wished for. His duty to his brotherhood called.

"I have to go," Ian said. He got out of bed and pulled on his shirt. "I'm supposed to rent a place for us to live." He fetched his waistcoat, stockings, and breeches from the drafty floorboards, and finished dressing in a rush.

Sidonie got up. She shivered in the cold room as she pulled on her dressing robe.

Ian shrugged into his coat. "I'm late. Colm was expecting me to muster at dawn."

Sidonie pulled his hair into a ponytail at the nape of his neck and secured it with the ribbon she removed last night. She kissed his neck.

Ian moved toward the door. He paused, and then turned around. "I'm supposed to kiss her before I leave," he said to himself.

She smiled, and breathed a laugh.

He pulled her into his arms and studied her face. His lust was quiet and satisfied. "How should I kiss you when I don't desire sex from you?" he asked.

Ian asked her that question each time he left Charles Town to return to Garden Mountain. Each time, she slipped her hand into his crotch and stroked him until he understood how to kiss her. On that morning, Sidonie decided that it was time he learned how to express love. She had no idea if he was capable of learning that lesson, but she decided to begin teaching it anyway.

She kissed him softly.

~

The confrontation on Long Wharf had familiarized Seamus with the overall atmosphere of the waterfront. The friction between the British soldiers and the provincial fishermen, merchants, sailors, and dockworkers was hot enough to ignite a fire. He was ready to be in that cauldron.

Long Wharf was not the only dock serving Boston Harbor, but it was the largest. Clipper ships, schooners, and frigates with energetic names like *Lively* and *Invincible*, preceded by the letters HMS, were moored at the docks while others lay at anchor in the harbor. Some of those ships belonged to or were commissioned by colonial merchants such as John Hancock—men who had financiers in England. Because of the Continental Congress' plea to boycott British goods, many ships tugged at their moors loaded with tea, fine fabrics, furniture, china, refined sugar, and food stuffs.

Seamus walked through the crowds on the bustling wharf to dock 10 where the schooner HMS *Draco* and the warship HMS *Invincible* rocked on rough waters. He knew the only way to obtain useful information was to work on the docks or on a ship.

As he approached the HMS *Draco*, a young British soldier blocked his way and demanded, "What is your business here?"

"I'm lookin' for work."

The young soldier noted Seamus' gray eyes, gray-brown hair and neat beard, then examined him closer. *This man's rough clothes are dirty and disgusting. I have heard stories about men who live like animals with Indian heathens. This man is one of them. I am certain of it.*

"You do not look like the type to possess the skills required to work onboard a ship. What experience do you have?"

A flash of a memory of working the sails on an Irish cog crossed Seamus' mind. He blinked. The memory was gone.

"Answer me, bumpkin."

Seamus removed his beaver-hair felt hat and went about "shaping" the narrowed edged brim—an attempt to keep his hands busy and avoid pummeling the source of his anger.

He said, "Boy, unless you're doin' the hirin', shut your mouth."

Several other soldiers gathered around Seamus.

"If you know whose hirin', point me in the right direction. If you don't, then get outta my way."

The soldier pointed at the HMS *Invincible*. "There is a help wanted advertisement posted in the Boston Gazette."

Seamus replaced his hat and walked to the lowered gangplank of the *Invincible.*

A sullen sailor wearing a bicorn hat with a white cockade and the blue-coated uniform of a low ranking British naval officer stood at the foot of the gangplank. He'd seen the exchange. "What position have you come for?"

"I can do anythin'."

The sailor yelled, "Mr. Rickard! A man's here in response to your ad!"

A man emerged from the interior of the ship and walked the gangplank to the dock. His attire was the same as the sailor's, except the cockade on his bicorn hat was green. There was one other notable thing that differentiated Rickard from the other sailor—Rickard was drunk.

Seamus was given a job on the HMS *Invincible* with no clear understanding of what that job entailed. No matter, he was there for British information and gossip.

NINE

Liam sat at the cramped writing desk in a corner of the Greystoke Inn's taproom. It was no mystery why the desk was there. Quill and paper were powerful weapons.

He placed an inkhorn, pounce pot, and a single sheet of unsized paper on the desktop. Then, he extracted a quill and pen-knife from his coat pocket. After sharpening the quill, Liam sprinkled pounce on the paper, then bent to write the missive to draw out Henry.

> *I am a stranger in Boston, but I feel compelled to speak of the Brotherhood of which I am a part. These men sometimes speak like ancient angels who have seen and endured much. They are aware of Heinous beings that move quietly through the dark in the guise of men. Yet they stand firm to face what is to come. I am told of a man named Henry who stands well with the Enemy of freedom.*
>
> *He hath given signaled proofs of his attachment to the depths of darkness where he would have this Brotherhood chained for eternity. This man claims that he is dispatched in the name of God and his mission is blessed by the same to fetter those who beg for liberty in thought and action.*
>
> *As a part of this Brotherhood, I stand as a Beholder within an inner circle made up of brave links of a chain. Deceit has been forfeited in reverence to the truth. And, so I say to the man named Henry, come forth if you dare to challenge the Preceptors of Mysteries not easily explainable or known to lesser men. We await your arrival.*

Liam gently vibrated the sheet of paper to remove the loose pounce. He reread his writing, and then folded the paper. As he slipped the missive into the pocket of his coat, he heard a beautiful voice ask, "Mr. Kavangh?"

He looked up. There stood a young, petite brunette with a look of expectation.

"How do you know my name?"

"You are a recent acquaintance of my husband, John Adams. He described you as blue-eyed, dark-headed, and mid-thirties in age. My name is Abigail Adams."

Liam glanced at the men drinking and eating at the tavern's tables. "Is it wise for you to be here unescorted?"

"I am not unescorted. My brother, William, is here. May we speak privately?"

"Is your brother not curious about what you are up to?"

Abigail laughed. "His curiosity is reserved for what is in his cup."

"We appear to have privacy here." Liam beheld her modest confidence. *Her husband must have discussed the appearance of angels with her.*

"With all that is happening between the loyalists and the patriots and Great Britain, the sudden arrival of beings claiming to be angels is very unsettling."

Liam listened to her honest, intelligent words without responding.

"You do not seem surprised," she said.

"How much did your husband tell you?"

"I suppose he told me everything he knows about your…I believe you call it a brotherhood."

"Then you know you *should* be unsettled by our arrival."

"I believe what John told me, and I want to help you."

Her courage and faith confounded Liam. She was behaving as if the appearance of angels was an ordinary event. However, her lack of fear concerned him.

"Mrs. Adams…"

"Please. It is Abigail."

"Abigail, did John tell you what is pursuing us?"

She glanced at her brother, who was absorbed in the contents of his cup and the conversation he was carrying on with another who also enjoyed his drink. Her brown eyes darted back to Liam. She whispered, "Demons."

"Your husband did not believe Colm and Fergus when they spoke of the demon, Henry."

"John *did* believe them, but he cannot pass that information on to others without proof. Even with proof, there will be those who will call him a heretic or accuse him of something worse."

Her soft-spoken manner reminds me of someone I once knew, Liam thought. *Who?* He studied her delicate facial features for a moment before he said, "It is one thing to involve John in our struggle. It is quite another to directly involve you and your children."

"My father is a minister. Perhaps, he can do something to return these demons to hell."

"These demons are *not* from Hell. They were sent by God."

"You are wrong! The author of our being does not kill us!" She stared into his handsome face, waiting for him to tell her that he was wrong.

Liam's eyes darted around the tavern to ensure no one was eavesdropping. He looked at Abigail. "John did not tell you that the demons chasing us are God's creations, did he?"

She shook her head. Her heart pounded as she absorbed Liam's sudden declaration.

"Abigail, you must stay away from us." The words stung Liam's spirit. He wanted nothing more than to keep her close now that he knew she existed.

"Mr. Kavangh…"

"It is Liam."

She searched his eyes for a glimpse of his angelic spirit. "Liam, when John returns from Cambridge, would you call on me at my home?"

Liam frowned. "Abigail, I told you that you must stay away from us."

A small smile turned up the corners of her mouth and creased the smooth skin beneath her eyes. "I do not think that will be possible." Her eyes dropped to the pocket of his coat. "I waited to approach you until after you finished writing your letter. It was evident that the words flowed from your mind to the paper effortlessly. John is also a skilled writer."

The missive had slipped Liam's mind. He patted his pocket to verify that it was still there. "As a matter-of-fact, I am going to Cambridge to deliver this to your husband and ask that he have it posted in the local newspapers."

Abigail breathed a soft laugh. "Well, then, I consider the circumstances under which we met to be fate. Would you agree?"

Liam shook his head. "Angels do not believe in fate."

Colm sent Ian to meet with one of John Adams' colleagues. The lawyer was handling the rental of a farm southwest of Boston in Roxbury. The saltbox farmhouse was large enough to house eight men.

Colm heard that Joseph Warren had not left for the Provincial Congress. Now, he walked the streets of Boston and past Beacon Hill to Hanover Street where Joseph lived and worked in a rented house with his four children, their nanny, and his apprentice in medicine, twenty-two-year-old William Eustis.

"Colm!" Joseph said, surprised. "Please, come in."

Joseph led Colm to his study and closed the door. Joseph motioned to an easy chair and said, "Please, sit down."

Colm sat down and leaned back in the chair.

"What can I do for you?" He sat in the chair opposite Colm.

"I need to know why ya knew we were angels before me and Fergus revealed ourselves."

"It was obvious that was why you asked about angels."

"I'm asking for the truth."

Lines formed on Joseph's brow, and his handsome face appeared tense. He looked at Colm for a long time before the lines disappeared and his face relaxed. "Your emanation was bright and intense. I saw the green aura surrounding you before you displayed your wings. I have no explanation as to why. It just appeared to me."

"It didn't frighten ya?"

Joseph smiled. "You are not frightening. And you are not what I expected an angel to look like. It was rather a nice surprise."

Colm smiled, then became serious. "We're staying, Joseph. Ian's renting a farm for us in Roxbury. We want to join the Boston militia, but Mr. Revere doesn't seem amiable toward us, and I can't have him undermining our intentions."

"Paul can sometimes appear harsh. I will speak to him before I leave for Cambridge."

"Are ya going to the Provincial Congress?"

"Yes, but my eldest daughter, Elizabeth, is ill. She pleaded with me to stay home until she feels better. It is difficult to turn down the wishes of a nine-year-old girl." He paused, then said, "I must tell you that our Provincial Congress meetings are illegal. We move the meeting location often."

"Are ya organizing an army?"

"Not specifically. We are keeping an eye toward defense and self-governing. Would you consider attending the congress as my guest? I believe a firsthand account of our process would be beneficial."

"I'm not a politician."

"Neither am I."

"I'm not well-spoken or inclined to fair thinking."

"I disagree."

"Ya don't know me." But Colm knew in his angelic heart that Joseph Warren *did* know something about him because Joseph had seen his green aura.

The two men regarded one another for a moment before Joseph spoke, "Then, perhaps, we should get to know one another better."

Colm didn't know how to respond. If he went to Cambridge with Joseph, command would fall to Seamus.

Can Seamus handle Michael for a week? Colm wondered. *We're alone in a strange and hostile place, but if I don't go with Joseph and become involved in the patriots' politics, I won't understand how to protect them or my men from Henry.*

Joseph could sense Colm's struggle, but had no idea what it entailed.

"I'll go," Colm said. "When do ya expect to leave?"

"Monday morning."

Joseph leaned forward and asked, hesitantly, "Whose body do you possess?"

Colm gave the question some thought. "Eight men died fighting as brothers-in-arms in Ireland one night six hundred years ago. We took their human vessels to confuse Henry and the demons. My vessel and Seamus' vessel had younger brothers among the dead. For some reason, we can't let go of the need to overprotect them."

"That need is a palimpsest. Traces of what used to be, showing through what exists now. Which one is your younger brother?"

"Michael."

"And Seamus'?"

"Patrick."

"Then I shall take extra care to look after them," Joseph said, his conscience relieved.

Aside from Jeremiah Killam, his human friend on Garden Mountain, this was the first time in his existence that Colm felt something more than angelic duty for a human being.

On Colm's order, Brandon and Michael walked the streets near Boston Common, trying to understand their surroundings.

"This is stupid," Michael said. A cold wind pulled strands of hair from his ponytail. The black curls blew in circles against his red cheeks. "We got no idea where we are. Let's stop at a tavern."

"That's a bad idea," Brandon said. "If I'm drunk, I'll never figure out where we are."

They walked past Boston Common and on to Beacon Hill. There were more British soldiers on the streets in the well-to-do neighborhood than the angels had encountered all day. Many of the soldiers stood guard duty in front of the two and three-storied homes. They shivered in the cold wind and eyed Brandon and Michael with suspicion.

A particular group of soldiers unnerved Brandon. They were gathered in the front yard of a stately Georgian home with third-story dormer windows and a chimney on each end of the house. Gray smoke snaked from the chimneys and blended with the bleak gray February sky.

Brandon said, "We shou'd move quickly through Beacon Hill."

Michael pointed at a building with a sign above the door that read *Wilton's Inn*. "Let's stop in that tavern for a hearth and a draught."

"I don't think we shou'd be in a tavern in this part of town. We won't fit in."

"Ya starting to sound like Patrick."

"Patrick's got sense, unlike you."

"I know ya are as cold as I am. Come on."

The tavern in Wilton's Inn was crowded with British soldiers and well-groomed men dressed in finery. Michael and Brandon wore homespun and deerskin clothing and were obviously unkempt. They stood near the crackling fireplace where they hoped they were less conspicuous.

A skinny middle-aged black woman, with a look of predominance, purposefully approached the boys.

"We're in trouble," Brandon said. He tilted his head toward the woman. "She's gonna make us leave."

As she got closer, the expression on her face changed. She raised a hand to her throat, and slowed her pace. When she reached the boys, her eyes widened and her mouth dropped open. She touched her chest above her tiny breasts and took a deep breath. "I...cain...see...your...aura."

She moved her hand away from her chest and reached for Michael. He took a step back to avoid her touch. Her hand trembled. "Your...aura is blue. Youse an angel of God."

Michael was afraid to look away lest she touch him. He gave Brandon a sideways glance and said, "We shou'd go."

Brandon nodded but his eyes never left the woman.

She turned her attention to Brandon. "Your aura is…is…yellow. Oh Lord! Obadiah ain't going to believe this!"

Michael and Brandon ran to the tavern's front door. Just as they reached the threshold, the innkeeper and two British officers intercepted them.

"You will not be leaving," the innkeeper snarled. Contempt flamed in his orange eyes.

Brandon saw the black woman watching them. With rising dread, he saw her eyes change from brown to orange. She mocked him with a wink.

Michael realized why Brandon had a look of dread on his face. They had encountered demons without Colm to protect them.

"Lieutenant Oldman, seize these men," the innkeeper seethed to one of the British officers.

Lieutenant Oldman and the other officer, Lieutenant Shoemaker leveled pistols at the angels.

Michael sneered despite the nauseous fear in his spirit. He knew the orange-eyed demons meant that Henry was in Boston. The soldiers' eyes were blue, but it was no consolation.

Brandon slid his hand beneath his coat and reached for the pistol wedged between the waist of his breeches and the small of his back. Lieutenant Shoemaker shoved the muzzle of his pistol under Brandon's chin and said, "If you remove your hand, and you are holding a weapon, you are dead."

"Unless you're a demon, that shot won't kill me," Brandon scoffed despite his terror. "And if you're a demon, and I stab both your eyes out, you're dead."

"Do not call me a demon again!" Lieutenant Shoemaker warned. He increased the pistol's pressure under Brandon's chin.

Michael's hand darted into the pocket of his overcoat to the handle of his curved surgical blade. With one swift motion, he whipped the razor-sharp blade out of his pocket, across Shoemaker's wrist, and sliced off the soldier's hand. Lieutenant Shoemaker's hand and pistol dropped to the floor. Blood spurted from the radial artery.

Shoemaker screamed and flipped the stub of his wrist up closer to his eyes. Blood spattered the walls, the floor, the ceiling, the tables, and the patrons.

Lieutenant Oldman screamed at Michael. "WHAT HAVE YOU DONE?"

Chairs slid back and benches tipped over as men dashed to help Shoemaker. Men shouted. A woman screamed. Soldiers slid sabers from their scabbards. Aside from Oldman, no one was certain who had injured Shoemaker.

Michael and Brandon ran to the basement, hoping there was an exterior door there that exited onto the street. If they were wrong, they were dead.

The white innkeeper and the black woman ran after them.

Brandon kicked in the basement door. The boys leaped down the stairs. Their eyes swept every inch of the basement walls looking for a way out. The demons jumped from the basement door to the dirt floor.

The woman shoved Brandon, slammed his forehead into the stone wall, and knocked him unconscious.

The innkeeper attempted to hook an arm around Michael's neck. Michael ducked and swung his curved surgical blade in an arc. The tip of the knife impaled the innkeeper's right eye. Michael jerked the blade from the eye and sliced the innkeeper's left eyeball.

The impaled eyes erupted in orange flames. Sparks stung Michael's cheeks and singed loose locks of his hair. The innkeeper did not scream or claw at his burning eyes, face, or hair. His body flopped face first onto the floor. Michael knew the innkeeper was already dead when the demon had possessed him.

The woman ran at Michael with outstretched arms and open palms.

Michael evaded her by dropping to his knees beside Brandon. He shook Brandon's shoulders and screamed, "WAKE UP!"

Five British soldiers poured down into the basement.

Michael stood up and kicked Brandon in the side as hard as he could.

Brandon woke as the soldiers surrounded him. He groaned, got to his knees, and struggled to stand. He was seeing double, and all he saw were redcoats and sabers. He couldn't see Michael until Lieutenant Oldman shoved him inside the circle of soldiers surrounding Brandon.

Lieutenant Oldman laughed ominously. "General Henry Hereford will be pleased to hear you are in Boston. I am on my way for a visit."

Brandon rubbed his forehead and winced; he was confused.

"YA STINK!" Michael screamed at Oldman. "Ya have possessed a living human body too long. It's rotting alive. That explains ya blue eyes."

"What does he mean?" Corporal Jehu Morris demanded of Oldman.

Lieutenant Oldman snatched Michael by the hair, jerked him in close, and said, "You do not mean a thing, do you boy?"

Brandon's muddled mind suddenly cleared. He recalled what took place before he was knocked unconscious. Without turning his head, he looked at the basement walls. There *was* an exit door. He bent backward slightly, and to his relief, he felt the front sight on his pistol brush his breeches above his buttocks. He had not been disarmed.

Oldman yanked Michael's hair until Michael's chin touched his own chest. "Answer Corporal Morris, you sugar stick!"

"At least I got one between my legs," Michael said. His neck audibly popped when Lieutenant Oldman yanked his hair harder.

Brandon whipped out his pistol. He shot the soldier standing beside him in the right eye. Michael swung his surgical blade upward and cut off the lock of his hair from Oldman's grip.

Michael straightened and turned toward the sound of the gunshot. Brandon was running at a basement wall. Michael ran after him. What seemed to Michael to be a stone wall was a door in Brandon's eyes. Brandon twisted the loose knob and to his relief, the door popped open. He and Michael scrambled up the stone steps to ground level. They ran until they reached Faneuil Hall in Dock Square.

TEN

U nder the assumed name of Aengus Maguire, Ian knocked on the door of a two-storied brick building a block from the Green Dragon Tavern on Union Street. An old woman answered and let him in. She inquired after his business, and then left him standing in the front hall.

A few minutes later, a short, rotund, white-haired, well-dressed man greeted Ian with an extended hand. "Gavin O'Keefe," the man said with a jovial Scottish accent. "You must be Aengus Maguire. Are you newly acquainted with our mutual friend, John Adams?"

Ian considered Gavin O'Keefe's offered hand. He had no idea what the gesture meant. Colm shielded his men from the farce of human etiquette just as he shielded them from probing human questions, which deserved to be answered with the language of silence. Ian had not met John Adams. He looked at O'Keefe with passive pale blue eyes.

"Maguire." Gavin chuckled. "A good Gaelic Irish surname which, of course as you know, means the son of Odhar, the dark-colored one." He veered off the topic with no warning and asked, "Have you been in the colonies long?"

"Yes."

Gavin nodded and led Ian into the living room. "Please, sit down." He motioned to the small round table in the center of the room. The table top was smooth from all the years of sliding contracts back and forth between Gavin and his clients. "May I call you Aengus? May I offer you coffee?"

Ian sat at the table and said nothing.

"Get right to it then," Gavin said more to himself than to Ian. He rummaged through a stack of documents on the table, then pulled one out of the pile and handed it to Ian.

"This is a description of the farm that is for rent in Roxbury. The house has a very large living room and kitchen downstairs and four rooms above stairs. There is a front and back porch, a cellar, a new Dutch barn, a smoke-house, several privies, and a small room in the barn currently occupied by two Indian slaves. The farm previously employed two house women, a stable and carriage keeper, and four farm hands if you are interested in retaining those employees."

Gavin rifled through his untidy stack of papers until he found the one he wanted, which he removed with a flourish. "Here is the lease agreement." He slid it across the table to Ian and asked, "How large is your family?"

It was difficult enough for Ian to remember his alias let alone conjure answers to personal questions. He ignored Gavin and read the lease. When he was finished, he said, "I'll sign and pay the required advanced rent, but we don't want slaves."

"The farm is expansive. I assure you, they will be needed."

The matter of slavery was a human struggle that made no difference to Ian. The angels' presence on the farm would endanger the lives of the slaves. That was his concern.

"No slaves."

Gavin O'Keefe sensed the vibration of something he could not see. It frightened and soothed him at the same time. He was certain he had heard the rustling of wings.

Ian and Gavin regarded one another for a moment.

"No slaves then," Gavin said.

༂

Ian signed the lease on the farm in Roxbury and left the lawyer's office with a sense of accomplishment. That sense of deed was extinguished less than ten minutes later when he encountered Brandon and Michael near Faneuil Hall on their way back to Greystoke Inn.

The boys were walking with their heads down, a behavior Ian had never seen in either one. They appeared as if they were forcing themselves to walk instead of run. Michael's hair was loose and wild. Brandon's hair lay matted against his skull. Fear pounded Ian's spirit when he saw their blood-soaked overcoats. He ran to them without regard for the pedestrians on the walkway.

"What happened?" he asked.

Ian's voice was a small relief to the terror-stricken boys. They raised their heads and looked at him. They unconsciously gripped their weapons in their bloodied shaking hands. The gray leaden sky spit snow upon them as if it disdained their existence.

Ian said, "Oh no…"

"Colm wanted to draw it out. He wanted it to be a planned maneuver," Brandon managed to say. The words burned in his mouth.

A frightened non-verbal exhalation escaped Michael's throat. He realized he was clutching the handle of his curved surgical blade in his bloody right hand. He tried several times to shove it into the pocket of his overcoat before he was successful.

Ian removed the flintlock pistol from Brandon's badly trembling hand and said, "Let's get back to the inn."

Ian looked at the people who passed by. Those who took notice of the angels' blood-soaked overcoats passed them with haste. A clutch of enlisted British soldiers stood on the walkway ahead. Ian was certain that in their agitated state, the boys did not see them. He thought it would be wise to avoid the soldiers.

Ian also noted that no one or nothing appeared to be in pursuit of Brandon and Michael. That observation should have been somewhat comforting, but it wasn't.

When they arrived at the inn, it was nightfall. Snow continued to fall and the temperature dropped ten degrees. They ran through the backyard and stopped beside the warm fire pit.

"We can't go inside," Michael moaned. "We're covered in blood."

"Stay here," Ian said. "Colm has to be inside."

"Don't leave us!" Brandon said as Ian left.

Michael's green eyes moved constantly as he strained to see into the black night. A shaft of light moved through the darkness. A door slammed. Muffled movement pervaded the freezing air. Orange points of light scurried toward the boys.

Michael screamed at Brandon, "RUN!"

Colm, Ian, Seamus, Liam, and Patrick burst through the inn's back door.

The orange lights bounced in mid-air, and then shot skyward like embers from a raging fire.

Liam and Patrick were running and watching the orange lights. Brandon and Michael, in their terror, didn't realize the other angels were in the backyard, and they ran blindly toward the inn. They collided with Liam and Patrick.

Michael and Patrick fell into the snow. Colm and Seamus snatched them by the coat collar and jerked them to their feet.

Liam and Ian threw their arms around Brandon to keep him from bolting in a panic.

The orange lights went out.

Colm waited for the angels to gather their wits, and then he said to his panting and shivering brother, "So ya and Brandon managed to get the demons' attention?"

Michael worked to catch his breath. His older brother was a dim figure framed against the dying flames in the fire pit, but he was able to judge Colm's stance. Colm was displeased.

"Aye, in a tavern on Beacon Hill," Michael said. "The blood covering us isn't ours."

Brandon said, "Colm, we know you wanted to draw them out with Liam's missive. We—"

"—were freezing so we went inside the tavern," Michael said as he lowered his head.

Colm stepped in close to the boys so he could better see their faces. "Liam's missive is intended to draw Henry's attention. It doesn't matter that demons found ya. It doesn't matter if they've gone to Henry with that information. What matters is that ya are acting cowardly."

Michael's head shot up. "They attacked us and tried to kill us! We're lucky we got out of there alive!"

Colm set his jaw and looked his brother in the eyes.

Michael pressed his lips together and narrowed his eyes at Colm.

"Our time of being afraid has ended," Colm said. "Ya understand me?"

The angels shivered as the plummeting temperature began to freeze the heavy snow that wet their clothes. However, they would be obliged to stand there all night if that was how long it took Colm to back Michael down. They had endured the brothers' standoffs in the past.

"Michael, are you hearin' Colm?" Patrick said. "No matter what happens, we gotta stand and fight. Tell him you understand and take the order!"

Michael sneered at his best friend's advice.

"It's freezin' out here!" Patrick shouted. "Say it!"

Michael looked at Patrick, and then back at his brother. "Aye, I understand," he muttered.

I hope he's not dead when I come back from Cambridge, Colm thought.

The angels shivered in the cold, waiting for Colm to dismiss them. After a few minutes, he let them go.

Colm walked into the taproom and sat at a table in the shadows. He needed time alone to ruminate over what had happened to the boys. Jane Greystoke served him a tankard of rum.

A man stopped her when she turned to leave. He pointed at the tankard in Colm's hand and said, "Bring me the same."

Jane nodded and went to fetch the rum.

"May I speak to you?" the man asked Colm.

Colm looked up and studied the man. The man endured it without question or comment. Finally, Colm said, "Aye."

The man sat across from Colm. "My name is Gordon Walker."

Jane served Gordon's rum.

Colm drank from his tankard while he kept his eyes on Gordon's face.

"I'm a free black man, not a slave if that's what's worrying you."

"It's not."

"You got a name?" Gordon asked.

"What do ya want?"

Gordon glanced around, and then leaned forward. "I saw you and the angels you command outside. Do not tell me otherwise because I saw the blue auras surrounding the two angels who look alike. But that was not what gained my attention. It was the orange lights."

Colm said nothing.

"I've seen them in every tavern in Boston. It's demons, but they aren't from Hell. Demons from Hell don't have glowing orange eyes."

Colm remained silent.

"Are you going to just stare at me?" Gordon asked.

"Why are ya telling me this?"

"I heard rumors of a powerful demon with yellow-green eyes that's been recruiting human soldiers to fight in a coming war. These humans, some dead and some living, are being possessed by underlings of this powerful demon. I came up from Richmond, Virginia to see for myself."

Gordon saw silver light flash in Colm's eyes that led him to believe his suspicions were correct. The man he was sitting with was an angel, and not just any angel.

"Demons from Hell are not smart enough or have the desire to assemble an army," Gordon said. "Their damned souls escape Hell. When they're among mankind again, they realize that they're *still* damned. It infuriates them so they start terrorizing the living. *And* their eyes are *red*—not orange."

This man has the courage to keep talking because he knows I won't hurt him, Colm thought.

"Don't pretend you aren't interested in what I'm saying," Gordon said.

He's baiting me, Colm thought. *Why? He's not possessed; he's just a human.*

Gordon continued undaunted. "The Christian Bible only mentions three archangels by name although there are seven. Which one of the seven are you?"

Colm had no intention of discussing his failures as an archangel with this bold stranger. He said, "Leave—now."

"Hear me out," Gordon said. He took a deep breath and then exhaled. His brown eyes took on a faraway look. "A demon from Hell possessed my daddy when I was thirteen years old. My family were slaves at the time. We lived on a big plantation outside of Jamestown, Virginia. That demon killed my mother and all five of my younger siblings while they were working in the tobacco fields. Then, it did something horrible to my daddy. It made his body explode. His skin and hair and blood and innards splattered the tobacco and the people working nearby. I could hear the demon laughing the whole time. It's been twenty years, and I can still hear it laughing."

Colm knew the children of man were capable of deceit by purposely arranging the expression on their face and changing the tone in their voice. Gordon Walker had done neither of those things. His grief was apparent. His anger was well disguised. His fortitude was respectable.

"That demon left ya to suffer," Colm said.

Gordon clinched his teeth and nodded. Then, his grief slid below the surface of his emotions. "Mr. Jackson Walker gave me my freedom that very day. I learned how to track demons and how to kill them from the handful of people I came across who suffered the same thing. I don't know how to kill the demons with orange eyes, but I can find a way if I know where they're from and why they're here."

Colm leaned forward and set the tankard in his hand on the table. "I know ya are being honest. Come back in a few days. Then, maybe we can talk." He got up and left the taproom.

Gordon Walker sat back in his chair and smiled. He finished his tankard of rum and called for another. Although the man had refused to answer his questions, Gordon was certain he had just spoken to the archangel rumored to be in Boston.

ELEVEN

General Henry Hereford invited Robert Percy and Bethel Oldman to join him on a horseback ride through the countryside. The light snowfall from the previous night glittered in a rare occasion of sparkling sunlight from the late morning sun. The woods of Suffolk County were interrupted here and there by farms and frozen streams.

Even in the crisp morning air, Robert detected Bethel's body odor. It reminded Robert of the way his first pet dog had smelled the morning he found her dead behind the barn of his childhood home in rural Surrey County, England. He shuddered and glanced at Henry. The general was beginning to exude the same smell.

A wagon trundled the muddy road past the British officers. The male driver, his wife, and seven children, all dressed in rough homespun clothing, glared at the men on horseback. Less than an hour into the ride, a small band of colonial men and women, armed with various weapons, began to accumulate on the road behind the officers. Some carried muskets, while others held knives or shovels. Two young boys joined the band swinging long sticks.

An old woman clutching a crude bow and arrow in one wrinkled hand, shouted, "Wagtails!"

This development pleased Henry. He was certain the ragtag mob's intention was merely verbal harassment despite their display of weapons. This was his opportunity to kill Robert and incite terror in the hearts of these dirty ill-bred Yankees. When Robert was dead, and his soul was gone, Henry's second-in-command would leave Bethel's body for its new home in Robert's body. The final result would be the death of Bethel Oldman and the resurrection of Robert Percy's human vessel.

When they were west of Roxbury, Henry reined his horse and shouted, "HALT!"

Robert and Bethel reined their horses.

The colonists halted.

Henry dismounted and favored the colonists with a bright smile.

The colonists retreated several paces.

"What are you waiting for?" Henry asked Robert and Bethel. "Dismount! We must not be rude to our little group of admirers."

Robert felt uneasy. He dismounted slowly and remained close to his horse without engaging in eye contact with the colonists.

The old woman carrying the bow and arrow raised her right hand. The fingertips on her three middle fingers were wrapped in dirty strips of cloth. She knocked the arrow, raised the bow, aimed and shouted at Robert, "Remove your coat, boy!"

Chills ran down Robert's spine. "What are you doing, old woman? Put that down!" He looked to Henry for support, but Henry merely grinned.

"I will not tell you again to remove your coat!"

Henry was no longer grinning. "Do as she says, Robert, or I shall do it myself, and it will be terribly painful."

Robert slowly unbuttoned his coat, and let it slide off his arms and onto the ground.

"Now, say my name, boy!" the old woman demanded.

Terror stained Robert's blue eyes. He pointed at her and shouted, "Make the old woman stop!"

The colonists took another step back. The frightened British officer was pointing at them, but there was no old woman among their group.

Robert's legs refused to move when he tried to run.

"Say my name, Robert Percy!" the old woman prompted.

His eyes widened and his cheeks flushed when he screamed, "I DO NOT KNOW YOUR NAME!"

"My name is Serepatice!" She released the bow.

Robert flinched when the arrow pierced his heart. His eyes shifted against his will to Henry's face. He prayed for God to have mercy on his soul. He did not want to die looking into those eerie yellow-green eyes or smelling the odor of the dead.

Women screamed. Men shouted profanity. The colonists' desire to witness perversion outweighed their desire to flee, but what they desired made no difference. Henry had no intention of releasing his captive audience.

Robert collapsed onto the snow-muddied road and died before his mind could conjure another thought.

Lieutenant Bethel Oldman swooned. He fell sideways into the snow at the edge of the road. The sound of a single beating drum arose from the ground. A bell accompanied the steady drum beat; joined by a powerful throbbing rhythm. Voices spoke Latin in unison. The sounds swirled and blended and rushed on a current of cold air in and around the people standing in the road.

Henry removed his riding gloves and walked to the place where Robert Percy's body lay. He straddled the body and asked, "Who did God command to kill this man?"

The colonists covered their mouths and shrank from the look in his yellow-green eyes.

"Serepatice! Say Serepatice!" Henry plied with a grin.

A woman sobbed.

"SAY IT!" Henry commanded.

A very young man pressed the muzzle of his pistol between his eyes. A woman screamed, "NO, CHRISTOPHER!"

Henry took three long strides toward Christopher and ripped the pistol from his hands. He wrapped his hand around the young man's throat, shook him and said, "SAY IT!"

Tears streamed down Christopher's face. Henry broke his neck and flung his body away.

The horrified people said, "Serepatice."

"SHOUT IT!"

"SEREPATICE!"

Robert Percy's body got to its knees then stood up. The demon within tested the movement of its new, younger human vessel. It flexed its arms and stomach. It turned its head from side to side. Robert's eyes flamed.

The colonists looked at Bethel Oldman, and then they looked at Robert and the arrow protruding from his chest. They murmured prayers. *God, rid of us of these demons and send your angels to protect us!*

"Please, sir, let me take my children home," a woman begged Henry. The two boys she pulled into an embrace were not her children, but no one refuted her claim.

Henry regarded the woman. She wore rough dirty clothing, and her dark hair was pulled severely away from her thin plain face. He said, "Come here."

She recoiled.

"I will not ask again."

She inched forward until she was within arms' reach of Henry.

He viciously ripped out the pin that held her hair away from her face. Dull dark hair tumbled in curls to her shoulders and down her back. She cast her eyes down. Henry clutched her shoulders and pulled her close.

A stocky gray-haired farmer thought, *I cannot let this continue even if it means the demon kills me.* He spoke, "Please, sir, let my daughter take my grandsons home. We mean no harm to you."

Henry ignored the farmer. He gripped the bodice of the woman's dress and the shift beneath it with one powerful hand. Both garments ripped and exposed her breasts. Her chin quivered and tears wet her thin cheeks. Henry slid a hand over her breasts.

Bethel groaned from the edge of the road.

Henry shoved the woman onto the road. She curled into a ball and cried.

Bethel rolled on to his back.

Henry strode forward, placed the heel of his boot on Bethel's throat, and applied pressure. Bethel's eyes flew open. He wrapped his hands around Henry's calf. He kicked and arched his back and tried to force Henry's boot from his throat.

The horrified colonists murmured their prayer again, *God, rid of us of these demons and send your angels to protect us.*

Bethel stopped struggling. He lay on his back, looking skyward with dead eyes.

Henry removed his boot from the dead man's throat. Robert extracted the arrow from his chest and handed it to Henry. With a flourish, Henry jammed the arrowhead into Bethel's windpipe. Blood and bile oozed from the wound.

"Captain Percy, our work is done here," Henry said with satisfaction.

Robert nodded. He picked up his coat and put it on. Then, he mounted his horse.

Henry looked at the woman lying curled up on the muddy road. He kneeled beside her, slid his fingers through her hair, and jerked her head up so he could kiss her lips. Then, he slammed her head down. Her eyes rolled back in her head. Henry shoved her skirt up over her waist and then began to unbutton the front of his breeches.

"General, I do not think what you are about to do is prudent at this time," Robert advised.

Henry considered Robert's advice. "I believe you are correct." He stood up, brushed at the mud on the knees of his breeches and mounted his horse.

Robert and Henry spurred their horses into a gallop. The horror-stricken country folk were released from the demon's restraint.

❧

Jeremiah Killam arrived in Boston the morning after Michael and Brandon encountered the demons on Beacon Hill. He and Colm ate breakfast in the Greystoke Inn tavern. Colm told Jeremiah about the Sons of Liberty and, in particular, Dr. Joseph Warren.

"I want us to join the Boston militia, but we need guns. My hunting rifle and a few pistols is all we have," Colm said. "Actually, we need any kind of weapons: muskets, rifles, pistols, sabers, and knives—anything ya can get without causing suspicion. Take them to the farm in Roxbury where we'll be living. Don't carry them through the streets so everyone can see what ya are doing or where ya are going."

"Do I look like an ijit?" Jeremiah asked.

Colm frowned. "Just be careful."

❧

Two days out, northwest of Boston, Jeremiah learned from a sympathetic member of the Pokanoket tribe that the patriots were stockpiling arms and gunpowder. Tatoson was hunting turkey when he encountered Jeremiah washing his hands and face in a rocky fast running creek.

Tatoson's grandmother claimed he was twenty-three years old. His head was shaved except for a scalp lock, and his deerskin mantel covered the tattoo of a turtle on his shoulder and a bear paw on each breast. Tatoson took to Jeremiah's plainspoken manner.

"I'm lookin' for weapons," Jeremiah said when Tatoson asked what he was doing wandering the snowy backwoods. "Me and my brothers are newly arrived in Massachusetts. We traveled unarmed because we didn't want ta stir up trouble."

"No one travels unarmed," Tatoson said. "Unless you *want to* get killed."

"You callin' me a liar?"

Tatoson's eyes fell on the haft of Jeremiah's skinning knife that poked out from the pocket Mkwa had sewn on the thigh of his deerskin breeches.

Jeremiah ignored the innuendo, stood up, and dried his face with the hem of his bearskin coat. He shoved his disheveled blond hair out of his face and said, "You speak good English, which makes me wonder why we're talkin'."

"My grandmother says I am meddlesome."

Jeremiah narrowed his eyes at the young man. "Like I said, I need weapons, but I don't want anyone ta think I'm totin' 'em ta start a war."

"Then stay out of Concord," Tatoson said. "I have been there. The patriots are stockpiling arms there."

"Ain't no Indian waltzing inta Concord."

"I do not know what *waltzing* means. What I mean is you just got lucky."

"You Indians ain't luck ta me. I got me one back home whose gonna have my baby. I ain't never gonna see her again. Do you know where I cain buy muskets or not?"

Tatoson tilted his head northward and began walking.

Jeremiah fell in step beside him. "Where're we goin'?"

"Fort at Number 4. It has been abandoned, but Algonquians from Quebec squat there and sell French muskets they steal from trappers."

"They killin' trappers ta git 'em?"

Tatoson shrugged. "You want guns?"

Colm ain't gonna like it if he finds out I'm buying blood guns, Jeremiah thought. *But I ain't got time ta be scoutin' for another source. Damn Indian's right. I got lucky.* He asked, "So you can just stop what you're doin' and lead a white man you don't know ta gun buyin'?"

"If you buy their guns, I get something for my trouble."

"Should've known. Why do you trust me not ta kill you?"

"The way you talk and the way you dress tells me that you are from the mountains somewhere south," Tatoson said. "I have never met a vicious mountain man."

"How many you met?"

Tatoson shrugged.

"You're an uppity cuss. Who taught you ta speak English?"

"A man in Concord. Redcoats killed my mother and father when I was ten. He felt sorry for me and took me in."

"He educates you then lets you loose in the wild?"

"It was not like that."

"What was it like?"

"The British murdered most of what was left of my tribe during the war. The general who governs Massachusetts was one of them. Those who survived, including my grandmother, ended up living with another tribe. When I was old enough, I left to find her. I live with her now."

"The French and Indian War?"

Tatoson nodded.

"So that's why you cain waltz inta Concord. And you hate the British so the rebels trust you."

Tatoson nodded.

"You buyin' guns from these Canadian Indians for the rebels?"

"No. I am not allies with the rebels. I just know some of them."

"Well, I'm havin' trouble reckonin' the way you talk with the way you look. Skinny Indian boy talkin' like a dandy."

Tatoson laughed.

"How far is Fort at Number 4?" Jeremiah asked.

"Four hours walk with all this snow on the ground. How many guns do you want to buy?"

"As much as I can carry."

"Carry to where?"

"Roxbury."

Tatoson reached into a small deerskin pouch around his waist, pulled out a hunk of deer meat, and offered it to Jeremiah. Jeremiah took it and tore off a bite.

"How are you going to get the guns back there?" Tatoson asked.

"You're gonna help me."

"No."

"I ain't buying 'em unless you do. I need you ta take a message ta someone in Boston, and return with his reply."

"Unlike Concord, I cannot just ride into Boston."

"You ain't gonna ride inta Boston. One of your Concord people is."

Tatoson thought for a minute, and then said, "I know someone who will oblige."

"Do you think them Canadians will let me stay at the fort until you git back?"

"If you give them a reason to let you stay."

"Pay 'em?"

Tatoson nodded.

"The things I do for them angels," Jeremiah grumbled. He tore off another bite of deer meat.

Tatoson looked surprised. "Do you mean angels of God?"

"Don't tell me you believe in the Christian God."

Tatoson said nothing.

❧

Colm and Joseph arrived in Cambridge on the afternoon of Monday, February 6. Snow showers blew in while they were traveling. The horses struggled to pull the carriage through the heavy wet snow. The miserable journey took twice as long as it should have. Colm's apprehension over leaving his men was not lost on Joseph as they sat in the cold, cramped carriage.

When they were situated in front of the fire at Irving House, Joseph said, "You are distressed about something. Perhaps I can help."

"Either ya are very observant or I'm failing to hide my concerns," Colm said.

Joseph smiled. "I have been told that I am observant."

Colm drank from his tankard of rum before he said, "They've found us."

Joseph leaned in close to Colm and whispered, "Your demons?"

"Aye. Michael and Brandon were discovered. It's the way they reacted that worries me."

"They were frightened?"

"Aye."

"I do not understand why that is a concern."

"John Adams has seen to it that our missive to draw Henry out will be published in the Boston Gazette tomorrow. The intent is to display our boldness. We've been afraid for millennia. If we betray our fear, Henry will use it against us."

Colm drained his glass of rum and rose without comment. He went to ask the server to bring another glass of rum.

Joseph contemplated the menace his children and their nanny could be exposed to if he allied with the angels. He supposed it was too late to take that concern under consideration.

Colm returned and sat down. "While I'm here, my men are moving to the farm in Roxbury. I hope that'll confuse the demons long enough..." He realized that he was exposing his worries by speaking them out loud.

"Long enough for what?"

Colm's green eyes searched Joseph's blue eyes for the trust he so desperately needed in a peer. It was there.

Joseph heard Colm's wings rustle. He repeated his question. "Long enough for what?"

"I don't know, and that scares me."

The following morning, Joseph and Colm attended the Second Provincial Congress of Massachusetts. Fergus was also in attendance. Colm sat in silence and witnessed the resolve of men who would not allow other men to suppress them.

Fergus and Joseph were one of several men appointed to the Committee of Safety. The committee members were charged with the duty to observe all persons who would attempt to carry out the execution of the British Parliament laws by force. Those attempts would alarm, muster, and cause a completely armed militia to march to a place of rendezvous for the purpose of opposing such attempts.

Colm found their decree to offer the highest gratitude to their Supreme Being for a government that allows land ownership equality for all men no matter their societal standing discomforting, for he knew God had nothing to do with it.

The week came to a close. The Congress adjourned until Monday, February 13. On that Friday night, Colm dined with Fergus, Joseph, John Hancock, Samuel Adams, John Adams, and Dr. Benjamin Church. The elegant inn, the decadent meal, and the conversation made Colm feel out of place. Fergus, on the other hand, looked as if he were created for it.

While Samuel talked of the success of their second week at congress, Colm thought of the moment he and his brotherhood had been banished from Heaven. Before that moment, he was also a part of a family of archangels—God's most fierce warriors—yet always benevolent toward the children of man. He wasn't a politician, though he felt these men needed him to understand their politics. It was then he realized that he had to become a part of these men. Think like they thought. See what they saw. Understand what they had at stake and make it his conviction.

He realized that Fergus was succeeding in doing just that. Fergus was assimilating. He was earning respect. He was learning about and contributing to the operations of a rebellion by actively drilling with the Cambridge militia. Even the way he spoke was changing. He was on the road to attaining a lofty general's position if the Americans did indeed form an army.

"Colm, you have said very little tonight," John Hancock said. "I am interested to hear your thoughts on the resolves put forth by congress, particularly those regarding the Committee of Safety."

"I don't understand what ya have suffered at the hands of the British Parliament, but I'm learning. It seems Fergus is better acquainted with your challenges."

The men at the table nodded and murmured in agreement.

Fergus' handsome boyish face lit up.

Colm continued, "I believe ya understand ya vulnerabilities. Ya got no army—just a loose network of militia. Ya got small gun foundries and limited supplies of metal and gunpowder. Ya got no network to get supplies to the militia companies. Depriving the enemy of the resources to build a war machine on American soil is all ya got."

Samuel crossed his arms over his chest and frowned at Colm. "You gleaned this information from one week of spectating the meeting of our congress?"

Silver light flashed in Colm's eyes as he made eye contact with Samuel. Samuel looked away.

John Hancock noted Samuel's reaction. He and Samuel were close associates. Perhaps, not as close as Joseph's political apprenticeship to Samuel, but their relationship was evolving. John was one of the richest men in the Massachusetts Bay Colony. His conceit was well deserved from the effort he had put into business and personal attainments. He sipped his wine to keep the corners of his mouth from betraying a sarcastic smile.

He said, "Colm's a trained military man, unlike you, Samuel. Your obvious dislike for him is not a reason to deny the value he brings to the table."

I do not dislike him, Samuel thought. *I am afraid of him, but I do not know why.* He reached for the wine decanter on the table and refilled his empty glass.

Colm addressed John Adams. "John, the day Fergus and I revealed our identities, ya said ya would take my counsel under serious advisement when my demon arrived in Boston and not before."

"I remember," John said, slowly. He was reluctant to hear what Colm had to say regarding the matter.

Joseph drank the remainder of the wine in his glass and refilled it. Colm had not asked him to keep Michael and Brandon's encounter with the demons quiet, but Joseph had chosen silence to avoid undue stress during the congressional meetings. Now, he experienced guilt for doing so.

"I haven't found Henry, but some of my men encountered demons on Beacon Hill," Colm said.

John Adam's heart skipped a beat. He had hoped that Colm's claim of demons was unfounded.

That news alarmed John Hancock. He lived in a mansion on Beacon Hill with his Aunt Lydia Hancock. John's fiancée, Dorothy Quincy, visited the mansion often.

Dr. Benjamin Church leaned in closer to the table and lowered his voice, "Did you say demons?"

"Aye."

"Is that a code word for something?"

"No."

"You cannot be speaking of demons from Hell!" Benjamin almost shouted.

John Adams felt responsible for pushing Colm to speak of his demon. *This is my reprimand for flouting the word of an archangel. How could I have questioned even a banished angel's word?*

Samuel motioned at a server to bring more wine to the table.

John Hancock saw Joseph and Colm look at one another. There was an allegiance between them: a developing brotherhood of which John was jealous.

Benjamin also saw the exchange. His eyes darted between Colm and Joseph. "What is it that I do not know? Joseph, answer me!"

The server brought three decanters of wine. Joseph snatched one and refilled his glass. Then, he leaned forward so Benjamin could clearly hear him. "We should not have kept this from you, Benjamin. You are an integral part of our cause, and you deserve to know. In our defense, we needed time to let what we have learned settle in our hearts and in our minds."

"Judging from the exchange I just witnessed between you and Colm, I would venture to say it has already settled in your heart."

In thinking about his wife's wisdom, John Adams had managed to gain confidence in what their immediate answer to Benjamin's question must be. "I insist we convene to a place of privacy. I suggest the home of Reverend Ralph Walton. He and his family are on holiday in Europe. Reverend Walton has a spacious basement. Joseph, Colm, do you agree?"

"I shall not convene anywhere until I understand the nature of this conversation," Benjamin said. "John, we have been friends for thirty-nine years; our entire lives. Surely, you are not sacrificing our trust and friendship for these—" He cast his eyes at Fergus and Colm. "—strangers."

"That is not what we are doing."

Fergus realized that he needed to demonstrate his ability to command and to discipline himself to make important pronouncements in Colm's presence; something he had never done in all the millenniums he had been with his archangel.

"Dr. Church, what we speak of must be kept amongst trusted compatriots such as you, thus John's suggestion to continue elsewhere."

This statement contributed to Dr. Benjamin Church's self-importance as Fergus hoped it would. Benjamin agreed to the change of venue.

Samuel gave Fergus a nod of approval.

But Samuel's approval was not what Fergus was seeking. He looked his former commander in the eye. Colm's expression remained neutral and that was what Fergus had hoped. Colm had truly released him.

Twelve

Boston, Massachusetts

Henry and Robert returned to Province House on Beacon Hill. When they rode up the short lane from the road to the house, the old house servant, Squire, was walking from the kitchen to the stables to deliver supper to his fifteen-year-old grandson, Will.

Robert dismounted and whistled for the stable boy to fetch the horses.

Will emerged from the stables and ran to do as he was bid. Squire stopped to watch. Henry handed his horse's reins to Robert. Robert handed the reins to Will, and then delighted in flashing his orange eyes at Squire.

That demon kilt Captain Percy while they was on their horse ride, and now, his dead body is possessed by a demon, Squire thought. *We cannot pray to God to protect us from his own demons. God does not care.*

"Captain Percy, sir. Where is Lieutenant Oldman?" Will asked innocently. "His horse did not go lame, did it?"

Robert found this to be a perfect opportunity to begin his existence in his new body. "Oldman took up with a whore at the tavern we stopped in for lunch. Do not expect to see him or his horse today."

Will suppressed a laugh and said, "Yes, sir!"

Squire continued on to the stables and waited for his grandson inside.

Will led the horses into the stables. Upon seeing his grandfather, he said, "Evenin', Pappy." He looped the reins of both horses over a hook in the door of a stall and sat at a tiny rickety wooden table with one chair.

Squire set the plate on the table in front of his grandson. Will picked up a piece of salted cod and shoved it into his mouth.

"Will, do not look them men in the eyes, do you hear me?"

Will broke off a piece of biscuit and shoved that into his mouth. Without looking up from his plate, he said, "Why?"

"Because I say."

Will glanced up at his grandfather. "Did you bring me some buttermilk?"

Squire realized he was still holding a pewter mug in his hand. He set it on the table.

"This is beer," Will said disgusted. He drank it anyway and made a face as if it was sour.

"Look at me boy."

"I am about starved, Pappy. Can we talk of it later?"

Squire snatched Will's hand away from his plate. "Look at me!"

Will looked at his grandfather, and tried to twist his skinny wrist out of Squire's grasp.

Squire's lined face shined with sweat. "I thank the good Lord that your momma, dada, and brother is dead; that they do not have to see the evil God has sent to Boston."

Will stopped twisting his wrist and studied his grandfather's face with big brown eyes.

Squire jerked Will's wrist so hard that the boy's body lurched toward him. "Promise you will not look at their eyes! Speak an oath to it!"

Sweat ran in rivulets down Squire's dark cheeks and dripped onto his chest. He feared for his grandson's eternal soul. Without a doubt, he knew that Captain Robert Percy's soul had been sacrificed for General Henry Hereford's needs. Squire believed that death by a demon guaranteed damnation, even if the executed soul was innocent.

Fear penetrated Will's youthful heart. "Pappy, what are you talkin' about?" His eyes shifted wildly to the stable's double entrance doors. *Did I hear the doors rattle?*

Squire's eyes also shifted to the doors.

The doors rattled and bowed in and out as if they were breathing. He unconsciously released Will's wrist.

Will abruptly stood up and knocked his chair backward. He spilled the tiny rickety table sideways. The remaining cod, biscuit, and untouched carrots littered the straw-strewn stable floor.

The stable doors exploded into javelins that flew through the air as if hurled by the hands of giants. The javelins pierced the horses' brains, and their bodies fell to the floor with a heavy slap. Will and Squire's stomachs were impaled. Their bodies were lifted above the straw floor. They hung in midair with mouths gaping, urine soaking their breeches, and death claiming their last breaths.

Robert Percy's eyes bathed the stables in a flash of orange light and flames. The straw carpeting the stable floor caught fire. Robert ran to warn the Gage household. It would not do to have the beautiful home, in which he and Henry were quartered, catch fire and burn to the ground.

Patrick saw the flames on Beacon Hill as he walked to the Green Dragon Tavern to meet Seamus. Seamus and Patrick had been meeting there every night for the past week after Seamus was done with his work on the HMS *Invincible.* The fire wouldn't have alarmed Patrick except that he knew John Hancock's mansion was on Beacon Hill, and John was in Cambridge.

Patrick broke into a run, but slowed to a walk when he realized that by running, he might attract unwanted attention. When he reached the Green Dragon, there was a clutch of men and a few British officers standing outside watching the fire. Seamus was among them. He turned and walked away from the tavern. Patrick followed. When they neared Faneuil Hall, Seamus stopped and waited for his little brother to catch up.

Patrick considered the orange glow on Beacon Hill. "Do you get the feelin' that fire's got somethin' to do with Henry?"

"It ain't just a feelin'. I'm pretty sure it does have somethin' to do with Henry because I found out he's quarterin' with General Gage."

"I think we shou'd see what's burnin'," Patrick said.

Seamus nodded.

The brothers walked toward Beacon Hill.

"How'd you find out where Henry's stayin'?" Patrick asked.

"Mr. Rickard's a demon."

"The man who hired you?"

"Aye. We learnt from Michael that reekin' demons are possessin' livin' people too long. Rickard smells like a rottin' corpse. He drinks all the time and talks too much. He started to talk to me."

"He don't know who you is?" Patrick asked.

"He's too drunk to notice. Oh, I ain't' had a chance to tell you—me and Ian is goin' out to the farm tomorrow. I got a message from Jeremiah sayin' he found what he's been lookin' for, and he's takin' them to the farm."

"Who delivered the message?"

Seamus laughed. "Dr. Samuel Prescott. I figured he'd stay away from us after how Colm described his reaction the day he seen we was angels."

"Jeremiah don't know Prescott. How'd he get a message to him?"

"How shou'd I know?"

"Fergus' been drillin' with the Cambridge militia. We shou'd be drillin' with the Boston militia. Why won't Colm let us?"

The brothers heard the click of sears releasing the cocks on flintlock pistols, and the brush of steel as sabers were pulled from scabbards.

"I believe you are the Cullen brothers," a voice from behind said. "You are both under arrest."

Seamus reached for the butcher knife he had tucked in his coat pocket and stopped walking. The brothers turned around. Seamus unconsciously moved in front of his little brother in a protective gesture.

Patrick stepped around Seamus to stand beside him. Patrick didn't understand Seamus' brotherly shield until Seamus spoke.

"What're you doin'?" Seamus asked the armed redcoats.

The young officer in charge leveled his pistol at Seamus' face. "If you resist arrest, we *will* bear arms against you with deadly intent."

Patrick's eyes darted to each British face. It was difficult for him to judge their eye color in the dark, but he saw no orange glow. If these men were just men, they were incapable of killing the brothers physically or spiritually, but Patrick was uncertain. Seamus was trying to determine that by asking questions.

"We have been sent by General Gage to arrest you for arson to his stables, and the murders of two slaves," the officer in charge said.

A young soldier wielding a saber shoved the sharp tip into Patrick's left breast. Another soldier whipped the tipped edge of his saber under Patrick's left ear. One quick slice would sever Patrick's jugular vein. His human vessel would take a long time to heal from a horrible wound like that.

The officer in charge frowned and said to Seamus, "If you do not come with us, we will kill your brother."

Seamus didn't understand how these soldiers knew who Patrick and he were. He gripped the bloodstained handle of the old butcher knife he had used to kill countless wild boars on Garden Mountain. These men weren't demons. He could see that now.

He looked at Patrick's calm façade. Seamus' vessel was thirteen years older than Patrick's vessel. Aside from their gray eyes, medium height, and speech pattern, the Cullen brothers had little physical resemblance to one another. Seamus wondered if Patrick's resemblance to Michael had caused the soldiers to confuse the two boys, and that this order had come from Henry based on the boys encounter with the demons on Beacon Hill.

Still, it was nearly impossible for Seamus to be mistaken for Brandon, and these soldiers knew the brothers' last name was Cullen.

Seamus said, "Kill him. I ain't goin' with you."

The officer in charge looked puzzled. *Why would a man agree to let his brother die unless that is not really his brother? Have we been misled? No! This man is hoodwinking me!* But the officer hesitated to give his next order.

He studied the Cullens, and said, "Why are you not denying the charges?"

The officer saw a faint silver light emanate from the brothers. It winked out the moment he perceived it. He blinked, and then said, "I think we have the wrong men. Let them go."

"But, sir, we were told…"

"I know what we were told! Stow your weapons and return to General Gage's house!"

The soldiers removed their sabers from Patrick's body, stepped back, and followed the order.

The young officer stared at Patrick and Seamus, searching for the silver light he was certain he saw.

The brothers changed their original course. Continuing on to Beacon Hill would entice more trouble. They walked back toward the Green Dragon.

The British officer watched them until they disappeared into the night. He left his detachment of soldiers, walked to the harbor, and down to the shore. The water lapped the rocks and promised peace within its depths if that was what he was seeking. The young man looked at the pistol in his hand, and then back at the faint orange glow on Beacon Hill. He waded into the freezing black water up to his chest.

The pistol shook when he held it to his right temple. Evil dwelt on Beacon Hill. He could never go back there. If he was worthy, Heaven awaited him, and he knew now that it existed because he had seen God's angels tonight. He prayed his pistol would not misfire when he pulled the trigger.

A fisherman found his body floating in Boston Harbor the next day.

The confirmation that demons were indeed in Boston, and the Cullens' confrontation with British soldiers, distracted Ian from his sexual urges. Sidonie was the furthest thing from his mind.

She fell into despair when she realized the angels left the Greystoke Inn for good, and Ian did not said goodbye. It was yet another lesson learned about Ian's loyalty to his brotherhood. She was an afterthought. Her vow to teach Ian how to express love seemed impossible.

But it wasn't his fault that he did not say goodbye.

The brotherhood walked through Boston Neck toward Roxbury under a white February sky. British soldiers stopped them at the guard post on the Neck to question their business and destination, and then let them pass. The cold wind daggered their freezing faces. Their hats constantly threatened to blow off their heads. Their cloaks and coats rippled in the wind.

"I'm gonna start lookin' for horses tomorrow," Patrick said as he buttoned his coat. "I'll stay at the farm with them even if we ain't ready to move yet."

"We are ready," Liam assured him.

"No, we aren't," Michael said. "Otherwise, we wou'd have checked out of the inn."

"You got somethin' there you need?" Seamus asked.

Michael shrugged.

"Then we're checked out," Seamus said.

Brandon said, "Why didn't you tell us we were moving today?"

"Too many ears is why."

"Seamus thought there would be less of a chance that demons would follow us," Liam said.

Michael asked, "How come ya knew?"

"I am more perceptive and smarter," Liam answered with a straight face.

"Fuck ya!" Michael spit back.

"Put a period to it and listen," Seamus warned. "We're gonna start drillin' with the Boston militia as soon as I talk to Paul or William. Me and Ian is goin' back to Boston to do that, and a few other things. Patrick, you cain go with us and start lookin' for horses."

"Ian, ya aren't fooling us," Michael said. "Ya are going to fetch that ghost girl ya brought with ya from Charles Town. Ya think we didn't know? Where's she at? Granary Burying Ground?"

Ian ran at Michael, shoved him and said, "Sidonie's none of your concern!"

Michael shoved him back. "She is if she's distracting ya!"

Ian jumped on Michael, and they fell into a drift of new fallen snow. Ian fisted his hand and pulled it back to strike Michael's face. Seamus caught his fist before it connected with Michael's nose.

"Get off him!" Seamus ordered.

Michael spit in Ian's face.

Ian jerked his wrist from Seamus' grasp. He put both hands on Michael's chest and pushed until Michael was submerged in the snowdrift.

Seamus bear-hugged Ian and tried to pull him away, but Ian tightened all of his muscles and pushed on Michael's chest harder. Liam wrapped his arms around Ian from a different angle to help Seamus.

"WHAT'RE YOU DOING, IAN?" Patrick screamed. "LET HIM UP!"

Michael could neither move nor breathe. Ian was killing his body. Just before he passed out he thought, *where's my spirit going to go?*

Patrick ran to the snowdrift screaming, "GET OFF HIM!" He waded in past Michael's head and kicked Ian in the face. Ian's head snapped back, and his tightened muscles relaxed. Liam and Seamus pulled him off of Michael.

Patrick and Brandon dug Michael out of the snowdrift. They moved his body to a snowless area of ground. The boys tried to revive him by calling his name and slapping his pale face until it was red.

Ian panted and struggled to calm down and catch his breath.

Seamus said, "Damn you, Ian! Fightin's tolerated. Killin' each other ain't! Now, I gotta come up with a way to punish you."

The sound of Michael groaning was relief to all the angels. Patrick and Liam helped him to his feet. Brandon fetched Michael's wet hat from the snow. Michael coughed hard. His eyes watered. He was soaked from head to toe. He shivered in the freezing wind.

Ian's remorse was evident from the downcast expression on his face.

Seamus looked at the apprehensive brotherhood. What just happened scared them, and Colm wasn't there to soothe them.

"Let's get movin' before we all freeze solid," Seamus said.

Patrick stayed by Michael's side the rest of the journey. No one spoke nor did they look at one another. Ian's remorse pressed heavily on their spirits. That remorse was punishment enough for all of them.

Jeremiah Killam waiting for them on the farmhouse porch was a welcome sight that eased their oppression. Jeremiah lived most of the forty years of his life alongside the angels. He knew when things weren't right with them.

Liam led the disheveled angels to the porch. Jeremiah and Liam embraced. "It's good ta see you," Jeremiah whispered. "Tell me what's happened when they git warmed up and settled in."

Liam nodded.

One by one, the angels embraced Jeremiah as they filed into the blissfully warm house. A fire crackled in the living room's open brick fireplace, and a jug of rum waited on the mantel. Michael sat on the brick hearth that was level with the floor. The layer of ice that coated his hair and clothing began to melt and muddied the ash-littered hearth.

The room was far from cozy. There were two wooden couches against opposite walls, and a large, round wooden table surround by six slat back chairs. An empty china closet and built-in shelves flanked the big fireplace. Three wrought iron floor candle holders held the remains of partially burned tapers. There were no rugs on the dirty floor.

Patrick took the jug from the mantel and handed it to Michael.

"There's guns in the barn," Jeremiah said as he sat in a slat back chair near the fireplace. This announcement somewhat soothed the angels' disquiet. Weapons equated to security.

Michael guzzled rum from the jug. Patrick took the jug from Michael's outstretched hand, drank from it, and passed the jug to Ian.

Angels did not hold grudges against one another.

Ian handed the jug to Liam.

Liam drank from it, and then announced to Jeremiah, "Ian tried to kill Michael."

Seamus frowned. "It ain't your place, Liam."

"Jeremiah asked me to tell him what happened."

Ian's eyes shifted to Michael then to Jeremiah.

"You gonna tell me why?" Jeremiah asked.

Ian shook his head.

Seamus walked to one of the two windows in the living room, and looked out over the snow-covered landscape.

"I ain't no angel, and I ain't been runnin' from demons for thousands of years," Jeremiah said. "But your bodies are human just like mine, and humans git tired eventually. It just took you much longer ta git ta the point of bein' exhausted. That's why this happened."

"No it ain't," Seamus said as he turned from the window to look at Jeremiah.

"I ain't sayin' you're weak. I'm sayin' take this time ta rest your bodies and spirits because all Hell's gonna break loose. You gotta help them patriots *and* put a stop ta the demons once and for all. I'm glad I ain't you."

81

Thirteen

Boston, Massachusetts

Margaret Gage became increasingly uncomfortable as February came to a close. She noted her husband's propensity to discuss gubernatorial and military strategies with General Henry Hereford was growing. However, the discussions, which often took place at supper, were not her primary concern.

Thomas was under the direct command of the British Parliament and King George III, and therefore obliged to follow the orders of the British-appointed Secretary of State for the colonies, Lord Dartmouth. Communication between Gage and Dartmouth was painfully slow because Dartmouth was in London. It took at least two months, sometimes three, from the time Thomas Gage sent a letter to London until he received a reply.

Margaret believed that Henry was taking advantage of her husband's anxiety over waiting for Dartmouth's cross-Atlantic replies.

There was no strategic conversation at supper the night after the stables burned. Margaret and Thomas spoke of their grief over the death of Squire and his grandson, Will. While their standing supper guest, Captain John Brown, expressed his condolences, Margaret measured Henry's reaction to the Gage's loss. In her opinion, there was none. Nor did she see any reaction from the general's aide-de-camp, Captain Robert Percy.

Margaret listened without comment as Thomas, Henry, Robert, and John discussed rebuilding the stables and replacing the dead horses. Her eyes wandered to Henry's face on occasion. He was a living oxymoron—devilishly handsome, and in deeply religious colonial Boston, the devil was a serious matter.

When the meal was over, the men at the table stood and waited for Margaret to rise.

"Please excuse me. I am going to retire," she said with the brightest smile she could muster while Henry stared at her as if she were dessert, and he was waiting to be served a slice.

Thomas kissed her cheek and said, "Good night."

Margaret mounted the stairs as the men walked to the living room. She gripped the banister in her sweating palm and thought, *I have not been able to sleep well since General Hereford has arrived. As soon as possible, I will seek a doctor who can prescribe something for sleep; a doctor who is not attending Thomas or his officers.* From behind, Margaret heard the living room double doors close with a loud click.

Robert, Thomas, and Captain John Brown each poured healthy glasses of wine before they made themselves comfortable.

"Thomas, we must discuss undertaking a mission to determine provisions which might be had off the land and from the local farms in the countryside," Henry said.

"I am waiting to receive a course of action regarding my admonitions to Lord Dartmouth," Thomas said.

Henry sat in a winged easy chair and crossed his legs at the knees. "What was that advice?"

"I believe if a respectable force of soldiers is visible in and around Boston, the rebel leaders are seized, and pardons granted to others, the government will come off victorious to the opposition."

John lit his clay pipe and took several puffs from it before he said, "I am in agreement with that counsel."

"I will admit that it is sometimes difficult to contain my patience when situations here change before I receive a reply from London," Thomas said. He did not want what he had just said taken for insubordination so he quickly followed it with, "I am sure it is equally difficult for Lord Dartmouth to control his patience when waiting for my report."

That was the moment Henry found a way to barge in through the door of not only the King's military might in Massachusetts, but matters of government. If he could circumvent Dartmouth's replies, he could become a master of puppets over the loyalists.

Thomas Gage was a loyal soldier of King George, but he was not a royalist. His concept of government leaned toward the government of Parliament and men. That political ideology was useful from the standpoint that he believed he had a right to make decisions if pressed upon. Henry was well aware of Thomas' beliefs.

Henry took a sip of wine before speaking. "Have you seen a change recently?"

"It is not what I have seen, but what I deem has become more pressing," Thomas replied. "My concern is twofold: the rebels' powder and armament stores, and our access to local provisions."

"I see no harm in gleaning information about what might be had off the land and local farms west of Boston—provisions such as cattle, horses, and straw. If the King's military presence needs to be increased those things may be useful, especially if Dartmouth does not want to comply with your counsel."

Thomas pressed the back of his head against his chair back. Henry's body odor was offensive. *Perhaps that is why John lit his pipe,* Thomas thought.

John silently puffed at his pipe. He had detected an offensive smell all evening, but he did not equate it with Henry. The pipe did little to curtail the stench.

"Henry, I will take your idea under advisement," Thomas said.

"There is not time to ponder uncertainty," Henry reprimanded.

John recalled a campaign Thomas and he had participated in during the French and Indian War. Thomas had been hailed for his foundry of light infantry in America. The tactic was a far cry from the stiff ordered European practice of marching in neat columns toward an enemy assumed to march in the same formation. Light infantry was capable of moving through heavy woods with the stealth of American Indians. "What about scouting the terrain?" he advised.

"Yes, a clandestine reconnaissance," Thomas replied. "Tell me more."

"We could sketch areas that may be defensible by the rebels and also sketch the general landscape—rivers, passes, hills, and fords."

Henry leaned back satisfied. His work was done for the evening.

Two days later, on February 22, 1775, General Gage gave Captain John Brown and Ensign Henry de Berniere the order to travel as inconspicuously as possible through the Massachusetts countryside to complete the discussed mission. The officers, poorly disguised as farmers, took Captain Brown's manservant along and passed through Charlestown toward Cambridge. Their first mistake was lack of consideration for the fact that farmers did not have manservants.

On the same day, Colm and Joseph left the Provincial Congress in Cambridge on horseback headed to Boston. Fergus stayed behind. The Committee of Safety had appointed him a major in charge of the Cambridge-Watertown militia.

"I spent my youth on a farm in Roxbury. I am the eldest of four sons," Joseph said. "My family grew russet apples. My brother, Samuel, and my mother, Mary, still live on the farm. I do not see them as often as I should what with my medical practice and growing political involvement."

"And ya father?"

Joseph sighed. "He died when I was fourteen; I had just begun my education at Harvard. He fell off a ladder and broke his neck. My youngest brother, John, only three years old, witnessed it."

Colm wanted to soothe Joseph's obvious pain, but he was unfamiliar with the appropriate social comments regarding the loss of loved ones.

Joseph continued his lament, "My wife, Betsy, died in 1773. I fear only the eldest of my four children will remember her." Then, to Colm's surprise, he chuckled. "People delight in speculating about my relationship with my children's nanny, Mercy Scollay."

"Why is that amusing?" Colm asked.

"It is…well…, it does not matter."

"Then, why did ya say it?"

Joseph chuckled again. "Religion is an integral part of our lives. We believe that we are devout and well educated on the subject. Then here you are, and I realize I know nothing about the celestial attendants of God. I am having difficulty believing I am befriending an angel."

Colm smiled. "Ya need to meet Jeremiah Killam. Ya can talk about the challenges of befriending angels. He's the only human friend we've ever had."

As they approached a slight curve in the road, Colm and Joseph saw three men walking toward them dressed in brown clothing with red handkerchiefs around their necks. When they were past the curve, Colm saw two men in the woods shadowing the walkers to their right.

"Do those farmers' clothes look right?" Colm asked.

"Questionable, indeed. The man walking behind them carries himself like a servant."

"They're being shadowed," Colm said. He tilted his head toward the woods to his left.

"Ignorant British officers," Joseph scoffed. "Whatever it is they are doing has been discovered."

"Shou'd we stop them?"

"No need. The local folk have this in hand."

The walkers bid them a good day as they passed. Joseph delivered a curt nod in response. Colm said nothing.

They rode in silence for a time before Colm said, "I need to ride on to the farm. Would ya come with me and stay the night? I'd like ya to get to know my men. I can't promise ya will be comfortable sleeping."

"Angels sleep and eat, yet you cannot have a woman," Joseph stated. "Why do you adhere to God's rule if he has banished you from Heaven?"

"If we create Nephilim, God will destroy the children of man like he did in the Flood of Noah…Michael and Seamus struggle with their urges, but they've managed them. Ian went to extremes to satisfy his."

"And you?"

"I'm an archangel. A warrior. We're the closest spiritual entities to God. Our spiritual burdens are none—"

"—of my concern?"

"Aye."

"But you also carry the spiritual burden of others."

Colm's attention shifted from Joseph to the road ahead. He didn't want to talk about his failures as an archangel—how he'd failed to stop his flock of Grigori angels, and Seamus, Ian, and Michael from creating the Nephilim. Spiritual burdens were what he deserved.

Joseph now saw Colm differently—as a gentle brave king who did not need to don the guise of finery or pretense. Colm's actions were for the ones he loved, not his own comfort.

"I would very much like to get to know your men."

Colm didn't understand why, but he was relieved that Joseph agreed to go to the Roxbury farm.

❧

The farmhouse's downstairs' windows were backlit with soft yellow light. A single candle burned in an above stairs window.

Michael, Brandon, and Patrick burst through the front door and into the yard. They slowed so they wouldn't startle the horses as they yelled, "Colm!"

They are greeting him just like my children greet me when I have been away for a long time, Joseph thought.

Colm and Joseph dismounted.

Colm's relief at seeing Michael warmed his freezing body. He wrapped his arms around Michael, hugged him, and then let him go.

Michael looked at Joseph. "Are ya Joseph Warren?"

"Yes. And you must be Michael Bohannon."

Michael nodded.

Colm embraced Brandon and Patrick. His boys were safe. "Joseph, this is Brandon O'Flynn and Patrick Cullen."

"I'll tend to your horse, Joseph," Patrick said. "Brandon, cain you tend to Colm's horse?"

Brandon and Patrick led the horses to the barn behind the house. Michael went with them. A dim light flared inside the barn. The horses softly whinnied. Although Colm had never been to the farm, he knew he was home.

Joseph followed Colm into the house. The remaining members of the brotherhood had gathered at the door, anxious to greet them.

Liam stepped forward. "I am Liam Kavangh," he said, bowing slightly to Joseph.

Joseph introduced himself and did likewise.

Seamus and Ian followed Liam's example of formal introduction.

Jeremiah handed a tankard of beer to Joseph. "Welcome, Joseph. Sit and warm yourself by the fire. I'm Jeremiah Killam, and I ain't no angel."

"Where'd ya get those manners?" Colm asked Jeremiah suspiciously.

"I ain't a complete heathen."

"I got news of Henry," Seamus announced. "May I speak freely?"

Colm looked at Joseph, and then nodded at Seamus.

"I learned from a drunken demon that works on the HMS *Invincible* that Henry's quarterin' on Beacon Hill at the home of the Royal Governor of Massachusetts, General Thomas Gage. We ain't been able to verify it, but I think he was tellin' the truth."

"I need to return to Boston. My children..." Joseph said, alarmed.

"Your children is safe. Henry don't know we know," Seamus said. "But me and Patrick think Henry knows we're here. Not here at the farm, but in or around Boston."

Whispered voices floated down the narrow steps that led above stairs. The wooden risers creaked. Those in the room turned their attention to the sound. Ian was descending with someone behind him.

Ian stepped into the living room. The woman who followed him alit from the last riser. Colm had never seen her, but he knew she was Sidonie Roux Denning, Ian's ghost woman—his object of lust.

This thin plain man was not what she had anticipated. But when Sidonie looked upon Colm, fear burned in her heart.

"She can't stay," Colm said before Ian could speak on her behalf. "Her presence will make ya vulnerable. Send her back to Charles Town tomorrow."

"Colm—," Ian implored.

"I know she was at the inn in Boston," Colm said. "I'd hoped ya had enough sense to send her home, but clearly ya didn't."

Michael, Patrick, and Brandon entered the living room and fell silent when they realized what was happening.

Ian said to Colm, "I'll find somewhere else for her to live."

Sidonie looked down and whispered, "Ian, I will return to Charles Town. He does not want me near you."

"Look at me," Colm said to Sidonie.

She did as he bid.

Colm was astounded at how much she looked like Ian. "I'm not trying to be cruel. Ian lets his *needs* cloud his judgment. Do ya understand me?"

"Yes."

Colm felt Joseph's stare. "Ya got something to say?" Colm asked him.

"Are my thoughts welcome?"

"Aye."

"What is your name?" Joseph asked Sidonie.

"Sidonie Denning."

"Can you cook?"

"Yes, of course."

"I believe I can position you as a cook with my friend, Colonel James Barrett, in Concord. They have a large farm and his wife, Rebeckah, needs kitchen help," Joseph said.

"No," Colm said. "If Henry finds out who Sidonie is, and where she is, he'll go after her. He'll kill ya friend to get to her if he has to."

"I assure you my friend is not feeble."

"Why are ya doing this?"

"As I have said, a man's needs are important."

Michael and Brandon snickered.

"Do you disagree?" Joseph asked them.

Michael frowned. "Ian's an idiot."

"Stop antagonizin' him," Seamus told Michael. "I think Ian's got a right to his woman if she ain't in the way. If she starts distractin' him, then she needs to go back to Charles Town."

"I said that a week ago, and the fucker tried to kill me for it!" Michael said.

"Brother," Patrick said to Seamus. "I agree with Michael. She *is* a distraction. You was one of the fools who went off fuckin' human women, but you ain't *keepin'* a woman. Michael ain't either."

Liam said, "I agree with Seamus."

After some consideration Colm said, "I'll allow it. Traveling somewhere as far away as Charles Town might be dangerous now that Henry knows we're here."

"Then it is settled," Joseph said. "Who will take the message to my friend in Concord?"

"I'm the least likely to be seen by demons because I can hide my aura from them," Brandon said. "Can I ride, Colm?"

"Aye; at first light."

Ian afforded a glance at Sidonie.

"Very good," Joseph said. "Do you have quill and paper?"

Liam went to the china closet to fetch them.

Ian's relief was short lived. Colm said to him, "Did ya try to kill Michael?"

"Oh Lord," Jeremiah said. "Colm, we done talked about this among us. He ain't gonna do it again."

Colm said, "Ya *did* try to kill Michael."

"I did," Ian admitted.

Jeremiah said to Colm, "Your boys is worn out. Cain't you see that? Let it go."

"This is none of ya business," Colm warned.

"It is if I'm livin' in this house with you," Jeremiah countered.

Colm said, "Ian, I'll feed ya to Henry's demons if ya try to kill any of us again. That includes Jeremiah…and Joseph. Now, we got an important guest who deserves to relax and rest. Sidonie, make yaself useful and make up a bed for Joseph—in his own room. Liam, get draughts."

"Please, I wish to be a friend and no burden," Joseph said, smiling.

"You ain't got no idea what you're askin' for," Jeremiah grumbled. "Damned angels will talk poesy then act like jilts."

"Yet you stay loyal," Joseph pointed out.

Fourteen

Boston, Massachusetts

March 1775

The fifth anniversary of the Boston Massacre fell on a Sunday. Therefore, the patriots observed the annual commemoration of the tragic clash that took place between British soldiers and town's residents on Monday, March 6. Joseph Warren had given the oration in 1772. He was asked to speak again this year because of the passion he vehemently shared with his fellow patriots.

The events of that fateful day were well-known, how British grenadiers fired on Boston residents, killing five colonists. Those actions were countered the next day when a mob of 4,000 gathered, demanding the British troops be removed to an island in Boston Harbor, and that British Captain Thomas Preston and his men stand trial for murder. Their demands were met. John Adams defended the British soldiers. They were acquitted.

There was much excitement to hear Joseph speak among the people gathered in the Old South Meetinghouse. Thirty British soldiers dressed in their brilliant red coats occupied the front seats. Fergus Driscoll, Samuel Adams, John Hancock, Dr. Benjamin Church, John Adams, Abigail Adams, Paul Revere, and William Dawes sat near the soldiers waiting for the orator to arrive.

Samuel Adams and John Adams feared that Joseph might fall victim to revenge and bloodshed from the loyalists. The Adams cousins went to Colm with their fears before the meeting, and asked for Joseph's protection. Colm stood behind and to the far-right side of the pulpit, watching the crowd. If anyone threatened Joseph, Colm would strike them dead. The realization that he would kill the children of man for Joseph troubled him.

Are human emotions infiltrating us? he wondered. *Is that why Ian tried to kill Michael?*

The smug soldiers turned a watchful eye on Colm. The inner circle of patriots who knew about Colm and his men were silently amused by the Redcoats' ignorance.

Michael, Patrick, and Brandon were stationed in the middle of the meetinghouse. Liam and Fergus were seated among the patriots near the pulpit. Seamus and Ian watched from opposite sides of the meetinghouse. Jeremiah stood in the back with the farmers and country folk who came to Boston for the occasion. None of the brotherhood had a firearm.

Liam smiled at Abigail Adams. He had not called on her as she had asked him to do when her husband, John Adams, came home from Cambridge.

Colm and Fergus made eye contact in readiness for a possible skirmish. Millenniums together as commander and second in command were impossible to erase. Fergus' blue eyes sent a message to Colm: *I am ready, and I am watching.*

At last, a carriage pulled up and Joseph and his apprentice in medicine, Dr. William Eustis, alighted at the door of the apothecary shop across the street. William had a garment draped over his arm.

Colm and John Hancock left the church and went inside the shop to meet Joseph. Colm raised an eyebrow when he saw what Joseph was wearing over his breeches and shirt.

"It is a toga," Joseph said, amused. "It is a garment of freeborn Roman citizens, a symbol of virtue and dignity."

John interrupted, "The church is packed. It will be almost impossible for you to make your way to the pulpit through the crowd. We do not want you roughly handled before you get there. William Dawes is placing a ladder against the building by a window behind the pulpit so you can climb through into the church."

"Is that really necessary?" Joseph asked.

"Please, Joseph. Just do as we ask."

Joseph looked at the archangel.

Colm nodded.

Once they'd all climbed through the window of the Old South Meetinghouse, Joseph stepped behind the black-draped pulpit. Colm returned to his station and ensured that his men and Jeremiah were still at their posts. William Dawes, William Eustis, and John Hancock seated themselves.

Joseph looked out over the crowd. He spoke with a language that gave an air of calm civility inside the meetinghouse.

"It is not without the most humiliating conviction of my want of ability that I now appear before you. I am obligated to obey the calls of my country at all times, together with an animating recollection of your indulgence exhibited upon so many occasions, has induced me once more, undeserving as I am, to throw myself upon that candor which looks with kindness on the feeblest efforts of an honest mind."

Joseph's oration was filled with religious references as was appropriate for the deeply religious men and women of the colonies. But his religious views had deviated since meeting the sons of God. He looked out over his captive audience. They were there watching over him—the angels and their human friend. Did he ever doubt there was truly a Heaven? Yes, because he was not a blind servant. He was certain all men capable of simultaneous self-loathing and self-respect doubted what they could not see.

"The tools of tyrants have rack'd their inventions to justify the few in sporting with the happiness of the many; and, having found their sophistry too weak to hold mankind in bondage, have impiously dared to force religion, the daughter of the king of Heaven, to become a prostitute in the service of Hell."

He described the events of the Boston Massacre.

A British officer standing just below the pulpit held up his hand and showed Joseph the butt of a pistol. The display enraged Colm, and alarmed Liam and Fergus. They were the only angels able to see the threat.

Colm's rage overwhelmed his spiritual restraint. His green aura lit the Old South Meetinghouse. It took every ounce of fortitude he possessed not to release his gold radiance in anger. The spellbound audience could not see the light, but the officer who threatened Joseph could. The officer's eyes brimmed with orange light. The demon that possessed the now deceased Captain Robert Percy made eye contact with Colm and mouthed the words, "I see you archangel, and your new friend is dead."

The brotherhood saw Colm's aura and felt his rage.

Joseph brought his oration near to a close:

"Our country is in danger, but not to be despaired of. Our enemies are numerous and powerful—but we have many friends. Determine to be free and Heaven and Earth will aid the resolution. On you depend the fortunes of America.

You are to decide the important question, on which rest the happiness and liberty of millions yet unborn. Act worthy of yourselves."

Rustling wings backdropped the conclusion of Joseph's oration. The brotherhood was alarmed. Michael reached into his coat and gripped the handle of his surgical blade. Brandon cloaked his yellow aura. Patrick forced himself not to look at his brother standing against the wall to his left. Seamus and Ian willed themselves not to move until they were ordered to do so.

Samuel Adams, John Hancock, and Paul Revere rose and came forward to the steps that lead up to the pulpit platform.

Colm's eyes were still on the demon's face.

Samuel, John, and Paul approached Joseph. Samuel's arm was out-stretched to reach for Joseph's hand in a congratulatory manner.

Jeremiah managed to shoulder his way through the dispersing crowd until he was standing behind Robert Percy.

Seamus, Ian, Brandon, Michael, and Patrick waited for Colm's orders.

Samuel and Joseph shook hands as Samuel said, "Thank you for that elegant oration. I move that you speak next year to commemorate the massacre."

Fergus saw Jeremiah. He didn't want to raise an alarm, but he also didn't want Jeremiah near the demon. He agonized over what course to take, and then decided that their human allies needed to recognize and become aware of what a demon was capable of.

The four British soldiers who remained in the nearly empty meeting-house moved in closer to Robert and pulled their sabers from their scabbards.

Colm ran to the edge of the platform and jumped to the floor in front of Robert.

At the same moment, Jeremiah slid his skinning knife into Robert's lumbar spine.

Orange flames shot from Robert's eyes, and he emitted a wolf-like howl. The black cloth that draped the pulpit caught fire. Liam's green aura flashed when he jumped onto the platform and dived at Joseph. They both fell to the floor.

Paul jumped to the floor alongside Colm. William Dawes ran to aide them.

The four British soldiers ran to the exit at the right of the pulpit platform.

Ian, Seamus, and Patrick ran toward the pulpit.

Jeremiah slid his knife out of Robert's back. There was no blood on the blade.

Robert laughed and doused his orange eyes. They returned to the blue eyes that belonged to his human vessel.

Colm called on every ounce of restraint he had to keep from killing the demon before they had a chance to find out if it knew anything about Henry.

Ian and Seamus shielded Paul Revere and William Dawes. Fergus and Patrick did the same for Abigail Adams, John Adams, Benjamin Church, and William Eustis. Brandon jumped onto the pulpit platform. Samuel and John Hancock flinched in surprise and stepped backward.

John Hancock knew without a doubt what he was witnessing, but still asked Brandon calmly, "What is happening?"

Robert sneered, "Pray to your God. Pray to these angels. Beg for forgiveness for your sins, because Hell on Earth is about to commence."

"Who *are* you?" Hancock demanded.

Robert snickered. "I am Captain Robert Percy, General Henry Hereford's aide-de-camp. The general read the missive the angel called Liam had John Adams publish in the *Boston Gazette.* He sent me here to determine if those brave and daring words were true."

Robert looked at Colm, "But more important to his desires, the general sent me here to make certain that you were with your men, archangel."

"Henry sent you instead of comin' himself?" Jeremiah asked. He still held his bloodless skinning knife in his hand. "Sounds ta me like he's a coward."

Robert turned around and took note of the knife in Jeremiah's hand. "Ah, so *you* are the man who stabbed me. You are *just* a man. Am I right?"

Colm stepped between Robert and Jeremiah.

"Do not worry, preceptor, I have no business with this man despite what he did—at least not yet," Robert said. Then he addressed Jeremiah. "General Hereford is awaiting my return. I will convey your sentiments to him."

He walked out of the meetinghouse. Colm let him go.

Liam and Joseph got up from the floor. Brandon stomped on the burning cloth until the fire went out. The men on the pulpit platform slowly descended the steps and joined the others standing on the floor in front of the pulpit. Paul Revere and William Dawes worked to control their breathing. John and Abigail Adams, Benjamin Church, William Eustis, and the angels gathered around Colm.

The patriots' religious world was badly shaken. It had been difficult enough to hear Colm recount God's banishment and deliberate release of demons to kill his own angels, but to *see* that abomination at work sparked a fear for which there were few words.

John Adams addressed Colm. "Is God punishing us for our rebellious actions?"

"Colm is not here to minister to us," Joseph said. "He is not here to soothe the terrors that are walking this Earth. He is here to protect us and his brotherhood from a death we cannot even imagine."

He paused to look at the tense faces of the eight other patriots huddled among the angels, and then continued, "We must accept what our eyes have seen and set aside our religious doubts if we are going to find the courage to move forward. We must accept the intentions of the angels who have come to dwell among us, and fight for us. We must be meritorious men and women who continue to serve God as he expects us to serve him, because *we* are the children of man."

Colm heard the angels' wings rustle. They were still uneasy.

"We shall," Hancock said. "Colm, please accept my apologies. I beg that of you and your men."

"We don't understand the purpose of apologies," Colm said. "But as Joseph said, we must move past our doubts and band together, or we'll all suffer."

Dawes said, "I believe shedding doubt is the simplest obstacle we will have to overcome in the coming months."

Abigail smiled at Liam. Then she said, "Yes, my dear William, I will accept the angels without doubt."

She turned her attention to the tall, thin angel with green eyes and a silver ribbon securing his neatly queued brown hair. "You must be the archangel, Colm Bohannon. John has spoken of you and the reverence he holds in his heart for you."

Joseph saw the tension drain from the angels' faces, but something was still amiss. He quickly looked about him in alarm, and said, "Colm, where is Michael?"

Wings rustled, and a breeze swept through the meetinghouse.

The angels scattered to search the meetinghouse. John Adams and John Hancock ran to the exit to the right of the pulpit. Jeremiah looked up at the ceiling horrified that he might see something hanging from the rafters. Paul, Samuel, and Colm ran toward the front door.

The meetinghouse door swung open just as Paul reached to turn the knob. A bruised and bleeding Dr. Samuel Prescott stumbled through the door.

੭

Colm's rage distressed Michael because he perceived Colm as always in control of his spiritual force.

The man, who once lived in Michael's human vessel and had died in Wexford, Ireland in 1169, idolized his older brother. The ghost of that spiritual idolatry haunted Michael. It was Michael's palimpsest—traces of what used to be showing through what exists now.

While Captain Robert Percy advised John Hancock to pray to his God, Michael stood alone near the front of the meetinghouse. He heard someone call his name. He turned around and saw Dr. Samuel Prescott, the twenty-three-year-old patriot who lived in Concord, standing in the front doorway. Samuel looked as if he needed someone to keep him from falling into distraction.

"Praise God you are here with me!" Samuel said, relieved. "Was that...a...demon?"

Michael went to soothe Samuel's fears. Suddenly, musket muzzles were jammed into the young men's backs.

"Do not issue a sound!" The man with the musket to Michael's back said.

Samuel felt the musket press hard into his kidney. "What are—?"

"Shut your mouth forthwith!" a man growled at him.

Michael had no idea if their assailants were demons or just men. Before he was able to act, a blow to the back of the head rendered him unconscious.

Samuel heard several men grunting as they dragged Michael away. Someone said to him, "Walk out the door, turn right, and turn right again. If you try to do otherwise, you will be shot."

The young doctor could not see the men who marched him out of the meetinghouse and into the narrow adjoining alley. The musket remained jammed in Samuel's back while two large men pistol-whipped him. He passed out when one of the men brought the butt of his pistol down on Samuel's clavicle for the fifth time.

Then, the men turned on Michael.

੭

"Joseph! William! It is young Dr. Prescott! He is severely hurt!" Paul shouted.

Samuel collapsed into Paul's arms, and William Dawes and Colm helped him get Samuel seated. Joseph and William Eustis arrived right away and began assessing Samuel's condition.

"Who has done this to you?" Paul demanded.

"We did not see them. They came from behind. They knocked Michael unconscious right off. He is lying in the alley."

Colm and Eustis ran out of the meetinghouse and into the alley. Patrick and Brandon followed. William knelt and began examining Michael. Patrick fell to his knees beside William.

Joseph and Paul hurried into the alley. Joseph said, "Patrick, stay out of the way so we can help him. Go back inside, and take Brandon with you."

Patrick made no response.

Colm put his hands on Patrick's upper arms. Patrick stood up, but kept his eyes on Michael.

Brandon asked, "Is he dead?"

"He is not dead," William assured.

"I will get Fergus to go with me to fetch a wagon," Paul interjected. He ran back inside the meetinghouse.

Joseph knelt beside William. The two doctors conferred briefly, and then Joseph removed his cravat and used it as a tourniquet on Michael's upper left arm.

It was then that Colm saw blood saturated the left arm of Michael's coat. Blood pooled in the dirt beneath his forearm. He was bleeding from a wound that would prove to be fatal if his assailants were demonic.

Colm tried to keep his attention on what Joseph and William were doing to care for his brother. It was difficult to concentrate on one member of his brotherhood when he knew they were all in danger.

John Hancock, Samuel Adams, Benjamin Church, and John Adams entered the alley.

As a lawyer, John Adams' inclination was to note the evidence left behind by the assailants. There was little to note except the amount of blood on the ground where Samuel and Michael had fallen. After a last glance at Michael's bloody coat sleeve, he said, "If this was meant to frighten us, it has failed. It has only served to embolden our courage."

Inside the meetinghouse, Jeremiah and William Dawes remained near the pulpit and the side exit doors in case of an unexpected intrusion.

Samuel Prescott shivered uncontrollably. Ian removed his coat and wrapped it around Samuel's shoulders. Samuel groaned. The weight of the coat increased the pain from his broken clavicle bones. He thought of his fiancée, Lydia Mulliken, who lived in Lexington. She would be frantic when she received the news of his attack.

Ian sat beside Samuel. He answered Samuel's silent prayers to God. "They've gone to fetch a wagon to get you to Dr. Warren's house. You'll recover from your physical injuries. The damage to your soul from what you've seen today will need more time to heal, but I assure you it will heal."

Liam and Abigail hovered near the meetinghouse front door while she waited for John to return to take her home. He stared at her lovely face, trying to think of something to say.

Abigail felt the weight of his stare. "Are you aware that staring is impolite?"

"No."

"Well, it is. Do you wish to say something?"

"Yes, but I am not certain about what I wish to say."

She laughed. "You are candid. I must remember to censor my questions lest I get an answer I do not wish to hear."

A carriage pulled up in front of the meetinghouse. A footman stepped from the back of the carriage and opened the passenger door.

John Adams climbed the meetinghouse steps. He smiled as he approached Abigail. He looked into her eyes. She did likewise. He offered his hand. She accepted it and returned his smile.

Liam watched their unspoken exchange like a child who had no conception that a loving relationship could exist between his mother and father.

Abigail said to Liam, "Thank you for protecting our dear Joseph."

"What are you saying?"

She smiled into his blue eyes. "Mr. Bohannon said angels do not understand the purpose of apologies. It appears you do not understand the purpose of showing gratitude, either."

"Perhaps you can teach me," Liam said, solemnly.

"She is a very patient teacher," John said with a tender smile. "Shall we go, Abby?"

"One moment, John. I would like to invite Mr. Kavangh to our home one afternoon for coffee and conversation. Are you agreeable?"

"Of course, my dear." John blinked. *We have invited an angel to our home. How odd.*

Michael awoke groggy in a shadowed and strange place. It took him a moment to realize there was another bed in the room, and the noise he heard was snoring. There was a figure silhouetted against the window to his left. Judging from the delicate features in his profile, and the long straight black hair pulled into a ponytail, it was Ian.

Michael focused his eyes on his bandaged forearm in the gloomy room.

"I told Colm I'd stay with you until you woke up," Ian said.

Michael sat up and threw his legs over the side of the bed. The back of his head pounded in time with the throbbing in his forearm. His face felt raw and swollen. "What happened?"

"You and Samuel Prescott were attacked. We aren't sure if it was just men or demons."

Michael remembered nothing. He stood up, and reeled with dizziness. He plopped on the bed.

"Is that Samuel snoring?"

"Yes. He's got broken bones, but he'll be fine."

"Where are we?" Michael asked.

"Joseph Warren's house."

"Where's Colm?"

"With Joseph."

"Where's Patrick?"

"Colm sent the rest of us back to the farm."

Michael attempted to stand again. Dizziness pushed him back down on the bed. He raised a hand to wipe away the sweat on his face, and then thought better of it.

Samuel exhaled a loud snorting snore and groaned.

Michael looked at the vague mound in the other bed that was Samuel. He said to Ian, "Those men or demons could've killed him, but they didn't. Why?"

"They're trying to scare us and the patriots. John Adams told Colm it didn't work."

Michael lay on the bed and stared at the ceiling. He remembered what he was thinking when Samuel had called to him in the meetinghouse. "When ya tried to kill me, did ya feel like there was something there that wasn't a part of ya spirit?"

"Something where?"

"Something within ya anger."

"Do you mean something that belonged to the human man, Ian Keogh?"

"Then ya did?"

Ian was unsure, and that uncertainty lingered like an intruder near his spirit. "I don't know. Did you feel something like that?"

Michael nodded at the ceiling.

Joseph opened the bedroom door. Colm followed him into the room.

Joseph smiled and said, "It is good to see that you are with us." He picked up the candle from the bedside chest, lit it, and then sat on the bed beside Michael. "How do you feel?" he asked, holding the candle up so he could see Michael's face.

"What do ya mean?" Michael asked.

"How is your pain?"

"I'm not in pain."

Joseph frowned and unwound the bloody bandage. Michael's forearm was mauled from elbow to wrist as if an animal had clawed it. The tendons were ruined.

"It is impossible for you to suffer no pain from this injury."

"Are ya asking me if my arm hurts?"

"Yes."

"The arm hurts, but I'm not in pain."

"I do not understand."

Michael didn't know how to explain.

Joseph looked at Ian and Colm's calm faces. It did not appear that an answer was forthcoming from either of them. *Angels must have a different perception of pain,* he thought. *Yet, Michael said his arm did hurt.*

Joseph continued his examination, and then dressed Michael's forearm with a clean bandage. "I will have to attempt to repair the tendons in your arm. Otherwise, you may never regain full function in your hand."

"What does that mean?"

Colm said, "Joseph, wait a few days. If men did this to him, his arm will heal on its own. If it was demons—"

"—I'm gonna die," Michael said. There was no fear in his voice.

Joseph looked at Colm. *How can I possibly respond to that statement?* Then, he looked at Michael and asked, "Are you hungry?"

"Aye. Can I have beer, too?"

"Of course." Joseph smiled. Michael looked like a little boy who was happy just to be alive. The contrast between the Bohannon brothers' demeanor astounded Joseph.

William Eustis stepped into the room. "Did you ask for me, Dr. Warren?"

"Yes, we need to remove Samuel's clothing so he may be more comfortable. I will wake him, but he may not be agreeable."

As if in answer, Samuel groaned from beneath his blanket. Joseph got up and went to his bedside. He pulled the blanket away. The young man's clothing was drenched in sweat, and he was shivering.

"Samuel," Joseph said. "Samuel, wake up."

Samuel moved his head and shoulders, which caused his broken clavicle bones to shift and grind. His eyes flew open, and he screamed. William tried to calm him by promising to give him whiskey.

Colm leaned against the wall and crossed his arms over his chest.

Joseph rose and took the few paces from the bed to stand in front of Colm. "This man is in terrible pain, and you lean back and take it in as if you are watching a cow birthing a calf? I thought angels eased human suffering! Or is that not the function of an *archangel*?"

Ian and Michael glanced at one another, surprised.

Joseph continued, "I tried to understand your unfamiliarity with appropriate social responses, but this is pure brutishness! If I prayed to God to help Samuel, of the eight of your brotherhood, which angel would he send?"

Colm walked out of the bedroom.

Joseph looked at Ian and Michael. "How could I have said that? I am so sorry."

"He knows you're upset," Ian said.

Joseph went back to Samuel's bedside. He and William helped Samuel remove his clothing and don a sleeping gown. As promised, William brought Samuel a bottle of whiskey.

After Joseph and William left the room, Samuel drank too much whiskey, and then threw up all over himself. He tried not to whine like a child, but his pain was horrendous, and he could not stop shivering. He felt like he was going to die, and he murmured a prayer.

Ian sat on the bed beside Samuel. He helped Samuel out of his vomit-stained nightgown, and then wiped the sweat from Samuel's face and chest and trembling arms.

Michael watched in silence.

"Don't pray to God," Ian said to Samuel. "He won't hear you because there are so many voices begging for mercy. I'm here, and I'll help you. I can't heal you, but I can assure you that you aren't alone. Lay your head down and close your eyes. Think of Lydia. Think of how she feels when you bed her."

Samuel managed to say, "I have not…"

"I know what a woman feels like. It was my downfall, and I realize it's my weakness, but it's your gift. When you go home, she'll come to nurse you. Her tender hands and loving words will heal you. There now. Close your eyes. Sleep and dream of Lydia."

Ian stroked Samuel's sweating forehead. Samuel drifted away into Lydia's arms.

Joseph stood in the bedroom doorway watching Ian soothe Samuel. He turned and quietly closed the door. He went to lock up the room he used as his medical office. Then he went to his study. Colm was sitting in a chair near the fireplace, drinking whiskey. Joseph poured whiskey into a crystal glass, and then sat in the chair across from Colm.

Colm didn't look at him.

"I was wrong," Joseph said. "I will *never* say something like that again."

Silver light flashed in Colm's eyes.

"Your ways are foreign to me. I did not understand your reaction to Samuel's pain."

"I'm not angry with ya," Colm said. He drank some of his whiskey.

"Is this about your spiritual burden, which is none of my concern?" Joseph asked.

"It *was* none of ya concern." Colm drank more whiskey. "When that demon threatened ya in the meetinghouse, I experienced something I've never experienced before. And I projected it onto my men."

Joseph waited for Colm to continue.

"I felt rage, Joseph. My men and I have protected humans in the past, but this time, I experienced an emotion triggered by a threat to a human being. Archangels don't invest emotions in the human condition. We're merely beholders and preceptors. I felt *involved* when that demon threatened ya. I shou'd only feel emotionally involved when it concerns my men."

"That is why you had no reaction to Samuel's suffering," Joseph said.

Colm nodded.

"Jeremiah is your friend. Have you not experienced the same thing with him?"

"No."

The study door flew open, and four rambunctious children spilled through the doorway. Their nanny, Mercy Scollay, came in behind them.

"Joseph, the children wish to say goodnight," Mercy said. She produced an alluring smile for his benefit.

She and Colm had met the first time he had come to the Warren house to speak to the doctor. She dipped her head. "Mr. Bohannon."

Joseph Warren's children were climbing into his lap or hanging on his shoulders. They stopped what they were doing when they noticed Colm. Five-year-old Richard and two-year-old Mary curled up in their father's lap and buried their faces in his chest. The older children, Elizabeth and Joseph stared at Colm.

"I'll let ya have private time with ya children," Colm said, rising from his chair. His experience with children was limited to those he saw in public places. He had never spoken to one nor had he had any sort of contact.

"Please, stay. I want them to meet you." The children in Joseph's lap turned their heads slightly and stole a peek at Colm.

"Come forward," Joseph said to his oldest child, nine-year-old Elizabeth. "Miss Elizabeth Warren, may I present Mr. Colm Bohannon."

Seven-year-old Joseph watched his big sister's reaction so that he may follow her example when it was his turn to be introduced.

Colm had no idea what the rules of etiquette were when being introduced to a child. He looked at Joseph for guidance, but Elizabeth took the lead. She went to him and demurely offered her hand, not as a handshake, but as a queen who expected to be kissed on the back of the hand. The gesture was not intended to be regal. It was intended to be polite.

"Mr. Bohannon, I am pleased to meet you," she said as if she were an adult. Her blue eyes sought Colm's attention.

His eyes shifted to look at her offered hand. Elizabeth let her hand drop.

"I prayed to you when my mother was dying," she said. "Why did you not save her?"

Colm had no answer. *She looks like Joseph,* he thought.

"You are God, are you not?"

"Betsey, that is quite enough," Mercy scolded.

But Elizabeth could not stop looking at Colm. His tranquil features were calming. He was quiet, unlike other men, who asked her silly questions and talked too loud. Above all, she saw the green light he emanated. No, Mr. Bohannon was not God. He was an *angel* of God, and her scolding nanny would not change her mind.

"Betsey, you are being rude," Mercy said in a stern voice. "I said that is quite enough."

"I will say when that is quite enough," Joseph warned Mercy.

He knew Colm was not going to respond to Elizabeth in a manner in which she expected, but at least she could gaze upon the archangel for a little longer. He urged his son, Joseph, forward to introduce himself. Then, he insisted the two youngest in his lap turn around to behold Mr. Bohannon.

Two-year-old Mary cried.

"All right children, kiss me goodnight; then off to bed," Joseph said. He pulled Mary in close and kissed the top of her blond head. Mary stopped crying and plopped a thumb in her mouth.

Mercy took Mary from Joseph. The three older children kissed their father and bid him a goodnight. Mercy herded the children out of the study, but not before she attempted to garner Joseph's attention. Her greatest wish was to become the next Mrs. Joseph Warren.

Joseph did not acknowledge her.

Colm poured himself a whiskey and sat across from Joseph.

Joseph chuckled, "When children are present, most adults try to appear amused by their presence and give the pretense that the youngsters are adorable. You looked absolutely terrified."

Colm gulped down the whiskey. "I'm not terrified of children."

Joseph laughed. "I believe you are. Do you not know any cherubs?"

"What are cherubs?"

"Angels that appear as chubby cheeked children."

"Joseph, ya need a lesson in the realities of Heaven."

Joseph became serious. "Then enlighten me. Why was Michael confused when I asked him if he was in pain?"

"Ya question confused me and Ian, too."

"Are you saying your body does not feel pain when it is injured?"

"Is that what ya were asking Michael?"

"Yes."

"We feel pain in our spirits because that's what we really are. We aren't flesh and blood. Michael's body may hurt, but that's not where he feels pain."

"If a demon injures your body, the injury will kill you?"

"If a demon injures our body it's only a visible sign of the attack on our spirit, and if a demon injures our spirit, we will die, but not in the human sense of death. It's true the body won't heal and the body could die, but our bodies and our spirits are not the same thing any more than ya body and ya soul are the same thing."

Joseph frowned and nodded.

"Humans associate life and death with a living body. Angels don't because we weren't created with a physical form."

"How *does* an angel die?"

Colm got up to refill his glass. He stared into the fireplace, drank down the whiskey and returned to his seat.

"Colm," Joseph insisted, "how does an angel die?"

Damn ya, Joseph, for making me say the words. "We're chained in eternal darkness."

FIFTEEN

On March 7, the day following Joseph's oration at the Old South Meetinghouse, a meeting of the Committee of Safety under the illegal Massachusetts Provincial Congress was held. Samuel Adams was notably present for the first time.

The Suffolk Resolves, which Joseph penned in cooperation with other delegates of the Suffolk Convention in September 1774, called for a boycott of British goods in Massachusetts. At that time, Samuel Adams and John Adams were attending the Continental Congress in Philadelphia. Joseph had written to Samuel before the convention began, seeking his advice on the matter of the resolves; however, Samuel's reply did not arrive in time.

Paul Revere served as courier and carried the Suffolk Resolves to Philadelphia and the Continental Congress. The congressional delegates unanimously approved the opposition that their countrymen in the Massachusetts Bay Colony were presenting to the latest unjust, cruel, and oppressive acts of the British Parliament.

This was the boycott Jeremiah had told Colm about the day before the angels left Burkes Garden for Boston. It was the first time Colm had heard of the Continental Congress.

Under the Suffolk Resolves, the poor of Massachusetts would have suffered if not for the generosity and patriotism of the colonies including Montreal, Canada. The loyalists despised this show of support and hoped that Boston might suffer more.

With the support of the Committee of Safety, Samuel Adams wrote endless letters of thanks to the colonies that sent donations to Boston. He never failed to include encouragements to the greater patriotic movement.

John Adams, who regularly published under the pseudonym Novanglus, did not openly write of inevitable independence, but his pen scratched out missive after missive regarding the liberties of the colonies and the dangers they faced.

These writings did not go unanswered by the pen of the many loyalist pseudonyms.

On March 14, the Committee of Safety focused on a proposed army, and the activities necessary to watch the movements of the British soldiers and the loyalists in Boston, Concord, Cambridge, and Roxbury. Fergus Driscoll and Brandon O'Flynn were among the new committee members under Chairman Joseph Warren.

Paul Revere organized a meeting at the Green Dragon Tavern to organize the watches. By now, it was commonly agreed upon that there was a traitor in the Provincial Congress. Paul was so concerned about the secrecy of the meetings that each man was required to swear upon the Bible that their transactions would not be revealed to anyone. Paul allowed the angels' refusal to make such a vow to God.

Fergus was now living in Cambridge. His new appointment to major of the militia there made him the natural choice for command of the Cambridge watch.

Brandon was given the rank of lieutenant and elected as commander of the Roxbury watch. Dr. James Prescott, Dr. Samuel Prescott's third cousin, was in command of the Concord watch. Joseph, John Hancock, Samuel Adams, and Benjamin Church took turns, two by two, watching the British soldiers by patrolling the streets of Boston all night.

The Provincial Congress renewed its session in Concord on March 22. The meeting under its newly elected president, John Hancock, immediately stated the necessity for putting the Colony of Massachusetts Bay in a state of defense. The congress concerned themselves with the rules and regulations of a constitutional army although they desired no war.

∼

Similar preparations to those in Boston were taking place throughout the colonies. In Richmond, Virginia, the colonial legislature reconvened in St. John's church after the royal governor dissolved its proceedings in the capital at Williamsburg. One of the delegates, George Washington, a planter from Westmoreland County, promised to review Richmond's militia, which he commanded. There was much debate on Virginia's action on a plan of military preparedness among the delegates, including a man named Patrick Henry.

Henry urged his fellow Virginians to arm in self-defense. In his closing appeal he uttered, "I know not what course others may take; but as for me, give me liberty or give me death."

Another round of debate took place. Then, by a majority of votes, Patrick Henry was named chairman of a colony-wide militia plan. Among those on his committee were George Washington and a plantation owner, Thomas Jefferson.

≁

The Gage's had been in Boston six months. Margaret joined the other British officers' wives in weekly games of Whist, which was more about gossip than cards. She listened with a disinterested ear about a handsome young widower—a doctor named Joseph Warren and his relationship with his children's nanny, Mercy Scollay.

On the morning of March 9, Margaret took it upon herself to seek Dr. Warren's medical attention. She was free to leave her home to do as she pleased as long as her personal maid, and the military guards appointed by her husband for her protection, escorted her.

Wanting to be unencumbered by others, she claimed she was afflicted with a female matter and needed to remain in bed. To her relief, or suspicion, her personal maid, twenty-six-year old Constance McCaskey was absent. Constance had developed a perverse carnal attraction for General Henry Hereford and Margaret believed that Henry was enjoying Constance's favors often.

Margaret slipped out of the house, cloaked and hooded, and hurried through the streets of Beacon Hill to Hanover Street. She paused at Dr. Warren's front door. What was she going to tell him once she was inside?

She could not confess her true identity nor was she certain she was able to convey the source of her sleepless nights without appearing as if she had the vapors. Her doubt intensified when a woman, who she assumed was Mercy Scollay, opened the door.

Mercy raised one delicate eyebrow when she saw Margaret.

"I am here to see Dr. Warren," Margaret said.

"As a patient?"

"Of course as a patient!"

Mercy regarded her with doubt. It was not unusual for unescorted women to seek Joseph's attention—medical or otherwise. *What is this beautiful elegant woman's real intention in seeking out Joseph? One would think she has her own family physician.*

Margaret felt judged by this *servant* and an element of self-satisfaction emboldened her. "Is Dr. Warren in?"

"He is with a patient. In fact, he has appointments all morning. Unless your condition is dire, I suggest you write your name, address, and symptoms in the daybook. Either Dr. Eustis or Dr. Warren will call on you as soon as one of them is available."

"That is not possible. I must see Dr. Warren today. I will wait until he can see me."

"As you wish," Mercy huffed. She had no choice but to let this woman enter the house. "Follow me."

Margaret crossed the threshold. She heard hushed voices as they passed a closed door on their way to the dining room that served as a waiting room. Mercy stopped near the open doorway and motioned for Margaret to enter. Margaret stepped into the warm room.

She immediately noticed a large painting of an unadorned, very young woman hanging on the far wall. Donned in a beautiful sweeping dress and lounging in a chair, the woman looked bored.

"Fill out an entry in the daybook with your name and a description of your discomfort. Once you have done that, I will inform Dr. Warren," Mercy instructed. "The book is on the table to your right."

Margaret's eyes remained on the painting. "Who is that woman?"

"Elizabeth Hooten Warren. She is…was Dr. Warren's wife. She passed on two years ago."

Joseph's oldest son ran into the room. "Mercy! Mrs. Revere brought the food for our picnic! Can we go now? Pleeezzz?"

Mercy made no excuses nor did she scold young Joseph for entering the patient waiting room, although it was forbidden. She smiled at the boy and said, "Yes, we may go now. Be sure to bundle up. It is cold outside."

"Betsey! Mercy said we may go now!" Joseph shouted to his unseen older sister. He darted out of the room. Mercy followed without a backward glance in Margaret's direction.

Margaret waited all morning and into the early afternoon as patients came and went, escorted by a young man they addressed as Dr. Eustis. She heard the grandfather clock in the hallway chime half past one.

"Miss Kemble?"

She looked up into his smiling face.

"I am Dr. Warren. Please, follow me."

She signed the daybook with her maiden name, hoping to maintain anonymity, but the fear of being discovered for who she really was dissolved. The descriptions of his beauty did not hold a candle to his true appearance. His blue eyes were alight with vigor. His neatly coiffed sandy-blond hair framed the perfect oval of his face. The tales of his kindness as a physician were evident in his gentle composed demeanor.

In that moment, Margaret knew that she needed no powders or potions to sleep at night. All she needed was to experience the touch of this younger man. The fantasy brushed her inner thighs like the wings of an angel. In horror, she realized her right hand had traveled to her lap.

"You *are*, Miss Kemble?" Joseph asked. Margaret was not alone in the throes of sexual admiration. Joseph was taken somewhat aback by his new patient's elegant beauty. And, like Mercy, he found it difficult to believe she had merely wandered into his medical practice in need of a family physician.

Mrs. Thomas Gage rose in answer to Dr. Joseph Warren's question. He turned and walked out of the waiting room. She followed. Then, they were alone in the examination room. Joseph did not remember offering her a chair. Margaret did not remember sitting down.

He said, "I read the complaint you wrote in the daybook. I apologize, but it was unclear to me whether you are having difficulty falling asleep or staying asleep."

Her mind heard his words and understood none of them. "What?"

Joseph's eyes drank in her unblemished face, brown eyes, straight nose, and mass of brown hair piled in seductive curls on the top of her head. His eyes dropped to the hint of ample cleavage that peaked over the bodice of her elegant dark blue gown. Her breathing quickened. The rise and fall of her chest was hypnotic.

He blinked to break the trance. *This woman is a member of a social circle far beyond my reach, yet she sought me out. She is hiding something, and if I allow her to stay, I will be a party to her deceit.* But that intrigue was the reason he *did* allow her to stay. "Miss Kemble...is it?"

She forced herself not to look away. "Yes."

"I find it hard to believe a lovely woman such as you is unmarried, but I suppose that is none of my affair." He waited for her reaction and when none was forthcoming, he said, "As I asked before, are you having trouble falling asleep or staying asleep?"

"Both, I suppose."

He moved closer to her and slipped his hand under her chin so he could look into her eyes. They were bright and clear. "Is there something in particular that troubles you so that you cannot fall asleep? Pain or discomfort? Perhaps a disturbance?"

"I am not suffering from vapors if that is your meaning," she said, insulted.

Joseph slid his hand out from under her chin, frowned, and took a step back.

There, I have broken this ridiculous lascivious game, she thought. But the stirring she felt between her legs longed for this to be anything but a game.

"I am not insinuating anything, Miss Kemble. You have come to me in need of a physician to treat you for sleeplessness, and these questions are necessary for me to issue a proper diagnosis and treatment to restore the balance of your bodily humors."

"I apologize. Yes, I have been experiencing anxiety due to an unwanted house guest." She looked down at her sweating clasped hands.

Joseph fought the urge to pull her up out of the chair and kiss her lips. He swallowed and said, "I understand. I will prepare a remedy for your insomnia. It should not take long."

The sound of William Eustis' voice in the hall snapped Joseph out of his insensibility. "I will escort you back to the waiting room."

Margaret nodded and stood up. She followed Joseph.

Thirty minutes later, she was on her way back to Province House. She had gotten what she had come to get from Dr. Warren. Much, much more than she had hoped for.

SIXTEEN

Michael's injuries healed on their own, which meant he and Dr. Samuel Prescott had been attacked by ordinary men. When Ian rode to Concord to visit Sidonie on March 20, he called on Samuel to see how he was recovering. As Ian had predicted, Lydia Mulliken was there caring for her fiancée, who was feeling much better.

With Colm, Seamus, and Brandon engaged in the proceedings of the Provincial Congress and the Committee of Safety, the remaining four members of the brotherhood and Jeremiah were tasked with ensuring the farm was in working order, the house and kitchen were supplied, muskets and pistols were cleaned and oiled, cartridges were prepared, and horses were cared for.

On March 24, under Colm's order, Patrick, Michael, and Liam went on foot to Boston to drill with the militia on the eastern edge of Boston Common where Gage's troops were not bivouacked.

Liam's mind was on the visit he had arranged with John and Abigail Adams after the drills.

The boys kept glancing at him. Finally, Patrick asked, "Why are you wearin' them fancy clothes, Liam?"

Liam had merely emulated what he had seen, believing that it was a step toward assimilating into human society. He had taken note of the Adams' clothing at the Boston Massacre commemoration and had gone to William Dawes to ask where he could get similar clothes. William had raised an eyebrow and recommended a tailor.

"I have no money," Liam admitted.

"Then offer something in exchange for a new shirt and breeches."

"What do you mean?"

William thought for a moment, then said, "I will take care of the payment."

Liam now realized that his new clothing was an attempt to please Abigail. He glanced at the boys. To his relief, they seemed to have lost interest in the answer when Patrick said to Michael, "Let's go to the Green Dragon while we're waitin' on Liam."

Michael shook his head. "I want to find a tavern where there's pretty girls. I never see any at the Green Dragon."

"That's because there ain't no whores at the Green Dragon. Besides, it's safer at the Green Dragon. There's less of a chance we'll get attacked by demons there. You're lucky them men that went after you and Samuel was human."

"I'm not scared of demons," Michael protested. "Colm doesn't want us to be scared so I'm not scared."

"Who're you tryin' to convince?"

Michael shrugged.

"I'm surprised Colm's lettin' us split up like we've been doin', considerin' the demons know we're here," Patrick said. "He hated it when any of us left Burkes Garden, especially without tellin' him."

Liam spoke up. "Things are different now."

"They're worse," Patrick said.

They entered the commons and walked toward a gathering of men.

"He wants you to think for yourself; understand the consequences of your actions," Liam said.

They stopped walking.

Liam looked at them. "Colm has protected us for millenniums. If something happens to him who will protect us?"

Michael's pouty lower lip quivered and Patrick thought of Seamus chained in the eternal darkness of death. Both boys' wings rustled.

Liam heard the rustling and was aware of the boys' distress, but he continued anyway, "We may have to stand on our own without Colm."

Michael shoved Liam, and yelled, "Why are ya saying that?"

"Because it is important," Liam affirmed.

Michael reached for the front of Liam's coat, but Liam dodged him.

Patrick jumped between them. "Stop it, Michael! Them men are watchin' us!"

"Why did ya say that?" Michael insisted.

"Do you not understand the gravity of what we are facing? What Colm is facing?" Liam asked.

"NO, I DON'T UNDERSTAND!" Michael screamed. He was shaking under the weight of his anger and apprehension. "Something's happening to us that has nothing to do with demons!"

"Michael, lower your voice," Patrick warned.

Michael ran a hand across his mouth. His chest heaved; he panted as if he had been running for miles. His palimpsest cried for attention. He pushed it away. It was a stranger who had no business interfering in his relationship with his brotherhood.

"Do ya feel him? Do ya?" he demanded of Patrick.

"Who?"

"I feel him. I think Ian might feel him. FUCK!" Michael turned in a circle, put a hand to his forehead, let his hand drop and ran toward the gathering of men on the common.

Patrick's beautiful effeminate face contorted with foreboding. "What's he talkin' about?"

Liam was uncertain, but whatever it was made him uneasy. He struggled to keep his green aura from bursting forth. His wings rustled. He regained control and walked across the common.

Patrick followed. The men of the Boston militia watched the angels' approach with expectation.

William Dawes went to meet them. Their tension oppressed him to the point that he felt like praying.

Michael stormed past him and fell in with the other militia members.

"What is wrong?" William asked Patrick in alarm.

He saw Patrick's blue aura flash as Liam and Patrick walked past. "Patrick, stop," he implored. Something was changing between the angels and their patriotic alliance with humans; something deeper than even Dr. Warren had proclaimed at the Old South Meetinghouse.

"I stand with your pain as you stand with mine," William offered.

Patrick and Liam stopped. They looked at William.

"Please, what is the matter?" William asked.

Liam said. "They are upset with me for telling the truth of what I see." He continued toward the waiting men.

The Boston militia, under the watchful eyes of British soldiers, drilled on the muddy grounds of Boston Common under the sun washed skies of a spring day. It would be their last drill. General Thomas Gage passed an ordinance two days later, forbidding any type of provincial military-like drills in the Massachusetts Bay Colony.

The ordinance was a relief to the angels. It was nearly impossible for them to follow another commander other than Colm.

∾

After drills, Patrick convinced William and Paul to join him and Michael for a draught at the Green Dragon. Liam kept his appointed visit with the Adamses.

A young man answered Liam's knock on the door. He frowned and asked, "Sir?"

Liam experienced an unsettling emotion he did not understand. He considered leaving. If Abigail had not come to the door, he would have left. Her smile lit up his world.

"Bertie, this is Mr. Kavangh. Please allow him to come in."

Bertie scowled, but he stepped aside to let Liam pass.

"This is John's nephew, Bertie…Bert Adams," Abigail said in introduction. "Bertie, Mr. Kavangh and I will be visiting in the living room. You are welcome to join us, but your attendance is not required."

Bertie was a young, skinny, unattractive prig with a pimply forehead and chin. Liam sensed that Bertie posed a threat, but the nature of it was beyond his understanding.

On the other hand, Abigail was aware that entertaining Liam alone would set the stage for unfounded idle gossip that would begin with her sour-faced nephew. Yet, she did not extract herself from the situation. Her husband had prior knowledge of the angel's visit and had not deterred it.

"John is at our home in Braintree on unexpected family business. He extends his apology for his absence," Abigail said as she led Liam into the living room.

There was a decanter of wine on a drop-leaf table in the living room. Abigail poured a glass and offered it to Liam. Their fingertips brushed when he took the glass from her hand. She filled her glass, sat on the couch, patted the seat beside her and said, "Please sit with me."

Liam winced from the stab of a spoken memory his spirit did not recognize. *Sit with me, son.*

He sat beside her. Despite the unsettling false memory, the sulking nephew, the absence of her husband, and the unfamiliar surroundings of her living room, his enthusiasm for the visit had not waned. However, he had no idea how to begin a conversation.

Abigail saw his conundrum cloud his face. She asked, "How are the accommodations at the farm in Roxbury?"

"The farm is suitable."

There was a long pause. Abigail continued, "I read the missive you wrote when it was first published in the *Boston Gazette*. I appreciated its eloquence. Following the confrontation with that demon in the meetinghouse, I read it again. I have read it many times since, and now I hear your voice in those words."

"What are you saying?"

"I am saying, now that we are better acquainted, I have more appreciation for your writing."

"The advertisement was a simple challenge."

"Please, do not be so modest."

Liam frowned. "Is this considered *polite* conversation?"

"It does sound that way," she tittered.

"I wanted so much to see you again, but this is a mistake. I should not be here without John in attendance." Liam rose from the couch. "My presence without the protection of a man in the house is endangering you and your children."

She smiled inwardly. Apparently, Liam did not consider Bertie a *man*. "My children are in Braintree. I will join them in a few days. Please stay."

Liam sat down and drained his glass of wine. He had no powers of resistance when it came to Abigail Adams.

She continued her conversation, "In your missive, you used the term *preceptors of mysteries* in reference to yourselves. That demon called Mr. Bohannon a preceptor. What does that mean?"

"When humans pray to God, we, the angels, answer those prayers. You ask for signs that God has heard you. You ask for signs of miracles. You ask for guidance. Angels reveal the mysteries of God in answer to the lessons you have asked for."

"Angels consider those lessons?"

"Yes."

Abigail feared the answer to her next question, but she asked it anyway. "Does God love us?"

"Abigail, I do not think that—"

"I am sorry. I did not intend for this to turn into a religious discussion."

"*We* are not discussing anything. You are questioning me about a God who does not love me or my brotherhood."

She looked at him with shame.

"I understand your need for religious answers. It is an archetype we have encountered throughout the millennium. But you are searching for those answers from a banished angel. I have no right to offer you heavenly guidance or assurance."

"Again, I offer my apologies."

"Why do humans apologize? I fail to see the purpose."

She smiled. "It is a societal habit intended to smooth ruffled feathers, but you are right, apologies have no real purpose. If we learned from the cradle that honesty is not an insult, apologies would not be necessary."

Liam had no reply.

"We have much to learn from one another," Abigail said. "I shall leave the matter of God in the hands of the church."

Liam found her enchanting.

She said, "I saw Mr. Bohannon's angelic light. What of yours?"

"His name is Colm."

"Yes, I am aware."

"It is rare that a human can perceive our light unless we are under extreme duress. Or unless we allow it."

She hoped that he would allow it.

He understood her expectation and said, "I cannot."

"Are we to become better acquainted or not?"

Liam offered a smile.

"The idea of your angelic spirit is enthralling. I so want to see and feel it."

"Abigail, what you are asking of me is the same as asking me to walk naked in front of you."

"Please, do not become exasperated. We are learning together. Remember?"

"I am not exasperated with you. If I give in to the vulnerabilities I have for you, I am afraid of how far I will let them go."

Abigail was surprised and stifled the urge to issue an apology.

"Did John tell you why we were banished from Heaven?" Liam asked.

"No."

"There were those of us who could not resist our vulnerabilities. We, with the Grigori angels, fulfilled our lust for human women. Some of us created Nephilim."

"You defied God's command?"

"Yes, so *do* you understand why I cannot give in to you?"

"You have…known a woman?"

"No. Ian, Seamus, and Michael created the Nephilim. The rest of us, under Colm's command, tried to stop them, but we were too late."

"Why was Colm commanding the charge?"

"He is the archangel who shepherded the Grigori angels."

"So, all of you were punished?"

"Yes."

She struggled with this new knowledge, and the religious implications. God was not the just being she believed him to be.

As Liam watched her inner strife cloud her beautiful brown eyes, his resolve to remain invulnerable weakened. The urge to soothe her strife overcame him. He rose from the couch and placed his empty wine glass on the drop-leaf table.

He closed his eyes and summoned the pageantry of his heavenly being. His wings unfurled as silently as snow falling in the dead of night. They swept the parlor from floor to ceiling. Silver crystals rained upon everything in the living room. They gathered on the furniture and drifted against the walls.

Abigail watched in awe as his shimmering wings fluttered over the drop-leaf table without disturbing any of the delicate glassware on top. His luminous aura illuminated the parlor with green light.

She fought the instinct to fall to her knees in reverence.

Liam furled his wings and doused his aura. Abigail's smile and obvious adoration fulfilled his need to please her—until he saw Bertie Adams standing in the living room doorway. Bertie flashed his orange eyes at Liam.

Liam's actions shook him to the core of his angelic spirit. He had committed an act that bordered on creating a Nephilim. Not only had he disobeyed a direct standing order from his commander; a demon had witnessed the act. Liam was certain that when he first arrived, Bertie was not possessed.

Bertie smirked at Abigail, and then walked away.

She went to Liam's side. "We have done nothing wrong! There is nothing Bertie can say that John is not already aware of. If he speaks of what he saw to those who do not know of you, they will think him distracted."

"What I just did is forbidden."

"Who forbids it?"

"Colm."

"Why?"

"It makes no difference why. He is my superior."

Abigail stepped closer to Liam. When he looked at her, his eyes appeared calm. "Are you going to tell him?" she asked.

"Yes."

"You are not afraid of the consequences?"

"I am terrified."

Despite his words, she saw no terror skewing his countenance, and that confused her.

"This is my fault." She pressed a hand to her breast as if her heart was breaking. "I will plead with John to speak with Colm on your behalf. I will beg him to have mercy because you were tempted by my sin."

"You will not beg! Colm is not God! When will you understand that we are not here in the name of religion?"

She had no answer.

"We struggle just as you struggle in the pursuit of life and liberty," Liam said. "Understand that. Then, perhaps you will open your eyes to me."

With remorse, she realized that she was projecting human emotions and reactions onto a being that was not human. It was no different than expecting a dog to speak English or a horse to use table manners.

"You are right. I did not see *you* before."

Liam wanted to touch her cheek or take her hand, but he did neither. He said, "It may be a long time before we meet again. I will have to face the consequences of my actions today. It is not your burden to carry."

Abigail nodded and led him to the door. Without any thought for the lurking Bertie, she stood on her tiptoes and kissed Liam goodbye on the cheek.

Her kiss left a strange sensation on his skin. He hesitated to leave Abigail alone with her nephew. Bertie's sudden demonic possession was worrisome, but Liam could not linger in the Adams house like a fabled guardian angel. He took his leave.

As he walked to the Green Dragon, he contemplated his behavior. He had envisioned the visit in a completely different vein. He had assumed that the visit would be one of many lessons he would learn about the society in which the brotherhood was trying to assimilate.

His humanistic urge to please her confused him. It lurked near his angelic spirit, and it was satisfied because what had happened was what *it wanted*.

SEVENTEEN

Liam entered the Green Dragon at five o'clock in the afternoon. Michael, Patrick, and William were very drunk. Liam was not looking forward to their journey back to the farm.

"Have a draught!" Michael suggested. "Ya just missed Paul."

"I think Paul wearied of us," William explained as he tried to control his drunken tongue. "He called us stupid kids. I am thirty years old! I've a wife and four child'en!" He elbowed Patrick in the side and pointed at Liam. "Tell 'im Patrick."

"It's ture," Patrick confirmed.

Michael howled laughter. "*Ture?* That's not a word!"

Liam looked around the shadowed candlelit tavern. Points of orange light flared here and there. Demons were watching. He said, "We need to go."

Patrick stood up and stumbled sideways.

Michael and William tried to stand, but instead fell backward off the bench where they were sitting. They burst out in laughter as they lay on the floor, looking up at the ceiling.

Liam left the tavern and ran down Union Street toward the North End. He found Paul on his way home.

"I need help getting Michael, Patrick, and William out of the tavern. I do not think they are aware that demons are watching them. I am sure the demons were watching you as well."

Paul raised an eyebrow, but then realized he should not have been surprised.

"Can you return to the tavern and ensure William gets home?" Liam asked. "I will not be able to get him and the boys out of there on my own."

"You angels are a demanding bunch," Paul said, exasperated. He knew John Adams was in Braintree, and wondered why Liam had kept his appointment with the Adamses anyway. He also knew that John's dolt nephew was staying with the Adamses. In Paul's opinion, Bertie was useless as a chaperon or as anything else, for that matter.

"I will assist, but only for Mehitable's sake," Paul said referring to William's wife. "Are those demons going to follow us home?"

"I cannot answer with certainty, but I see no purpose it would serve."

Patrick, Michael, and William were sitting outside of the Green Dragon when Paul and Liam arrived.

"Can you stand?" Paul asked William.

William looked up at Paul and burped. "I am gonna puke."

Michael and Patrick struggled to get to their feet. They stumbled into one another and bounced off the tavern's brick outer wall. Liam was reminded of their drunken sprees with Brandon in Burkes Garden. The boys often spent those nights woods-running. Liam longed to be back on Garden Mountain living in seclusion.

Paul helped William to his feet and steadied him.

William said, "I tole ya…" and vomited on his boots.

Michael and Patrick threw their backs against the tavern wall and erupted into raucous laughter. The noise drew the attention of several British soldiers.

Paul did not look at the angels as he urged William away from the tavern toward home.

Liam managed to corral Michael and Patrick by pointing out the soldiers striding purposefully toward them. Michael and Patrick were too drunk to make sense of the danger posed by the soldiers' approach, but they were not too drunk to run. The angels made it to Orange Street and escaped Boston without being detained at the Neck. The soldiers at the Neck's guard post had no interest in what they believed to be ignorant drunken Yankee farmers.

Patrick tripped and slid headlong on the slick muddy road. Tree roots, downed branches, and rocks ripped his cloak and breeches, and cut his face and hands. Michael stumbled to a halt and dropped to his knees beside Patrick.

Patrick spit mud from his mouth and said, "I cain't." He threw up.

Michael pitched sideways.

Both boys passed out. Liam shivered in the freezing Massachusetts March night; he sat on the muddy road guarding Colm's and Seamus' little brothers, contemplating his disobedience.

❧

Patrick felt the toe of a boot nudge his ribs and heard, "Wake up, Brother." He rolled onto his back and tried to focus his eyes. The waning crescent moon cast little light on the road. It took him a moment to realize Seamus and Colm were standing over him with their arms crossed. He didn't know where he was or why he was there, but he supposed that meant that Michael was with him, and they had gotten very drunk.

"Get up, Brother," Seamus calmly said.

It took Patrick a full minute to get stable footing in the mud. His mud-caked clothes were wet and heavy, and he smelled vomit. He detected movement to his right. Michael was standing, but he was unsteady.

"You're lucky you weren't spotted by patrols," Seamus said.

"Where are we?" Patrick asked.

"Outside the Neck. Let's go home."

Michael focused all his energy on staying upright.

Patrick took two tentative steps, and then stopped.

Liam picked up Patrick's musket from the road. He slung the musket onto his shoulder alongside his own. Colm had already dispossessed Michael of his musket.

"Come on now," Seamus said to the drunken boys. "I ain't carryin' you."

Patrick burped and gagged and swallowed the bile in his throat.

Michael took a step, stumbled, and fell. Colm broke his fall and stood him up.

The boys were finally able to walk. Liam was exhausted. He dawdled along behind them until Colm took up the rear to protect his charges from anyone lurking in the woods. It took them over an hour to walk the mile to Roxbury.

Just before they reached the perimeter of the farm, they encountered Brandon and the newly formed Roxbury watch.

"There's movement north from Dorchester," Brandon told Colm. "The watch there sent a rider. They aren't sure if the patrol's returning to Boston or coming our way."

Abijah Cunningham, a twenty-eight-year-old farmer and the brotherhood's closest neighbor, observed Patrick's muddy condition. "You and Michael were to be on watch with us tonight. Where were you?"

Colm said, "Liam, go in the house. Patrick, Michael, go with him."

Brandon could see and smell why they hadn't joined the watch.

"Abijah, don't ever question my men when me or Seamus is with them," Colm warned.

Despite Colm's calm demeanor, Abijah was afraid to rebuff the order. There was something about Colm that frightened him. Abijah stepped back.

"This is the last point of our patrol tonight," Brandon said to the men of the watch. "Dawn's less than two hours off. Go home and get some sleep." He failed to address Michael and Patrick's absence from the watch. Belittling or making excuses for his brotherhood for the benefit of outsiders wasn't done.

The farmers, blacksmiths, lawyers, and saddle makers of the Roxbury watch dispersed.

"I'm gonna stay on alert until dawn in case that British patrol is coming our way," Brandon offered. He looked at the one dimly-lit living room window and cocked his head. "Where did you find them?"

"Lying on the road outside the Neck," Colm said. "Me and Seamus got back from Concord late, and they weren't home, so we went looking for them."

Seamus said, "Liam was with them. He weren't drunk. He was just sittin' there guardin' them."

"Why wasn't Ian and Jeremiah looking for them?"

"They was sleepin'."

"Brandon," Colm said. "I'm proud of ya for taking the responsibility of commanding the local watch."

A comment like that from Colm was rare and cherished. It helped Brandon come to terms with the difficulties he had getting the human men to form some kind of ranks. For the most part, they had been cooperative, but they were strong-willed, independent thinkers who were competitive and sometimes argumentative. It didn't occur to him that Colm faced those challenges every day.

Colm said to Seamus, "Go get some sleep. I'll stay with Brandon. I don't want him out here alone."

࿇

That afternoon, Jeremiah, Liam, and Seamus were in the living room cleaning and oiling muskets and flintlock pistols. Colm sat with them while he cleaned the long rifle he used for hunting. The large round table in the middle of the room was littered with guns, various knives, a whetstone, and balls, powder, and paper for cartridges.

Ian and Brandon were in the kitchen preparing supper. Both hated to cook, and they often made food that caused the men to suffer later in the night. It had been weeks since the men had eaten a meal together.

Michael and Patrick were outside washing their muddy clothes. They shivered in the early spring breeze. The only coat and cloak they owned was in the washtub.

This domestic harmony had been learned from Jeremiah and Mkwa. Before that time, the angels streaked through the cosmos like a flock of birds unable to roost. When they took human vessels, they had no example of domestication that they understood. So, they wandered like sheep with no shepherd whom they could look to for shelter.

Colm thought about Jeremiah's Shawnee woman, Mkwa, and wondered how men felt about leaving a woman behind while they marched off to war. Love and shared responsibility between human men and women was a curious attachment. Aside from Jeremiah and Mkwa, the angels paid little attention to that relationship.

"Ya child's a boy," Colm announced to Jeremiah.

Jeremiah looked up from the musket he was oiling. His hands stilled. "What? How do you know?" Jeremiah rolled his eyes. "That was a stupid thing ta say. 'Course you know. You're omnipotent."

Colm frowned. "I'm not omnipotent."

Liam and Seamus did not look up from the pistols they were cleaning.

A son, Jeremiah thought. He said, "I ain't never gonna meet 'im. I'll never make it back ta Burkes Garden. Do you see that in your visions archangel? My death?"

"No."

"Then you ain't been lookin'." Jeremiah returned to oiling the musket, but his mind stayed on his son.

"Supper!" Ian yelled from the kitchen.

Colm was the principal game hunter among the brotherhood. Since they moved to Roxbury, his many absences left a void in the pantry, which Michael and Patrick were happy to fill. Jeremiah skinned and prepared the game for cooking or salting or smoking depending on the animal that was laid on his skinning table.

Now, on this early evening in the last week of March, the angels and their human friend gathered in the warm living room to eat supper.

Colm noticed that Liam did little more than stare at his food.

The sound of horses galloping toward the farm along the road from Boston Neck didn't alarm the eight men in the living room. What did alarm them was the sudden silence of clattering hooves. There was banging on the front door.

Colm put his plate down and reached for his long rifle. He nodded at Jeremiah and Seamus to take up arms, and then he shifted his eyes to Brandon,

Michael, and Patrick. The boys armed themselves and retreated to the kitchen. Ian and Liam were already armed with pistols. They ran to flank the door.

Colm leveled his rifle at the center of the front door.

"Colm, open the door!"

"Joseph?"

"Let us in!"

Colm nodded at Ian. Ian disengaged the bolt. No one moved from their stance.

Joseph burst into the house with Paul and William on his heels.

Liam closed the door and threw the bolt.

Colm called for Brandon, Patrick, and Michael. The boys were alarmed at the patriots' presence. However, they kept quiet. "Take their horses to the barn. Stay there on the defensive until I say otherwise," Colm ordered.

The boys took the order.

Joseph looked at the cache of weapons piled on the table in plain sight. "Hide those!"

Colm pointed at Seamus, Jeremiah, and Ian, and then pointed above stairs. "The attic."

They scrambled to clear the table of weapons except the knives and whetstone. William and Paul collected the powder horns, scooped up the balls and cartridges, and dumped them into the cartridge boxes. All five men ran up the steps that lead to above stairs and the attic.

"What's the alarm?" Colm asked.

"Someone has tipped off Lord Patterson to the presence of dangerous rebels in Roxbury," Joseph said as he walked to a window.

"Who's Lord Patterson?"

Joseph surveyed the road through a small diamond-shaped window pane. "He is a ruthless royalist who is known for taking matters into his own hands without consulting General Gage. He has dispatched regulars to make arrests."

"The presence of rebels living in the surrounding towns and villages is well-known," Colm said. "Why's this different?"

Joseph turned away from the window. "Something happened yesterday that caused this sudden aggressive move. That event concerns me because we have not been able to identify it."

"How do ya know they're coming here?"

The five men thundered down the stairs to the living room.

"I was told the captain commanding the regulars referred to the Maguire farm as the starting point," Joseph said. "That is the surname Ian used to lease this farm."

"Henry's gotta have a hand in this," Seamus said.

"Perhaps you should consult with Liam," Paul spat.

Seamus noted the guilty disbelief on Liam's face, but it wasn't his place to ask questions when Colm was present.

Colm gripped the butt of his rifle. *This can't be because of Liam. Liam is intelligent and thoughtful and dependable and reasonable.*

Liam had intended on confessing his disobedience after supper. What shocked him was the idea that John Adams' nephew had gone to the loyalists and reported what he had seen take place between his aunt and Liam. Even more puzzling was the fact that this Lord Patterson had believed a story about an alleged angel.

No, Liam thought. *That is not correct. Bertie Adams made other accusations. That has to be the explanation for what is happening.*

"How did ya get through the guard post on the Neck?" Colm asked Paul.

"William talked our way through."

"Talk ya way back through."

"No. William and I are riding to spread the alarm that the regulars are marching with malicious intent toward citizens."

"Seamus, get the boys and ride west as fast as ya can," Colm said. "Ian and Jeremiah take your muskets and start walking the road to Menotomy. If a patrol stops ya, ya are traveling from Hartford to Menotomy. Ya can all circle back at dawn."

Jeremiah and the brotherhood swiftly carried out their orders. Paul and William went with Seamus to the barn. They mounted up and left to spread the warning throughout the countryside.

Colm leaned his long rifle against the wall beside the fireplace. He stacked the eight abandoned dinner plates, shoved them into the china closet, and said, "Joseph, go home."

"And leave you and Liam to face this alone? No."

"Joseph, do as Colm has asked," Liam said quietly. "I must pay penance for what I have done."

"What *have* you done?"

"Ya are interfering, Joseph."

"Is that really what you believe?"

126

Colm crossed his arms over his chest and set his jaw. He tried to stand his ground, but he realized there was nowhere to get even footing. *Damn this man who is capable of shaking my resolve. Damn this man who I'd do anything to protect and makes me feel the human need to explain.*

"We don't know how many soldiers are coming or if they're demons or if Henry's with them," Colm said. "I won't expose my men to an unknown situation if I can help it. I won't let them die like that. I won't let ya die like that."

"But you will let Liam die like that?"

Colm clenched his jaw.

"Answer me, Colm."

Colm's jaw muscles flexed and tightened.

"You and Liam came to my aide and protected me at the Boston Massacre commemoration," Joseph said, undaunted. "I will not turn my back on either of you."

Horses galloped the road toward the farm, and then came to a stop. A man shouted. Sabers clattered. Boots thudded across the porch.

Colm slid his long rifle under a couch to avoid provoking gunfire. Then, he snatched the wrought iron poker from the fireplace mantel.

The front door trembled under the punishment of a man's fist. "The King's troops! Allow us entry!"

Liam walked to the door.

Colm tightened his grip on the wrought iron poker.

Joseph touched the butt of the pistol that was tucked in his coat pocket.

Liam threw back the bolt and opened the door.

An officer and eight troops stormed into the living room. The soldiers quickly assessed how many men were in the room and their activity.

The young captain in command pointed at Liam and said, "Detain and disarm him." Two soldiers shoved Liam against the wall and held crossed sabers to his throat while another soldier seized Liam's pistol.

"Subdue this man as well. Search him for weapons."

Joseph was propelled face first into a wall by two overzealous soldiers. They patted his coat and extracted the pistol.

The captain began to approach Colm, but his knees buckled as he suddenly experienced a vision. He saw an angel with long flowing brown hair and unfurled wings etched on a stained glass window in the wall of a meetinghouse. The male image of the angel wore a breastplate, carried the scales, and brandished a sword as he trampled Lucifer with his sandaled feet. It was the archangel, Michael. He represented God's love *and* God's wrath. The archangel had terrified him since he was a boy.

He shook his head to clear the vision. The archangel brandishing the sword vanished. The stained glass window dissolved. The captain's overwhelming reverence and fear of God remained. In his heart, he knew that the man—no the being—who stood before him gripping a wrought iron poker was the embodiment of his childhood terror, for this being was the archangel Michael's brother.

The pious young captain's fear turned inward, and he berated his blasphemous heart. *This man is not one of God's warriors! How dare I presume to entertain the notion! This is Lucifer's foolery!*

Despite his emotional denial, the young officer forced himself to look at Colm. It took every ounce of fortitude he possessed to keep focused on Colm's serene face when he said to his ensign, "If this man moves, break his arms and legs. Or better, bash his brains in."

The ensign acknowledged the order and four soldiers moved closer to Colm.

Colm's green eyes reflected a powerful captivation that made it impossible for the captain to shift his attention away from the archangel's face.

With the knowledge that the regulars were mere men sent to the farm to confirm his whereabouts, Colm asked, "What's ya name?"

He's attempting to unnerve me. Still he answered, "Captain Levi Chitwood."

"Tell ya men about ya vision."

"I do not know what you are referring to."

Silver light flashed in Colm's eyes.

"BASH HIS BRAINS IN!" Captain Chitwood shouted.

The soldiers did not move. General Thomas Gage had issued the strictest orders to his soldiers to treat the colonists with lenity and justice.

It was not just the strict orders that caused the soldiers to ignore a direct order. There was a sense of reverence surrounding the tall man standing on the fireplace hearth, holding a wrought iron poker. The soldiers could not imagine bashing his brains in as Captain Chitwood had ordered.

Colm said, "Tell them about ya vision, Captain Chitwood."

A sound like water streaming from a tipped bucket surprised the silent soldiers.

Joseph realized the streaming water was Captain Chitwood pissing himself. Strangely, he thought that the captain's breeches should have absorbed the piss and muffled the noise, but it sounded as if he had pulled out his penis and aimed it at the living room wall.

Colm dropped the poker. It clattered loudly on the brick fireplace hearth.

The soldiers released Liam and Joseph then fell back in astonishment at their commanding officer's actions. The stunned soldiers shifted their eyes between the captain and Colm.

Captain Chitwood's ensign mustered the fortitude to shout, "All out!"

None of the regulars obeyed.

The ensign approached Captain Chitwood cautiously. "Sir, let us retreat. This has been a mistake."

Captain Chitwood shivered and murmured, "An archangel."

"Sir?"

Without looking at anyone in the room, the captain turned and walked out of the house.

Colm signaled for Liam and Joseph to gather near him. He said to the ensign, "Give these men their pistols back."

The soldiers holding the confiscated pistols looked at the ensign. The ensign took the pistols and ordered the soldiers to leave the premises. When the soldiers were outside, the ensign handed the pistols to Colm, and asked, "What did you do to Captain Chitwood?"

"What do ya think I did?" Colm asked. His eyes flashed.

Chills ran up the ensign's spine and down his arms. He backed away from Colm then turned and ran out of the house.

Joseph walked to a window and watched the British regulars urge their horses back toward Boston. Satisfied that they were gone, he turned to Colm and said, "What *did* you do to Captain Chitwood? He was terrified of you."

"He conjured his own fear."

"And you helped him along."

"I don't manipulate human fear. They're either fearful of me or they're not."

"And what of Liam? You did not ask him what he did to disobey you."

"Those regulars were sent here on a fool's errand," Colm said with anger. "They came here without bravery, truth, or fairness. They pretended they were strong. They pretended they were carrying out God's will. Liam isn't like them. He doesn't lie to himself about his behavior. He knows he was disobedient, and he knows the price of that disobedience."

"Joseph, I beg of you, let this go," Liam said.

"I cannot."

Colm reined in his anger and calmed his tone. "Joseph, I know ya see our ways as cruel, but it's the only way we've been able to survive. Everything has gotten so much worse. Fergus is gone, and Seamus has been thrust into second. We're trying to protect ya. We're trying to live among ya. We're trying to face Henry and his demons."

"And with all that, letting Liam die at the hands of a demon is still an acceptable punishment? You did not punish Fergus for his disobedience!"

"He was released from Colm's command," Liam said. "We suffer the same fate. We have no one to protect us now."

The demon that possessed Bertie Adams reported to Henry that he heard Abigail Adams ask the angel they called Liam about his accommodations at the farm. Henry, in turn, ordered Lord Patterson to dispatch Captain Chitwood and his regulars to verify the angels were indeed living on a farm in Roxbury.

Word of Captain Levi Chitwood's breakdown traveled throughout the Massachusetts Bay Colony. There was much erroneous speculation over the reason for the captain's utterance of the words, *an archangel,* after he pissed himself. None of his soldiers admitted to the reverence they felt for Colm Bohannon, but one reported that he believed one of the men in attendance at the farm was Dr. Joseph Warren.

Further, there was loose talk concerning Abigail Adams and Liam Kavangh. It was not particularly ruddy gossip, but it was enough to alert Henry to the possibility that Liam had been disobedient and was suffering under the archangel's punishment.

These developments pleased Henry and Robert. Surely, Joseph Warren would finally realize that Colm Bohannon was as cruel and dangerous as any demon. Although John Adams' wife was in Braintree with the rest of her family, Henry could not help but wonder if John Adams was unhappy with the angels.

In late March, Henry convinced General Gage to send Captain John Brown and Ensign Henry de Berniere on another clandestine mission to search for munitions, this time north to Concord. Their route took them through Roxbury and Brookline along the direct road to Concord. In Concord, their appearance was greeted with more open hostility than their previous mission, which ultimately led them to Worcester.

But General Gage had accomplished something that even Henry had not—Gage had successfully planted a spy among the rebels' innermost circle.

~

Two weeks before, on March 13, Henry, Robert, Thomas, and Margaret attended a social at the home of Francis Shaw. Scottish Major John Pitcairn of the Royal Navy Marines was the host. Pitcairn was quartered in Shaw's home. Paul Revere was Shaw's next door neighbor.

Fifty-two-year-old Pitcairn was the father of ten children, and was regarded for his integrity, honesty, and sense of humor even among many patriotic Bostonians. His gatherings were a place where British officers and locals could air their views with civility.

Paul had invited Joseph to attend John Pitcairn's social gathering. Pitcairn greeted them as they entered the Shaw home, "Dr. Warren, it is an honor to have you here tonight," Pitcairn exclaimed with an edge of humility. "I look forward to your contributions to our conversations."

"Thank you for the kind words, Major," Joseph replied, smiling. His eyes darted to a man standing among a group of British officers on the other side of the room. He had never been introduced to General Thomas Gage, but he knew what the general looked like.

The major saw the curious look on Joseph's face. "Come, Dr. Warren. I will introduce you to General Gage."

The three crossed the room. The group of British officers silenced upon their arrival. Thomas was already aware of Dr. Warren's reputation and physical appearance. They politely shook hands and murmured their pleasure when Pitcairn introduced them.

A runner with an urgent message for Joseph interrupted them. Joseph read the note, and then said, "If you will excuse me, I need to tend to a patient. I am afraid it cannot wait." He issued a vague polite bow and swept out of the house.

A moment later, Margaret entered the room and joined her husband's conversation with the group of British officers.

When Henry, Robert, and the Gages returned home after the social, Thomas requested that Henry and Robert take a night cap in the living room.

"I have received another communication tonight from my rebel informant describing the exact location of the hiding places of munitions in Concord," Thomas said smugly. "This communication also contained secret deliberations conducted by the leaders of the Massachusetts Provincial Congress."

Henry took a glass of wine from a servant's offered hand. "Thomas, I do believe your cunning has gone unrewarded for too long. Who are these leaders you speak of?"

"You do not know?" Margaret sneered. "I *am* surprised." It was not a surprise but rather disgust she felt with Henry's manipulation. She resented the way her house smelled because of his presence.

Henry attempted to subdue her by leering at her, but she scoffed at him. This American-born woman was a challenge he was not used to.

"Margaret, please temper your comments," Thomas warned. Being the loyal soldier that he was, he needed to hear praise aside from the constant barrage of shortcomings Lord Dartmouth never failed to fire at him. "The rebel leaders have been identified as John Hancock and Samuel Adams. There is a clash among the delegates within the Provincial Congress concerning the organization of a formal army. Some delegates believe it would be seen as an offensive posture unlike the local militias. However, they are soliciting the opinions of their constituents. Apparently, Dr. Joseph Warren is using his quill to convince others that an army is of great importance. In fact—I was introduced to Warren tonight"

Henry leaned in toward Thomas. "Warren was at the party?"

"Briefly. He was called away during our introduction."

The mention of Joseph Warren sent a shock wave of guilt through Margaret's heart and mind. Although she had done nothing more damaging than seek his medical care, the lust she harbored for him since the day they met would not leave her alone. It constantly tempted her to return to him.

Thomas droned on.

She uttered a sigh before she realized that Robert was watching her.

He grinned and nodded as if to say, "I know what you are thinking."

Margaret's desire and lust overcame her sensibilities. The excuse she used to slip out of Province House the week before served her well one more time. She returned to Joseph's home on an overcast and bitterly cold Saturday morning in mid-March. She took a deep breath and knocked on the door. Silence.

She knocked again. A cold wind gusted and blew the hood of her cloak off her head. The Warren house creaked in response. Disappointment devastated her. She turned to step from the small portico when the door swung open.

"Miss Kemble?" Joseph recognized the tumble of her brown curls.

If I turn around, I will go through with what I have come for if at all possible, she thought. She turned around. Her cloak fluttered in the wind, but she took no notice. All she saw was him.

"Please, come in out of the cold," Joseph invited.

The sound of his voice stirred the feathers of her desire. They brushed her thighs and nipples. She did not remember crossing the threshold or removing her cloak.

"Are you experiencing new symptoms?" Joseph asked, although he was certain of the cause of her malaise and how to cure it.

Her brown eyes drank in the intoxicating nectar of his sexuality. "Yes."

The moment he saw her on the portico, Joseph's arousal had awakened. Now, it throbbed hard and strong. He clutched her upper arms and pulled her to him.

She exhaled a small cry of relief.

He slipped a hand behind her head and brushed his lips over hers.

Her mouth fell open.

His tongue darted into the moist warmth of her mouth.

She wrapped her arms around his neck.

His free hand encircled her waist, and he forcefully pressed his erection against the front folds of her skirt until he could feel what lay beneath. He tried to lower her to the hall floor.

She resisted. "Not here," she breathed. Her desire for him was blinding, but she wanted to see his young naked body. She wanted to ensure that no one would interrupt what they were doing.

He took her hand. They climbed the steps to above stairs and his bedroom. Once inside, Margaret had a sobering moment. "Where are your children?" she asked as his hands parted the lace-trimmed opening on the bodice of her dress.

He cocked his head and smiled at her. "I suppose that is a fair question, Margaret. You have children of your own. What mother would not worry about being overheard in the throes of passion?"

"How do you know—?"

"That you are Margaret Gage? That I am playing with fire by being with you like this?" Joseph's blue eyes sparked with intrigue and spunk. He lowered his head. His tongue traced the crease of cleavage that peaked over her bodice.

Her hands sought his crotch. She squeezed his erection through the cloth of his breeches.

EIGHTEEN

BOSTON, MASSACHUSETTS
APRIL 1775

John Hancock, Samuel Adams, and Joseph Warren had a rebel intelligence network of tradesmen and skilled workers who frequented the Green Dragon and other Boston taverns. These members of the Sons of Liberty noted British troop movements, ship arrivals and departures, and anything out of the ordinary. They reported these observations along the secret network that led to the Committee of Safety of the Provincial Congress, which was now adjourned in Concord.

On April 7, the rebels observed longboats being moored under the sterns of British men-of-war in Boston Harbor for ready access and concluded that an attack somewhere was imminent.

The next day, Paul saddled up to carry a message of alarm to Concord given the stockpiles of munitions and supplies located there. When Paul burst through the door of the meetinghouse, John Hancock, Samuel Adams, Colm, Fergus, Seamus, and Joseph Warren rose in alarm.

"What news?" John asked Paul.

Paul relayed the observations of the rebels.

Seamus had permission from Colm to speak as he saw fit now that he was second in command. He said, "I spent a short time workin' on the wharf. It was overrun with demons. So, the question is, who's behind this? Thomas Gage or Henry Hereford? If the answer is Henry, then demons will be sent to Concord."

"Does it matter?" John asked. "Both will send demons."

Seamus' purple aura flickered in distress. He tried to hold his temper. "Why cain't you understand the difference between the evil God's demons possess and the evil that humans conjure on their own?"

"Do pray tell, what is the difference?"

"Let us leave that determination to holy men," Samuel advised.

Colm bristled, but he had no intention of interfering with Seamus' given authority.

"Please, gentlemen," Joseph said. "Paul's warning is ominous, and if Seamus is correct, and Henry does indeed send demons to Concord, or anywhere else, the human inhabitants may die without a shot being fired."

"My men will be ready to set a watch for demon possession as well as battle, if the British regulars are dispatched," Colm said.

Paul said, "Without Fergus, there are but seven of you. How many demons can Henry set afoot?"

"Maybe thousands. I don't know," Colm admitted. "But we're all ya got."

"The angels must be alerted first if an alarm is raised," Joseph said. "Do we agree?"

It was agreed.

John and Samuel were egotistical, but they were not fools. They acquiesced to Seamus' forewarning, but the decisions they made that day after the Provincial Congress retired had nothing to do with angels or demons.

It was obvious to both men that things had deteriorated with the British to the point that it was not safe for them to return to Boston before setting out for Philadelphia and the Second Continental Congress scheduled to convene on May 10. John managed to get word to his aunt, Lydia Hancock, his fiancée, Dorothy Quincy, and his young clerk, John Howell, to leave Boston and take refuge at Reverend Jonas Clarke's house in Lexington.

John was very familiar with the Clarke house. It was from that house that he had been taken away, as a seven-year-old boy, by his uncle and aunt, Thomas and Lydia Hancock, to be raised in the world of Boston business.

Samuel's wife, Betsy, left their house on Purchase Street in Boston and went to stay in the home of her father in Cambridge. Samuel's nineteen-year-old daughter, Hannah, his child with his deceased wife, Elizabeth, joined Betsy in Cambridge. His son, Samuel, Jr., who studied medicine under Joseph, elected to remain in Boston.

During this time, Joseph was making arrangements to move Mercy and his children out of Boston. Confusion over their destination—Roxbury or

Worcester—led to a delay. In the meantime, he continued to tend to his patients, but his friends were concerned for his safety.

As William Eustis returned from caring for a patient one evening, he passed a party of British soldiers on watch near newly constructed gallows from which a thief swung by his broken neck.

"Eustis!" one of the soldiers called. "Relay a message to Warren." The soldier jerked a thumb at the gallows. "Tell Warren we are waiting for him!"

The others nodded and laughed in agreement with the insinuation.

When William arrived home, he entered the medical office. Joseph was preparing his medical bag. "I do not think it is a good idea for you to be walking the streets alone."

Joseph glanced at him, "I have a patient to visit in Cornhill this evening. If you are worried about my safety, come with me." He latched his medical bag and walked to his study.

William followed him. "This is a serious matter, Joseph."

Joseph set his bag on the desk. He opened a drawer, extracted a pistol, checked to make sure it was loaded, and then shoved it in his coat pocket. He extracted a second pistol from the same drawer, offered it to William, and said, "I *am* taking this seriously."

William's eyes dropped to the pistol. Guns made him nervous, therefore he was a terrible shot, but he took the gun anyway.

"It is loaded," Joseph said. He picked up his medical bag, smiled, and asked, "Shall we go?"

As they passed the British watch by the gallows, one of the three redcoat soldiers asked Joseph, "Did Eustis relay my message?"

William and Joseph kept walking without comment.

"Go on, Warren; you will soon come to the gallows."

Joseph stopped and looked at the soldiers. "Which of you spoke?"

He received no reply.

Joseph smiled and exhaled a laugh. "Just as I thought. Your words come easily. I will not die at the gallows! You fellows say we will not fight, but by heavens I hope I shall die up to my knees in blood if it comes to that!"

William's brow furrowed with concern that Joseph's bravado would be retaliated, but the British soldiers remained silent.

The doctors continued on to Cornhill without further harassment that night.

❧

The members of the Massachusetts Provincial Congress feared that the sudden rapid decay between England and America would thrust them into war. All those in attendance recognized the portent and the need for preparedness.

The Committee of Safety put a military command structure in place, incorporating existing militia companies and regiments, and their officers. They promoted six men, of various military abilities, to generals.

Fergus was tasked with tightening the Cambridge-Watertown militia into a well-trained fighting force. Despite his aspirations, Fergus missed his brotherhood. Yet, when Seamus asked to speak with him after congress adjourned, he felt ensnared.

"Will you consider comin' to the farm for a day?" Seamus asked.

Colm stood quietly; his attention on his two men.

Fergus frowned. "We share the purple aura of angels foreshadowed to carry the burden of leadership that is not truly ours; yet it is nearly as painful to our spirits as it is to our archangel's spirit. I can't face that again."

"It ain't your job no more, Fergus. It's mine."

"Then you understand why I can't go to the farm."

"No, I don't understand. I'm askin' you to do this for the others. I think it would do them good to see you."

"No."

"Fuck you!" Seamus shouted. "You've deserted us at a time when we need to stand closer together than we've ever needed to stand in our existence! Michael and Patrick are scared! Brandon's tryin' to grow into a leader. Liam and Ian have been disobedient! We're your family!"

Fergus just walked away.

On April 11, five days before Lord Dartmouth's long-awaited orders on how to deal with the rebels reached General Thomas Gage via the HMS *Falcon*, the general's clandestine patriot informer noted, "A sudden blow struck now or immediately upon the arrival of reinforcements from England would cripple all the rebels' plans."

Based on this intelligence, Thomas asked Henry to assist him in drafting operational orders.

Thomas cited exact details from his informant's letter. "See here, Henry. There are four brass cannons and two mortars and quite a number of smaller arms in the cellar of the house of Mr. Barrett. Mr. Barrett's farm is about a mile from the North Bridge in Concord."

Henry whispered to Robert, "See to it that we have men planted in Concord. I am sure you will have no trouble assembling volunteers."

Robert set his glass of wine aside and rose from his chair.

There were many disembodied demons awaiting instructions from their overlord.

Lord Dartmouth's council arrived from England on April 16. Two days later, Thomas received a missive from his patriot informant that all but a small number of powder barrels had been removed from Concord to nearby towns as a result of the rebels anticipating a strike by British troops. He also received intelligence that the leaders of the rebellion, John Hancock and Samuel Adams, were in Lexington.

Lord Dartmouth's council specifically ordered that these men were to be arrested and shown no mercy.

Thomas ignored the order.

The night before, Henry and Robert patronized a tavern that was rumored to shelter rebels and their secret meetings—the Green Dragon. The demons watched and heard the humans fall into drunkenness as the sun set and the moon rose to influence the tide of men who came to the tavern in search of relief from the struggle to stay afloat in the deep waters of conflict.

Then the tide stilled, and a man entered the tavern. The patrons called him by name and reached to touch his cloak. A younger man accompanied him who displayed the pride of their intimate medical association.

Robert reined in the urge to let his blue eyes erupt into orange flames at the sight of Joseph Warren. He leaned in closer to Henry and said, "How delightful. The archangel's new pet has made an appearance. He is the man wearing the cloak. I sensed Margaret Gage's carnal longings for him the night of Major Pitcairn's social."

Henry was aware of Warren's association with the patriots, but this was the first time he had laid his yellow-green eyes on him. Joseph Warren and the angel, Michael Bohannon, had come together to form the archangel's greatest weakness.

"Perhaps, it is too late to plot the dramatic death of Warren before the first battle of our war is fought. However, we can make certain that he will be the first tragedy Bohannon suffers in a war that will stretch out long enough to rape his spirit in ways not yet imagined. In fact, we will see to it that Bohannon is so weakened by loss, that he will die from the agony of his ruined spirit."

"That shall be an excellent game!" Robert gloated.

"Who is the man with Warren?" Henry asked.

"Dr. William Eustis. He's Warren's apprentice in medicine."

Henry and Robert watched Warren and his companion cross the room to a table occupied by six men. There was much tension among the men and much drinking to relieve that tension.

Joseph removed his cloak and sat beside Benjamin Church. Benjamin was distracted by a group of British officers sitting at a nearby table. The curious look on his face caused Joseph to regard the officers. He recognized Robert Percy.

"That is the demon from the meetinghouse," Benjamin whispered to Joseph. "And the general with him is no doubt Henry."

Paul leaned across the table toward Joseph. "They have infiltrated our tavern, and I do not like it one bit."

"We will not allow them to unnerve us," Joseph replied. He shifted his attention to his fellows at the table.

William Eustis and William Dawes exchanged nods. One word from any of the men seated around their table, and they would be more than happy to start a row with the British officers.

Henry asked Robert, "Who is that man seated beside Warren?"

"I believe that is Dr. Benjamin Church; however, I cannot be certain. Quite a few men, along with one woman, lingered in the meetinghouse during my confrontation with the archangel."

Henry took note of the faces around the table with Warren and sketched them into his mental notebook. Then he said, "Tomorrow morning, it will begin. Gage has received his orders from Lord Dartmouth. I will ensure that he executes those orders without delay."

Three British officers approached Henry's table. Robert's closest demonic advisors were in temporary possession of the officers' bodies. He was expecting their arrival.

The officers performed the etiquette required when acknowledging higher ranking officers. Without speaking, they clapped their hand to their hat and bowed. Robert gave them permission to be seated, and then motioned to a server to bring them tankards of beer.

When the draughts were provided, Robert said to the officers, "The general wants a report of who will be among the British troops deployed to Lexington, and who will be among the patriots in Lexington, as well as the patriots in Concord."

"I request that I may stay in possession of this man," Lieutenant William Sutherland said. "His capabilities are superior, and his ego is fine."

Henry nodded, pleased with the request because he understood the value of an ego.

"The population of Lexington and Concord is small. Therefore, I believe we need but a few dozen of our servants among the citizens," Sir Rupert Weller, a Captain in the 10th Regiment of Foot, said. "They have already been dispatched."

"I have fifty rascals on the ready to possess soldiers dispatched with Colonel Francis Smith," Lord Asa Dinmore, a lieutenant colonel in the 22nd Regiment of Foot, boasted.

Henry was satisfied that his war was beginning as he had hoped. He afforded a glance at Joseph Warren and his compatriots.

Joseph did not attend the Committee of Safety sessions held in Concord after April 8. He resolved to eventually abandon his medical profession in favor of politics and warfare, but he felt that he needed to take a step back first. The committee had already laid plans for a watch and couriers to alarm the countryside of suspicious British army movement, and he was well-versed in those plans.

On the evening of Tuesday, April 18, a vigilant patriot informed Joseph that an impressive aggregate of British companies, perhaps as many as 800 enlisted men and 70 officers, had assembled in Back Bay across the Charles River from Cambridge by order of General Thomas Gage. Further, there appeared to be special purpose units within the regiments—grenadiers and light infantry, but supply wagons and field pieces did not seem to be among their equipment. This movement alarmed Joseph to the possibility that the British were commencing to arrest John Hancock and Samuel Adams in Lexington and strike at the heart of the rebel resistance.

This hodgepodge of companies had been placed under the command of Colonel Frances Smith, with Royal Marine Major John Pitcairn as Smith's second in command. The result was disorganization as junior officers were forced to report to a command they were unfamiliar with. On the other side of the coin, Colonel Smith and Major Pitcairn had no knowledge of who among their ranks possessed what skills.

Colm was with Joseph in the Warren home when the news arrived from a trusted source. Soon after, a member of the Sons of Liberty arrived

ANGELS & PATRIOTS, BOOK ONE

to inform Joseph that the Charles River crossing was moving slowly for the British. They were crossing in Royal Navy longboats and against the incoming tide. It took up to an hour for the boats to ferry a group of soldiers across the river and then return for another group. All of this was taking place under the watchful eye of the British man-of-war, HMS *Somerset,* which lay at anchor in the river.

Joseph, pent up with anxiety and frustration, paced his study.

"Joseph, why are ya walking back and forth? It doesn't seem to have a purpose," Colm said.

Despite his uneasiness, Joseph found Colm's confusion endearing. "My friend, this is what we humans do when we have no outlet for our helplessness. Our friends, John and Samuel, are in danger, and I cannot deliver them relief. Where is William?"

The possible seizure of rebel armaments in and around Concord was of secondary concern to Joseph. He knew that most of the weaponry was well hidden or moved out of Concord in the early weeks of April.

Someone banged on Warren's front door. William Dawes strode into the study.

Joseph relayed the news to him. "You are to ride through the guard post on the Neck. I know you can convince them to let you pass. Take word to Seamus first; he is ready to deploy. Then ride on to Lexington to Reverend Clarke's house to warn John and Samuel that the British regulars are on the move."

William asked Colm, "Are your men to go without you?"

I need to be with them, Colm thought. *But I won't leave Joseph because Henry will go after him if he thinks I'm not protecting him.* He said, "Aye, for now."

William supposed the archangel's motives were none of his affair, but the idea of Colm's absence from Lexington was unsettling. Henry may have already sent demons to kill John Hancock and Samuel Adams. He scolded himself for wasting precious time worrying about something he could not control.

"Godspeed!" Joseph said to William as he departed.

"Ya can't let William bear the burden of reaching Lexington alone," Colm said. "If he's arrested or…worse, then ya have no backup plan."

Another knock on the door provided Joseph's answer to Colm's concern. Paul hurried into the study in answer to Joseph's previous summons. Joseph instructed Paul to cross the Charles River to Charlestown and ride to Lexington with the same warning William was delivering.

Like William, Paul wondered why Colm was lingering behind with Joseph instead of making haste to join his men.

NINETEEN

Even at the late hour of near midnight, William was able to get past the guard post on Boston Neck by cajoling guards he knew from prior trips. He rode to the farm in Roxbury, dismounted, and banged on the farmhouse door.

Jeremiah opened the door almost immediately and let William in.

"If you're here, it means the Brits is movin'," Jeremiah said.

The saltbox farmhouse quivered as six angels stampeded down the steps from above stairs.

"They are crossing the Charles River to Cambridge," William told Seamus. "Joseph wants us to get to Lexington and warn John and Samuel!" He gave Seamus a brief description of the village of Lexington.

"We're goin' on foot," Seamus said. "We're ready, so go on now."

William ran out of the house to continue his ride.

The angels slung muskets, cartridge boxes, canteens, and knapsacks over their heads and across their chests.

Seamus paused to watch Liam. *Liam didn't hesitate to prepare, yet he has the most to lose if he's attacked by a demon. We cain defend him, but if the demon is too strong…*

Jeremiah snapped Seamus out of his reverie. "I know what you're thinkin', and it's scarin' you. Colm punished Liam by leavin' him unprotected and that scares me, too."

"As long as Colm ain't with us, we're all vulnerable," Seamus said. He shoved his butcher knife in the waist of his breeches, and said, "Let's get goin'."

❧

In Boston, Paul went to the home of Robert Newman to alert him of the situation. The twenty-three-year-old married man, with two children and expecting a third, had to sneak out of his house through his bedroom window because British officers where quartered at his home. Paul and Robert had prearranged the lantern signal that would be hung in the steeple of Christ Church in the North End of Boston—if by land one, if by water two.

It would be two lanterns. The signal would display for only a minute, long enough for the rebel leaders in Charlestown to observe the dim signal. It was also long enough for the British to notice it.

After returning home to prepare for his ride, Paul hurried to Back Bay. Two friends rowed him to Charlestown across the Charles River where, unlike the crossing the British were traversing, it curved eastward and took advantage of the incoming tide.

As Paul's rowboat silently glided past the HMS *Somerset,* he wondered who the traitor was among his close-knit band of rebels, and what, if any, hand that person had in what was about to commence.

Several men, including the rebel leader Colonel William Conant, met Paul on the shores of Charlestown. Paul told the waiting men what was happening, and that he was in need of a horse. A horse was secured and saddled and he was off to Lexington.

Between midnight and one o'clock in the morning on April 19, Paul reached Lexington and Reverend Jonas Clarke's house where John Hancock and Samuel Adams were sheltered. There were eight armed men stationed around the Clarke house due to a British patrol that had passed through Lexington around eight o'clock the night before. The sergeant in charge tried to intercept Paul as he approached the sleeping household, but Paul side-stepped him and pounded on the door.

John threw open a bedroom window and looked out into the darkness. "Who is there?"

"Let me in!" Paul hissed.

Samuel and Reverend Clarke joined John in the living room while Paul swept through the front door. William Dawes arrived as Paul was issuing Joseph's message.

William said, "The ang…" He stopped himself from saying *angels* in front of Reverend Clarke. "Seamus Cullen and his men are on the way."

John understood and said, "Where is Colm?"

"He is with Joseph in Boston."

Paul and William could not linger. They left immediately to ride west toward Concord to spread the alarm that the British regulars were on the march.

On the road, Paul and William encountered Dr. Samuel Prescott, returning from an evening with his fiancée, Lydia Mulliken, in Lexington. The three of them knocked on doors and spread the word. Midway between Lexington and Concord, Paul scouted the road ahead for British patrols while William and Samuel stopped at a large farmhouse to warn the residents.

The bright moonlight shadowed the woods on either side of the road. Two British officers rode out from the shelter of the trees, surprising Paul.

"We have been seen!" Paul shouted in warning to William and Samuel.

Two more heavily armed regulars emerged from the shadows. The unarmed patriots' only choice was to flee.

Samuel thought of the underhanded attack on him and Michael at the meetinghouse the day of the Boston Massacre commemoration, and knew he could not hesitate. He urged his horse over a stone wall and escaped into the darkness of the woods.

William was mounted on the slowest horse. He rode in the opposite direction until he found the shelter of an abandoned farmhouse.

Paul attempted to outrun the British, but six more regulars blocked his path. He was taken prisoner along with three other rebels captured earlier in the morning.

An officer ordered Paul to dismount, and then asked him where he had come from and when.

"I have ridden from Boston just hours ago," Paul quipped.

The officer was surprised that someone like this man had slipped out of Boston and had ridden this far. "What is your name?"

"Paul Revere."

The officer nodded and said, "You are known."

"Well, you will not find what you are after whether that is men or arms," Paul sneered. "I have warned the countryside all the way from Charlestown."

Another officer rode at Paul at a gallop. The officer identified himself as Major Edward Mitchell. He then held a pistol to Paul's head and said, "You will answer my questions or I will blow your brains out."

After more detailed questioning, Major Mitchell ordered Paul to mount his horse. A regular took the reins, and Paul and the other captive rebels were led eastward. As they neared Lexington, the boom of a signal gun reverberated through the cold dawn air. Mitchell questioned Paul about the signal. Paul shrugged and repeated what he had already said twice before.

Soon after, the bell at the meetinghouse on Lexington Green began to ring. One of the other rebels, Jonathan Loring, snapped at his captors, "The bell's ringing, the town's alarmed, and you are all dead men."

Major Mitchell and his regulars forced the rebels to dismount. One soldier drew his sword and cut the horses' bridles and saddles off and drove the horses away. Major Mitchell's patrol took Paul's horse with them.

Major Mitchell's regulars were the patrol that had passed through Lexington the evening before. Rebels had followed his patrol and were subsequently captured. They were forced to walk back to Lexington along with Paul.

Meanwhile, Samuel Prescott rode to Concord and sounded the alarm to arms along the way.

❧

At 2:00 a.m., after slogging through the wetlands of the Cambridge marshes, Colonel Francis Smith's and Major John Pitcairn's regulars reached the road to Lexington. The wetlands had not been the sole reason for their delay.

Colonel Smith was physically rotund and a stickler for established British army practices. He prided himself on open-field parade ground maneuvers and arrangement of his order of march. This strict adherence caused disorder among the disjointed regiments unfamiliar with his command.

Further, the different regiments wore distinctive headgear with different colored cockades and facings. Their respective uniforms were impressive, but impractical for slogging through marshy tidal flats.

As the column of regulars marched toward Lexington, Seamus and his men arrived. Unlike Concord, the village of Lexington was an unfamiliar landscape to Seamus. A tavern lay ahead that was abutted to a long, triangular field of about three acres. It was here that the road from Cambridge split northward toward Bedford and westward toward Concord.

At the farm, William had given Seamus a brief description of the layout of the village and from that he deduced the field was Lexington Green. The Clarke house was located on the green behind the intersection. Buckman's Tavern stood across the road to Bedford.

The call to arms had spread throughout the countryside. Men were arriving two or three at a time to assemble under the command of Captain John Parker of the Lexington militia. The tall and hardened countryman had honed through some of the toughest fighting during the French and Indian War. Now, he was dying of tuberculosis. Like most men of his caliber, duty came first.

The angels and Jeremiah made little noise as they entered Lexington Green. The brotherhood was foreign among the gathered hardworking neighbors and friends related by blood or marriage.

"Seamus, can we stop for a minute?" Ian asked. He had spent the walk to Lexington worrying over the possibility that the angels would be forced to kill the children of man to protect the rebels against demons in possession of living human vessels.

Ian's wings rustled as Jeremiah and the angels gathered in a tight circle. The other angels' wings rustled in response. He sensed that they, too, had contemplated the grievous possibility.

Lord, Colm. You shou'd be here. Your angels is facin' a horrible reality, and you've left them in favor of Joseph Warren, Jeremiah thought. He was grateful for the darkness that shrouded the dismay and fear on their faces.

Seamus was ashamed of his inability to soothe the angels. It had taken Fergus thousands of years to learn the art of soothing, and still, his ability was a far cry from the comfort their archangel could offer. But Seamus had to do something.

The soft brush of rustling wings was now a snapping flutter and in a moment, their wings would unfurl. Once that happened, they would lose control and release their auras in their desperation to soothe themselves. Faint, glints of green, blue, red, and the purple light of his own aura, threatened to disintegrate Jeremiah's gratitude for the darkness. Only Brandon would be able to maintain control of his yellow aura.

Liam made eye contact with Seamus. With quite deference he asked, "May I speak?"

"It ain't your place."

Liam did not look away.

Michael and Patrick huddled closer together.

"Let 'im speak," Jeremiah said. "Otherwise, let 'em comfort themselves. If there's demons out there, they cain see your auras anyway."

"Brother, let Liam speak," Patrick agreed. "It ain't gonna hurt nothin'."

Seamus let go of his shame, and said, "I know you need soothin', and I ain't able to give it. Liam, go ahead and say your piece."

Michael blurted out, "No! I don't want to hear ya talk about what we're going to do if we don't have Colm to protect us, like ya did the day we went to Boston to drill with the militia! " It was almost impossible for him not to worry about Colm's death. But he saw someone who eased his immediate fears.

A young black man was standing among the militiamen. Michael's experience with black humans was extremely limited, and he was drawn to the man. It didn't occur to him that the black man might be a slave.

149

Michael said to Patrick, "Come with me."

The young black man appeared confused and dismayed as Michael and Patrick, bathed in the light of the bright moon, approached. But it wasn't the moonlight that caused the man to temporarily forget his own existence. It was Michael's and Patrick's bright blue auras illuminating the grass as they crossed Lexington Green.

Prince Estabrooke beheld the angels with an unbelieving shocked soul. They came to him, looking so much alike with medium statures, curly black hair, beautiful countenances, and open smiles.

Since forming a close alliance with the rebels, Colm had lifted the restriction of saying their names in front of strangers; therefore, Michael and Patrick were free to introduce themselves.

"Ya got a name?" Michael asked the staring young man.

"Who *are* you?" Prince asked. He squinted against the brightness of the angels' auras.

"I already told ya," Michael said frowning. "Is there something wrong with ya?"

"I think he sees our auras," Patrick whispered to Michael. "He's squintin'."

"That can't be. What's ya name?"

Prince felt his lips move in answer, but he didn't hear himself speak.

"Prince, what color is the light?" Patrick asked.

Prince was overawed. "Are we all gonna die this mornin'? Are you angels here to take us to Heaven?"

Michael rolled his eyes.

Patrick thought, *it's difficult to pull the children of man up from the depths of religion.*

Prince, however, saw Michael roll his eyes. That action brought him to his senses. "You *is* angels."

"Aye." Michael saw no use in denying it.

And we're here to fight, same as you," Patrick added.

Prince blinked. "What's that blue light you're givin' off?"

Michael and Patrick glanced around the green to make certain no one was paying attention to them. Satisfied, Michael said, "It's our auras. The children of man normally can't see them unless we let them. It's strange that ya can see them."

"I *am* gonna die!" Prince shouted.

"Shhh!" Patrick hissed. "You ain't gonna die."

Prince let out a sigh of relief. "Then can you put out the blue light? It's too bright."

"We don't know how to douse our auras from humans who can see them," Michael said. *Maybe Colm knows. But he's not here. He shou'd be here,* Michael thought.

Patrick saw Brandon walking across the green toward Captain John Parker. He waited until Brandon and Captain Parker were engaged in conversation before he said to Prince, "Can you see the man who's talkin' to Captain Parker?"

Prince nodded.

"Do you see anythin' odd about him?"

"I don't see a light, uh, an aura if that's what you are askin'. Is he an angel, too?"

"Aye," Michael said. "Will ya come with us? I want ya to meet him."

As the boys neared Brandon, Patrick said to Michael, "Call Brandon 'Lieutenant.'"

"Why?"

"Because he *is* a lieutenant. The children of man value their military ranks."

"Like Fergus?" Michael asked. A thought occurred to him. *Is Fergus' need to be a general something that belonged to the man, Fergus Driscoll, when he was alive?*

Patrick and Prince reached Brandon. They stood aside while Brandon finished his conversation with Captain Parker. Then, Captain Parker walked to the center of Lexington Green. He coughed hard, and then called muster.

Brandon and Patrick thought, *Captain Parker's dying of consumption.*

Michael caught up with the boys. The four of them stood in a small circle as the men, who had come to answer the alarm in Lexington, streamed past them toward Captain Parker.

"Patrick said I shou'd call ya 'Lieutenant'," Michael blurted out to Brandon.

Brandon laughed, "You shou'd." He saw the anxious young black man standing beside him. "Who're you?"

Prince stared at Brandon. *Am I really standing among angels? No, this can't be. I gotta be dreaming.*

"Answer him," Michael insisted.

Prince forced himself to blink. Then he said to Brandon, "I am Prince Estabrooke."

151

"Why are staring at me?"

"I just now seen your yellow light—um, aura."

Brandon frowned. He looked at Patrick and Michael with suspicion. "What's he talking about?"

"He cain see our auras. He knows," Patrick said.

"If he goes spouting off that we're angels—"

"—he's not going to do that, are ya Prince?" Michael asked.

Prince's eyes widened, and he rapidly shook his head, but the burning question on Prince's mind could not go unasked. "Why don't you have wings?"

"We do. At least ya can't see those, too."

Seamus, Jeremiah, Liam, and Ian passed the group of boys. Seamus motioned at them to join muster. The four boys fell in with the rest of the men.

Earlier in the morning, Captain Parker had sent two scouts down the road toward Cambridge to locate the approaching British regulars. They returned around four o'clock in the morning, and reported no appearance of movement. Given this report and the cold morning air, he announced to the men gathered on the green that they were dismissed, but needed to stay within earshot of drumroll and ready to reassemble.

Seamus gathered his men. Prince Estabrooke gathered with them. Jeremiah raised an eyebrow at Prince, but he said nothing.

Seamus said, "Most of the men are goin' to Buckman's Tavern to warm up and have a draught. Me, Michael, Patrick, and Brandon will walk the first patrol while the rest of you go on to the tavern. Keep an eye out for—"

"Seamus," Jeremiah said as he jerked his head toward Prince.

Seamus looked Prince over and studied his eyes. Then he asked, "Who're you?"

Prince was no longer overawed. He smiled. "I am Prince Estabrooke. Your aura is purple."

Seamus sighed. He thought, *now I'm forced to figure out what Colm wou'd want me to do because this ain't never happened before.*

"Liam, get Prince out of the cold and take him to the tavern," Seamus said. To Prince he said, "You ain't gonna talk about no auras or angels or nothin' like that, do you hear me?"

Prince nodded. The flame of happiness he had found with his new angels dimmed a bit.

When Liam, Ian, Jeremiah, and Prince had gone on to the tavern, Seamus looked at Michael, Patrick, and Brandon. He knew they shouldn't have gotten Prince involved, but decided he'd address it if they survived the next few days.

&

Seamus led his small posse of men toward the Clarke house. Soft yellow candle-light flickered behind a few windows that overlooked the green. The eight-man guard remained stationed in various spots around the property.

They eluded the two men stationed in the front yard by swinging out wide before they got close enough to be seen. Seamus formed a V-shape with the fore- and middle fingers of his right hand. He pointed the fingers at Michael and Brandon, and then bent the ends of the fingers, indicating that they were to split off and walk around the right side of the house. From that, Patrick understood that he was to stay with Seamus and circle the left side of the house.

Michael removed his curved surgical blade from the pocket of his coat. Brandon slid his loaded flintlock pistol from the small of his back to his hip. The boys slipped out of Seamus' sight.

Patrick gripped his musket ramrod, thinking it would fit nicely into an eye socket. Seamus held his butcher knife in his left hand, blade tip up, just inside the breast of his coat.

Michael and Brandon crept along the west side of the Clarke house, as bright moonlight shone down upon them. Seamus and Patrick slipped through the shadows on the east side of the house.

A point of orange light flamed to Seamus' left. He heard a grunt and then a sound like a foot splashing in a puddle. He didn't want to panic, but he was sure something had happened to his little brother. As he turned to retrace his steps, a memory flickered in his spirit.

Seamus, I'm sick. Máthair warned me not to… The boy's voice silenced. *Patrick?*

Seamus shook off the false memory in time to see that he was about to be run through with a saber. He dodged the demon-possessed man, jerked his butcher knife out from under the breast of his coat, and stabbed the man in one orange eye, then the other.

Flames erupted from the demon's eyes. Sparks stung Seamus' face and hands. The orange light went out. The man made no sound as he fell to the ground. The demon had been in possession of a corpse.

Seamus whirled around and backtracked along the side of the house. The word *Brother* welled up in his throat. He tried to swallow it, but it rushed out of his mouth in reaction to the sound of someone panting.

"Brother!" Seamus said in a loud whisper. "Where are you?"

"Here."

Seamus looked down.

Patrick was on his hands and knees working to slow his breathing. He still had a grip on the musket ramrod.

Seamus kneeled beside him and looked him over. The brothers heard footsteps coming toward them. Seamus stood up and tightened his grip on the haft of his butcher knife. Lanterns chased the shadows away. Michael, Brandon, and three guardsmen arrived.

Seamus and Michael bent to help Patrick.

Patrick ignored their offer of help and got to his feet. The knees of his breeches were wet and caked with mud. He wiped at the mud with the palms of his muddy hands, which did little more than ground mud deeper into the deerskin.

A guardsman asked Patrick, "Are you alright?"

"He's fine," Seamus said to shield his little brother from having to answer questions. It's what Colm would have done.

"Are you Seamus Cullen?" another guardsman asked.

"Aye."

"Lieutenant O'Flynn said that you are acquainted with Mr. Hancock and Mr. Adams."

Seamus glanced at Brandon and nodded. "Joseph Warren sent us here to look after them."

A downstairs window slid open. All the men turned to see Hancock lean through. He asked, "Is that you, Seamus? Brandon?"

Seamus said, "Aye, John it's us."

John shuddered. He and Samuel knew that Joseph had sent the angels and why. He said, "Is all quiet?"

"We ain't leavin'."

It was obvious to John that Seamus' answer meant they *had* seen demons. He shut the window and returned to the debate he was having with Samuel on their next course of action.

The guardsmen returned to their posts. To the angels' relief, the men had not seen the corpse lying on the ground near the house.

❧

Stripped of his horse by Major Edward Mitchell and his patrol, Paul walked into Lexington three hours after he had delivered Joseph's message to John and

Samuel. He walked through the town cemetery to avoid Lexington Green on his return to the Clarke House. He encountered Michael and Patrick on the west side of the house.

"Did ya lose ya horse?" Michael scoffed.

Paul sneered at Michael. His tolerance for the brash angel was wearing thin. He skirted around the guard and went to the front door. Reverend Clarke let him in. Paul was surprised to find his friends were still ensconced inside, and embroiled in debate.

Neither John Hancock nor Samuel Adams had any sort of military training save for Hancock's leadership in a cadet corps, which was more for show than naught. However, his considerable ego led him to believe that if he had his musket, he was capable of standing on Lexington Green and challenging the enemy with the militia, and those who had come to answer the alarm. Samuel had no interest, whatsoever, in military participation. His elation stemmed from the idea that the revolution he had championed over the past decade may finally be at hand.

A constant stream of Reverend Jonas Clarke's male congregation came and went. The men had hung on the fiery words of Reverend Clarke's sermons on the doctrines of civil and religious liberties. His patriotic preaching had readied the men of Lexington for the moment that was upon them.

John's fiancée, Dorothy Quinn, wanted to return to Boston to check on the welfare of her father. Dorothy was thirty-eight years old; the same age as John. If she had not been betrothed to him, she would have been considered an old maid. Her facial features were sharp and well-defined—almost a mirror image of her beloved John.

"No, Dottie, I will not allow it," John said in response to her plea.

"May I remind you, Mr. Hancock, that you are not yet in charge of me?"

"That may be so, Dottie, but returning to Boston is unwise."

Dorothy considered her fiancé's distracted mind and flounced out of the living room.

"Paul, I am trying to convince John that we should vacate and retire further away from Lexington, but he is under the impression that he is a qualified soldier who must stand and fight," Samuel said as he glanced at John, who was now cleaning his pistol.

John's aunt Lydia brought Paul a beer. He thanked her and drank most of it before he said, "Samuel's right, John. Your pistol is no match for British bayonets."

Lines formed on John's forehead as he realized he must concede.

"I see the angels are on watch," Paul said. "Did they—"

"—detect anything?" John asked. "Yes, they did."

"Then, I suggest you leave now while we are able to procure an angelic escort," Paul said.

Reverend Clarke raised an eyebrow.

John said to his trusted young clerk, John Howell, "Go fetch Seamus Cullen and Brandon O'Flynn."

"Did Mr. Revere say angelic?" Howell asked, stunned.

"That is what I said, Howell," Paul snapped. "Go on now."

Howell reluctantly left.

"What's happening that I am not aware of?" Reverend Clarke asked.

"Paul, do you care to explain the situation to the good reverend?" Hancock asked.

John Howell returned with Seamus and Brandon. The angels hesitantly entered the house. They stood in the living room and shouldered the un-comfortable weight of Howell's stare and Reverend Clarke's scrutiny. Paul explained the angels' presence while John and Samuel prepared to leave.

An hour later, with John and Samuel tucked away in a distant safe house, Seamus, Brandon, Paul, and John Howell returned to Lexington and walked to Buckman's Tavern. Reverend Clarke and ten other men were standing out-side. Seamus and Brandon remained outside with them.

Paul and John Howell entered the crowded tavern. They slipped through the noise and dim candle light. They found Jeremiah and Ian leaning against a wall near the fireplace.

"What is happening?" Paul asked Jeremiah.

"Nothin' right now. We're ready ta assemble on the green at the sound of a drumroll."

"Where is Liam?"

Jeremiah tilted his head. "There."

Liam was at the bar, drinking rum, and watching every man who passed through the tavern door. He saw Paul and John Howell when they entered, but he chose not to draw attention to himself by acknowledging them.

A man burst through the door and raised an alarm that the British col-umn of regulars was a half mile from the tavern and marching into town. Captain Parker left the tavern and ordered a roll of the drum. Men poured out of the tavern and rallied to assemble on Lexington Green.

Paul and John Howell scrambled up the narrow stairs to the tavern's attic to fetch John Hancock's huge trunk. Loaded with papers and correspondences from the Provincial Congress and the Committee of Safety, it was the last thing they wanted to fall into British hands.

Men ran to Lexington Green from all directions. A number of spectators, including women and children, gathered on the edge of the green.

The angels and Jeremiah moved quickly to muster with Captain Parker's militia. Reverend Clarke and the ten men with him did the same.

Prince Estabrooke ran across the green to stand beside Patrick and Michael.

"We can't protect ya," Michael said to Prince. "Ya *do* understand that?"

"I understand."

As dawn lightened the sky, Major John Pitcairn and his troops in the vanguard approached the intersection adjacent to Lexington Green. The major heard the roll of a drum. *This obvious call to battle is not what I expected,* he thought. He shouted to his troops. "Halt! Hold your fire!"

Captain John Parker positioned his men in a line along Bedford Road from the tavern to the Clarke house. He struggled to control his persistent cough before he shouted, "Let the troops pass by, don't molest them without them being first."

In the meantime, Paul and John Howell had lugged John Hancock's unwieldy trunk out of the tavern and were now passing through the line of Lexington militiamen.

Neither the rebels nor the British wanted armed conflict. The stand that the men of Lexington made was intended to show the British that they couldn't march through their town unnoticed and unchallenged.

"Stand your ground. Don't fire unless fired upon," Captain Parker warned his men again. He coughed hard, and then added, "But if they mean to have a war, let it begin here."

Major John Pitcairn's troops continued along the road to Concord under the watchful eye of the Lexington militia and those who had come to spectate. Major Edward Mitchell and his exhausted men scurried on horseback around the advancing infantry.

Then the vanguard, led by Lieutenant Jessie Adair, veered the wrong way at the intersection and marched up Bedford Road toward Captain Parker's forces.

What is Adair doing? Major Pitcairn thought in horror. He spurred his horse and galloped toward the vanguard shouting, "Halt! Adair! Halt the van!"

In the dim early morning light, it was impossible for Captain Parker and his men to assess how many British regulars were bearing down on them.

A militia man, Elijah Sommers, fell in beside Ian. He had seen Ian in the tavern and couldn't shake the feeling that Ian's presence represented Heaven.

Prince Estabrooke stepped in closer to Patrick and Michael.

Seamus moved to shelter Liam.

Brandon cloaked his yellow aura, entered the woods, and back tracked the road from Cambridge. He took note of Colonel Francis Smith's infantry and grenadiers, who had not yet entered Lexington. A familiar face rode among the soldiers—Captain Robert Percy.

A general with yellow-green eyes rode in the rear guard. He surveyed the woods that flanked the road. Brandon stepped back further under the cover of trees. General Henry Hereford and his aide-de-camp would shortly converge on Lexington.

Brandon prayed to his archangel, "Colm, where are you? Have you forsaken us?"

As the last of the rear guard passed by, Brandon heard leaves crunch and twigs snap in the woods to his right. A horse with no rider was cautiously moving toward him. When the filly reached Brandon, she snorted and nudged his shoulder with her nose.

From the look of the horse's tack, Brandon thought she probably belonged to a local farmer, and she'd been spooked by the noise of the British marching the road. He stroked her nose and took hold of her reins. He led the horse through the woods toward Lexington Green to deliver the news to Seamus that he had seen Henry.

TWENTY

Ian thought of Sidonie as he watched the misguided Lieutenant Jessie Adair lead his troops toward Buckman's Tavern.

In the confusion, Major Pitcairn, Major Mitchell, and demon-possessed Lieutenant William Sutherland, galloped across the line of British troops marching along Bedford Road. The officers spread across the green toward the assembled militia.

Elijah Sommers would later swear that he saw one of the British officers riding with a pistol in his hand.

The colonials couldn't swear which British officer yelled, "Throw down your arms, you damned rebels, and disperse!"

"Hold your fire!" Captain Parker ordered his militiamen.

Then a shot rang out.

The British regulars rushed furiously toward the front line of the dispersing militia.

Major Pitcairn saw rebels running toward the cover of low stone walls. He shouted to the regulars in the vanguard, "Hold your fire and maintain ranks!"

But the regulars kept advancing.

The Lexington militiamen turned to defend themselves.

Shots were volleyed at close range.

Paul and John Howell were still hauling John Hancock's trunk across the green. They dared not stop to ascertain what was happening.

Lieutenant William Sutherland's horse bolted at the sound of musket fire. The demon that possessed Sutherland gripped the reins as his horse galloped unchecked along Bedford Road toward the Clarke house.

The first of Colonel Francis Smith's grenadiers and infantrymen marched into Lexington. The rebels dashed for the cover of the low stone walls as a new wave of British regulars surged across the green.

A thick veil of gunpowder, discharged from hundreds of muskets and pistols, settled on Lexington Green. The morning sun was little more than a fuzzy globe of distant light.

Prince Estabrooke, in his enthusiasm over the angels, and the certainty there *was* a Heaven, leaped over the wall where he, Michael, and Patrick had taken cover. He ran at the advancing regulars and disappeared into the gloom.

"Fuck!" Michael shouted. He scrambled over the wall in pursuit of Prince.

Patrick stood up cautiously. Points of orange light infiltrated the veil of smoke. They bobbed up and down and sideways as the human vessels the demons possessed moved through the battle. He was afraid that Michael had forgotten about the demons in his pursuit of Prince.

Patrick reloaded his musket, then leaped the stone wall into the pandemonium. With relief, Patrick saw Michael not far from the wall.

Michael also saw Patrick. He grasped Prince's wrist and shouted, "Follow me!"

Anxious, Seamus and Liam had not taken cover. *How many demons had Henry sent?* The smoke-shrouded green made it difficult to tell if demons were in possession of living or dead human vessels.

Seamus tried not to lose sight of Liam lest a demon found him unprotected. He thought about his little brother out there somewhere in the fog of gunfire, and hoped that he hadn't gotten separated from Michael.

A musket ball punched a hole in Seamus' beaver felt hat. He seized the narrow-edged brim before the hat flew out of his reach. *I'm gonna get myself killed because I'm worryin' too much,* he thought.

Ian and Jeremiah were together near the meetinghouse. They had a cloudy view of the road from Cambridge. Two men with whom Ian had a brief and pleasant exchange with while waiting for Captain Parker's orders, Asa Potter and Jacob Harrington, were guarding the powder cache in the meetinghouse. They were both shot to death by a British infantryman. Ian didn't see their deaths, but he felt the struggle their souls endured as their bodies died. He ran blindly toward them to offer comfort as they left their earthbound lives.

Jeremiah immediately lost sight of Ian. He blinked to clear his eyes of the stinging smoke, and saw two men dressed in redcoats bearing down on him with bayonets flashing in the gloom. A musket fired. The redcoats scattered. A man coughed hard. Jeremiah caught a glimpse of his defender moving away through the haze—Captain John Parker.

Prince and Michael and Patrick became separated. It was impossible for any of the boys to determine where they were on the green or if they were *still* on the green.

Michael stopped to reload. He bit off the top of a cartridge, poured a small amount of gunpowder into the pan, and closed the frizzen. With his musket primed, he lowered it to his left side so he could drop the rest of the powder, paper, and ball down the barrel. He pulled the ramrod from its holder under the barrel.

As he seated the cartridge, he heard a grunt to his left. The continuous noise of musket fire made it difficult for him to identify the importance of the grunt. He removed the ramrod from the barrel of his musket and returned it to the holder.

"Michael? Patrick? Can someone hear me?"

"Prince?" Michael asked. He strained to see through the heavy smoke. "Are ya down?"

"I'm down. I'm hit in the leg."

Michael turned toward the sound of Prince's voice, took one step, and stumbled over Prince's wounded leg. Prince grunted when Michael fell on his stomach.

"FUCK!" Michael said as he got to his knees. Musket balls whizzed through the surrounding air. He crawled closer to Prince's legs.

A musket ball had ripped through the tattered stockings on Prince's left calf. The furrow was bleeding, but Michael didn't think it was bad enough to cause Prince to bleed out. He removed the filthy sweat-stained scarf from Prince's neck and wrapped it around the wound.

"I have to get ya out of danger," Michael said. "Can ya see Patrick's aura? I can't see him."

"I can't see much of anything from here," Prince said. He was so relieved to have Michael with him that he had little concern about the danger he was in.

Amid the noise of the battle, Michael and Prince heard the clatter of metal upon metal. Even from his disadvantaged view on the ground, Prince saw the line of British infantry running directly at them with bayonets.

Prince turned his head and shut his eyes so he wouldn't see the bayonet that would run him through and leave his guts spilling on the ground. Michael threw his body on top of Prince, and tried to unfurl his wings to frighten the charging infantrymen.

Prince thought, *I'm gonna die with an angel. Thank you, Lord.*

Michael's extreme distress crippled him, and he was only able to rustle his wings. He braced his vessel for the onslaught. Muskets fired and bayonets clashed. Horse hooves trampled the ground. Hands pulled him to his feet. Hands lifted Prince from the ground.

Prince shouted, "Patrick!"

The horse and its rider circled Michael several times. Michael saw that the rider was Brandon.

Brandon spurred the horse and galloped at what was left of the bayonet-brandishing line of British infantry. They scattered like startled birds.

Seamus materialized out of the black haze. He shouted, "Fall in!" and motioned for Michael to follow him. They ran toward the buildings on the northern edge of the green. Liam and Jeremiah broke away from the militia ranks and fell in beside them.

Liam had been firing from his position beside Jonas Parker, Captain Parker's much older cousin. Jonas remained in the militia ranks with his musket balls and flints on the ground between his feet. Before he had a chance to reload, he was shot. Jonas struggled on the ground as he attempted to reload his musket. William Monroe, who was standing beside Jonas, witnessed two regulars run Jonas through with their bayonets.

West of the spot Jonas Parker died, the angels and Jeremiah took shelter inside the blacksmith shop located between the two Harrington brothers' houses, near the edge of the green. They paused to catch their breath in the smoke-filled shop.

Patrick burst into the shop, panting and coughing.

"Where's Prince?" Michael asked.

Patrick swigged water from his canteen. When his thirst was quenched, he wiped the back of one filthy hand across his mouth, and said, "I got him to a house where they took him in."

Seamus tried not to sound worried when he asked, "Has anyone seen Ian? Him and Jeremiah got separated."

Patrick, Liam, and Michael shook their heads.

"Well, I sent Brandon to look for him."

"By himself?" Patrick asked, stunned that Seamus would send one of them off alone during a battle.

"Are you forgettin' that he's the only one of us who cain hide his aura from demons?"

Patrick shook his head.

"How'd Brandon get a horse?" Michael asked.

"I didn't ask him," Seamus said. He bit the paper off the top of a cartridge and dropped it down the barrel of his musket.

"The green is crawling with demons," Michael said. "I know those fuckers did something to Ian! I'm going after them!" He reached into his cartridge box, and began to reload his musket.

"No, you ain't," Seamus warned. "Brandon saw Robert Percy, and who he's sure is Henry, ridin' with Colonel Francis Smith's infantry and grenadiers that're behind Pitcairn's van. They're marchin' into Lexington as we speak. Me and Brandon think Ian might've broke ranks and went to Concord because Sidonie's there. That's where Brandon's headed."

Michael plunged the ramrod down the barrel of his musket. His beautiful face contorted with anger and fear. He was angry with Colm for leaving them and was afraid because Colm wasn't with them.

"I am not staying with you," Liam blurted out. "Seamus, I am aware of what you are doing, and I will not let it continue."

The men stopped and looked at Liam.

Seamus looked Liam in the eye and said, "You ain't leavin'."

"Brother? What's Liam mean?" Patrick asked. "You ain't doin' somethin' stupid just because Colm punished Liam—are you?"

The Cullen brothers' eyes met. They shivered as a memory that belonged to the souls of human brothers slid through their angelic spirits and vanished.

"He is, as you say, doing something stupid," Liam said. "He is overprotecting me because of the punishment Colm has effected on me. Seamus is afraid that I am too vulnerable."

"Where *is* Colm?" Michael demanded. "Why isn't he with us?" He stood up and turned on Liam. "Ya knew this was going to happen! Ya were going on about it the day ya went to visit the Adamses in Boston! How we might have to stand on our own without Colm!"

"Stop actin' like a baby!" Jeremiah shouted at Michael. "You've fought countless battles! I ain't never been ta war before today, and I ain't whinin'."

Before Michael had a chance to react to Jeremiah's insult, the rhythm of a beating drum rolled across Lexington Green. Colonel Francis Smith and his regiments had arrived.

❧

Colonel Smith was aghast when he saw the dead and wounded rebels littering Lexington Green. Major John Pitcairn's companies of the advanced guard were in disarray. Major Edward Mitchell's company was in a state of exhausted confusion. The British troops were so wild that they could not hear the orders to assemble.

General Henry Hereford rode out from the rear of the column to survey the shambles beside Colonel Smith. Captain Robert Percy acknowledged General Hereford's passing by momentarily revealing his orange eyes. Lieutenant William Sutherland rode to meet the colonel and the general near the meetinghouse on the green.

"Find a drummer and order him to beat to arms," Smith ordered Sutherland.

Colonel Smith searched for hope within the dreadful situation and found it. *It appears we have suffered no casualties*, he thought. In his shocked state, Francis Smith failed to note Henry's presence.

Major John Pitcairn arrived on horseback. He raised one blond eyebrow in surprise when he saw General Hereford. John recalled that the general was among the guests at the social he had hosted on March 13. His unnatural yellow-greens eyes were impossible to forget.

John acknowledged his superior officers by clapping a hand to his hat. Henry felt no obligation to remain while the major attempted to explain his junior officers' and troops' conduct to Colonel Smith.

Henry's single interest was locating the archangel and his men. He rode back and fetched Robert from his regiment. Together, they returned to the southern edge of the green at a slow pace. The possessed William Sutherland joined them. The three officers carefully watched the movements of the rebels.

As enlisted officers goaded their men back into ranks, Colonel Smith held commissioned officers' call. The objective of their march had never been revealed to the colonel's subordinates, in order to maintain the element of surprise that General Gage had assumed Colonel Smith and he were operating under. That element of surprise had disintegrated with the carnage in Lexington.

"We are marching on to Concord," Colonel Smith told his officers. "The true objective of this mission is to capture stores of armaments and powder the rebels have hidden there."

"Colonel, you cannot mean to go on with this after what has happened here!" A mortified young captain pronounced. His eyes swept the dead rebels. "We did not come here to kill men, no matter their allegiances to our King!"

"I am in agreement with Captain Duncan!" one of Major Pitcairn's other captains shouted.

"By God, we shall fulfill our orders from General Gage!" Colonel Smith decreed. "We will not return to Boston with a report of a failed mission! Now, let us rally and demonstrate our fortitude!"

When the British regulars were at last under control and assembled on the green, Colonel Smith ordered his command to fire their weapons in a victory salute and raise three huzzas. The roar of eight hundred muskets shook the town.

Colonel Smith gave the order to march toward Concord. As the column of regulars marched the westward road, Henry and his demon officers crossed the green. They encountered rebels just arriving from outlying farms.

The new arrivals joined the battle's survivors in stunned disbelief at the sight of dead and wounded friends and relatives. Residences streamed from all directions toward the green to aide those in need and gather their casualties. John and Ebenezer Munroe had fought with the militia that morning. They found their father dead near the place the militia line had formed. John Harrington's family found him dead almost on his own doorstep on the edge of the green. Jonas Parker's wife, Sarah, sobbed as her sons removed their father's body.

Henry and his posse of demons stopped at the edge of the green near David Harrington's house. The possessed deceased Captain Sir Rupert Weller and the living Lieutenant Jasper Durnford, both of the 10th Regiment of Foot, crossed the green from the Clarke house and approached Henry. Robert had dispatched Weller and Durnford to Lexington earlier the previous evening. They were to locate the angels, if they were indeed in Lexington, and keep them in their sight.

Henry and his officers dismounted and walked to meet Weller and Durnford. The five demons converged in front of the blacksmith shop where the angels had taken cover.

Inside the shop, the uneasy angels struggled to keep their wings still. The demons would hear even the slightest flutter. Jeremiah crawled to the wall that faced the green and squinted to see through a crack.

"The angels are here," Lieutenant Durnford told Henry. "Before dawn, the one with the purple aura killed the demon possessing the dead saddlemaker. He and two other angels remained with the human guardsmen at the Clarke House until they moved the patriots elsewhere."

"Where were the other five angels?" Robert asked.

"We only saw three."

Robert had a difficult time believing that the archangel would send only three angels to guard the ignorant human patriots. He stepped close to Jasper. "Where are the three now?"

Jeremiah crawled closer to Seamus and whispered, "They think there was only three angels guardin' Hancock and Adams last night." He crawled back to the crack in the wall.

Jasper shot Rupert a nervous glance. "We lost track of them in the fighting."

Henry strode over to Jasper. He wrapped one gloved hand around the lieutenant's throat and squeezed. The lieutenant choked and his face turned red. He struggled with Henry, but it was as effective as a child pushing away a two-hundred-pound grown man.

Henry's yellow-green eyes flared. He addressed Captain Rupert Weller, "Is Jasper telling me that, not only did you lose sight of those angels, you *did not* locate the archangel? HE HAS TO BE HERE! HE WOULD NOT LEAVE HIS ANGELS UNPROTECTED!"

Henry snapped Lieutenant Jasper Durnford's neck. The demon that possessed Jasper exploded into a shower of orange sparks. Henry let go of the dead human body, and it crumpled to the ground. Lieutenant Jasper Durnford would become the overlooked British causality of the Battle of Lexington.

"Robert," Henry said with his eyes still on Rupert. "Kill him. Then you and I and William will destroy every door in Lexington if that's what it takes to find the angels. Bohannon could not possibly have left his pets unprotected!"

Jeremiah crawled back to Seamus and whispered, "We gotta get outta here. They're gonna start searchin' for us."

Seamus nodded and moved to confer with the angels.

Henry muttered, "Oh!"

"Sir?" Robert asked.

Henry's eyes lit up. "The preceptor did *not* leave his pet unprotected! I have changed my mind Robert. There is no need wasting our time scouring this town for three angels. Let's move on to Concord."

Jeremiah watched Henry, Robert, and William saddle up. They spurred their horses, galloped off the green, and up the road to Concord.

A drumbeat reverberated in the late morning air. When the last British officers rode toward Concord, Captain John Parker reassembled his militia.

Blood had been spilled on the grass of Lexington Green, and the rebels would march to exact revenge.

☙

Ian knew he was risking British capture or a demon attack, but Asa Potter's and Jacob Harrington's deaths convinced him that he needed to go to Concord to protect Sidonie.

As he walked alone in the woods, on the edge of the road to Concord, he thought, *All I have to do is stay alert.* However, his vigilance slipped when his thoughts turned to the prospect of satisfying his lust with Sidonie.

"Aren't you the pretty one?"

The question startled Ian. A young woman stepped in front of him and blocked his way. She held a butcher knife in her right hand. Her eyes were blue, but he knew she was possessed by a demon because no human woman would be alone in the woods, especially with the British moving through the countryside.

"Why are you away from your flock, angel?" she sneered.

Ian slipped his dagger from his coat pocket.

She raised the butcher knife over her head and lunged at him.

Ian jumped backward. His shoulder hit a tree trunk and he jolted to a stop. She jabbed the butcher knife at him. The tip embedded in Ian's coat just above his collarbone. She raked the knife down the front of his coat to his waist.

He felt a sharp sting as the knife ripped through his clothing and grazed the skin on his chest and abdomen. He stabbed his dagger into one of her blue eyes. The eye immediately burst into orange flames. The human woman, who the demon possessed, screamed in agony. The demon plunged the butcher knife into Ian's coat and slashed his chest and abdomen again.

The physical pain he felt was strange and surprising. His dagger slipped from his hand. The demon whipped the butcher knife up and tried to stab him in the face. He dodged it by stepping behind the tree. The demon fell forward and onto her knees.

Ian ripped his musket off his shoulder. He gripped the barrel and attempted to slam the butt into the top of the demon's head. She laughed, jerked the musket out of his hand, and slung it over his head. The musket hit the ground with a dull thud.

As the demon got to her feet, Ian dived for his dagger. He fell hard on his stomach. The fall knocked the wind out of him, but he was able to get a grip on his dagger. He immediately rolled over onto his back.

The demon tried to stab him in the chest. The knife caught in the fabric of Ian's coat. The demon slashed at Ian's coat repeatedly until she lost her balance and fell on top of him.

"Don't touch me with your demon filth!" Ian screamed. He buried his dagger up to the hilt into the demon's other eye.

Flames ignited in the eye and licked the living woman's face and hair. Her screams were excruciating.

Ian's consciousness flickered and threatened to go out. It took more effort to shove her off than he'd expected. She sprawled on the ground face up. He rolled over, got to his knees, and then fell forward, unconscious.

∼

Brandon found Ian on the edge of the woods along the road to Concord, less than two miles from Lexington Green. Ian's red aura blinked as if it was depleted of energy. Brandon reined his horse, dismounted, and then led the horse into the woods.

Ian was lying face down on the cold damp ground. His hat was missing. The ribbon holding his ponytail was gone, and his hair draped both sides of his face. Brandon kneeled and rolled Ian onto his back. The front of his buttoned coat was slashed to ribbons, but there was little blood on the woolen material.

From Ian's hips down, Brandon saw nothing more damaging than filthy breeches, torn stockings and dirty boots. He searched for Ian's musket, and found it on the ground nearby. When he reached to pick it up, he saw, out of the corner of his left eye, a mound covered in brown homespun cloth.

He slung the musket over his shoulder and went to investigate. The dead woman, who made up the mound, lay on her back. Ian's dagger protruded from her open right eye. Her left eye was a hollow pitted shell. Her eyelashes and eyebrows were burned off, and the upper layer of skin on her cheeks and forehead was burned away to reveal a layer of pink skin that sweated blood beads. Singed blond hair framed her forehead. She clutched a butcher knife in her right hand.

Brandon guessed she was no older than thirty. It was apparent that she had been a living woman, possessed by a demon, and that she had used the butcher knife in an attempt to kill Ian.

Someone is going to think Ian murdered her, Brandon thought. *I have to get us out of here before someone sees.*

His wings rustled. He pulled the dagger out of her eye socket and slipped it in his coat pocket. That was when the air and sounds in and around the woods fluctuated. The shift was caused by the approach of the British. Colonel Smith's infantry and grenadiers, and Major Pitcairn's vanguard now marched as one. The parade of 1,600 boots was ominous.

Brandon had to get himself and Ian on the road without being observed by the advancing British, and stay well ahead of them. He ran back to Ian and picked up his limp body. Ian's head lolled and his mouth dropped open.

The sharp notes of a fife and the roll of a beating drum announced the arrival of the British column. It was too late to escape on horseback. He shifted Ian in his arms, and walked further into the woods until he realized the horse was following him.

The noise they were making as they walked—the snap of breaking branches and twigs, the crunch of dead foliage on the ground, and the crack of disturbed underbrush—was sure to attract attention if Colonel Smith had grenadiers flanking the road in the woods. He laid Ian on the ground and sat beside him. The horse nudged Brandon with her nose.

Brandon struggled to keep his wings from rustling, and his yellow aura hidden. Ian's red aura was a dim flicker in the woods.

Brandon was uncertain of how much time passed before he realized something was wrong. His horse whinnied and trotted away. He heard the approach of horses as they trampled the dead foliage and underbrush. Robert Percy, and two lower demons that occupied the bodies of living enlisted men, were upon Brandon before he could get to his feet.

The demons dismounted. Brandon slowly stood up. If his wings rustled, he would be found out. There was nothing he could do to protect Ian, because killing all three demons at once was impossible. The best he could do was to ensure that his angelic spirit went undetected so he could go for help if they took Ian.

Robert approached Brandon with a sneering grin and flaming orange eyes. He considered Brandon's calm face.

What if he remembers me from the meetinghouse? Brandon thought.

Ian's aura flickered. The lower demons saw it and started toward him. Robert whipped out his right arm as a sign for them to stop. He went to Ian, straddled Ian's prone body, and looked down at him. His grin transformed into a wide smile.

"Tie him to a horse," Robert said to the demons as he stepped aside.

They carried out the order and reached to haul Ian's body up from the ground.

Brandon's spirit screamed in his head: *DON'T TOUCH HIM, YOU FUCKERS!* His concentration slipped, and his wings rustled.

Robert Percy whirled around at the sound. He went to Brandon and stared at him with his orange eyes. Brandon tried not to flinch.

Finally, Robert asked, "Why are you with the angel?"

Robert's direct reference to *the angel* startled Brandon. He stupidly asked, "Angel?"

Robert continued to study Brandon while the demons heaved Ian into the saddle of one of the horses. Ian's upper body fell forward and draped the horse's neck. The demons secured him in place with a rope.

"Search the area for the demon that attacked the angel," Robert ordered.

The demons fanned out.

Robert backed away from Brandon a few steps without taking his skeptical eyes from Brandon's face.

Brandon remembered that he had Ian's dagger in his coat pocket. If he killed Robert, the other demons might run off, but he couldn't be sure that would happen, nor could he be sure they wouldn't kill Ian.

The lower demons returned and reported that the demon that attacked the angel was found dead.

Robert supposed it was time to deliver his prize to Henry. He concluded that he would let the young man live. It would be more sporting to watch him die horribly in a battle that was yet to be fought. He doused his eyes so they would appear blue again.

When the demons were gone, and Brandon was sure they were well down the road, he comforted himself by spreading his wings and freeing his yellow aura. Delicate silver crystals dusted the surrounding woods and set it aglow as if the sun touched it.

"Colm, where are you?" he murmured. "Henry has Ian. We need you."

TWENTY-ONE

General Thomas Gage was awakened at 5:00 in the morning of April 19 by the arrival of a messenger whom Colonel Smith had dispatched with a request for more troops.

Smith's appeal for reinforcements was passed on to Lord Hugh Percy's brigade major, Captain Thomas Moncrieff. From that point, several events took place that caused Smith's relief to be delayed for hours.

The troops of the First Brigade should have been at the ready to march at a moment's notice. However, they were asleep and had to be roused.

As the First Brigade prepared to march, Lord Hugh Percy waited for the battalion of Royal Marines to arrive. Two hours after General Gage had been roused with the message of Colonel Smith's solicitation for assistance, the marines had not answered the call. The marines were also asleep because the orders for reinforcements had been sent to Major John Pitcairn's quarters, and at that moment, Major Pitcairn was marching toward Lexington.

Word of Lord Hugh Percy's activities and what had occurred in Lexington reached the Warren residence at 8:00 a.m. Joseph and Colm had not been able to sleep and prepared to leave for Concord.

The two youngest Warren children, Richard and Mary, woke while their father was speaking to William Eustis in his medical office.

"William, please take care of my patients and medical practice," Joseph implored. "I do not know when I shall return."

I hope this is not the last time I see you, William thought as Joseph said his farewells. The thought made William feel sick, and his hands shook. His first inclination was to pray to God to keep Joseph safe. He glanced at Colm and decided prayers were a waste of time.

William's distress and doubt was obvious to Colm. He left the medical office and waited for Joseph outside.

Mercy brought Richard and Mary to Joseph. "Kiss your father children. He must run an errand," she said.

Joseph squatted so he could hug Richard and Mary. The children allowed their father to pull them in close and press their little bodies against his chest and shoulders. He kissed their foreheads and breathed in the aroma of their love. Joseph closed his eyes for a moment as he thought of their dead mother, Betsy. Then, he let his children go and stood up.

"Shall I awaken Elizabeth and Joseph?" Mercy asked.

Joseph longed to say farewell to his eldest children, but they would ask endless questions for which he would have no answers. "No. I do not want to worry them."

He turned to leave.

Mercy's mournful voice stopped him. "Joseph, please…" Her eyes watered with unshed tears.

Joseph cupped her cheeks in his hands and kissed her on the mouth.

She wrapped her arms around his neck and pulled him closer until she felt the curve of his ribs press against her breasts.

He untangled himself from her embrace, looked into her eyes, and said, "I will see to it that you and the children are safe."

Then, he was gone.

Colm and Joseph rode through Boston to the Charlestown ferry; prepared to be stopped at every corner. Joseph, the patriot and physician, was a recognizable figure. They made it to the dock with no trouble. Before they boarded the ferry, an elderly man, John Adan, recognized Joseph. Adan looked for encouragement from the idolized young man.

Joseph smiled. "Keep a brave heart! They have begun it, and we will end it!"

Colm and Joseph did not speak as they rode the ferry to Charlestown. Each man's burden was too great. Colm bore the weight of guilt and blame for leaving his men unprotected and alone to participate in a battle no one had expected. Joseph struggled with the fate of his friends, and the undefined conflict that lay ahead. Yet, both Colm and Joseph could not imagine being in the company of anyone else on that decisive morning.

The ferry landed in Charlestown at 8:30 a.m. The town was in turmoil and confusion over rumors of war to the west. Joseph managed to procure a pair of mares with help from Colonel William Conant; the same rebel leader who had provided Paul with a horse.

Colm and Joseph caught up with Lord Hugh Percy's troops and the marines as they passed through Cambridge. They tried to pass the column, but were stopped by bayonets.

"I recognize you, Warren. Where are the troops?" a British soldier demanded.

"I do not know."

The soldier wondered, *Is he telling the truth?* Despite the cold morning air, beads of sweat formed on the soldier's forehead and armpits. He forced himself not to turn his head and look at the man with Dr. Warren.

"You are free to move on," the soldier muttered.

"We need to make haste to Menotomy," Joseph told Colm as they veered past the British column. "The Committee of Safety is scheduled to meet there at the Black Horse Tavern."

"How am I going to sit through a political meeting? I'm worried about my men."

"Perhaps the men at the meeting will have news. It may not ease our minds, but it may alert us to what we have in store on our journey to Concord."

Joseph was gifted with a rare laugh from Colm. "I've got a lot to learn about working with human men during times of war. Ya should be in command—not me."

Despite Colm's laugh, Joseph heard the shame in his friend's voice.

The haunting quiet along the road to Menotomy was a stark contrast to the loud discussion of the news of war on the streets of Menotomy. As Joseph and Colm made their way to the Black Horse Tavern, wagons filled with families fleeing town to safer havens and militiamen marching toward Concord, passed them on the streets.

In John Hancock's absence, the members of the Committee of Safety looked to Joseph as their chairman. Benjamin Church and Paul Revere were in attendance. Paul had managed to make it safely to Menotomy after John Howell and he delivered John Hancock's trunk to the safe house. Benjamin had escaped Boston an hour before the messenger arrived at the Warren home to alert Joseph of the latest news.

Colm was pleased to see Fergus among the attendees. Fergus, however, didn't stay long. He rode off to Watertown to meet up with the militia there.

While the committee discussed their business, messengers came and went with the latest news. The committee members hoped that the British had fired the first shot in Lexington as that would justify the actions the Americans were about to take.

Colm's need to be with his men and his anxiety over their well-being grew as the morning dwindled. Still, he sat quietly by while Joseph did what he needed to do as a man and a patriot. Colm left the meeting when Lord Hugh Percy's troops marched through Menotomy. He mounted his horse and, from a distance, followed Percy's column.

Fifteen minutes passed before Joseph noticed Colm was gone. He asked Benjamin to stand in for him as chairman for the remainder of the meeting, and then left the tavern.

Paul followed Joseph outside and stopped him before he mounted his horse. "Are you sure it is wise for you to be with Colm?"

"Why do you say that?"

Paul sighed. He and Joseph were longtime friends. Joseph was the grand master of the St. Andrews Masonic Lodge of which Paul was a member. They were fellow patriots, and Sons of Liberty. Paul knew Joseph's brother, Dr. John Warren, and remembered the now deceased Elizabeth 'Betsy' Warren. Paul's first wife, Sarah, had died within weeks of Joseph's wife. His children played with Joseph's children.

"You are not thinking with a clear head," Paul cautioned. "Not in regard to the archangel. Colm's first allegiance is to his men. Our cause is secondary. Who do you think he would choose if he had to make a decision between his men and us? Between his brother, Michael, and you?"

Joseph and Paul regarded one another in silence for a moment.

Paul said, "You are already deaf to my words. Why?"

"I know you have been tolerant of the angels because there is no other choice. However, I would venture to say that some of us have found a kinship with them. I cannot predict Colm's decisions any more than I can predict your decisions, my old friend."

Joseph mounted his horse.

"I pray that God keeps you safe," Paul said. He saw doubt in Joseph's eyes. "I shall also pray that your archangel keeps you safe."

Joseph spurred his horse and galloped out of Menotomy. He took a little-known crossroad leading from Watertown to Lexington where he encountered Fergus and his Cambridge-Watertown militia marching toward Lexington.

"Colm has left me," Joseph confessed. "He must be on this road."

"He's here. He's lagging on the left flank."

Joseph turned his horse to find Colm.

"Wait," Fergus said.

Joseph halted his horse.

"It's his way to take on the shame and the blame so that we, and now you, do not have to bear that burden. We were, and still are, incapable of helping him because we aren't his equals. But you—" Pain clouded Fergus' eyes, and lines marred his handsome face. "—you can help him, Joseph."

"Fergus, I am but a man. How can I possibly help God's creation?"

"You too are God's creation." His blue eyes held Joseph in an angelic embrace. "Go to him." Then Fergus spurred his horse and galloped to his place at the head of the militia formation.

Joseph urged his horse into a gallop. He saw Colm lagging behind the formation and drew his horse up beside him. "Please, Colm, speak to me," Joseph implored.

The anguish that radiated from Colm's eyes hurt Joseph so bad that he winced. "They're in pain. They're afraid. They're separated. They've seen Henry," Colm said. "I can't linger here. Come with me."

No matter if you choose Michael over me, if that is what it comes down to, I will still stand with you, Joseph thought. *Curse you, Paul! Why did you insinuate that Colm would be forced to choose between Michael and me? Why did you try to place doubt in my heart?*

Colm's guilt-ridden spirit perceived it as a sign that Joseph harbored doubts about their friendship. The pain of that doubt tormented him and he lost control. The reins tangled in his hands as he tightened them into fists. Green light shot out from his body in all directions. Golden light flashed like distant lightning. His horse reared to rid itself of its rider's terrifying authority.

The hair on the back of Joseph's neck bristled in response to a faint current of static electricity. His mare whinnied and cast one fearful eye at Colm's horse, but Joseph did not hesitate. He reached up and snatched the reins on Colm's horse. He jerked them downward and toward him so the rearing horse would have less leeway.

Ahead, like the faraway sounds of a dream, Joseph heard men shouting and horses whinnying.

Colm's horse reared again. The leather reins slipped through Joseph's hands and burned the palms. The horse tried to bolt off to the right and into the woods. In the madness, Joseph could not confirm if Colm was still on his horse.

Joseph was yanked from his saddle. He tried to release the reins of his own horse, but the leather reins refused to slide from his sweating and bleeding palms. There was no pain when his body slammed into the road face down. For a moment, the lack of pain made him believe he was dead. He blinked to clear his eyes of dust, and spit until he felt like he was no longer going to choke on the dirt in his mouth.

The bedlam calmed. Joseph rose slowly. Horses trotted in hypnotic circles. Fergus' purple aura tinted the men, the horses, the woods, and the road. Fergus had ripped the reins from Joseph's hands and broken his fall.

Colm was on his knees; his magnificent wings were unfurled. Silver crystals showered the road and drifted into the woods. Fergus sat beside him like a father waiting to take a sick child into his arms.

The members of the Cambridge-Watertown militia were kneeling in the silver crystals. Many were acquainted with Colm Bohannon and the men who lived on the farm with him in Roxbury. The manifestation of Colm's heavenly embodiment was stupefying.

Joseph kneeled beside Colm. In a pleading whisper, he said, "You must tell me what has happened so I may help you."

Colm's eyes were bright with mania. He didn't understand how to react to Joseph's plea. In the thousands of millennia of his existence, Colm had never had anyone say those words. Confessions and protection were his provinces.

"Let him help you!" Fergus insisted.

Although Fergus had no authority to issue an order to an archangel, Colm heard Fergus' words and took them to heart. He doused his aura and said, "I heard Brandon pray to me for the second time this morning. Henry has Ian. I'm unable to tell if Ian's been hurt because I can't sense him." His confession calmed him somewhat. His wings fluttered and with ethereal delicacy, they became volute, and furled into obscurity.

Fergus' eyes drifted to Joseph so he could calm his panic before speaking to his archangel. "We will find Ian." Fergus looked at Colm. "Despite what Seamus thinks, I will not turn my back on any of you."

Colm took strength from Fergus. He let the last of his angst evaporate and then got to his feet.

Sensing his calm, the two did the same.

Fergus ordered the awestruck militiamen to rise.

As they rose, not one man shifted his eyes away from Colm. With all the confusion that had surrounded Colm's display, the men were unaware that Fergus had been emanating a purple aura. With Joseph and Fergus by his side, Colm let the children of man do what they needed to do to ease their awe.

Gideon Eldon, a shaken twenty-five-year-old sergeant, asked, "What have we just witnessed?"

Seth Walters saw unbridled innocence in Colm's eyes. Like Captain Levi Chitwood, Seth had had a vision of the archangel Michael, but his hadn't been frightening. As a child, he'd seen a painting of Michael hanging in the home of the rector of the Anglican Church in New York.

Seth smiled. "Do you not see, Gideon? One of God's most transcendent creations is among us."

Afraid, Gideon fueled his boldness from Dr. Warren's presence and took a step toward Colm.

Fergus stepped toward Gideon.

Gideon paid him no mind. "Why would you frighten us with such a display of power?" he asked Colm.

Colm's eyes flashed.

Gideon stepped back until he was well behind the group of awestruck militiamen.

A forty-five-year-old veteran of the French and Indian war, Sergeant Abe Rowlinson, was acquainted with Colm and his men. Abe was not easily shaken by chaos and unexplained phenomenon. It was not only the display of Colm's power that had frightened the other men, it was also the words Major Driscoll and Dr. Warren had exchanged with Colm as they knelt on the ground.

"Colm, you accidentally revealed who you are, did you not?"

Colm's jaw tightened.

Abe was undaunted. "You were under duress from news you received regarding Ian Keogh. I heard you speak his name. What has happened to him?"

Colm realized that Abe's concern was genuine. "Ian's been captured by the British. They may have mortally wounded him."

Abe understood Colm's evasiveness. He was convinced Colm was an archangel because the pain he saw the archangel suffer hurt his soul. He wanted to reach out and ease Colm's turmoil. The urge to do so seemed strange.

Colm said, "Brandon O'Flynn was with Ian. I don't know where he is now."

177

"Then we must find them," Abe said.

"Major Driscoll, I wish to ask something before we move on," Seth Walters said.

Joseph intervened. "Listen to me," he whispered to Colm. "We are facing unknown peril. Not just this day—but all the days to come. Man or angel, we are facing the same enemy."

Colm looked away.

"Look at me." Joseph insisted.

Colm looked at Joseph.

The men of the Cambridge-Watertown militia stood silent as they watched the inaudible exchange between Colm and Joseph.

"I saw the expression on Abe's face," Joseph said. "He knows what you are, and he sees your affliction just as I do. Seth knows what you are. He just needs to hear it from your lips. These are deeply religious men. You and your angels can give them the hope that God is on their side—"

"—our presence has nothing to do with hope."

"That makes no difference. Let them have their beliefs."

"It's a lie."

Joseph sighed. "Perhaps, but it is not a lie you told. It is a lie man has passed on for thousands of years. It is all we have to cling to in a world where life and death hold no answers to our existence."

Colm's jaw muscles quivered.

"You are an angel. Give them comfort," Joseph pleaded.

Fergus saw the faraway look in Colm's eyes, and thought, *he has given in to Joseph.* He nodded at Seth as an indication to ask his question.

Seth gathered his fortitude and faced Colm. Colm's eyes flashed. Seth did not back away. "Are you one of God's archangels?"

Why is this so difficult? Why was I able to admit it to Joseph without feeling like a martyr? His wings rustled. "Aye, I am."

There was murmuring and sighs of relief among the militia.

"Fergus was once under my command," Colm said to Seth.

"The purple light was his," Seth said. He felt a rush of happiness.

Gordon Walker, the free black man who had come to Colm at the Greystoke Inn, stepped forward. "Colm, tell them why you and your angels are here."

The question took Colm off guard. He regarded Gordon for a moment. Then, he turned and went to soothe his horse.

Abe Rowlinson challenged Gordon. "Why do you not tell us why the angels are here, Mister...?"

"Gordon Walker." He decided to keep Colm's secret until the day brought its conclusion. "I venture to say they are here to fight beside us as rebels and Americans."

Abe eyed Gordon with doubt, but he remained silent.

Fergus ordered the militia to fall into formation. Lexington awaited them no matter whether they were human, angel, or demon.

Joseph mounted his horse and urged the mare to fall in beside Colm's horse. The archangel's jaw muscles formed small mounds, but he was calm. His tone was set when he said, "I'm riding ahead, Joseph. I think now ya wou'd be best served by staying with the militia."

Joseph laughed. "Say it plain. You think my *safety* is better served with the militia."

"Aye."

"I do not need your protection, Colm. I'd be part of this fight whether you were here or not."

"No, Joseph. The war ya wou'd wage if I wasn't here wou'd not include demons." He spurred his horse into a gallop.

"You are wrong, Colm," Joseph whispered to the retreating figure. "You are wrong."

TWENTY-TWO

CONCORD, MASSACHUSETTS

Concord and Lincoln had been on the alert since Dr. Samuel Prescott galloped to spread the warning that the regulars were out, after eluding Major Edward Mitchell's patrol.

While the Concord militia assembled, a saddlemaker, Reuben Brown, was dispatched eastward to Lexington to gather intelligence. He witnessed the initial firing from the far western edge of the green and hurried back to give the alarm without waiting for the outcome.

But there was no doubt doom was on its way to Concord.

Unlike in Lexington, there were men designated as being able to assemble and march in the shortest time possible. These men converged upon the town and reported immediately to their captain, David Brown. Twenty-three-year-old Corporal Amos Barrett was one of those minutemen. He took his captain's orders to march to Lexington.

From the Concord town square, an abrupt ridge flanked Lexington Road for about a mile. Where the ridge leveled off into the surrounding plain, they heard fifes and drums and saw the British regulars coming. The minutemen were ordered to about face. They marched back to Concord to the intimidating pulse of their own fifes and drums.

As the minutemen fell back, there was debate about whether the militia should form and defend the town or withdraw to surrounding high ground to both learn the regulars' intentions and to await the arrival of more militia.

The commander of the combined Middlesex County regiment of the militia, sixty-four-year-old Colonel James Barrett, advised the latter and his counsel prevailed. Colonel Barrett led them across the North Bridge over the

Concord River, and up to the high ground of Punkatasset Hill, a mile north of Concord Common.

At 8:00 a.m., Colonel Francis Smith's men marched into Concord unopposed and came to a halt opposite the long rectangular common. From the common, the main road curved north through town toward North Bridge. The British commanding officers assessed the nearly 500-armed militiamen and minutemen assembled on the hills on the other side of the river.

General Henry Hereford and Captain Robert Percy, joined Colonel Smith as he assessed the situation. The colonel was unsure why a general he didn't know was riding in his rear guard, and it irritated him. He took note of the horse Robert was leading and the man draped across the horse's neck.

"Who is that?" Colonel Smith asked Robert.

"He attacked General Hereford as we left Lexington," Robert said. "I was forced to stop his aggression. I thought it was best that he was not left to die on the road."

Colonel Smith huffed. The pungent odor of depraved death that clung to General Hereford stung his eyes and caused them to water. The colonel sat up straighter in his saddle and tried to pull in his rotund belly before he issued a clear sign of disgust by purposely pinching his nostrils together.

Hereford favored Smith with a broad smile, and thought, *the human man Henry Hereford will die tonight, and I will be rid of this stink.*

Smith did not return the smile. He shivered under the gaze of Henry's yellow-green eyes, and then shook the feeling off. *You disgust me,* Francis thought, then he moved on to pressing matters.

"Captain Parsons!" Colonel Smith shouted.

"Sir!" Leslie Parsons answered.

"Take six companies to the bridge to the north. Then take three companies on to the Barrett farm beyond the bridge. We have intelligence that powder and other munitions are hidden there."

Smith, you bastard! You are overtly bypassing my command after what happened in Lexington, John Pitcairn thought as Parsons attended the colonel.

Leslie Parsons was an adolescent-faced young man of twenty-six years. He smirked as he hailed his companies into formation. Pitcairn confronted Parsons. The two men conducted a short-lived standoff of wills.

Captain Parsons marched off for the North Bridge with six companies of light infantry. The hundreds of militiamen and minutemen assembled on the hills near the bridge watched as Parsons marched three of the companies across the bridge to Colonel Barrett's farm.

This was the move Henry anticipated, and he, Robert, and William Sutherland accompanied Parsons. A month ago, General Gage, at the urging of Henry, sent Ensign Henry de Berniere and Captain John Brown on a clandestine mission to search for munitions in Concord. There *was* a stockpile at the Barrett farm. But at the bidding of the Committee of Safety, Paul rode to Concord on April 8 to warn of the British movement detected by the Sons of Liberty at Boston Harbor. The only muskets still at the farm had been *planted,* by Barrett's sons, in a recently plowed field.

Meanwhile, Colonel Smith assessed the other routes rebel forces could take to converge on Concord, as well as their current stance in the hills and woods to the northwest. Smith shouted for the captain of his Tenth Regiment's grenadier company.

With Captain Munday Pole in attendance, Smith issued his orders. As some of the British officers took refreshment in local taverns, Captain Pole's detachment advanced to the South Bridge. A number of his grenadiers held the bridge. The others commenced a search in that area for hidden munitions.

Colonel Smith kept the remaining companies of light infantry and the bulk of the grenadiers in the center of Concord under his direct control, but his forces were now spread thin. He had 100 men at the South Bridge a mile west of the common; 120 at or near the North Bridge a mile to the north; another 120 with Captain Parsons a good two miles beyond that assigned to digging around Barrett's farm; and the remaining number of about 500 searching the buildings in Concord proper.

British Captain Walter Laurie had only thirty men of the light company guarding the North Bridge, and no communication with Captain Parson's and his companies nor the Fourth and Tenth light regiments positioned atop the knolls about four hundred yards beyond the bridge. He had no exchange of information with Colonel Smith in his rear in Concord proper. The steady increase of numbers among the colonials on the heights above the bridge made Captain Laurie nervous.

Two companies of 38 minutemen under the command of gun maker, Captain Isaac Davis, arrived from Acton. Forty men from Bedford, and many from Lincoln and other surrounding areas, joined the force of aroused rebels on Punkatasset Hill above Concord. As Captain Parsons' men passed, the rebels on the hill saw the unmoving man tied to a horse led by a British officer. There was no doubt, judging from his clothing, that the man was a colonist. The sight fueled the rebels' simmering anger. They shouldered their muskets and rifles.

In Concord proper, the grenadier companies were searching for weapons and supplies. What little remained in town was hidden in various ways.

Mill owner Timothy Wheeler had caches stored in barrels of flour, wheat, and rye in his barn. When he protested that the British had no right to search what belonged to his livelihood, the officers agreed that they did not injure private property and withdrew.

The incident at the house of Ephraim Woods was repeated throughout many homes—women refused the British entry into their bedrooms where caches of military stores were hidden. Many stores were saved by feminine persuasion.

Tavern keeper and town jailer, Ephraim Jones, had custody of important papers from the provincial treasurer. He was arrested at bayonet point, but the officers soon decided that they would be better served if Mr. Jones opened his tavern and set up a round of drinks.

At residences around Concord, hungry troops paid the women of the households for breakfast; after which, the troops searched the houses.

The searches turned up a meager supply of munitions including three iron twenty-four-pound cannons. The munitions were piled and set on fire near the courthouse on the northernmost corner of the commons. The fire soon became out of control and set the courthouse on fire. This was visible from the knolls to the west of the bridge that Colonel James Barrett's Middlesex County militia, Major James Buttrick's Concord militia, and Captain Isaac Davis' Acton minutemen occupied.

For a few minutes, the militiamen and minutemen stared at the smoke curling upward from the courthouse.

"Colonel Barrett," a militiaman from Lincoln asked, "are you to let them burn the town down?"

This set them in motion. Colonel Barret commanded the militia to march. The minutemen from Acton led the column. As fife and drum played, they marched down the hill and toward the North Bridge with no regard for Captain Parson's companies searching the Barrett farm a mile and a half to the west behind them.

❧

Satisfied that he had used the unconscious angel to stir the embers of hostility among the colonial rebels, Henry focused his attention on breakfast as did the other officers. At the farm, the hungry regulars offered to pay Mrs. Barrett for breakfast, but Rebeckah Barrett was not amiable. Her disdain for the British, who occupied her home and scavenged her farm while her husband, Colonel James Barrett, was with the militiamen near the North Bridge, was apparent. To make matters worse, she saw the poor man tied to the horse.

Dr. Samuel Prescott also saw him.

Samuel was at the Barrett farm tending to Rebeckah's fever-stricken son, eighteen-year-old Silas Barrett. Samuel left the house by way of the back porch and circled around to the front. He approached the horse and swept the man's hair away from his face. Samuel recognized the angel, Ian Keogh. Ian had comforted him when Michael Bohannon and he were beaten outside the meetinghouse the day of Dr. Warren's Boston Massacre oration.

"Damn!" Samuel shouted without thinking. He began to untie Ian.

His shout of profanity attracted the attention of an infantryman stationed near the horses. The soldier called for Captain Parsons, and then ran to stop Samuel at bayonet point.

Captain Leslie Parsons, Henry, Robert, and several other officers ran out of the house. Rebeckah and her cook, Sidonie Denning, stepped onto the front porch.

When Samuel looked at Robert, the demon purposely flared his orange eyes. Samuel remembered Robert from the incident at the meetinghouse. He had no doubt that the man with the yellow-green eyes was Henry. He was afraid of Henry, but he wanted to get Ian away from the demons.

"I am Dr. Samuel Prescott. Please allow me to administer care to this injured man," he said to Henry.

The regulars gathered and watched the scene in front of the Barrett house.

Henry weighed his options. *What value does the angel fulfill at his point? The archangel will come to his rescue sooner than later. Or…perhaps he won't. Bohannon has others to protect, such as his new pet, Joseph Warren.*

Henry considered the attending officers and infantrymen.

If I refuse the doctor's request, the men in Parsons' companies will see me as a brute, and that could result in loss of respect for me. Does that matter? Yes, it does for now. In the end, I will see to it that all the angels die.

"Parsons, untie the man and take him in the house so Dr. Prescott may tend to him," Henry ordered. He walked back to the house. As he crossed the porch, he looked at Sidonie.

Her heart quickened, and she looked at him with wide eyes.

For a moment, he thought he saw red light flicker in her pale blue eyes. An angel's aura was not visible in their eyes; therefore, he dismissed the illusion.

"Why are you staring?" Henry asked. Without waiting for an answer, he pushed his way past her and into the house.

Sidonie watched while two infantrymen cut the ropes from the man on the horse. His name bubbled in her throat. She swallowed hard.

The infantrymen carried Ian past Sidonie and into the house.

Rebeckah had them lay Ian on the bed she shared with her husband.

On his way into the house, Samuel stopped and asked Sidonie, "Do you know him?"

She bit her lower lip and nodded.

"Then you understand why I may not be able to help him."

She nodded again.

He walked past her. She followed.

After Captain Parsons and his officers ate a breakfast of smoked ham and hard biscuits, they started to search the Barrett house. Suddenly, everyone in and around the Barrett farm heard scattered shots coming from the direction of the North Bridge, a mile and half away.

Brandon was observing the activity at the Barrett house from the woods on the western edge of the farm when he heard the shots. As soon as Captain Parsons, his companies, and the demons marched back toward the North Bridge, Brandon dismounted and led his horse to the farmhouse. He tethered the horse, and looked around to ensure he wasn't drawing unwanted attention before he knocked on the front door.

Rebeckah Barrett answered. Although Brandon's homespun clothing told her that he was not a redcoat, she frowned and asked, "Who are *you*?"

"I'm Brandon O'Flynn. I'm a friend of Dr. Prescott's. I need to speak with him."

Samuel heard the knock, and then the exchange of words. He went from the bedroom to the living room where he saw Brandon. "Follow me," he said.

Brandon avoided eye contact with Rebeckah and followed Samuel. Sidonie stood in the hall that lead to the bedroom. Brandon recognized her from the few days she'd spent at the Roxbury farm.

"Come with us," Samuel said to her.

Rebeckah watched them. *What is taking place here in my home and why is Dr. Prescott not in the least bit surprised?*

185

Brandon and Sidonie entered the bedroom. He sat on the bed beside Ian. He stroked Ian's forehead. *What will help him? What comforts him? What makes him strong?*

He looked at Sidonie. *They touch each other through copulation, and I know that comforts him. Perhaps, she may help.*

"Be with him, Sidonie," Brandon said as he rose from the bed. "I don't understand copulation, but I think it will help him. At the least, it may help him awaken."

Samuel thought of the day he was attacked at the meetinghouse, and how much pain he had suffered. Ian had soothed his pain by telling him to think of Lydia's touch.

Brandon's inference embarrassed Sidonie, but she asked the question anyway, "How am I to make love to him when he is unaware of my advances?"

"I…don't…know," Brandon said. "Samuel, can you answer her?"

Samuel's young hormones found the idea erotic. He smiled and blushed like a virgin. "I dare say that he will respond if at all possible."

When Brandon and Samuel were gone, Sidonie closed the curtains over the one small window in the room. She removed her dress, shift, shoes, and stockings, and unpinned her black hair so it draped her shoulders and fell down her back. Then, she sat on the bed beside Ian.

"Why do I love you?" She stroked his face. "Neither of us is real. Not in the human sense. There is no *life* for us to live together. We can neither be husband and wife nor have children. We have no future."

She kissed his cheek, and then removed his filthy clothing. His body was grimy with gunpowder, blood, and dirt. He smelled of sweat. Yet, none of those things existed in her senses. She slid her slim naked body on top of him and kissed his neck.

She sat up and straddled his hips. In her mind's eye, she saw the movements Ian made with his hips when he fucked her, and she tried to emulate that motion. "Wake up, my angel," Sidonie whispered. "I love you with all my heart."

෨

Captain Laurie and his troops at the North Bridge were genuinely surprised by the sight of the rebel column coming toward them from Punkatasset Hill. This was not Captain John Parker's small band hastily gathered on Lexington Green and just as hastily dispersed, but a well-drilled military column of apparently disciplined troops.

As they advanced, Captain Laurie thought, *We should have maintained position on the Concord side of the bridge.*

Laurie ordered his three companies to fall back across the bridge. As they retreated, Lieutenant William Sutherland and two companies from the knolls joined them. Sutherland ordered some of the regulars to rip up the planks on the bridge to impede the rebels' progress.

This destruction of property did little more than irk the minutemen and militia. Colonial Major James Buttrick thought they should continue to advance across the bridge. His men concurred.

"Load your weapons! Do not fire first, but if fired upon, return it as fast as you can," Major Buttrick ordered.

Captain Isaac Davis and his Acton minutemen ran to the bridge with the militia column following behind them.

The plank-ripping regulars scurried across the bridge and fell back into ranks on the Concord side.

Then a shot rang out.

Corporal Amos Barrett saw a ball strike the water in the Concord River to his right. Several more shots were fired over the rebels' heads.

Then, the British fired a full volley.

Captain Isaac Davis gave the order to return fire, which his Acton men did.

The regulars fired another volley.

Isaac Davis and a man among his ranks, Abner Hosmer, were shot dead.

Major Buttrick shouted, "Fire, for God's sake!"

The militia fired at Captain Laurie's troops. They wounded several of his officers and killed two privates. The captain sent a lieutenant to dispatch a plea for assistance from Colonel Smith.

Colonel Smith and Major Pitcairn were in Concord proper, supervising the searches and watching a bucket brigade put out the courthouse fire. The sound of gunfire and the sudden appearance of Captain Laurie's lieutenant set Colonel Smith into action. He assembled two companies of grenadiers and personally set off for the bridge.

Two more British soldiers were killed at the North Bridge. Captain Laurie signaled his troops to retreat. They encountered Colonel Smith and his band of reinforcements on their flight toward the common.

Captain Laurie halted his companies and addressed Colonel Smith. "Sir, we have three privates dead and four officers and five other ranks wounded! It was necessary to fall back!"

Lieutenant William Sutherland galloped up to meet the officers. The right breast of his redcoat was slightly frazzled which indicated he had suffered a minor wound. The demon that possessed Sutherland was unconcerned.

Major Pitcairn was upset with all the unexpected blood spilled that morning. He had endured quite a berating about what had occurred in Lexington from Colonel Smith. Now, it seemed that bloodshed was inevitable no matter who was in command.

At the North Bridge, colonial Major James Buttrick stared at the dead body of Captain Isaac Davis of Acton. "What has just taken place?" Major Buttrick asked Colonel James Barrett as if he had no recollection of the exchange of musket fire.

Minuteman, Corporal Amos Barrett and his captain, David Brown, squatted next to the body of nineteen-year-old Henry Mackey. Mackey's body was sprawled in the dirt near the bank of the Concord River in a dark pool of blood. Brown murmured, "Henry's mother will be beside herself with grief. He was her last surviving child."

Captain Parsons and his men marched from the Barrett farm into this disconcerting moment. There was not a redcoat to be seen, only stunned colonial rebels with guns in their hands standing on or near the damaged North Bridge.

Henry found the moment delightful. He saw the missing planks in the bridge, and like Parson's regulars, wondered if it was a rebel tactic to slow their pace. *No matter*, he thought. *Robert and I shall ride ahead of Parson's men, past the ignorant humans in rough clothing, and over the bridge. If they wish to fire at us, it will be glorious. In fact, I will bring one of my favorite human game pieces along for the ride.*

"Ensign de Berniere! Captain Percy! Attend!" General Henry Hereford shouted as he rode to the front of the column. The irritation on Captain Leslie Parson's face pleased Hereford. Accompanied by Robert and Henry de Berniere, Hereford galloped over the North Bridge unmolested by the still-stunned rebels. Then, Captain Parsons led his companies across the bridge and passed without harm.

While growing numbers of rebels covered the ridgelines and surrounding hills, Colonel Smith gathered his troops on Concord common. Major Pitcairn assembled the companies that had been searching the town's buildings. Their wounded were cared for.

At noon—two hours after the first shots at the North Bridge were fired—Colonel Smith gave the order to march back to Boston. Francis Smith prayed that they would encounter the reinforcements that he had requested from General Thomas Gage eight hours before.

The rebel militia regrouped, and as the disconcerted shock of what had happened not only in Concord, but also in Lexington, wore off, they went from a stance of armed frustration to outright vengeance.

TWENTY-THREE

Colonel Smith's column heard a shot resound through the crisp spring air at Merriam's Corner. The shot was just the beginning of a long afternoon of relentless rebel attack on the regulars from the fields and woods flanking the road on which the British retreated to Boston.

As the exhausted British infantrymen fired a poorly aimed volley, Captain John Parker's militia was at the ready two miles to the east in the heavily forested terrain along the Lincoln-Lexington town line. He had deployed his men in an ambush along the high wooded ridge above the road. This position offered a good view of the road to the west, and the ridge rising higher to the north offered a good defense against any flanking attempts by the regulars.

Like the other colonials awaiting the arrival of the British column, Jeremiah, Seamus, Patrick, Liam, and Michael suffered from anxiety and fatigue. But the angels' heightened apprehension over what had happened to Ian and Brandon, and their deprivation of Colm's protection, was taking a toll on them.

From where he stood quietly conversing with Captain Parker, Jeremiah watched the angels struggle to keep their heavenly traits hidden. He knew the gestures they used to comfort themselves were the very things they couldn't reveal.

Liam sat on the ground with his back against a tree. His green aura flashed from time to time with no warning. He could not control it, but he could wrap its glaring brightness in a cloak he had weaved from comforting thoughts of Abigail Adams.

Seamus sat opposite of Liam. He ran the blade of his butcher knife back and forth between the thumb and forefinger on his left hand until a blister formed. Seamus concentrated on the strange feeling of the blister, which kept his silver wings from unfurling.

Patrick, Michael, and Prince sat side by side on the wooded ledge and dangled their legs over the edge. Prince refused to let his wounded leg deter him from the fight. Michael polished his surgical blade over and over with the hem of his coat. Patrick snapped inch-long lengths off a twig until the twig was only an inch long. Then, he picked up another and did the same.

"What'd you think happened to Brandon and Ian?" Patrick asked.

"I don't want to talk about it," Michael responded.

"We gotta talk about it. If we live through what's about to happen, we gotta find them."

Michael shot Patrick a sideways glance.

"Colm's gotta have some idea about what's happened to them," Patrick said. He flicked the one-inch twig over the ledge and then picked up another long twig. "If Ian went to Concord…if Henry was in Concord…what if Henry saw Brandon on the road to…"

Michael snatched the twig from Patrick's hands. "Stop talking!"

Patrick looked at Michael, surprised. "There was fightin' in Concord! Demons was probably there! You cain't pretend nothin' bad's happened!"

"Demons?" Prince was alarmed.

"Shhh," Michael warned. He stood up. "They're volleying up the road to the west."

Patrick stood up. Prince stood up.

Suddenly, the militiamen were on their feet and alert. They all heard the shots.

"Spread out and load your weapons!" Captain Parker ordered. "Watch the flankers! And pray to God to watch over you!"

Seamus reluctantly took the order, which forced him to leave Liam's side.

Liam moved closer to the edge of the ridge with a group of men.

Jeremiah took a position near Michael and Patrick.

The Lexington militiamen saw Captain Leslie Parsons and his ragged company first. Colonel Francis Smith rode just behind them, at the head of the main column with a light infantry regiment directly following. Next, Captain Walter Laurie's company came into view.

The exhausted British regulars had been under rebel fire since leaving Concord. They saw and heard the swarming rebels in the woods on the ledge above them and in the woods on their right. The British officers, wearing bright redcoats and brandishing bayonets, pressed the need for speed. Colonel Smith's flankers lagged behind when the column moved from open farmland to the terrain they were navigating now. The rocky narrow road dipped and rose, slowing the frazzled regulars.

There was one important difference between the previous rebel snipers and those who were about to open fire on the column. Captain Parker and his men were determined to avenge their dead family members and neighbors who had fallen on Lexington Green.

The Lexington men unleashed a ferocious volley that slammed into the column's left flank. Colonel Smith was shot in the thigh. Captain Parsons was wounded in the arm. There was a volley of rebel crossfire that killed a British captain and several men in his company along the column's right flank.

Major John Pitcairn rode forward and directed a counterattack while the rebels continued to fire at will. The major ordered grenadiers from the rear to assault Parker's men on the right and left flanks.

Liam and the men closest to the edge of the ridge to the left of the British column, were overrun by the grenadiers. Three grenadiers with orange eyes swung around and converged on Liam.

He jerked the ramrod out of its holder beneath the barrel of his musket, and fired at one orange eye. The musket ball destroyed it. Liam leapt forward to stab the ramrod into the demon's other eye. He was shoved to the ground.

The one-eyed demon walked over and put a boot on Liam's chest. "So, you are the angel that has been forsaken for disobedience. Am I correct?"

Liam was terrified, but he experienced an emotion he had not expected—anger. He jammed the ramrod into the demon's balls.

The demon extracted the ramrod and tossed it aside. He leaned over. His one orange eye showered Liam with sparks that stung his cheeks. The demon asked, "Is that your answer?"

"Yes."

"I suppose it makes no difference," the demon said. "We shall see if you can die."

A young rebel shot at, what appeared to him to be, British grenadiers harming a fellow rebel. His musket ball struck a demon in the back of the head. The demon turned, aimed his musket at the young man's right eye, and fired. The musket ball pierced its target. The stunned man staggered backward a few feet, then collapsed and died.

The demon placed its boot on Liam's chest and said, "Stand up, angel!"

Liam complied. He heard musket fire, saw black smoke, and smelled gunpowder—the last sensations his physical body would ever experience. His spirit was saddened, knowing he would not have a chance to say goodbye to the angels with whom he had spent millenniums.

Something grazed his forehead. He tried to raise his hand to touch the wound, but he had no control of his arm. To his left, he saw a bayonet blade sail through the air toward him. *Who throws a bayonet like a knife? It is going to skewer my spirit. But it cannot bleed. Or can it? I wonder if Heaven's melodic music will mourn for me.*

Liam's deranged coda conjured a figment of a tall man with long curly brown hair that had slipped from its usual neat queue. The man stopped the bayonet's flight by seizing it in his right hand. The three demons and the dead men they possessed ignited into an inferno of orange flames, and then disintegrated in a shower of sparks.

Liam's spirit was plunging into the darkness from which he would never return. Then, he heard the beatific melody of Heaven, a tune so ancient no living thing could recreate the tones and chords. Green and gold sparks enveloped his physical body, and silver light washed over his spirit. He came to rest in the arms of his archangel.

Colm was there.

Liam lost consciousness.

Colm carried him to higher ground on the ridge, away from the volley of musket balls, and laid him on the ground. Then, he moved forward through the gray haze of gunpowder to the edge of the wooded ledge. On his right, Seamus knelt on the ground, reloading his musket.

When Seamus was done, he replaced the ramrod, and then looked around as if he had lost something. "Liam!" He stood up and shouldered his musket. "LIAM!"

There was a volley of musket fire from the regulars on the road. Seamus aimed at a regular with orange eyes. His musket misfired. When he stopped to reload, Colm was by his side. The relief Seamus felt was overwhelming, but he kept his attention on the battle as the regulars shot off another volley.

Then, for a moment, the only sounds were the redcoats' boots marching on the road and the clop of horses' hooves. Captain Parker's unexpected shout to retreat pierced the bright spring afternoon. There was confusion as the militiamen fell back.

Colm walked to the edge of the ledge and looked west down the road. The rear of the column was visible now. The rear guard flanked three British officers on horseback. He recognized Robert Percy, but he didn't need to see a physical body to recognize Henry. The archangel sensed the most heinous creation of God's wrath.

A shaft of light shined through the trees and lit up Henry's yellow-green eyes when he turned his head to say something to the officer riding to his left. Colm didn't recognize the officer, and he was unable to determine whether or not the man was a victim of demonic possession.

Colm's greater concern was distancing his men from Henry as much as possible. He needed to slow Henry's progress.

"Ya *do* know Henry and Robert are with the column?" Colm asked Seamus when he returned.

"Aye, but I don't know if they know how many of us is here," Seamus said. "Ian and Brandon is missin'. We think Ian might've tried to make it to Concord, and Henry might've gotten to him along the way. I sent Brandon to find him. They never came back."

Colm's eyes flashed.

He already knows, Seamus thought.

"Liam's been shot, and he's unconscious," Colm said. He pointed toward the higher ground of the ridge. "Stay with him until he wakes, then take him to Joseph so he can look at the wound on Liam's forehead. I doubt Joseph can do anything, but maybe—"

"You cou'dn't let him die, cou'd you?"

Colm's jaw muscles twitched. He pushed his hair away from his face and looked westward over the ridgeline. Finally, he looked Seamus in the eye and said, "I cou'dn't."

Seamus said nothing. He suspected Joseph had unknowingly influenced Colm's resolve to punish Liam. It was best to let his suspicion blow away on the winds of change.

"Joseph's with Fergus and his militia," Colm said. "They're about two miles east of here. The quicker ya can get Liam to him the better. They're going to be engaged in battle as soon as the regulars arrive at their position. I'm going to look for the others, and send them to ya. Then, I have to figure a way to slow Henry's pace."

"You ain't doing that alone are you?" Seamus asked, wearily.

Colm avoided answering the question by saying, "Keep them safe."

"Wait." Seamus reached into his coat pocket and slipped out his butcher knife. He offered the haft to Colm.

Colm grasped it, then turned and ran west through the woods along the ledge. A few minutes later, he came upon a group of militiamen bent over something on the ground.

A man said, "I am not savoring taking Jedidiah home to his family. His wife did not want him fighting at his age." The man who was speaking lapsed into a coughing fit.

He's dying of consumption, Colm thought.

When his coughing calmed, the man said, "We need to lift him."

"You heard Captain Parker," another man said.

They reached down, cradled the dead man in their collective arms and walked east toward Lexington. Colm saw two other men walking deeper in the woods along the ridge, carrying a dead teenage boy. Those killed were the reason Captain Parker had signaled a retreat.

Colm searched the hundreds of retreating militiamen for Michael, Patrick, and Jeremiah. Michael's voice couldn't have been sweeter if it had been Heaven's music itself.

"Damn, Prince! Why'd ya go and get shot again?"

Colm saw his little brother and Patrick near the high ridgeline. A young black man was sitting on a boulder. Patrick was sitting cross-legged on the ground in front of him.

"Come on, Patrick! Henry's coming. We have to go!" Michael looked over his shoulder as if he expected to see Henry or Robert. He blinked, turned around, and blinked again to make sure the man coming toward him wasn't a mirage.

The Bohannon brothers' palimpsests surfaced. Colm put his right hand on the back of Michael's head and pulled him into his arms. The brothers' tight embrace soothed their angelic spirits, and quieted the dread harbored by the ghosts of the souls that once belonged to the human men, Colm and Michael Bohannon.

When their spirits calmed and their palimpsests faded, the Bohannons let go of one another. Colm went to Patrick, embraced him, and patted his cheeks. It was a human act that made Patrick feel safe.

"Where's Jeremiah?" Colm asked.

"I ain't sure, but I think he went to help with a wounded man who was on the first line of defense back toward Merriam's Corner," Patrick said.

That means he might have to pass the rear of the column on his way back, Colm thought.

"Ya boys start moving east," Colm said. "Find Seamus and Liam and keep going until ya meet up with Fergus and his militia. And stay together!"

"Someone has to get Prince home," Michael said.

Prince looked as if he was experiencing the rapture. He beheld Colm with eyes that had never seen such omniscient beauty. He asked Colm, "Are you God?"

Colm's eyes flashed silver light when he looked at the young man.

"You are!" Prince exclaimed.

Michael rolled his eyes. "He isn't God."

"Go!" Colm said to Michael and Patrick. "I'll make sure Prince is looked after."

"Ain't you comin' with us?" Patrick asked. He didn't want to move on without Colm.

"No. I can't leave Jeremiah behind and—"

"—and what?" Michael felt the dread he had just shed return.

Colm's jaw tightened.

"NO!" Michael screamed. He felt his palimpsest panic. "HE'LL GO CRAZY IF YA DO THAT! NO! STAY AWAY FROM HENRY!"

Patrick's gray eyes widen with fear. "Who're you talkin' about, Michael? You were goin' on about this the day Liam went to see Abigail Adams! Who the fuck are you talkin' about?"

The sight of the angels' dissent and uneasiness made Prince forget his own existence.

Michael walked backward a few steps. He fisted his hands and clenched his jaw. "I'm talking about the soul of the man who used to be Michael Bohannon! Don't tell me ya don't feel the man who used to be Patrick Cullen! Don't deny ya don't worry about Seamus like a human worries about his brother!"

Colm went to Michael and seized his wrists. "Put a period to it! Do ya want Henry and his demons to hear ya?" He shook Michael. "Do ya?"

Michael was stunned by the tears that welled in his eyes. His human vessel had never cried.

"I have to slow Henry down," Colm said evenly. "I have to make sure he knows I'm here. I have to make sure ya are out of his way. We didn't come here today to die. We came here to fight as patriots."

Patrick was shaking. He had been denying his recent, abrupt dreams of Seamus shouting at him, in an old language, as he struggled to free himself from the arm his brother had wrapped around his neck.

"HENRY'S PROBABLY ALREADY KILLED IAN AND BRANDON!" Michael screamed at Colm. "WE CAN'T LOSE YA, TOO!"

"Stop shouting Michael!" Patrick said, trying to neutralize his own panic.

A small group of militiamen with shouldered muskets had gathered around the angels. A tall, rough looking man coughed and said, "My order was to retreat."

Colm let go of Michael's wrists and walked away.

Michael ran an unsteady hand across his sweating forehead.

Patrick took a deep breath. "Captain Parker, Prince needs help gettin' home."

John Parker knew his time on Earth was coming to an end. Now that his body was close to death and his soul would soon be free, he was able to perceive things beyond this world. He knew the man who had walked away, and these beautiful young men before him were angels of a god who no longer loved them. Parker wondered if he wanted to meet a god who could turn his back on such splendid creatures.

"We will take care of him," Parker said. "Now, do as your angel commanded."

Michael and Patrick moved off to the east without a backward glance.

"Farewell, angels," Prince whispered. "I hope I see you again someday."

From the wooded ledge, Colm watched the British regulars move eastward. The exhausted men marched through the rough terrain with a renewed urgency. Here and there, an enlisted man stopped to offer assistance to a wounded comrade. The names of the dead were noted before they were stripped of their weapons—and then left behind as the regulars continued east toward Menotomy.

Now, the rear guard of the column was directly below the place where Colm stood and watched. Rocks and dirt showered the road, impeding Lieutenant William Sutherland's way.

William looked up at the ledge. The source of the avalanche was not evident. He turned his horse back to circle around the debris in the road.

Colm considered his course of action. He wanted to avoid a confrontation with Henry. A showdown between the leader of the demons and an archangel would ignite a clash of power that would summon a tempest of collateral damage upon the hundreds of humans on the road and along the ridgeline.

It had happened in 1318 at the Battle of Faughart in County Louth in Ireland, four years after Henry had taken the body of the dead knight, Sir

Henry de Bohun. The fierceness of Heaven's warrior and the heinousness of God's wrath collided during the battle, and human casualties, including the brother of the King of Scotland, Edward Bruce, were the result.

Henry's obviously playing a game, Colm thought. *He somehow made Ian a part of his game, and he's not ready to end it.*

William Sutherland's horse cleared the debris. Colm gripped the haft of the butcher knife and jumped onto the road in front of Sutherland's horse, startling it. Sutherland, addled by his horse's sudden reaction tried to stay in the saddle, but his boots slid from the stirrups. He desperately tried to replace them to regain his balance.

The horse's front hooves plunged to the ground. Colm darted to the left. He grasped the saddle's cantle and pommel so he could lift himself up high enough to shove the toe of his boot into the empty stirrup.

Sutherland shoved the sole of his left boot into Colm's chest, which caused Sutherland to slip sideways in the saddle.

Colm slipped his foot into the left stirrup and threw his right leg up and over the back of the horse. He slid into the saddle behind Sutherland. The horse reared again. Colm tightened his thighs, threw his arms around William's waist, and gripped the saddle horn.

The archangel's spirit pressed heavily on the demon's spirit. If the pressure went on long enough, the demon's spirit would compress and disintegrate.

"Get control of ya horse," Colm said calmly.

"Fuck you, archangel! I will die before I let you use me to your advantage."

"Then ya have made ya choice." Colm brandished his knife and aimed it at one of William's eyes.

William's demon panicked. He reined in his horse.

Colm's sudden appearance on the road and the chaos that ensued caused the captain of the rear guard to shout at his weary men, "Make ready, but hold your fire!" He and his two lower ranking officers drew their sabers.

The captain walked toward Sutherland's horse and shouted at Colm, "Dismount immediately, Yankee!"

Forty muskets were aimed at Colm. If they fired, they would also hit the man with whom he shared a saddle, but he wasn't certain that would deter them from shooting. Gunshots fired by humans couldn't kill Colm, but he would be severely crippled until he had a chance to heal. He couldn't risk it.

He snatched the horse's reins out of William's hand, and urged the horse to walk in slow wide circles. This made them a moving target while soothing the horse.

As they rode in a circle, Colm's resplendent silver wings silently unfurled. Silver crystals showered upon the horse, the road, and the regulars of the rear guard. The crystals drifted into the edges of the woods and against the earthen wall below the ledge.

A few stupefied regulars fired accidental shots. Half of the men bolted into the woods on the other side of the road; propelled by a ravishment that erased their fear of rebels lurking there. The remaining men fell to their knees and thanked God for delivering an angel unto them.

Henry watched with smug satisfaction. He was far from tired of this game of cat and mouse with the colonists and the British. Besides, the game became more interesting with the arrival of the angels, so there was no need to rush the outcome. *What was another few years compared to a few millenniums?*

"Preceptor, there you are!" Henry said, as if Colm had been out of his sight for two hours instead of two centuries. "I must say, I have forgotten the spectacle you are capable of producing!"

Colm reined the horse to a stop and tightened his grip around William's waist.

Henry grinned. "Have you left Joseph Warren without the benefit of your protection just to steal a horse?"

Colm struggled to restrain the urge to use his gold radiance to kill Robert Percy in response to Henry's sarcasm. That struggle intensified the pressure Colm's spirit was inflicting on the demon possessing William.

William exhaled a cry of pain. "Henry, the archangel is killing me! Make him release me!"

Henry did not acknowledge William.

Colm furled his wings. They had served their purpose by defusing the threat from the men of the rear guard. "Where's Ian?"

"Oh!" Henry exclaimed. "Joseph Warren is not the only one deprived of your holy protection. You have lost an angel. What a pity."

Colm sliced off William's ponytail with one smooth motion of his butcher knife.

William screamed, "Henry! He—"

Colm sliced the back of William's sweat slicked neck from hair line to shoulders.

"Henry, he is cutting me with a knife! Tell him where the angel is! Make him release me!" William tried to throw his body forward and away from the archangel's blade, but Colm's grip was an iron manacle around his waist.

"Are you murdering humans now?" Robert sneered.

"That is a good question, Robert!" Henry chortled. He narrowed his yellow-green eyes in a gesture of false suspicion for he could have cared less about the answer. "Are you and your angels losing control—again? The angel you call, Ian, killed a possessed living woman outside of Lexington. She seemed to have gotten the better of him before she died. Robert discovered the angel unconscious and bleeding."

Colm's voice thundered. "WHERE'S IAN?"

The nervous horse brayed like a frightened donkey.

Robert smirked. "We took your angel to Concord. He died on the way."

He's baiting me, Colm thought. *But Ian is in Concord. Robert didn't see Brandon or he didn't recognize that Brandon is an angel. They're safe for now.*

The demon that possessed William felt the pressure on his spirit increase. "HENRY! GET THE ARCHANGEL AWAY FROM ME! HE'S KILLING ME!"

Henry remained unfazed by William's plight.

Robert's eyes remained on Colm when he spoke to Henry. "The preceptor killed three demons that possessed living vessels in defense of the angel they call Liam. I was under the impression he had forsaken Liam."

"I believe Robert has provided a perfect example of your loss of control, archangel. To forsake or not to forsake…." He pointed his index finger at Colm, "…*that* is the question."

Colm's rage erupted. He removed his arm from William's waist, whipped his butcher knife outward, and stabbed William in the right eye and then in the left. William's scream was bloodcurdling. His hands flew to his eyes and face. The horse reared. Its front hooves came down and hit the road with a hard jolt. William tumbled head first over the saddle horn. His forehead struck the ground, and his neck snapped. The demon's compressed spirit shot from William's dead eyes in two tight shafts of orange light and then disintegrated in mid-air.

Henry's horse spooked and bolted a hundred rods to the west.

Colm threw his butcher knife at Robert, but Robert caught the knife by its hilt before it could do damage to his eyes.

"Ya are next," Colm promised Robert.

Colm stroked his horse's neck. Then, he flashed his green aura to comfort the frightened regulars who remained on their knees.

He shook the reins and the horse trotted to the earthen wall that rose from the road to the ledge. The silver crystals from his wings still glittered in drifts against the wall. Dirt and rocks drizzled on the road. Jeremiah rappelled the wall and landed on his feet near Colm. Colm offered a hand to heave Jeremiah into the saddle behind him.

Well, well, look who we have here; the man who stabbed me in the back at the meetinghouse. Robert thought. He reached for the flintlock pistol hidden in the breast of his coat.

Colm spurred the horse. It galloped past the dead Lieutenant William Sutherland and eastward toward Menotomy before Robert could aim and squeeze the trigger.

Robert watched the horse gallop past the last two companies in the rear of Colonel Smith's column, and then bound into the woods to the south.

TWENTY-FOUR

Ian dreamed that he saw Sidonie's ghost floating above him as he lay on his back upon the leaf-strewn grave. He thought at one time he had given her a human body where her soul could dwell, but that must have been a dream.

No, it had not been a dream. It had been another life.

His wife and children were dead in the life he had now. The emptiness and the wretchedness of losing them was more than he had been able to bear.

Are they buried in this churchyard? Or am I lying in my own grave, dead of a broken heart and spirit?

"Ailbe, where are you?" Ian called out to his wife. Dirt filled his mouth. He spit it out, but the gritty grains remained.

Where are my children? He tried in vain to remember their names.

"Diareann, Fianna, and Quinn," Ailbe whispered. "They are here."

Ian's eyes stung with the dirt from their graves, and the saltwater in which he drowned in Wexford, Ireland.

When did I go off to war to fight with Colm Bohannon and his men? Ian thought. *Or was that a dream I never lived?*

Then, there was darkness.

The rebels had reorganized and leapfrogged to the head of the British column. The militia units took up positions along Fiske Hill. Michael and Patrick were among the group of rebels in the woods to the north of the road. Seamus had taken Liam deeper into the woods away from the gunfire.

Liam was awake, but not lucid. Seamus had a difficult time getting him to walk let alone maneuver the rough terrain. By the time the boys caught up with them, the militiamen where again swarming the woods around them.

Colm and Jeremiah were in the woods to the south of the road. Colm carefully guided the horse around boulders and underbrush. They encountered militiamen prepared to assault the British column's advance on Fiske Hill and joined them.

Major John Pitcairn was riding madly about, re-forming the head of the British column, when rebel volley fire raked them. Pitcairn's horse was hit and the major was thrown into the rocky dirt road, irate but unhurt.

The road over Fiske Hill was steep and heavily wooded—another box of rebel crossfire. For many of the regulars it was the end of any self-respect and discipline. The advance companies of the column stalled, causing following companies to collide into them.

Open anarchy swept through the British troops, and as they pushed past Fiske Hill, they were met with another obstacle on the outskirts of Lexington proper—Concord Hill.

Ensign Henry de Berniere saw that the light companies were so fatigued with flanking that they were scarcely able to act, and their great number of wounded were falling behind. The column's ammunition was nearly depleted.

The regulars began to run. The officers presented their bayonets to stop the uproar, but the panicked troops couldn't differentiate between death by rebel musket ball or bayonet.

As minutemen and militiamen closed in for the kill on Colonel Smith's column, just west of Lexington, there on the rise beyond Lexington Green, where all this had started ten hours before, stood a thick line of red uniforms. It was Lord Hugh Percy and his 1,500 British reinforcements.

The constant sound of gunfire led Lord Percy to draw a battalion up on a height overlooking Lexington Green. The sight of Colonel Smith's dirty, frightened, and worn-out troops, fleeing the rebels' volley, was evidence of their impending destruction. He was ready to avenge them.

"Captain Campbell, provide the field pieces for immediate firing upon the rebel forces! Target the woods to the north of the road and the other to the south," he ordered.

In the woods to the north, Michael and Patrick crouched behind a low stone wall that marked the boundary of a farmer's land. Patrick sat down to reload his musket. He reached into his cartridge box, pulled out a cartridge, and then bit the paper end off before he dropped it into the muzzle.

Michael aimed at the simmering eyes of a demon-possessed British infantryman running along the edge of the road. Michael's musket misfired when he pulled the trigger. He was resetting the flint when he heard cannon fire.

A black cloud of smoke swelled in the gunpowder choked air. The woods behind the boys were lambasted by cannonballs.

Panicked, Patrick and Michael abandoned their position behind the stone wall and stumbled through the hazy woods to ensure that Seamus and Liam were safe.

"SEAMUS!" Patrick shouted. "WHERE ARE YOU?" His distress caused his palimpsest to surface for the first time. The fleeting dream of Seamus shouting in an unknown language and grabbing him around the neck was little match for what Patrick's spirit experienced.

He was in a forest with Michael and Brandon. They were eleven-year-old kids. Acrid smoke irritated their nostrils and burned their throats. Suddenly, they were running. Patrick's consciousness shifted. They were standing in a clearing, which served as the commons, in the village where they lived. Everything was on fire. The tall canopy of trees roared in an inferno overhead. People were shouting and running in all directions. Some screamed in agony as their arms flailed in an insane attempt to rid their bodies of the flames engulfing them. Dogs, pigs, goats, and chickens scurried into the surrounding forest only to be incinerated in the furnace of burning underbrush. Embers and sparks snapped and popped within the thick roiling smoke.

Michael ran across the commons toward a cluster of burning huts screaming, "ATHAIR! MATHAIR!"

Brandon remained rooted to the place where he stood, and repeatedly cried out, "BRANNA!"

The smells and sights were inconceivable to Patrick. He didn't know whom among his loved ones were caught in this horrible calamity. *Had Seamus already left the village with Ian to fight with Colm?* Hot smoke choked Patrick and closed his throat. Embers and sparks burned his cheeks and hands. Then, the vision slid away, and he was falling into darkness.

Michael saw Patrick fall, but he no idea what had felled him. "No!" Michael shouted. He caught Patrick before he fell onto the forest floor. Patrick's body was unwieldy and limp. Michael stumbled.

Seamus ran to help Michael. He wrapped his arms around Patrick as Michael's knees buckled. With Patrick in their arms, the three angels fell to the ground.

❧

The rebels on the south side of the road heard the heavy sound of cannon fire from Lexington and knew that meant British reinforcements had arrived. They continued to volley at the British regulars.

Colm's spirit suffered from the agony of wounded and dying British and rebel soldiers. The children of man, no matter who they fought for, deserved comfort. Their duty to see to it that reapers ferried the souls of the dead to God's commanded final destination, was a millstone all the angels had to bear each time the brotherhood went into battle. Their fear for one another and the overwhelming number of dead kept them from performing their duty as they should.

Further, the spiritual noise of the battle deterred Colm from sensing the stress his men were enduring in the woods north of the road.

The British fired their cannons again—this time aimed at the woods to the south. A cannonball whooshed through the trees. The underbrush to Colm's right caught fire. There was momentary confusion among the militiamen. Someone yelled, "Hot fire from Lexington!"

Another cannonball trundled through the woods directly behind Colm and Jeremiah. The militiamen in the southern woods ceased fire and dispersed.

Colm, overcome with fear for his men, bolted toward the road.

Jeremiah went after him, jumped on Colm, and knocked him down before he got to the edge of the woods.

Colm tried to push Jeremiah off.

Jeremiah tried to keep him pinned to the ground.

Colm punched Jeremiah in the jaw.

Jeremiah returned the blow. He pinned Colm's wrists to the ground and said, "Listen ta me! The road's crawlin' with demons possessin' the dead! If they see you tryin' ta get ta your men, they're gonna follow you!"

"Ya got one second to let me go!" Colm hissed.

Jeremiah ignored the threat. "The Brits column has fallen apart. The militia has scattered, for now. You killed that livin' man—that lieutenant. This is exactly what Henry wants—bedlam among you and your brotherhood; bedlam among the humans. He wants you ta lose control. Ain't that the very thing that drove you ta hide in Burkes Garden? Loss of control?"

Colm's jaw tightened. *Why is he always right? He's just like Joseph.*

Jeremiah released him. They stood up. The woods were eerily quiet on both sides of the road.

"The rear guard's comin'," Jeremiah whispered.

"Get away from the road."

"I ain't one of your—"

"—GET AWAY FROM THE ROAD!"

Colm's shaking body scared Jeremiah more than anything he'd seen since they arrived in Lexington under Seamus' command. He wasn't sure who he was afraid for, but he knew if he didn't do as Colm ordered, Colm would have trouble controlling his angelic powers.

"I'll go fetch the horse," Jeremiah said, reluctantly.

Colm tried in vain to catch a glimpse of his men in the woods on the other side of the road. Within the momentary silence, he attempted and failed to reach out to Ian and Brandon.

The rear guard passed by. William Sutherland's body was draped over the horse that Robert had been riding and was now leading. Henry's attention briefly shifted to the southern woods.

Ya know I'm here, Colm thought. *Good.*

Thirteen demons, possessing dead British regulars and a few countrymen, trailed behind the rear guard.

The sight of the ghoulish procession of the walking dead, whose bodies were ruined in one fashion or another, induced yelling and sporadic gunfire from both sides of the road. The rebel forces ran east through the woods to stay on the flanks or get ahead of the British column.

When the rear guard disappeared from sight, Jeremiah led the horse out of the woods, and across the road to enter the northern woods.

Colm followed. With the immediate danger out of the way, he was able to concentrate on sensing his angels.

"They're deeper in the woods," Colm said. He ran until he saw Seamus' purple aura flashing in distress.

Patrick sat with his head lowered. Seamus sat beside him with one arm wrapped around his shoulder. Liam sat with his back against a boulder. His head had fallen to one side, and it nearly touched his shoulder. Michael stood on the boulder behind Liam's head and watched the rebels move out. He saw Colm's approach, jumped down, and went to meet his brother.

"What's happened?" Colm asked Michael.

"Patrick collapsed. Liam won't wake up." Michael's wings rustled loudly.

Colm kneeled in front of Patrick.

Seamus breathed a sigh of relief.

Colm slid a finger under Patrick's chin and raised his head. "What happened?"

At Colm's touch, Patrick's blue aura shimmered brightly. He looked into the familiar eyes of his archangel. "It's what Michael was goin' on about. It was him. I saw a vision of somethin' horrible that happened to the human, Patrick Cullen, and his village, when he was a boy."

For the first time since he occupied his human vessel, Patrick felt the strange sensation of tears drip from the corners of his eyes. The tears rolled down his cheeks.

"What did ya see?"

"I saw a horrible fire destroying a village. People was screaming and burning and the smell…" Patrick shivered. "Michael and Brandon was with me."

Colm cupped Patrick's cheeks. "Joseph called it *a palimpsest*. Traces of what used to be, showing through what exists now. Some of us are beginning to consciously experience it, and we can't control it. I know it's frightening. Close ya eyes, and let it slip away."

Patrick closed his eyes. He unfurled his wings to comfort himself. Silver crystals and blue light shimmered in the woods. The remnants of his frightening vision were washed away on the current of his archangel's benevolence.

A few straggling militiamen stopped to behold Patrick's wide-spread wings.

Jeremiah's arrival was announced by the noise of the horse stomping through the underbrush. Two or three startled men rounded on him with aimed muskets. They relaxed when Michael greeted Jeremiah.

"Liam's in a bad way," Seamus said to Colm. "His aura's gone out. He ain't gonna make it."

Colm moved to sit on the ground in front of Liam. He grasped Liam's cheeks with one hand, and turned Liam's head so that he could see his face. He brushed the fingertips on his other hand across Liam's wounded forehead.

"Liam, I know ya can hear me."

Colm's words drew no response.

The anxious angels rustled their wings. The nervous men rustled the leaves beneath their boots as they shifted their stance.

How can I save him from the death that awaits him? Colm thought. *There must be something that can counteract the poisonous evil that's killing his spirit. But what is that? Over thousands and thousands of years, we haven't been capable of understanding the cure.*

Michael thought about Colm's description of the impressions left behind by the souls of the men who once dwelled in the angels' human vessels. *Palimpsest. Some of us are beginning to experience it, and we can't control it.*

That had to be what drove Liam to disobey Colm. It would explain his odd behavior. Michael dropped to his knees beside Liam and unfurled his wings. The tips of the delicate feathers brushed Liam's dirty bloody face.

"That's why ya disobeyed Colm, wasn't it?" Michael said to Liam. "Ya showed Abigail Adams ya angelic spirit because *he* wanted to please her."

Michael's exclamation shot searing guilt through Colm's spirit. *Liam didn't deserve to be forsaken, if indeed, his palimpsest had taken control. No, that's not true. What he did didn't warrant a death sentence at all. Joseph tried to tell me, and I wouldn't listen.*

The militiamen quietly watched the angels. Patrick's and Michael's auras were a brilliant blue light in the shadowed woods. Seamus' aura cast glittering purple light over the horse, making it look like a mythical creature.

I have to rekindle Liam's aura or he'll be dead in a matter of hours, Colm thought. *At least I can give him more time. But how do I do that without killing him or myself? How do I do that without searing our spirits?*

"Close ya eyes, Liam. Think about Abigail Adams and hold on to her tight," Colm whispered.

Liam's hooded eyes closed. Abigail's voice stroked his subconscious: *"The idea of your angelic spirit is enthralling. I so want to see and feel it."*

He heard the echo of his reply: *"Abigail, what you are asking of me is the same as asking me to expose my spirit and walk naked in front of you."*

Colm released his green aura and golden radiance and held them close to keep his spirit and his power concentrated near his body. His angelic power began to spin in a tight ball of light no bigger than a man's fist.

Michael tried not to sound panicked. "What are ya doing?"

The ball spun faster and faster. Colm pulled it in a little closer to his body.

Seamus' spirit seized painfully with trepidation, and his wings involuntarily unfurled.

"WHAT ARE YA DOING?" Michael shouted at Colm.

The green light of Colm's aura and the gold radiance shot out from the ball in different directions. The unprecedented act he had committed out of desperation excruciated his spirit. He clenched his teeth and held his breath.

"NO, COLM! NO!" Michael screamed.

Electrical currents of gold lightning incited the woods. The men watching the angels experienced the effects of static electricity. It raised the hairs on their forearms and the back of their necks. They fled from Heaven's vehement violence.

The horse reared in terror. Jeremiah released the reins. The horse bolted toward the road.

Seamus screamed, "JEREMIAH, RUN! NOW!"

Jeremiah already felt electrical combustion building in his body. He ran east through the woods.

Michael took Colm by the shoulders and shook him. "STOP IT! STOP IT!"

Colm's eyes rolled back in his head as he tightened his grip on Liam's shoulders.

Liam's eyes opened. Blood dripped from the wound on his forehead. Liam's green aura sparked and flickered.

Colm lost control of his aura and screamed in agony. *It is what I deserve for abandoning my men in their time of need and for leaving Joseph to face demons without my protection. It is what I deserve for failing to prevent Michael, Ian, Seamus, and the Grigori angels from copulating with human women.*

Michael slapped Colm's face. "STOP IT!"

"LET GO OF LIAM, COLM! HE'S CONSCIOUS!" Seamus screamed.

Michael slapped Colm's face again.

Patrick clutched his brother's upper arms and shook him. "SEAMUS, MAKE COLM STOP!"

Seamus jammed his hands into Liam's underarms and tried to jerk him away from Colm's grasp.

Michael wrapped his arms around Colm's waist, pulled him backwards, and shouted, "Patrick, help me!"

Patrick threw his body between Liam and Colm, wrapped his legs around Liam's waist, and thrust their bodies to the ground. Seamus dragged Liam backward, breaking Colm's grip.

The fragments of Colm's aura that rekindled Liam's aura flashed and then went out. Liam issued a long moan. He looked at Patrick.

"Why are you laying on me?" Liam asked.

"It worked," Patrick said with a small smile. "Whatever he did worked. I cain see your aura. It's bright and strong. You look right!"

Liam and Patrick heard Michael say, "I won't leave ya."

209

Patrick got off Liam. They crawled toward Colm. Michael scooted in closer to his brother so the other angels could sit beside their archangel.

Colm lay on his back. He shook violently, unable to control the agony his spirit was suffering. His gold radiance swept through the woods like a flock of birds. Its amplitude was diminished by the loss of its other half—its spiritual light. It swirled and rose and dived as it coalesced with the scattered pieces of Colm's aura.

Seamus got up and watched the woods for demons. If Colm was attacked by a demon in the condition he was in, it could kill him.

The angels waited with trepidation for Colm's fate.

Liam had no memory of being attacked by demons or anything that ensued, yet he thought, *I am responsible for this.*

Colm's palimpsest tried to soothe him with a memory of his little brother. *Michael was only five years old when ya taught him how to hunt with a bow and arrow. Ya mother said he was too little to handle the weapon. But Michael pleaded with ya to teach him how to use it. Ya have never been able to say no to him. He loves ya. For that reason alone, ya will survive this.*

When the energy of the archangel's aura and power were rejoined as one, it flew home and roosted in his vessel.

TWENTY-FIVE

CONCORD, MASSACHUSETTS

Ian's mouth was dry and his eyeballs hurt when he opened his eyes. He smelled his own body odor, and something puzzling—his own semen.

It took a disconcerted moment for him to understand that he was lying in bed, and the probable reason he smelled semen. He was naked. He lay there thinking about the fading dream of Sidonie, human death, and a wife and children. Then, it slipped from his mind like the sun setting below the horizon. When it was gone, he felt spiritually exhausted.

Dim sunlight filtered through the curtains. He slid out of bed and searched the small shadowed bedroom for his clothes and boots. He found them piled in a corner beside a ladder back chair. When he reached to pick up his clothes, he became dizzy. He sat in the chair and lowered his head into his hands.

I'm going to faint. No, I'm going vomit. Bile rushed into his throat. He vomited on the floor between his feet.

The bedroom door opened, and then closed.

Ian vomited again. He looked up at the people who had entered the bedroom.

"Brandon? Samuel?" Ian asked, bewildered.

The relief Brandon felt when he saw Ian sitting in the chair was doused when Ian's red aura blinked weakly.

Samuel Prescott pulled a handkerchief from his vest pocket. He offered it to Ian.

Ian took it, and wiped his face and mouth. "Where am I?" he asked.

"In Concord, at the Barrett farm," Samuel said.

"Where Sidonie lives? Is she here?"

"Yes."

Ian gagged. When he was sure he wasn't going to vomit again, he reached down and plucked his coat from his pile of clothes.

"How are you feeling?" Samuel asked.

Ian remembered Joseph asking Michael that same confusing question. He dismissed it. Ian held his coat up so he could see it. The shredded coat was covered in gunpowder, dirt, leaves, and streaks of blood. He threw it on the floor. *Why am I so tired?*

Brandon saw Ian's exhaustion. The demon had gotten to his spirit after all.

Ian picked up his breeches and asked, "Who undressed me?"

"Sidonie did," Samuel said. "Brandon realized that she could help you by bedding you. You told me that same thing at Dr. Warren's house when I was in so much pain from my injuries. You told me to let Lydia ease my pain."

Ian looked at his filthy breeches, and then glanced down at his coat. "What happened? Why am I so dirty?"

Samuel sat on the bed and asked, "You don't remember?"

Ian's strange dream slid through his mind. He tried to hold on to it, but it slipped from his grasp.

"What's the last thing you remember?" Brandon asked Ian.

Ian's brow furrowed. "William Dawes coming to the farm, but I don't remember why he was there."

Brandon said, "Ian, get dressed. I need to get you to Colm so he can take care of you."

"I want to get a bath and see Sidonie first," Ian said. He was dizzy again. He put his head in his hands.

"I'll fetch her," Brandon said.

He found Sidonie in the living room with Rebeckah Barrett. Rebeckah's stare made him uncomfortable, and he struggled for a moment to avoid rustling his wings. Then he said to Sidonie, "He's awake, and asking for you."

She rose from her chair.

Brandon touched her hand. "He may be dying. Do you understand what *dead* means to an angel?"

"Yes. His spirit is chained in eternal darkness."

"He *is* a spirit. The human man you see isn't Ian. If his spirit is chained, *he* is chained."

Tears welled in Sidonie's eyes.

"Go to him. Wash him. He's unhappy about being dirty, but don't take long. Ian needs Colm."

"I'll gather the things I need." She ran from the room as tears spilled down her cheeks.

Samuel walked into the living room. Brandon drew him aside and whispered, "Sidonie may have awakened his spirit, but the demon that attacked him has damaged it. Ian's aura is very weak."

"Is there nothing I can do for him? He comforted me when I was hurt and in distress. I wish to return that comfort."

Brandon smiled. "You *are* returning that comfort by staying with him and offering your friendship."

Rapping on the front door startled everyone in the living room.

Brandon cloaked his aura, slid his hand into his coat pocket, and wrapped his fingers around the hilt of Ian's dagger. Rebeckah forced a calm expression on her face. Samuel strode across the room and threw the door open.

A young Pokanoket man stood on the porch. His head was completely shaved except for a scalplock. He wore English clothing—boots, breeches, and a linen shirt—that covered the tattoo of a turtle on his shoulder and a bear paw on each breast. The butt of the long rifle in his hand rested on the porch.

"Tatoson!" Samuel exclaimed.

Rebeckah Barrett relaxed. Brandon did likewise.

"Why are you in Concord when there has been fighting all morning?" Samuel asked.

"That is why I am here. Your alarm about the approaching British spread far beyond Concord." Tatoson smiled broadly. "I joined Colonel Barrett's militia this morning. He told me you were here tending to Silas."

Samuel's father, Abel, had taken Tatoson in under his care when the British killed most of the ten-year-old Pokanoket boy's tribe during the French and Indian War. Tatoson and Samuel spent their formative years as brothers.

Rebeckah said nothing to Tatoson nor did she invite him inside. She knew the young man would not enter her home under any circumstances, nor would she allow his entry despite his association with Dr. Prescott.

Samuel glanced at Brandon, then stepped out onto the porch and closed the door behind him. "Silas Barrett will recover from his fever. I am not so certain about the angel who Sidonie is caring for as we speak."

Tatoson raised an eyebrow. "One of the mountain man's angels?"

Samuel nodded. "Would you consider helping Brandon O'Flynn take the angel, Ian Keogh, back to their farm in Roxbury? Brandon is an angel, as well. He is very worried about Ian. It would be a kind gesture if you would accompany him. I assure you that Brandon will tell you the truth of what happened to Ian."

"You believe the angels need protection."

"I do…." Samuel glanced over his shoulder and whispered, "…from the demons crawling the countryside."

Tatoson's brown eyes studied Samuel's sincere but fearful expression. He knew that Samuel would never speak of demons unless he believed in his own words.

When Sidonie entered the dim bedroom, Ian was struggling with his latest bout of dizziness. He threw up what little was left in his stomach.

She had never seen him in a state of vulnerability. The motherly instincts that she had not had a chance to nurture rushed like a waterfall of emotion from her soul. The water in the basin she held in her arms, rippled as she placed it on the bed. She straddled the spreading pool of Ian's vomit and stood in front of him.

Ian threw his arms around her waist and pulled her close. He rested his head on her stomach. She stroked his filthy matted hair.

"Why am I so dirty?" Ian asked.

She slid her hands under his cleft chin and raised his head.

Pale blue eyes met pale blue eyes.

She would let Brandon explain the horrors of the battle in Lexington, and the demon attack. Her place was to care for the angel she loved.

"I will wash the dirt away," she said.

I'm feeling so much worse than when I first awakened, Ian thought. He tightened his arms around Sidonie's waist.

She gently removed his arms from her waist, and urged him to stand. Then she led him to the bedside and washed the dirt from his face and neck. Drops of water rolled down his chest and wet the small patch of hair between his breasts. He shivered.

"My clothes are filthy. I can't wear them," he said.

Sidonie kissed his lips. "And you shall not wear them, my love. I brought clean clothing."

Ian had never heard her say 'my love'. *Is she referring to me as love?* He wondered. Deep in his memory, he heard another woman say, "I love you, Ian." Her voice was familiar.

After Sidonie had washed and dressed her beloved angel, she opened the bedroom door and called for Samuel and Brandon. When they entered the bedroom, Ian was shivering *and* sweating. He reached out blindly for Sidonie.

She gathered him in her arms, and pressed his body against hers. *If you die, I die,* she thought. *I thought I was afraid of dying, but now I know I am not. I am afraid of your death, and your suffering.*

"It is time for Brandon to take you to Colm," she whispered.

Thousands of millennia with his archangel had conditioned Ian's spirit to look for comfort within Colm's spirit. Yes, he needed Colm. He needed his brotherhood.

Brandon put his hands on Ian's cheeks and kissed his forehead. That comfort gave Ian the strength to walk out of the dim bedroom. Brandon led Ian from the house.

Tatoson brought around the horses.

Brandon helped Ian into the saddle. Then, he jumped into the saddle in front of Ian.

Rebeckah, Sidonie, and Samuel walked out of the house and onto the front porch.

Samuel went to speak to Ian.

Ian looked at him with tired pale blue eyes.

Samuel said, "You will get through this. Think of Sidonie, and know she loves you. Think of me, and know I am your friend."

Colonel Smith's column moved through the ranks of Lord Hugh Percy's brigade and found shelter around Munroe's Tavern east of the green. With Percy's regiment forming a shield and marksmen sniping at rebels who ventured too close, Percy ordered all buildings burned that offered cover for rebel gunfire.

Percy saw this as a militarily sound decision. His troops saw this as an opportunity to plunder homes as they burned. The infuriated rebel sharpshooters were indeed driven from the cover of those buildings, but the destruction only drove them down the road to Menotomy.

Lord Percy inspired the British by riding through their scarred ranks. He permitted his troops to share their rations with Smith's besieged men as they rested for thirty minutes along the roadside around Munroe's Tavern.

With satisfaction that he had offered necessary relief to the exhausted regulars, Percy held a conference with his regimental commanders, as well as, Colonel Smith and Major Pitcairn.

"This shall be the order of march," Lord Percy said. "I want the overly fatigued companies of grenadiers and infantry to move off first. My brigade will cover them."

"I request that my grenadier companies march in the van," Colonel Smith said. "They have suffered less than the infantrymen; therefore, they can also provide cover."

This meant that Captain Mundy Pole of the grenadier company that had guarded the South Bridge in Concord would go first. Lord Percy allowed it.

As the British fell into formation and marched from Lexington, the rebel forces dogged them along the road from every direction despite the flankers deployed by Lord Percy.

Henry and Robert remained among the rear guard. If Henry's human vessel arrived in Charlestown intact, Robert would perform the necessary ritual to make General Henry Hereford's body a permanent vessel for the demon leader.

On the rebel side, command above the regimental level was introduced by the arrival of Major Fergus Driscoll and his militia. When they arrived near Lexington, Fergus engaged in re-forming a rebel regiment that had been scattered by Lord Percy's artillery.

He had expected to see Colm and the brotherhood among the two thousand rebels. He realized that within such a large number of men, spotting the angels would be difficult, but he expected that Colm, at the least, would seek him out.

It wasn't just their absence that concerned Fergus. He sensed that they weren't together and they were struggling. What they were struggling *with* was unclear.

What *was* clear was the need to reorganize. Although Fergus was their commander and the militia followed his orders, the rebels looked to the familiar strength of Dr. Joseph Warren. He heralded the cause for which they fought, and he had not been shy in his exclamations.

That reverence and mystique caused Gordon Walker to seek Joseph out. He found Joseph standing in a smoke-hazed clump of trees near the edge of a field with a group of thirty other men. Some of the men were participating in a volley while others were reloading.

Gordon had to raise his voice to be heard. "Are you Dr. Warren?"

Joseph looked up from loading his musket. "Yes, I am."

"You were with Colm Bohannon when he had his archangel fit on the road this morning."

Joseph frowned. "I would not call it a *fit*."

"What would you call it?"

Joseph skirted the question. "I recall that you spoke to Colm with familiarity, and challenged him to explain why he was here."

Gordon laughed, but it wasn't born of humor or cynicism. "Do you know that you're regarded with reverence as if you were an angel yourself?"

"I know I have my admirers, but your comparison is—"

"—sacrilegious?"

Joseph set the sear on his musket and said, "I fail to see the point of this conversation. There is a battle to be fought. I suggest you fall into ranks as Major Driscoll has ordered."

"I track demons from Hell and kill them," Gordon said undeterred. "Those demons marching with the British column aren't from Hell, but you already know that. I told Colm I'd figure a way to kill them aside from stabbing or shooting them in both of their filthy orange eyes, and I intend on doing that. But I need your help. I need your faith in those angels."

"What are you asking of me?"

"I don't know yet, but I saw the exchange between you and Colm on the road outside of Menotomy after he had his fit. You appeared as if you were brothers born from the same womb."

The sound of gunfire quieted.

Fergus approached Joseph and Gordon. He ignored Gordon and said, "Joseph, the angels need help, and I can't go back to look for them."

"What has happened?"

"I can't be sure because the only color I see is green. I know you promised Colm that you would stay with me, but if you move west to look for them, the threat from the British will be much diminished as they move in the opposite direction."

"Are you asking me to backtrack and look for them? Are you feeling that alarmed?"

"Yes."

Sergeant Gideon Eldon, the man whom Colm had terrified when he had his angelic fit, approached. "Major Driscoll. Dr. Warren. The militia regiments are mustered and ready to fall out. The other rebels have moved out of Lexington to keep up the assault on the column's van."

Fergus nodded. Then he addressed Joseph. "We are moving on toward Menotomy. I'm leaving you in charge of a company of fifty men from the Watertown militia. I've order two regiments to stay with you to assail the last of Lord Percy's flankers as the rear guard moves out of Lexington."

Fergus considered Gordon's presence. "You must be the man who claims he can kill demons. Colm described you as black-skinned and honest."

Gordon said nothing.

"Stay with Joseph. That's an order from your commanding officer not from an angel. Do you understand me?"

Gordon acknowledged the order with a somber, "I understand—sir."

"Stay safe," Fergus said to Joseph. "Help the angels if you can."

"I shall do my best."

The Americans sounded off a volley from beyond the field. The British answered in kind.

The company and the two regiments left behind to attack the British column's rear guard moved into the woods, skirting the Lexington town line. The pleas and moans of the injured and the dying contaminated the woods. Joseph was conflicted between his role as a doctor and his role as a commander engaged in warfare that resulted in the loss of human life.

Joseph was not accustomed to military leadership, but he was familiar with inciting passion in the hearts of men with the spoken word. The noise of battle made audible commands difficult. He dropped behind a low stone wall that marked the boundary of a farmer's field and signaled the company of fifty men to do the same.

The British column's rear guard was approaching. Lord Hugh Percy's flankers beat the woods on the north side of the road where Joseph's company was positioned.

"Corporal Trumble," Joseph said to the twenty-six-year-old man beside him. "Take twenty-five men and do your best to eliminate the flankers."

Corporal Jeb Trumble acknowledged with a curt nod and carried out the order.

The remaining twenty-five men followed Joseph and took cover behind trees and boulders along the perimeter of the road. Gunfire was heard as the Americans shot dead three British flankers. In retaliation, two Americans were killed.

Joseph stepped from the shelter of a tree. A flanker aimed at his head and fired. The bullet struck a hairpin that held Joseph's hair out of his eyes. The blow knocked him to the ground. For a moment, he lay there disoriented.

"Dr. Warren!"

Joseph blinked and looked up. He recognized Sergeant Abe Rowlinson from the Cambridge militia.

Abe held his hand out to Joseph.

Joseph grasped it, and Abe pulled him to his feet.

The British rear guard was passing the Americans. Joseph shouted the command to fire. He ran to the edge of the road and leveled his musket. He saw two British officers in his site. They both turned and looked at him.

He heard Gordon Walker shout, "Move away, Dr. Warren!"

The British captain's eyes simmered with orange light. Joseph recognized Robert Percy. The general riding beside Robert smiled broadly at Joseph.

Joseph hesitated.

Henry urged his horse toward the edge of the road. He grinned and pointed at Joseph. "I will kill you, Warren, while the archangel is forced to watch."

Gordon snatched Joseph's wrist and dragged him away from the road to the shelter of the trees.

The Americans volleyed at the British. Screams and pleading announced the suffering of the injured and the dying on both sides.

"What were you thinking standing in view of those demons?" Gordon demanded. "The one with the yellow-green eyes is their leader!"

Joseph jerked his wrist from Gordon's grasp. "I am aware of that! And do not presume to question me! I am not afraid!"

"You should be! That demon's going to kill you just to prove that Colm can't protect you!"

"War has begun! I will not let demons impede my way!"

Gordon saw movement in the woods behind Joseph.

Corporal Jeb Trumble cautiously picked his way through the underbrush, militiamen, and sporadic shower of musket balls. He was returning to report the death of two fellow company men. On his approach, he heard the words spoken between Gordon and Joseph. He thought, *Did I hear Dr. Warren speak of demons?*

It was the last thought Jeb Trumble, husband and father of four from Lincoln, Massachusetts, would think. An orange-eyed rebel wearing the bloody tatters of a homespun shirt slipped out from behind a tree. The demon-possessed rebel stabbed Jeb in the back and severed his spinal cord. Jeb dropped to the ground like a ragdoll.

The demon yanked the knife from Jeb's back then lunged at Joseph. Gordon shoved Joseph out of the way.

Joseph stumbled sideways a few steps.

Gordon leveled his musket and shot the demon in one eye. It slowed the demon long enough for Gordon to reach down and pull a butcher knife from a deerskin sheath in his boot.

Joseph recovered and whirled around.

The demon kicked the knife out of Gordon's hand.

Joseph fired his musket. The ball obliterated the demon's other eye. Orange flames flared and licked the skin off the demon's vessel's face. The dead body dropped silently to the ground. The acrid smell of burning hair and skin co-mingled with the smell of gunpowder. The flames caught the tattered sweat-soaked homespun shirt on fire.

Gordon extinguished the lazy flames with the sole of his boot.

Joseph stepped backward and nearly stepped on Jeb Trumble's wide flung arm. Jeb lay on the ground face down.

Abe and two other militiamen approached. They halted beside the smoldering body.

"So, this is the reason the angels are here!" Abe shouted at Gordon with disgust. "*You* should have spoken of the demons when you challenged the archangel to speak of it. I hold you responsible for the death of that young father. I will see you punished, black man. Even if I have to do the deed myself!"

"This had nothing to do with black or white!" Gordon shouted. "This is evil produced by the God you worship! Did you expect me to make that exclamation in the presence of three hundred men who were already frightened by the appearance of an out-of-control archangel?"

"Desist speaking!" Joseph ordered. "Jeb has died! Which of you wishes to deliver his body to his family?"

Abe and Gordon said nothing.

"The rear guard has passed us," Joseph said. "It is time for us to retreat to the west to find the angels. Sergeant Rowlinson, delegate responsibility to ensure that Jeb's body is delivered to his family. Then, assemble the company to move out."

As the two regiments Fergus left behind to assist with attacking the British rear guard moved east toward Menotomy, Joseph and his company withdrew westward. They covered less than a quarter-mile when Joseph ordered the company to stop. He felt the need to be forthright and allow these men the freedom to choose their actions.

Joseph's eyes swept the gathered men. "We have been sent on a mission by an angel—the man you know as Major Fergus Driscoll. The archangel, Colm Bohannon, and his angels are in peril from demons God created."

Quietude passed over the men and hung in the air. A musket fired in the distance.

"I release you from my command if the idea confuses or frightens you." Joseph said.

Rufus Williams, a middle-aged redheaded man surprised Joseph. "How can we help the angels?" he asked.

The quietude moved away.

"I suppose by killing as many demons as we can," Joseph guessed. He glanced at Gordon. "Perhaps, there are other ways that we do not yet understand."

"It was a demon that killed Jeb," Abe interjected.

"I saw its orange flaming eyes. I see no difference between the enemies who have killed Americans today, and the enemy with orange eyes," Rufus said.

"Did you hear what I said?" Joseph demanded. "These demons were created by God! God wants these angels dead! The battle we are about to face is for the angels' cause, and you *must* believe in that cause. If you have *any* doubt, then you cannot stay."

The men murmured amongst themselves.

A man beside Abe stepped forward. "Dr. Warren, my name is Lemuel Grady. I am a lawyer from Acton. We know of your good reputation, but we are nevertheless doubtful that angels are among us let alone one who has bid us to help them."

Sergeant Gideon Eldon said, "I can assure you that Dr. Warren's claim that Major Driscoll is one of them is founded. I saw not only his angelic aura, but I also witnessed the archangel, Colm Bohannon's, terrifying display of power."

"I as well," Abe affirmed.

Gordon said, "I'm acquainted with the archangel. Dr. Warren, however, has a very close relationship with him and the angels."

Rufus Williams was afraid of God's punishment, yet he said, "I will stay and fight if necessary."

"I shall do the same," Sergeant Eldon declared.

Lemuel Grady and ten others looked doubtful as each man in the company, in turn, pledged their loyalty to the angels' cause. When it was the lawyer's turn to say yea or nay, he paused to confer with the small group of doubters.

The company was alarmed by thrashing through the underbrush. The men presented their muskets before the order was given. The panting and sweating band of straggling rebels, who fled when Colm lost control of his aura, burst into view, and then came to a sudden halt. Some bent to place the palms of their hands on their knees to catch their breath. Others seemed confused.

"You ain't goin' in their direction," a scruffy man warned. "What has happened back there ain't for mortal man to see!"

Another asked, "Who is in charge here?"

Joseph stepped through his gathered company and asked, "What have you seen?"

"It was unbelievable! We saw men with wings surrounded by glimmering colors! One of them shot gold and green light outward from his body! It was as if God's power was on Earth and among us! You shou'd all flee!"

The terrified rebels fell in together and hurtled eastward past the company. Without a word, Lemuel Graves and the doubters hastened to follow. While the men in the company were trying to make sense of the panicked words they heard, a lone man stumbled from the western woods.

Joseph recognized Jeremiah Killam. *If Jeremiah fled what happened among the angels, the situation was dire.* Joseph ran to him.

"Joseph?" Jeremiah panted. "What...?"

Joseph allowed Jeremiah a moment to catch his breath before he asked, "What has happened? A group of terrified men just passed us."

Jeremiah looked at the company with uncertainty. "Joseph, cain we talk without ears overhearin'?"

"These men have pledged to help. Speak plainly."

Jeremiah's eyes roamed the faces of the men. Abe was the only man he recognized, although they were not formally acquainted. His green eyes shifted back to Joseph. "Colm tried ta re-light Liam's aura...the power he let loose was...Seamus told me ta run! I've known them angels for twenty-five years, and I ain't never seen such bedlam among 'em. This's what Henry wants. He wants 'em ta lose control!"

"Are you willing to return to them with me?"

Jeremiah gave a deep sigh and nodded.

"Reload, and move quickly!" Joseph ordered his company.

Forty deeply religious, God-fearing men—some who had to shift their religious paradigm in a matter of seconds—loaded their muskets and followed Joseph Warren. Their dauntlessness was the image of the courage they nurtured in order to fight for their right to have influence on a British monarchy and parliament 3,000 miles away, which taxed American property at their whim.

TWENTY-SIX

Fear fluttered in Michael's spirit.

Some of the angels were experiencing uncontrolled memories that belonged to their palimpsests. Ian was impossible to sense, and although the angels could sense Brandon, they were uncertain of his whereabouts. Fergus was not with them. Colm was on his feet, but he seemed unsteady. Despite Liam's rekindled aura, he was in obvious spiritual pain.

Henry's minions were skulking through the woods in a stealthy attempt to surround the five angels.

"Ya got ya blade?" Colm asked Michael.

Michael knew if he didn't control his emotions, Colm would force him to do so. He rustled his wings to calm himself and said, "Aye."

"Give me ya musket and cartridge box."

Michael did.

"Seamus, get Liam up and bring him to me," Colm said.

Patrick moved in close to Michael.

Seamus helped Liam get to his feet.

Colm looped the strap of Michael's cartridge box over Liam's head and settled it across his chest. He took Liam's shaking hands and placed the musket in them. "Ya can do this, Liam."

Liam looked into his archangel's soothing eyes. The usual silver light that flashed there was dim. *He has injured his spirit to help me,* Liam thought. *I do not deserve it.*

The smell of smoke dissipated on the gentle breeze.

The summer afternoon was raped when dozens of demons swarmed from the northwest. Some wore brilliant redcoats. Others wore homespun. Unless their vessels were ruined, it was impossible to tell if the possessed were living or dead. The badly outnumbered angels recoiled. If they did not discard their heavenly duty to protect the children of man, they would perish.

Colm tried to soothe his angels by ingesting their panic into his already maimed spirit. He bore the burden of Ian's and Brandon's disappearance, Liam's faltering aura, the uncertain nature of the game Henry was playing, and his own unfamiliar fear for the humans he loved—Joseph and Jeremiah.

Patrick was calm enough to realize that the demons were armed, but none had raised a weapon. *The demons are only storming us. Something is wrong.*

Colm noticed the same anomaly, but was distracted by the sound of men thrashing through the woods behind him. He turned and saw a smaller group of demons scurry like rats from the woods to the south. Michael was the only angel facing south. The other angels forced themselves not to turn and defend him until Colm gave the order.

But the order never came. Colm summoned his destructive power. The effort was more than he expected, but once it was amassed, it shot from his spirit like jagged gold lightning. The fleeing demons exploded in a blaze of orange and gold light. Skin, bones, hair, clothing, and muskets disintegrated in the inferno of the archangel's gold radiance. Living or dead, the human vessels were pulverized.

Then, he turned his fury on the demons to the northeast. They stood silently in the woods. Lazy sparks popped in their simmering orange eyes. Patrick saw them drop their weapons. The demons were baiting Colm; feeding his fury until he could no longer control it.

Patrick's attempt to communicate his suspicions to Colm was drowned out by a sound rumbling through the woods. Green light flashed. Static electricity charged the air. Golden radiance detonated the silent demon-possessed vessels and eradicated them.

Suddenly, men shouted in the woods east of the angels' position. A horde of possessed British regulars weaved around trees and trampled the underbrush as they opened fire on the angels.

Michael and Patrick didn't wait for Colm's order to retaliate. They swung around and flanked Seamus and Liam. Patrick fired, then stepped back to reload while Seamus and Liam fired.

Sweat soaked Colm's face, neck, chest, and back. Stray locks of hair stuck to his cheeks and forehead. The angels' desperation, as they tried to defend themselves, was the force that fed his mania, and he threw his arms outward and channeled his power into tight beams of light. He was deaf to Seamus' shouts.

225

"They're purposely firin' high!" Seamus shouted at the others. "Them demons ain't tryin' to kill us!"

Patrick's blue aura brightened in distress. He ripped the ramrod out of the barrel of his musket and moved closer to Seamus. "I think they're baitin' Colm! I tried to—"

"FUCK!" Michael screamed.

Colm channeled his power. At the same time, Jeremiah, Joseph, and the company of colonials surged through the woods from the east.

Seamus, Patrick, and Liam allowed their eyes to dart toward Michael for a split second.

"FUCK! STOP HIM!" Michael screamed. If Colm released his channeled power, the woods would be annihilated along with every living thing that existed there. Michael lunged at his brother and swung his fists down on Colm's outstretched arms. "NO, COLM! YA WILL KILL THEM! JOSEPH AND JEREMIAH ARE HERE!"

Jeremiah, Joseph, Gordon, Abe, Gideon, Rufus, and the others in the company took cover behind trees and brush. They experienced the effects of the static electricity charged air. Every strand of hair unsecured by a queue or ponytail stuck to their foreheads, cheeks, and the back of their necks. The demons turned and volleyed into the woods. The rebels returned fire.

Colm neither felt the blows to his arms nor heard Michael's warning.

Michael shoved Colm. "YA ARE GOING TO KILL THEM!"

Seamus sprung at Colm and slapped his face.

Colm snapped out of his trance-like concentration. He heard Michael's warning: "JEREMIAH AND JOSEPH ARE HERE! YA ARE GOING TO KILL THEM!"

Through the haze of gun smoke, Colm saw the truth. Henry released his minions, and in doing so, laid a course for Colm to inadvertently kill Joseph and Jeremiah while defending his men. *But that failed; therefore, Henry's going to use my love for Joseph and Michael as a pawn in his hideous game. He's going to make me choose between them.* The event was inevitable. The logistics were indeterminate.

Colm's epiphany had distracted him from the battle between the rebels and the demons. The air was so heavy with black gunpowder that all Colm saw was the blaze of flint and powder, and the orange flash of dying demons.

He ran into the thick haze to find the angels and stumbled over someone lying on the ground. Colm stopped and kneeled beside him. He was neither a demon nor a man—only a boy of sixteen. Demons had ravished his young life. A bleeding, ragged, seared hole exposed the boy's viscera. Tears of pain and fear soaked his pubescent cheeks. Colm's wings unfurled. Heaven's silver crystals of solace showered upon the suffering boy.

Colm wiped the tears from the boy's cheeks and asked, "What comforts your soul?"

The boy's blue eyes were fading, but they were still able to recognize the angel who had come to ease his death.

"You," the boy breathed. Blood slid from his nose and the corners of his mouth.

"What is your name?"

"Michael."

For a fleeting moment, Colm wondered if this boy's impending death was a mockery.

The boy sighed as his life ended.

Colm escorted the boy's soul to its egress and summoned a reaper. The gossamer draped reaper slid through the woods. It regarded the archangel, then moved on to complete its task.

Colm furled his wings and stood up. He felt the sting of a musket ball hit his right breast. It served as an admonishment. There was a battle raging around him, and he had become disconnected and distracted.

"Colm," a soothing voice called.

"Joseph? Where are ya?"

"Here to your right, but you must take cover! You are unarmed!"

In contrast to the human men, Colm was heavily armed. He moved through the haze to his right and collided with Joseph behind a slim tree trunk. Both suppressed the need to demonstrate relief and joy over their reunion.

"Are ya all right?" Colm asked.

"Yes," Joseph said. His eyes were drawn to Colm's bloodied shirt. "You have been hit in the chest and are bleeding badly."

"I'm fine."

Joseph searched Colm's eyes for their silver light. "You are not fine. If you have been hit by a demon's ball—"

"I want ya to take Jeremiah and ya men and run," Colm interrupted, "I'm putting a stop to this."

As musket balls dashed clods of dirt and leaves upward from the forest floor and stripped trees of their bark, a yowling rose from somewhere in the black haze of the battle.

Michael saw demons pepper Gideon Eldon's abdomen with musket balls and heard him scream. Stunned, Gideon looked down at the neat row of wooden buttons on his rough, but fashionable vest. Crimson blood spread across the torn and burned flaxen homespun material. Gideon collapsed.

"Fuck!" Michael yelled. With his curved surgical blade in one hand, he ran to Gideon's side.

Abe and Gordon materialized from the gloom.

Michael unfurled his wings and sat beside Gideon.

Gideon wondered why Colm's distressed angelic display on the road outside of Menotomy had frightened him, now that he knew the young man sitting beside him with the curly black hair and green eyes was an angel.

Gideon asked calmly, "Why was I so afraid of Heaven's ascendancy?"

This question had been asked of Michael millions of times over the millenniums. He had no answer. His response was to bend and kiss Gideon's filthy sweating forehead and blanket him with his blue aura. The touch of Michael's angelic lips on his skin let Gideon die in peace. The light in Gideon's eyes went out. He stared blankly up at Michael's face.

Michael's wings rustled as he escorted the dead man's soul to its egress. A reaper moved like vapor through the woods in response to Michael's summons.

Gordon watched Michael with a close eye.

The woods quieted. The surviving demons and the bodies they possessed vanished. Men walked through the odd haze of gray gun smoke and yellow sunlight and gathered around Gordon and Michael. Joseph and Colm arrived. Joseph started to kneel beside Gideon to administer medical care.

Michael said, "He's already dead, Joseph."

Patrick, Liam, and Seamus emerged from the haze.

"Did Gideon's soul go to Heaven or Hell?" Gordon asked Michael.

The blunt question irritated Abe Rowlinson.

The question surprised Michael. Instead of looking to his archangel for guidance before answering an intrusive human question, he said, "Heaven."

"If his soul was bound for Hell, what would you have done? Are you capable of gaining entrance into Lucifer's den?"

Men grumbled at Gordon's insensitive inquiry.

Abe stepped toward Gordon and spat, "I have had enough of your—"

"—no, Abe," Joseph interceded. "I understand the motive behind his question."

Michael didn't understand the man's motive. Furthermore, he didn't like the man's audacity to question the role of an angel. Michael frowned at Gordon.

Patrick's eyes garnered Colm's permission to speak. Colm nodded.

"Angels each have their own way of guidin' a soul to its egress," Patrick explained. "But we don't chaperon the soul to its destination. That's the role of a reaper. They wait for our signal."

"And if you signal Hell?" Gordon asked.

"We don't know how the reapers take souls to Hell. Only God and Lucifer know that."

"If God marks their souls as Hell bound, does the dying deserve your comfort?"

Michael lunged at Gordon and screamed, "FUCKER!" He shoved his curved surgical blade under Gordon's chin and clutched the back of his neck so Gordon couldn't move his head without the blade slicing his throat.

A few men moved to help Gordon. Seamus and Patrick intercepted them. Liam sat on the ground. His was too exhausted to care.

Colm crossed his arms over his bloodied shirt and said, "Let him go, Michael."

Michael ignored Colm and dug his fingers harder into the back of Gordon's neck. "How dare ya presume that an angel would withhold comfort from *any* human just because God has decided their souls aren't worthy of Heaven!"

"Seamus, get Michael off Gordon," Colm ordered.

Seamus hesitated. A part of him believed Michael's anger was justified.

"Do you know him?" Seamus asked Colm.

"Aye. He tracks and kills demons."

"HE'S A FUCKER!" Michael screamed. "Stay away from me Seamus or I'll cut his head off!"

"Michael, please do not do this," Joseph requested. "It will serve to accomplish nothing."

Gordon concentrated on staying as still as possible. He remembered Michael's anger and stubbornness outside the Greystoke Inn. He had no doubt that Michael would kill him in a fit of rage. What Gordon didn't understand was why the archangel was standing idly by.

Seamus went to Michael and said, "I understand your anger, but you'll regret it if you kill him."

Michael spit in Gordon's face, and then released him. Without looking at anyone, Michael shouldered his way through the gathered men and ran up hill westward through the woods. Patrick went after him.

"Stop," Patrick said when he caught up to Michael.

Michael kept walking.

Patrick seized him by the upper arm.

Michael tried to pull away, but Patrick tightened his grip. "You ain't the only one of us that's fallin' apart! But we ain't attackin' humans for no good reason. Liam's dyin'! You're makin' his last days worse by havin' a fit and makin' him anxious!"

The angels were startled by the approach of a large animal through the woods to the west. Jeremiah appeared, leading an uncooperative horse.

"Damn horse! She bolted when she came across demons, then she bolted when she heard gunfire, then she bolted when she saw Colm," Jeremiah said. "What're you two doin' out here alone?"

The boys remained silent.

Jeremiah's eyes widened. "I'll be damned…" He ran down the slope to the road, pulling the confused horse behind him.

"What's he doin'?" Patrick asked Michael.

The boys looked down onto the road. They both jumped from the ridgeline on the hill and landed on the road. They ran to meet the men riding eastward as they yelled, "Brandon! Ian!"

The angels, men, horses, woods, and road were bathed in a burst of red, yellow, and blue light. Jeremiah had to shade his eyes to make out the rider on the other horse.

"I'll be damned! Tatoson! How'd you get bit inta ridin' with the angels?"

Tatoson smiled. "Mountain man, it is good to see you have survived the British incursion."

"Incursion? Can you talk normal?"

Tatoson shrugged. "The angel with the red aura is ailing. I told Samuel I wou'd make sure he is delivered to his archangel."

"You can see their auras?" Jeremiah asked, surprised.

Tatoson nodded.

Brandon dismounted. His jubilance was so great that he fought off a foreign erratic urge to weep. The angels' wings unfurled and Heaven's tenderness dusted the horses, Jeremiah, and Tatoson.

"They are beautiful," Tatoson remarked as he watched Ian's wings unfurl.

Patrick reached to touch Ian's weak red aura. "Are you dyin'?"

The question sobered Michael's joyful spirit.

"I'm tired and dirty," Ian said. Without Brandon sitting in front of him in the saddle, Ian had nothing to rest his body against. He fell forward. Once again, his upper body was draped over a horse's neck. His beautiful silver wings fell in gentle waves and blanketed his ailing spirit.

Colm, Seamus, Liam, and Joseph bounded down the slope and joined them.

The angels' emotional reunion caused them to let their guard down, and their angelic display was visible to the militiamen in the woods on the hill. The rebels watched the angels' joyful reunion.

Colm slipped his boot into a stirrup and pulled himself upward to balance on one foot as he encouraged Ian to sit up. Then, he got into the saddle in front of him.

Brandon and Jeremiah helped Liam climb into the saddle on the horse Jeremiah was leading. Jeremiah sprung into the saddle behind Liam. Tatoson leaned over and offered Seamus a hand. Seamus took the offer and Tatoson made room for Seamus to ride behind him in the saddle.

Joseph, Patrick, Brandon, and Michael fell in ahead of the horses. Wings were furled and auras doused. The weary men and angels moved eastward along the road toward Boston.

The militiamen gathered their dead. Gordon, Abe, Rufus, and those who remained of the company streamed down the hill, converged on the road behind the horses, and followed Dr. Warren and the angels.

For them, the long horrible battles of April 19, 1775 had finally come to a close.

Far ahead of the angels and the weary men who followed them, the British column led by, Lord Hugh Percy, Colonel Francis Smith, Major John Pitcairn, Captain Munday Pole, Captain Leslie Parsons, Captain Walter Laurie, and Ensign Henry de Berniere marched the road to madness through Menotomy.

The stretch of road through Menotomy marked the deadliest fighting that day. The British soldiers ransacked homes, searching for and killing rebels hiding inside. American civilians perished defending their families and property.

The Danvers militia, under the command of Captain Daniel Epes, suffered horrible casualties, yet those men, in conjunction with the Cambridge-Watertown militias under the command of Major Fergus Driscoll, and the

Menotomy minutemen under the command of Captain Samuel Whittmore, maintained ferocious pressure on the British.

When the day came to an end, the British suffered 73 dead, 174 wounded, and 26 missing. The American casualties totaled 49 dead, 40 wounded, and 5 missing.

Lord Hugh Percy led his surviving soldiers through Charlestown Neck on the evening of April 19.

As the waning gibbous moon rose over Boston, rebels and British soldiers alike wondered, *what have we done?*

TWENTY-SEVEN

SUFFOLK COUNTY, MASSACHUSETTS

On the night of April 19, instead of entering Charlestown with Lord Percy and Colonel Francis Smith, Henry remained outside the Neck while Robert delivered the sullied body of William Sutherland. An angel had killed the demon in possession of Sutherland, making future demonic possession of the body impossible. Once Robert completed his task, he summoned twelve disembodied lower demons to participate in a rare ritual—the preparation of a living human vessel for death and permanent possession.

The ritual would be different than the death and possession of Captain Robert Percy, which had taken place two months ago in the woods of Suffolk County while shocked locals watched. Because this possession concerned the powerful leader of the demons, the transformation required a precise protocol that had been attempted only once.

Many of the residents of Charlestown evacuated as the British troops quartered in tents and other buildings throughout the town. Robert rode back through Charlestown Neck among the throng of people escaping the British occupation. The disembodied demons moved through the crowd, possessed human bodies, and then with discretion so the human would not be immediately missed, they followed Robert.

Outside of the Neck, Henry reunited with Robert and the demons. They traveled due west through Suffolk County and far beyond Roxbury until the sound of humanity could no longer be heard. Overhead, the waning gibbous moon cast cold white shadows through the trees. This was the lunar phase suitable for rituals associated with letting go and banishing; a time to clear out the old and prepare for the new.

They arrived at a small clearing on the bottom of a heavily wooded hill. A fast running stream skirted the clearing to the east. Henry and Robert dismounted.

Robert pointed at two young possessed women and said, "Remove the tack from the horses then get them on their way."

Once the horses were driven from the clearing, twelve demons sat in a tight circle around Henry. Robert stood outside of the circle beside the stream. His orange eyes flamed brightly and lit the clearing as if it were aglow with flickering candlelight.

Henry took inventory of the possessed bodies surrounding him, pleased by their youth and beauty. "Stand," Henry said to the demons.

They stood.

Henry's eyes flashed. He stripped and stood naked before them.

The lower demons imitated Henry's actions, and when they were through, twelve naked young men and women stood in a circle under the moon's white shadows.

"Who does God command to kill this man?" Robert asked from the fringes of the circle.

The demons said, "Serepatice."

"Who shall release the demon from this living body until such time that it can return to its permanent abode?"

The demons said, "We shall."

A heavy expectation hung in the clearing. Then, the beautiful possessed bodies converged on Henry. They kissed his face, caressed his strong arms, fondled his penis, and licked his inner thighs. Henry's demonic spirit absconded from the human vessel it possessed in a shaft of yellow-green light that rocketed into the night sky. For a few seconds, it seemed as if the sun had risen only to realize its error and drop back below the horizon.

The man, General Sir Henry Hereford, returned. The Massachusetts night was cold and unfamiliar; it was frightening to the man whose consciousness had been quashed by another being. But what horrified his soul the most were the men and women who were molesting his body.

"WHAT IS HAPPENING?" he screamed. He tried to shove them away, but there were too many of them. He turned to run, but twenty-four hands groped him with ferocity. He was pushed to the ground. They swarmed his body like bees desiring to taste their queen's honey. Some kissed and licked his face, neck, chest, and abdomen. Others sucked his fingers, toes, penis, and nipples.

Henry pummeled them with his fists. "YOU ARE HURTING ME! GET OFF ME!" He tried to attain the leverage to get to his knees by digging his heels into the cold, damp ground and twisting his body.

His attempt to escape only served to intensify the demons' lust.

Robert watched their frenzy with delight, and shouted, "Serepatice! It is time!"

The demons scurried away from Henry and reformed their circle.

Henry Hereford, the man, scrambled to his feet. An old woman holding a bow and arrow appeared before him. She looked into Henry's eyes and said, "Say my name, boy!"

Henry realized there was no escape from this horrifying situation. Everything he had accomplished in his life—education, military advancement, Member of Parliament, and homeowner in the wealthy London West End district of Mayfair—was about to be obliterated.

The old woman raised the hand holding the arrow. The fingertips on her three middle fingers were wrapped in dirty strips of cloth. She knocked the arrow, raised the bow, aimed, and snarled, "Say my name, Henry Hereford!"

"Fuck you!"

"My name is Serepatice, and if I had my desires, you would do just that!"

When the arrow pierced his heart, Henry flinched more from disbelief than from pain. Confusion clouded his wide brown eyes. He crumpled to the cold ground and clung to life long enough to beg God to save his soul. In the woods of a foreign land in which he had no memory of entering, Henry Hereford drew his last breath.

The thrum of a single beating drum arose from the ground. A bell accompanied the steady drum beat, joined by a powerful throbbing rhythm. Voices prayed in Latin. The sounds swirled and blended and rushed on a current in and around the demons.

Robert stepped through the circle and straddled Henry's body.

The demons maintained their circular formation and crawled toward Henry's body. They rose to their knees and clasped hands.

Yellow-green light flashed like sheets of heat lightning in the sky. The celestial display was visible throughout the northern hemisphere.

Robert raised his eyes and arms skyward. The demons did the same. Fire burned hot and intense in their eyes.

Robert spoke loud and clear. "Now it came about, when men began to multiply on the face of the land, and daughters were born to them, that the sons of God saw that the daughters of men were beautiful; and they took wives for themselves, whomever they chose."

The demons chanted, "They will die in eternal darkness."

Yellow-green lightning flashed.

Robert continued. "The Nephilim were on the Earth in those days, and also afterward, when the sons of God came in to the daughters of men, and they bore children to them. Those were the mighty men who were of old, men of renown."

The demons repeated, "They will die in eternal darkness."

The yellow-green light disappeared from the sky.

Robert said, "For if God spared not the angels that disobeyed, but cast them down to Hell, and delivered them into chains of darkness, to be reserved unto judgment."

A bolt of yellow-green light seared the dark horizon of the night.

"He will be forced to choose," the demons said.

Robert smiled and pronounced, "And spared not the old world, but saved Noah the eighth person, a preacher of righteousness, bringing in the flood upon the world of the ungodly. And the angels who kept not their first estate, but left their own habitation, he hath reserved in everlasting chains under darkness unto the judgment of the great day."

"He will be forced to choose," the demons repeated.

Henry Hereford's body glowed with yellow-green light. The demons cast their eyes down to behold their leader's return. Their arms fell to their sides. Robert stepped from the circle. Henry breathed.

"Dress him," Robert ordered. He walked east toward the stream and faded into the black woods.

The demons dressed the eternal body of their overlord, and then sat upon the ground and waited for his resurrection.

When the waning gibbous moon dropped below the horizon, Henry Hereford arose strong and virile.

Joseph watched yellow-green sheets of heat lighting flash in the sky. He suspected that what he was witnessing was an inaugurate beginning to the end of the family of angels, whom he had become a member. He recognized that the allegiance was not restricted to Colm. It was a catholic kinship of love and devotion stronger than any he had ever experienced. And Joseph was deeply devoted to his fellow Sons of Liberty and their collective cause.

He thought of his beloved children, and the time he had sacrificed with them for the cause of American liberty. Yet his strong convictions to protect the rights of colonists drove him to stand under this ugly yellow-green sky and face demons God had created in all forms.

"Joseph, ya need rest."

"You are not resting, and do not tell me your body does not need rest. I know it does."

"My body isn't what's exhausted."

Joseph looked at Colm. "Your body *is* tired. You cannot help them if every particle of your being is weary."

"Do ya hear ya own words?"

"Now that this has begun, I will get little sleep. I need to ensure Mercy and my children are safe. My colleague, Dr. Elijah Dix, agreed to give them refuge in his home in Worcester." Joseph rubbed his forehead. "None of the Sons of Liberty dare return to Boston. We will be arrested on sight—probably hung. I have no means to dispatch my children to safety."

"I'll send Brandon to do whatever it is ya need to do. He can take some of his men from the Roxbury watch."

"No, I will not endanger lives."

"Someone has to go who can fight demons, if necessary. If Brandon gathers volunteers, then they go knowing the stakes."

"I would be greatly relieved," Joseph admitted. He looked skyward. "The eerie light is Henry, is it not?"

Colm followed Joseph's gaze. "Aye," he said. "The demons have killed the human, Henry Hereford. They're performing a ritual so the leader can take possession of Henry's dead vessel permanently without decaying it; or until it wants a new vessel."

"Do you know what the ritual entails?"

"No."

"Have they done this before?"

"Only once, in Ireland, over four hundred years ago."

"Are you afraid?"

"Aye."

"As am I. Not for myself, but for the future."

Dim silver light flashed in Colm's tired green eyes.

The dim light made Joseph think of Ian's dissipating aura. "Is there no way I can help Ian or Liam? Are their deaths inevitable?"

"Damn ya, Joseph! Why do ya make me talk about these things?" Colm sighed. "Before I met ya, I would have said that their deaths were inevitable. Now, I'm not so sure."

Yellow-green light bolted across the night's horizon.

"It is three o'clock in the morning," Joseph said. "We need sleep. The dawn will awaken us soon with demands that we carry out another day."

They turned and walked to the barn. Once inside, they laid their weary bodies in the hay near four sleeping men: Gordon, Abe, Rufus, and Tatoson.

Joseph woke when the sun was halfway to its noonday apex. He was disoriented until he saw Colm asleep in the hay a few feet away. He got up, walked to the stream that ran behind the barn, and washed black gunpowder from his hair and hands and face.

The smell of food floated on the breeze and reminded him that he was hungry. He heard Seamus rousing Colm. Joseph walked to the farmhouse, crossed the porch, and entered the kitchen. Colm and Seamus came in behind him.

Abe, Rufus, and Tatoson stood around the fireplace eating from bowls. Liam sat at the table drinking beer. In the living room, Michael and Gordon were immersed in a muffled argument.

Jeremiah took a bowl off the mantle, handed it to Joseph, and pointed at the black kettle hanging over the fire. "Help yourself. Brandon scraped together enough fixin's ta make stew. There's a keg of beer on the table."

"Where is Brandon?" Joseph asked after he had filled his bowl. "I need to speak with him."

"Him and Patrick is above stairs with Ian," Seamus said. Then, he said to Colm, "Your brother's holdin' a grudge against Gordon, and there's gonna be a fight."

"Let them fight," Colm said. "Go fetch Brandon."

Colm filled a bowl from the kettle and sat at the table. He saw that Liam's aura was still bright green.

Joseph sat beside Liam. "May I examine the wound on your forehead?"

Liam sought Colm's approval. Colm nodded.

Joseph examined the deep furrow caused by a musket ball. There was no scabbing. It looked raw, as if the wound was fresh instead of a day old.

Joseph sighed and turned his attention to Colm, "Do angels not suffer any physical pain? You were shot, yet you sit there as if nothing happened to your body."

"I told ya, I wasn't shot by a demon."

"And the ball lodged in your breast?"

"It will dissolve eventually."

"And what of your wound, Liam?" Joseph asked. "It was inflicted by a demon. Will it fester?"

"It will kill me," Liam said candidly.

The kitchen door swung open. Brandon and Seamus stepped through.

Colm said, "Brandon, Joseph needs ya to get his children and their nanny out of Boston and to Worcester. Do what he tells ya. Get some of the men from the watch to go with ya, and be honest about what ya are up to. I'm giving ya command of this mission."

Brandon saw the blood on Colm's shirt. "Have you been shot?" he asked, wide-eyed.

"I'm fine. Now, acknowledge the order," Colm warned.

Brandon swallowed his fear and nodded.

Abe placed his empty bowl on the table, and said, "I will go with you."

Rufus Williams glanced around the kitchen. He had pledged his allegiance to Joseph Warren and the angels yesterday and intended on keeping that vow. He said, "I will go."

"Me too," Jeremiah said.

"Are you fine with me goin'?" Seamus asked Colm.

Colm didn't like the idea of Seamus going with his purple aura shining like a beacon for the demons to see. It would endanger the others.

Joseph sensed Colm's hesitation. "Colm, please allow Seamus to go. I know you think that he will attract demons, but I am more concerned with the evil patrolling the streets of Boston under the command of General Gage."

Ya know I can't say no to ya, Colm thought. He gave Seamus a nod. Then he said to Joseph, "Before ya leave, come talk to me. I'm going above stairs to tend to Ian."

Colm rose from his chair. "Tatoson, come with me."

"Do not order me about, archangel," Tatoson retorted. "I am not a Christian."

Silence plunged into the kitchen.

Jeremiah shelved his empty bowl on the mantel. He turned and squeezed Tatoson's right shoulder. "You *cain't* be denyin' the existence of this archangel," he seethed.

Tatoson threw Jeremiah's hand off his shoulder. "I am not. What I am saying is that I do not revere them as you do."

"Well, that's the trouble. Colm ain't orderin' you as a servant of God. Whether or not you're a Christian don't make no difference. He's orderin' you as a man. You're a man ain't you?"

Tatoson frowned and narrowed his dark eyes.

"Understand somethin'," Jeremiah said, "if Colm wants you ta go with 'im, you will. He don't see no difference between you or me."

Tatoson crossed his arms over his chest in defiance. He stole a look at Colm. *You are beautiful,* Tatoson thought. He remembered thinking the same thing about the angels when they were reunited yesterday afternoon on the road from Concord. He wanted to dispute Jeremiah's claim, but could not.

Colm pushed the living room door open. Tatoson followed him through the door.

Michael had left the living room. Gordon sat at the big round table, sketching. He didn't look up when Colm and Tatoson passed on their way to the stairs.

The narrow stairs creaked and groaned as Colm and Tatoson's boots punished the risers. Above stairs, they entered the largest bedroom in the house. Ian sat on the edge of the bed with his head in his hands as Patrick looked through the single window in the room. The window afforded a view of the barn, the stream, and the woods beyond.

"Michael's run off into the woods," Patrick said without shifting his gaze from the window. "He thinks Gordon is intrudin' where he don't belong. I cain't convince him otherwise."

"I'll go after him if he doesn't come back soon."

Patrick turned away from the window and walked to the bed. Colm heard wings rustle when Patrick said, "Ian, I know you feel horrible. We ain't gonna let you die. Colm ain't gonna let you die." Patrick kissed the top of Ian's head.

Colm pulled Ian into his arms.

Ian rested his head on Colm's chest.

"Does ya body hurt?" Colm asked.

"Yes."

"Are ya in pain?"

"Yes."

"I won't let ya die."

"I'm dirty."

"I know," Colm whispered.

"Help me."

"Do ya need Sidonie?"

Ian nodded and cried.

"Go to Concord and fetch her," Colm said to Patrick. "Take Tatoson with you."

Tatoson remained silent. He intended to obey the archangel.

When Patrick opened the door, Colm released his aura to comfort Ian. Green light lit the bedroom.

Tatoson moved to leave the room with Patrick. He stopped to take one last look at the archangel's celestial magnificence. *I hope I shall be blessed with seeing you again*, he thought as he closed the bedroom door behind him.

"I'm so tired, Colm," Ian said.

"I know." Colm held him closer.

Joseph opened the bedroom door, crossed the room, and sat on the bed beside Ian.

"Ian, do you remember me?" Joseph asked.

Ian's pale blue eyes shifted toward Joseph's voice. "Joseph Warren."

"Good. Do you remember my occupation?"

Ian closed his eyes. "Doctor," he whispered.

"Why're ya asking him these questions?" Colm asked.

"I want to see if he is mentally aware. May I touch him?"

Colm nodded.

Joseph cupped his left hand under Ian's chin. Ian's skin was soft. There was no beard stubble.

Ian opened his teary eyes and looked at Joseph.

"I want to see his wounds," Joseph said to Colm.

It took Colm several minutes to coax Ian from his arms, pull off his shirt, and lay him down. Erratic, thin, and shallow lacerations, from the attack he had suffered under the demon's knife, covered Ian's chest and stomach. They were healing. Joseph and Colm's eyes met in surprise.

The bedroom door opened with ghostly placidness. Jeremiah, Brandon, Liam, Michael, and Seamus watched silently from the doorway.

"I heard my wife's voice," Ian said.

Colm tightened his jaw and covered his mouth with one hand. He sighed, and let his hand drop from his mouth to stroke Ian's hair. "What's her name?"

"Ailbe."

"Did ya see her?"

"No, I heard her speak to me," Ian said.

Colm pulled Ian into his arms.

Ian rested his head on Colm's chest and said, "I have children."

"What're their names?" Colm asked.

"Diareann, Fianna, and Quinn."

"She is *his* wife. They are *his* children," Colm said gently.

Ian cried.

"The human soul who occupied the body of Ian Keogh is still there," Colm said to Joseph.

"That's possible?" Joseph asked.

Colm looked at Jeremiah and the angels. Then he looked at Joseph and said, "It wasn't intended. The angel who came to escort the man's soul to its egress must have called his reaper after Ian's spirit took possession."

"Why is Ian dying now after six hundred years?" Joseph asked.

"The demon attack must have awakened the human soul, and it fused with the angelic spirit. A human soul infused with the essence of an angel is blessed. An angelic spirit infused with a human soul is crucified."

Wings rustled in the doorway.

"He's been copulating with Sidonie's human soul and body for twenty-four years. Perhaps they have created some kind of spiritual—"

"—don't say Nephilim," Colm warned. "They didn't spawn children."

Ian reached for Joseph's hand.

Joseph accepted Ian's grasp, and stroked his face. "Does my touch comfort your body?"

"Yes."

"Do my hands comfort your spirit?"

"Yes."

"Can you sleep?"

"I'm too dirty to sleep."

"What should I do to wash away the dirt?"

"I don't know," Ian said. He sobbed.

"Colm, I must go," Joseph said as he let go of Ian's hand. "I have things to attend to that cannot wait. The battles that occurred yesterday have changed everything."

Colm didn't look at Joseph.

Joseph stood up. "Colm, look at me."

Colm complied.

"I must do my part to see that this country achieves liberty from tyranny. I must ensure that we are not enslaved at the hands of King George III, the British Parliament, or any entity that would chain us. I must see to it that my children have a future in which they can reap the benefits of their labor without fear of it being taken away. Can you not understand that?"

"Why can't ya see that I *have* been trying to understand?" Colm asked quietly.

Joseph's allegiance was torn between his patriotic duty to his family and lifelong friends, and the archangel whom he knew only a short time. However, his relationship with Colm seemed eternal.

Michael watched the unspoken exchange between his brother and Joseph unfold.

"I'll saddle up a horse for you, Joseph," Seamus offered.

Joseph kept his eyes on Colm and said, "Thank you, Seamus."

"Why do ya both have to act like ya don't care?" Michael asked Joseph and Colm. He turned and ran down the stairs.

The tension in the room led Jeremiah to say, "I'll git ready ta go ta Boston."

Liam sat on the bed beside Ian and said to Colm, "I will stay with him while you help Joseph prepare to leave."

Colm let Liam take Ian from his arms. He got up and said, "I'll help ya with the horse, Seamus." Then, he pushed past Joseph.

Joseph said nothing as Colm and Seamus left the bedroom.

"Colm does not mean to make you feel guilty," Liam said to Joseph.

"Liam, are you sick?" Ian asked.

Liam continued without answering Ian. "Guilt is a human emotion. He is afraid for you. Do you not understand *that*?"

"I do."

"We see the spiritual bond you and Colm have, and it is bright and strong and ardent. We have never seen devotion like that between an archangel and a human. You are fortunate spirits."

Joseph pressed his lips together in an attempt to keep his emotions from spilling out on a wave of words. He sighed and said, "I see that with a clarity that I thought could not exist."

"Then tell him where you are going and what you are going to do. Tell him you will be back tonight. Do not let him bear the burden of Ian's death and my death alone. Do not let him bear the millstone of helplessness without your hands to uplift him."

"I will be back," Joseph promised. "I will do everything I can for Colm and Ian; although, I'm only a man."

"You are so much more than a man. Be careful. The British want you dead," Liam said.

Joseph's smiled and said, "When liberty is the prize, who would stoop to waste a coward thought on life?"

❧

After Joseph had gone, Colm went in the house. He started to go above stairs, and then realized that Gordon was still sitting at the table in the living room. Colm remembered that Gordon had been sketching earlier. Now, Gordon was staring at the paper before him. Colm sat down next to Gordon and said, "I'm not sure ya are going to want to stay. Ian's dying and things might get bad."

Gordon stayed focused on the sheet of paper. "What things?"

Colm had no answer. This was the first time angels under his care were dying. There was a time when the other archangels had shared stories with him about their own dying angels, and the suffering they had to endure. He had forgotten those ancient stories. He would have to face what was about to happen all over again when Liam died.

"What are ya doing?" he asked Gordon.

Gordon didn't look up. "I told Dr. Warren that I needed his faith in you angels to figure out how to kill those demons other than putting their eyes out. When I woke up this morning in the barn, and you and Dr. Warren were sleeping near me, I had a vision of this." Gordon pointed at the sheet of paper.

Colm looked at what was drawn on the paper.

Gordon saw Colm's jaw flex. "You know what it is, don't you?"

"Aye. It's the Sigil of Lucifer."

"I think you can use the sigil against the demons. Maybe to kill them. Maybe to ward off their evil. Perhaps not Henry." Gordon raised an eyebrow. "Unless…there's something you know that I don't."

"There are a great many things I know that ya don't."

"What I mean is…is there something about Henry that makes you think a sigil will kill him or repel him?"

Colm thought about the confrontation with Henry in 1318 at the Battle of Faughart. Henry's wrath had sheeted the sky with yellow-green heat lightning. Colm had lacerated the sky with sizzling bolts of golden rage. Two of God's most powerful creations had collided to form a tempest that had hailed death down on the children of man. Colm doubted that Henry could be destroyed by something as simple as a sigil.

He said, "No."

"Have you used sigils in the past?" Gordon asked.

"Aye, but not the Sigil of Lucifer. It belongs to my fallen brother. It has no place in the hands of angels."

"Nor banished angels?"

Colm said nothing.

"Are you going to stare at me or are you going to answer me?" Gordon asked.

"I have no answer."

"Well, I'm thinking about how to use it. Can you conjure spells?"

"Aye, but I haven't done that in a long time."

"What did you use them for?"

"Ian is dying, and unless this sigil is truly a way to combat the demons, ya are wasting the minutes of the last days I have with his existence."

"Are you going to sacrifice six angels for a few more minutes with an angel you can't save? Are you going to sacrifice Joseph Warren for the same reason? I know how demons think. Henry will kill Dr. Warren, and make you watch. He will rape your brother, Michael, and make you watch."

Rage bubbled to the surface of Colm's spirit. He fought to back it down.

Gordon saw the archangel's struggle with the things he had just described. *Good. This is the one way I can convince Colm that they have to try and use the sigil as a weapon.*

"What *did* you use spells for?" Gordon asked again.

TWENTY-EIGHT

BOSTON, MASSACHUSETTS

Boston, Charlestown, and Cambridge were in chaos. Fear and anxiety ran rampant.

Loyalists were aghast at the rebels' determined show of force. Rebels were as stunned by the violence. The British wondered how they, as soldiers of one of Europe's greatest armies, had suffered under the tenacity of backwoods colonialists.

There were many who found the rebel tactics of shooting from behind cover despicable. Lord Hugh Percy voiced this disdain in his official report to General Gage. Others in command of various British infantry companies deemed the rebels cowards because they would not fight in open fields by rank and file in the traditional European style of combat.

These reports among others, which included statistical numbers of dead, wounded, and missing, were gathered and assembled by General Thomas Gage, who softened the miserable results of April 19 in his report to Lord Dartmouth, Secretary of State of the Colonies. Masking the horrors of what had really happened, Gage flourished his report with acknowledgments of promotions, and recommendations for further promotions. He then assured Dartmouth that he was making preparations to raise artillery to oppose the rebellious Americans.

Loyalists living in the surrounding townships flocked to Boston to live under the protection of General Gage and his troops. But Boston quickly became an unpleasant place. Rebel troops, amassed outside of Boston Neck in Roxbury and Cambridge, had stopped deliveries of fresh produce from the countryside.

With the access to and from the mainland blocked at the Neck, Boston was left dependent on supplies brought in by ship. However, Boston was almost an island surrounded by dozens of smaller islands dotting a huge harbor that was in many places dangerously shallow and lurking with mudflats and rocks. The British warships were huge and cumbersome to navigate in the harbor waters, adding to the difficulty of getting food and supplies into Boston from the resource-rich surrounding islands.

There were many who wished to leave Boston, but could not. As well as the threat of war and martial law, was the horror of smallpox. People felt they were being forced to take sides, but it was hard to garner which side some residents were on—could you trust your neighbor? Both loyalists and rebels were nervous.

Mercy Scollay was desperate to leave Boston with Joseph's children. However, if she *could* get out, she had no idea where to go, because communication from outside Boston was stifled.

The Committee of Safety had been meeting almost nonstop. Joseph was elected president of the Provincial Congress in place of the absent John Hancock. The congress resolved to raise a provincial army of eight thousand soldiers to serve until the end of the year, although they were unsure how the soldiers were going to be paid.

Joseph issued a circular letter that was distributed throughout the colonies under the influences of the Committee of Safety, urging men to enlist in the provincial army headquartered in Cambridge. The letter was a forceful, almost threatening, plea. Joseph wrote that death and devastation were the instant consequences of delaying to enlist.

The committee summoned forty-seven-year-old General Artemas Ward from Shrewsbury to preside over organizing the new provincial army. Fergus was promoted to general and put in charge of the provincials stationed in Roxbury.

On April 20, after hearing about the events of Lexington and Concord, Colonel Israel Putnam left his farm in Connecticut and arrived in Cambridge the following day. Putnam was a French and Indian War veteran and the founder of the Connecticut branch of the Sons of Liberty.

In the days and weeks to come, militiamen from throughout New England arrived in Cambridge and Roxbury. These companies were made up of a diverse force of white and freed black men who were farmers, doctors, lawyers, artisans, merchants, and sailors.

Then, Joseph turned his attention to his ever-adored town of Boston—the patriots who could not leave, and the loyalists who could not get in. And in his heart and mind, specifically his entrapped children. He sent a respectful letter to General Gage declaring the need to settle on a policy regarding the inhabitants of Boston.

The irony of his plea to General Gage did not escape Joseph. He was forced to humble himself to a man whose wife had literally bared her most intimate parts to him.

A committee was appointed to take sworn depositions from participants and eyewitnesses to the actions of April 19. Elbridge Gerry, Thomas Cushing, and Dr. Benjamin Church made up this committee. The depositions were to draw up a narrative of the massacres at Lexington and Concord, and to be compiled and sent to England immediately. By use of the word *massacre*, there was not much doubt as to how the rebel media would portray these events.

John Hancock and Samuel Adams made their way westward to Worcester. The duo made up two of the five Massachusetts delegates to the Continental Congress, which was scheduled to convene in Philadelphia on May 1.

John Adams was also one of the five delegates to the Continental Congress. Before he left his home in Braintree to meet John Hancock and Samuel Adams, he rode to Cambridge to meet with militia officers, one of which was Fergus. John wanted to understand what had happened and the situation they were in now. He found circumstances distressful because the militia was lacking in provisions: clothing, weapons, and money.

As the news of what had occurred in Lexington and Concord was carried throughout the colonies via messengers on horseback, the Provincial Congress compiled a packet of the depositions they had taken with a cover letter written by Joseph. The cover letter was the furthest thing from a plea for reconciliation with the British. This packet was to be delivered to Benjamin Franklin, who was living in London, England. Once Franklin received the packet, it was to be distributed throughout England.

Joseph managed to relay the rebels' account of what had happened in the colonies to Lord Dartmouth and the rest of England before Thomas Gage did. And the American rebel cause was not without its sympathizers in England.

∂

A laundered General Henry Hereford, accompanied by his aide-de-camp, returned to Province House late on the morning of April 22. He prepared to dismount, and was pleased to see a young white boy dash from around the side of the house to his aide.

248

"Say your name, boy," Henry said with delight as the boy grasped the horse's reins.

"John Gage, sir!"

Henry smiled broadly. "Why are you in attendance of my horse instead of a stable boy?"

"Father said I should learn as much as I can about horses, sir!"

Henry and Robert dismounted with a chuckle.

The front door swung open. Margaret stood in the doorway. With brisk movements, Henry pulled his riding gloves off and strode toward Margaret.

"Mrs. Gage!" Henry exclaimed. "After the disturbing and exhausting events of the past few days, I must say the sight of you is good for sore eyes!"

Margaret was suspicious of Henry's absence after what had occurred in Lexington and Concord. She had not asked Thomas where the general and his aide-de-camp were during that time, hoping that they had fallen off the face of the Earth.

"General," Margaret said curtly.

Henry stopped beside her. "Your son, John, is a good lad. He must be aged eight or nine, yet he demonstrates superior manners."

Stay away from my children, she thought.

Henry's eyes dropped low to study the place where Margaret's womb resided. *I can smell the sweet amniotic fluid of her pregnancy.*

She willed herself not to shield her flat pregnant belly with her hands. Thomas had been told of her pregnancy only this morning.

"Robert and I are famished," Henry announced as he strode past Margaret and into the house. "Have breakfast prepared right away." He paused and turned to look at Margaret. "Tell Thomas I want to see him."

Margaret walked away without acknowledging Henry. Robert grasped her upper left arm and said, "You will do as the general has asked—now."

She regarded Robert's hand on her arm, then her brown eyes flitted upward to look into his scowling face. "Thomas is in private conversation and cannot be disturbed."

Robert's urge to reveal his orange eyes almost overcame him, but he contained it. He, too, smelled the amniotic fluid of her pregnancy.

Margaret's lovely face contorted with disgust when she said, "Remove your hand from my arm immediately."

Robert grinned and thought, *I will remove my hand this time. Next time, I will break your neck—or kill your unborn child.* His hand dropped from her arm.

Several of the Gage children peaked around corners and witnessed Robert's abusive actions. Margaret's oldest children were attending college in England. The children who remained at home were not old enough or brave enough to confront their mother's abuser.

Thomas emerged from his office with Dr. Benjamin Church. The two men were conversing as though they were long time acquaintances. It was evident to Henry, Robert, and Margaret that Thomas was pleased with his rebel informant's visit.

When it came to rebel secrets and plotting, only Samuel Adams, John Hancock, and Joseph Warren were more involved than Benjamin Church. But Benjamin had an expensive mistress, and spying brought the ready cash he needed to please her. He had no qualms about betraying his fellow patriots in exchange for the means to pay for the treasure between the legs of Phoebe Yates.

Benjamin recalled his announcement the night before to the Provincial Congress that he intended to go into Boston the next day. The other members were aghast.

"You cannot be serious, Benjamin! Hanging will be the fate of any of the committee members caught in Boston," Joseph had warned.

He urged his thoughts to the present moment. "Mrs. Gage," Benjamin said, somewhat surprised to see her dour expression.

Margaret went to her husband's side to impress her loyalty to Thomas. She knew Benjamin Church was betraying Joseph and the Sons of Liberty. The American-born part of her found him despicable. The part of her that was wife to Thomas Gage admired her husband for managing to hire an intimate member of Boston's rebel circle as an informant. The pregnant hormonal part of her wanted to run to Joseph and whisper the betrayal in his ear while he made love to her.

"Thomas," Margaret said. "Please take tea with me when your guest has gone."

Thomas fell into her pleading eyes. Her wish was his command each time she was pregnant.

Henry took note of the Gage's blissful exchange. He would allow them their private time before he questioned Thomas about the news his informant brought. It was important to stay abreast of Warren's activities and whereabouts, because the archangel would never be far away.

After Henry and Robert ate breakfast, and while the Gages took tea behind closed doors, a messenger arrived with news for Henry. The demon that once possessed William Sutherland was now in possession of a British ensign. He entered the living room where Henry and Robert were relaxing. The general had promised the demon a permanent captain's vessel if he brought something valuable in exchange.

The ensign touched his hat in salute and then removed it. "General Hereford, sir! Am I free to speak?"

"Robert, make sure there are no eavesdroppers," Henry said. "Oh, and find Margaret's personal maid, Constance, and tell her I want to see her."

Robert nodded and went to do as he was ordered.

"Sir, I bring news of the angels. Paul Revere has joined Joseph Warren and the Committee of Safety that is adjourned in Cambridge. Warren was overheard telling Revere two of the angels are dying."

"So, the angel they call Ian suffered fatal wounds after all. Who is the other angel?"

"The one they call Liam. Our men shot him outside of Lexington."

"Very good! We shall kill them off one by one. The archangel may self-destruct under the weight of his own suffering and guilt. Delightful!" Henry paused for a moment in thought. Then he said, "I want you to spread the word among us that none of the other angels should be hurt until I allow it. I want the archangel to wallow in his grief for as long as possible. We have waited for this for so long, and now that the time is here, I intended to savor it."

"Right away, sir." The ensign lowered his head in deference to Henry and left Province House.

When Robert returned, Henry relayed the news to him.

"Once my order has been delivered, prepare a British captain for death and possession," Henry said to Robert. "A certain Captain Anthony Jameson comes to mind. Afterward, have some of us spread the word among the people of Boston that the poor living conditions here are due to the rebels' selfish need to keep fresh food, fodder, clothing, and arms to themselves."

"It will be my pleasure, sir! Afterward, may I threaten Joseph Warren again? Perhaps, even terrorize him?"

"What a splendid idea, Robert!" Henry sneered. "Now, the sooner you get on with my orders, the sooner you may go play! In the meantime, I shall speak with Gage and plan our next move toward inflaming this war."

Constance McCaskey lingered near the living room door. She stepped aside to let Robert pass, then entered the room and presented herself to Henry.

A satisfied smile played on her full lips. The general appeared a handsomer man than the last time they had met.

"Did you wish to see me, General?"

Henry rose. "Yes, I wish to see you in my bedchamber."

She produced a demure smile, and said, "As you command."

Brandon, Seamus, Jeremiah, Rufus, and Abe had a difficult time getting into Boston. After lingering outside the Neck, and observing all types of people trying to get in and out with no success, they decided to find a way to enter the city by water. The cover of night and slogging through shallow salt marshes slowed their unpleasant journey to the shore west of the Neck.

"Paul said the British man-of-war, the HMS *Somerset,* was anchored in the river near where he crossed to Charlestown on the night of the eighteenth," Brandon said. He looked out over the ghostly moonlit water.

"There's a battery to the north of the Neck," Seamus said, "We gotta avoid that, too."

"We ain't gotta worry about bein' seen because we ain't got no boat," Jeremiah said. He began walking the shore to search for anything that would solve their dilemma.

"If we *can* get to Joseph's kids, how are we going to get them out of Boston?" Rufus asked.

"Let us solve one problem at a time," Abe suggested. He watched Jeremiah's retreating figure for a moment, and then followed him.

Seamus and Rufus walked along the shore in the opposite direction.

Brandon continued to look out over the river. He saw dim lantern lights here and there, which were an indication that long boats were patrolling the waters. That gave him an idea. He squatted and groped the ground for large rocks. When he found one, he stood up and threw it as far as possible out over the water. The splash wasn't as loud as Brandon hoped, but he thought if he did it over and over again, someone in one of those patrol boats would hear it.

When Jeremiah and Abe returned from their unsuccessful search, Brandon had thrown a dozen rocks in the river. One of the lantern lights was moving toward the shore where he stood.

"Go get Seamus and Rufus," Brandon said to Abe. "I've attracted the attention of a boat. It's coming our way, and it's probably a British long boat."

Jeremiah double checked the pocket on his deerskin breeches for his skinning knife and shouldered his musket. Brandon had proved to be more resourceful than he thought was possible.

The others returned and prepared for the unknown occupants of the boat sliding toward them across the water.

When the lantern light grew close enough to see that it was indeed a British long boat, the five men stepped away from the water's edge. The boat slid onto the shore. The men stepped further back from the lantern-illuminated shoreline.

Six British soldiers climbed out of the long boat. One soldier remained in the boat. He lit another lantern and handed it to a soldier on the shore.

Brandon and Seamus hoped they would see orange eyes among the soldiers, but there were none. They both agonized over killing the children of man for no other reason than to protect another man's children. They watched as the six soldiers spread out along the shoreline. Yellow light from their lantern bobbed through the darkness.

Jeremiah ran toward the bow of the boat and fired his musket. There was a brief blaze of flint and gun powder before the ball struck and killed the soldier in the boat.

Abe and Rufus darted from the shadows, and shot and killed the two soldiers at the rear of the group.

The four remaining soldiers ran for the cover of the boat, but the bobbing lantern light betrayed their intent.

Jeremiah, Abe, and Rufus were reloading. Seamus knew that it was up to him and Brandon to cut the running soldiers down. He couldn't see these soldiers any clearer than he could see the British soldiers through the haze on Lexington Green.

"I volunteered for this mission so I gotta do this," he told himself, and raised his musket. He fired at the soldier carrying the lantern.

A man screamed, and the lantern tumbled to the ground.

I lured the men in that boat to their deaths. How could I have done that? Brandon thought.

Rufus fired again, but the shot went wide to the right.

Two soldiers jumped into the boat while one shoved the boat off the shore. Seamus and Abe ran for the boat. Abe shot the soldier who was pushing the boat in the head. The soldier fell into the boat.

Brandon discarded his guilt when the two remaining soldiers stood up and aimed their muskets at Seamus. One of the soldiers had orange eyes.

"Jeremiah, one of them is a demon!" Brandon shouted. He fired and hit the demon in one orange eye. Jeremiah shot out the other eye.

The demon howled. Flames and sparks spewed from its eyes. The living man it possessed burst into flames. He issued a long, agonizing scream.

The last surviving soldier quickly shed his heavy woolen coat. He jumped into the shallow water and swam away.

Brandon, Jeremiah, and Rufus ran to the boat. They tilted the boat until the burning man's body fell overboard. Seamus and Abe pulled the other dead soldier out of the boat and laid his body in the long grasses several feet from the shore.

"I hesitated," Brandon admitted to Seamus. "You need to take command."

"No, Colm wants you in command."

"Seamus, I—"

"Get in the boat," Abe barked. "You can argue over who is in command later. We cannot let the soldier in the water get away."

They climbed into the boat and doused the lantern. Rufus shoved the boat off the shore.

When they reached the swimming soldier, Jeremiah slid into the water and stabbed him to death with his skinning knife. The act made him feel like a murderer instead of a rebel fighting for the safety of a woman and four children.

Jeremiah heaved into the boat. He and Rufus rowed until the long boat became caught in the current of the outgoing tide. Using the oars, they guided the boat northward along the shore of Back Bay. It floated without a sound past the Common, where many of the King's troops were bivouacked. Then, Seamus and Brandon took the oars and rowed to the far north shore of Back Bay. They landed just before dawn, faced with a new challenge—get to Joseph's house without attracting attention from humans and demons alike.

Brandon cloaked his yellow aura. Seamus' purple aura would be visible to any demon they encountered. They had to avoid Beacon Hill where Henry was quartered. In order to do that, they had to ensure they landed far enough north of Beacon Hill so they could take a direct easterly route from the shoreline toward Hanover Street and Joseph's house.

They made their way east under a brilliant yellow and pink sunrise. The residents of Boston were up and about early. The streets were teeming with British soldiers.

As they approached the northern edge of Beacon Hill, they swung further north where they encountered a patrol. The ensign in charge of the patrol, Daniel Martin, had been a part of Major John Pitcairn's vanguard in Lexington. Seamus' beard and beaver felt hat stirred his memory.

Ensign Martin approached Seamus. "Are you enjoying your morning stroll, rebel?" The ensign's eyes moved to the musket slung over Seamus' shoulder. "More importantly, why are you walking the streets armed? Are you aware that is against the law?"

Damn! Seamus thought. *How come none of us thought to leave our muskets in the boat?*

The patrol encircled them and stripped the five men of their muskets. One of the soldiers saw Jeremiah's skinning knife, and reached to pull it from the pocket on his breeches. Jeremiah snatched the soldier by the wrist, and warned, "Leave it."

The soldier wrenched his wrist free of Jeremiah's hand and stepped back.

Curious people gathered to watch the British harassment.

"I cannot believe you have the nerve to enter the city after what occurred two days ago," Ensign Martin said to Seamus. "How did you get into Boston, and better yet, why are you here?"

Seamus made eye contact with the ensign and said, "Fuck you."

That answer drew the attention of all the soldiers in the patrol. They stared at Seamus in disbelief.

Brandon began to back out of the circle. Jeremiah, Abe, and Rufus understood Seamus' motive. They, too, took a step backward, and then another.

"You are not amusing, rebel," Ensign Martin said. "Answer me."

"You have my answer." Seamus' eyes stayed locked on the ensign when he stepped closer to him and said, "Fuck…you."

Brandon was no longer amid the patrol. He turned and walked away in one smooth move. Jeremiah and Abe stepped out of the circle. Rufus stopped moving when his elbow hit a soldier's forearm. The soldier pulled his red ponytail and jerked him forward. Jeremiah and Abe walked away.

Ensign Martin sighed as if he was sorry for what he was about to do. He said to Seamus, "Well, then, here is my answer." The ensign turned with a pistol in his hand and shot Rufus in the forehead between his dark red eyebrows.

Blood ran into Rufus' eyes and down his nose and cheeks. He raised a hand toward his face, but he could not maintain the motion, and his hand dropped to his side. His green eyes were filled with surprised pain.

The civilian onlookers scattered like frightened sparrows.

The British patrol fell apart when Rufus dropped to the ground. His body twitched.

Seamus felt the struggle Rufus' soul endured as his body died. His instinct was to comfort Rufus, lead his soul to its egress, and call a reaper, but he had to avoid being detained. He turned and ran. It was a horrible burden on his angelic spirit.

Ensign Daniel Martin looked at the pistol in his hand as if it were a grotesque monster. He looked at the shocked soldiers under his command. *What have I done?* Daniel thought. *The man I just killed was innocent.*

"Sir,…you cannot…believe…what you just…did…was acceptable," a young soldier stammered. His eyes shifted between Rufus' body and Ensign Martin's face.

Two soldiers of the patrol fled.

"Sir?"

Ensign Martin raised the pistol to his temple and fired.

The ensign's quick death hurt Seamus' spirit, but he kept running.

Brandon began running when he heard the first pistol discharge and didn't stop until he reached Joseph's front doorstep. He bent and put his hands on his knees so he could catch his breath. His angelic spirit felt Rufus' soul struggle as his body died, and he forced himself not to return to comfort him.

He heard voices inside the house. The front door opened.

"Brandon?" William Eustis asked in surprise. William looked beyond Brandon and saw no one. "Come inside before you are seen."

Brandon straightened up and stepped in the house. Jeremiah and Abe arrived before William closed the door. He let them inside.

"Why are you here?" William implored. "Is Dr. Warren all right?"

"He was when we left Roxbury yesterday," Brandon said. "We've come to get his children and their nanny out of Boston. You shou'd probably leave, too."

"William, who is here?" Mercy asked as she entered the living room. She faltered and said, "Oh."

"Joseph sent these men to get you and the children out of Boston."

She pressed a hand between her breasts. "Is Joseph safe?"

Brandon avoided eye contact. "As far as we know."

Mercy's sigh of relief filled the living room.

Jeremiah saw Brandon's discomfort. He stepped forward. "I'm Jeremiah Killam, Miss Scollay. Joseph wants us ta take you and his kids ta Worcester."

"Yes, now I remember," William said, nodding. "Dr. Warren told me that his colleague, Dr. Elijah Dix might agree to shelter the children if anything happened. Mercy, get them packed and ready for the journey right away."

"There ain't gonna be no packin'," Jeremiah said. "We'll be lucky if we cain get you out of Boston with the clothes on your back."

Joseph's children ran into the living room. They stopped, and clung to their nanny when they realized the men speaking to Dr. Eustis were strangers. Elizabeth, Joseph's oldest child, studied Brandon.

"There is no need to be frightened," Mercy said. "These men are your father's friends."

The youngest child, two-year-old Mary, stuck her thumb in her mouth, buried her head in Mercy's skirts, and began to cry.

Someone knocked on the front door.

The two middle children, Joseph and Richard, hid behind Mercy.

William opened the door and allowed Seamus inside. Seamus assessed the people in the living room. When he saw the children, he decided not to speak of Rufus' death.

Elizabeth Warren took a step toward Brandon. He looked at the floor to avoid her probing blue eyes that looked so much like Joseph's.

"Betsey, what are you doing?" Mercy asked. Chills ran down her spine. She remembered the child's reverent reaction to Joseph's new friend, Colm Bohannon, the night they were first introduced. Betsey appeared to have the same reaction to the handsome young man who kept his eyes downcast.

Elizabeth saw Brandon's yellow aura.

Brandon was painfully aware of her sighting, and he was puzzled by the fact that she could see his aura when it was cloaked. He was unaware that Joseph had seen Colm's aura the first time they met. Like father, like daughter.

"You are an angel just like father's friend—Mr. Bohannon," Elizabeth said. She turned and looked at Seamus. His purple aura was bright and strong. "As are you."

Mercy was so in love with Joseph that she wanted to believe anything he or his children had faith in; whether it be angels and demons, or Heaven and Hell. She asked Brandon, "What do you want me to do?"

Brandon forced himself to look at her. But he had no answer to her question. They had no escape plan. *How have we come to this? How have we come to protecting these humans from their own evil? We are merely soothers and beholders.*

257

Seamus sensed the source of Brandon's distress. He wondered the same thing. Then, Seamus realized that Jeremiah and Joseph had changed everything. The angels had taken Jeremiah's loyalty for granted because it had been limited to their life on Garden Mountain, but that was no longer the case. Jeremiah had left the sanctuary of their home in Virginia despite knowing he could die defending them. Joseph had, thus far, given everything he had to Colm despite knowing the risks.

"William, maybe you can get them through the guard post on the Neck if you say you have to doctor someone," Brandon suggested.

William said kindly, "I do not think they will believe that I need to bring four children and their nanny along to care for a patient. Furthermore, I promised Joseph that I would take care of his medical practice. Even if I *can* get out of Boston, I may not be able to get back in."

"You gotta help us, William," Seamus said. "After what just happened, we cain't be walkin' the streets with the children."

"What do you mean by 'what just happened?'" William asked evenly.

Seamus glanced at Mercy. "I'd rather not say just now."

William looked at Mercy and the children clinging to her skirts. They were Joseph's treasures. He owed Joseph their safety. "Mercy, take the children and feed them. Then, prepare them for a long journey."

"Where are we going?" seven-year-old Joseph asked William.

He went to the boy and squatted so they could speak face to face. "You are going someplace where your father can visit."

"Why can he not come home? Where is he?"

William sighed. He looked up at Mercy and then at the other children. The three oldest children were waiting for his answer. He did not know where Joseph actually was, but it would be safe to assume he was in meetings with the Committee of Safety and the Provincial Congress.

"Your father is in important meetings that he cannot leave. Do as Mercy asks so we do not worry him. Can you do that?"

Young Joseph nodded.

Mercy pulled Mary away from her skirts and picked her up. She turned to go. Elizabeth looked at the angels one more time before she followed Mercy out of the living room.

William gave Seamus an expectant look. "What just happened?"

Seamus relayed the incidents.

Jeremiah and Abe were surprised by the ensign's suicide.

"We gotta figure out how to get Rufus' body to his family," Brandon said.

"He is a widower with no children, just as I am," Abe explained. "Do not risk yourselves to get his body home."

"He ain't got no family at all?" Jeremiah asked. He stroked his dark-blond beard to comfort himself for the first time in his life.

Abe shook his head. That sad fact quieted the room.

Finally, William asked, "What is our plan to get the children out of Boston?"

"We got here in a British long boat and landed on the shore of Back Bay," Brandon said.

"The boat may not be there now," Abe pointed out. "If soldiers have seen it, they have probably moved it."

"Then we gotta go back and hide it," Brandon said. "If it's gone, then we'll figure out something else. Seamus, you shou'd go. You can keep out of sight of demons while you keep the boat out of sight of the British."

"And if the boat is gone?" William asked.

"I'll find us another boat," Seamus said, as if that was the obvious choice. "Either way, I'll be waitin' for you in Back Bay."

William's experiences were, for the most part, limited to church, school, administering medical care, and the occasional company of a lady. This dangerous mission sparked his adrenaline. He asked, "What should I do?"

"Get the children and Miss Scollay to Back Bay, but do it before nightfall," Brandon said. "Skulking through the streets at night will attract more attention."

"And you should have a story concocted about where you are going if you are stopped and questioned," Abe added.

William nodded.

"Abe, you go with them so they know where they're going. But stay out of sight," Brandon ordered. "Me and Jeremiah will leave after Seamus is gone. We'll make our way to Back Bay and hide somewhere until nightfall."

The long boat was still on the shore of Back Bay. They had landed that morning in a sparsely populated stretch of beach. Seamus shoved the boat off the shore, climbed in and sat down. He took an oar in each hand and began to row. The boat was wieldy and heavy. He cussed under his breath while he struggled to get the bow to turn away from the shore. When he finally got the boat turned around, he rowed toward a marshy area where he slipped into the cover of reeds.

In the meantime, Jeremiah and Brandon took a different route toward Back Bay than they had come. They walked further north toward Mill Pond, just east of the Green Dragon Tavern, then swung west toward the Charles River. This maneuver kept them north of Cambridge Street and away from the surrounding neighborhood. Once they reached the shores of the river, they moved south along Back Bay.

Brandon bent slightly backward to check the pistol he kept shoved between the waistband of his breeches and the small of his back. He felt the pistol's site reassuringly graze the top of his buttocks. Jeremiah removed his skinning knife from the pocket of his breeches and tucked it up the sleeve of his coat. That way, he could grab the hilt without obvious movement.

At the Warren house, Mercy was in the girls' bedroom dressing them in layers of clothing. If they were to travel with only the clothes on their back, she intended to ensure they took plenty of clothes.

Mary whined when Mercy slipped another frock over the one she already had on.

There was a knock on the bedroom door. "Mercy, we need to go," William said from the other side of the door.

"We are almost ready," Mercy reassured him. She said to Elizabeth, who was pulling at her layers of clothing, "Take your brothers to William."

"Joseph and Richard, come with me now!" Elizabeth told them.

The children left the bedroom with much noise. Mercy and Mary followed them a few minutes later.

"Are we ready?" William asked Abe.

"It seems so. Do you have Dr. Warren's pistols?"

William nodded and handed one to Abe. Then, he stashed the other loaded pistol in his coat.

Mercy said to Abe, "Wait a moment." She said to the children, "You will not speak while we are on our walk. You will not answer any questions asked of you. Tell me you understand."

The three oldest children said, "We understand."

Mercy picked up Mary and set her on her hip.

It was six o'clock in the evening when they left the Warren house. This was the supper hour for most people, including the British soldiers. The streets would not be as crowded, and that would make their way to Back Bay easier.

They took Hanover Street to Cambridge Street, with the intention of moving through the neighborhoods. This route would take the least amount of time to reach the shore, but William feared it would draw them the most attention. He was right.

From behind William, a male voice commanded, "Stop immediately!"

William and his group of escapees did as they were told. They slowly turned around to face a British corporal. A small troop of soldiers stood behind him.

"Dr. Eustis?"

William's heart sank. The corporal was one of his patients.

"Corporal Webb," William acknowledged with a surprisingly steady voice.

"Why are you out and about at the supper hour with Dr. Warren's children?" The corporal took another look at the children. "They *are* Dr. Warren's children?"

Abe backed away so he would not be seen.

Mercy was extremely nervous, but she kept her eyes on the corporal so she did not appear guilty of being on Cambridge Street.

"Yes, they are Dr. Warren's children," William answered. "We have already had our supper and are taking a stroll to enjoy the cool evening."

Corporal Webb narrowed his eyes and asked, "Where is Dr. Warren?"

Sweat wet William's underarms and the back of his neck.

Young Joseph forgot his nanny's warning not to speak. He said, "Father is at a meeting."

Corporal Webb looked at the little boy. He had children of his own, and he knew that children often told the truth, when the truth was what the adults were hiding. He knelt and asked, "What meeting is your father attending?"

Joseph looked at William.

The corporal stood up. "What meeting is Dr. Warren attending?" he asked William, impatiently.

William relaxed. "I have no idea. He is not in Boston."

Corporal Webb smiled and said, with no regard for the children, "I have heard that he and his cohorts will be hanged if they are found."

The corporal's statement upset Mercy, but she bravely hid her distress. She asked, "May we continue our walk?"

"Yes—Miss Scollay—is it?"

She nodded.

The soldiers let them pass.

❧

Abe rejoined them when they were out of sight of Corporal Webb and his patrol. The supper hour had passed, and people were leaving their homes for various reasons—to visit friends or run the last errands of the day.

The children were already tired of their journey. Mary cried and kicked at Mercy to be put down. Richard whined that he was too tired to walk anymore. Joseph hit Elizabeth in the arm while he accused her of stepping on his feet.

"Hush," Mercy hissed at the children. She tightened her grip on Mary's flaying body.

When they finally arrived at the sloping shores of Back Bay and reached the spot where the long boat had landed that morning, Abe stopped them.

The sun was setting. Ribbons of pink and orange clouds streaked the sky. Abe's eyes swept the darkening bay and the shoreline. He saw something unusual and murmured, "That is odd."

William looked northward and said, "What is it, Abe?"

Abe lifted his chin toward what he saw on the shore. "Do you see three British officers at the water's edge?"

William strained to see in the fading light. "Yes, I see them." Then, he saw what Abe had deemed unusual. "There is an old woman with them. She appears to be holding a bow and arrow."

Oars swished the water. Seamus was approaching with the long boat. Brandon and Jeremiah were with him. Abe ran to the boat as it slid onto the shore.

The last remaining light of the day turned crimson gray as Brandon and Jeremiah got out of the boat.

Abe took Brandon aside, pointed down the shore, and relayed what he and William had seen. A vague outline of the officers and the woman was still visible.

William took Mary from Mercy's arms so Jeremiah could help her into the boat. Seamus tried to keep the boat steady.

A bow twanged as it released an arrow. The sound vibrated across the waters of the bay. The darkening sky back dropped the arrow's arching flight. It hit one of the British officers in the chest.

Brandon's eyes widened. "We gotta get them out of here!" He ran to the boat.

Abe ran after him, and asked, "What is it?"

Mercy and the three oldest children were seated in the boat. William handed Mary to Mercy.

Brandon jumped in the boat and startled the children. Richard and Mary began to cry. Brandon said to Seamus, "Serepatice is here, and if she's here, Robert Percy is here!" He pointed down the shore.

It was nearly pitch black. Seamus couldn't see anyone, but he saw two pairs of orange lights flare.

"Shut them up!" Jeremiah growled at Mercy.

Mary and Richard howled louder, though Mercy tried to quiet them. Joseph shouted, "I want father!" He, too, began to cry.

Abe scrambled into the boat.

"Get down so Robert and Serepatice can't see your aura!" Brandon said to Seamus. He took off his coat then shoved Seamus into the bottom of the boat. He threw his coat over Seamus. Jeremiah also removed his coat and draped it over Seamus. The angel's purple light was still visible, but shaded.

Elizabeth bent to comfort Joseph. She stroked the top of his head and said, "Don't cry. The angels are taking us to see father."

As William pushed the boat off, they saw lanterns and heard oars break the water's surface. Two British long boats were coming toward them.

The sound of a single beating drum rolled across the water from the place where Robert and the other demons stood. A bell accompanied the steady drum beat.

Brandon tried not to shout when he said to Jeremiah, "Get us out of here!"

Jeremiah and Abe each manned a set of oars.

The British long boats' oars silenced. For a minute, all three boats just floated.

The steady drum beat intensified into a powerful throbbing rhythm. Orange lights flared on the shore.

Elizabeth had managed to quiet Joseph, but Mary and Richard were still crying. She whispered to Brandon, "You can quiet them."

"I can? What shou'd I do?"

Men were talking among themselves in the British long boats. Another lantern flared. An officer stood up in one of the boats.

Voices praying in unison rose from the northern shore. The Latin words flew like a flock of birds across the bay.

"What in the devil is that noise?" the officer shouted. He saw orange lights flare again. "Swing the boat portside and move north toward those voices."

A confused soldier asked, "Are we to abandon the boat with the crying children, sir?"

"Take the order! Row!" the officer ordered.

Elizabeth got up and pulled her wailing two-year-old sister toward Brandon, and sat her down beside him. "Touch her cheek," Elizabeth instructed Brandon.

Brandon traced the wet trail of tears down Mary's cheek with his fingertips. She looked into his face. Her cries settled into sniffles. He touched her cheek again, and she quieted.

The British long boats moved away to investigate what was taking place further down the shore.

Robert Percy was performing the ritual to give a lower demon a permanent human vessel. This particular vessel once belonged to the living Captain Anthony Jameson. By performing the ritual on the shore of Back Bay, Robert had unknowingly helped Joseph Warren's children escape Boston.

Twenty-nine

Sidonie lay beside Ian in his bed. The light of his red aura had gone out. She held him tight against her body and tried not to cry.

Twenty-four years earlier, Ian energized Sidonie's dying soul with a part of his essence—his red aura. Now, she felt it burning brightly within her soul. *If I could give it back to him, perhaps he would not die.*

Ian shivered in her arms.

Sidonie whispered to her dying angel, "I love you. Feel that love. I know you can feel it in your heart even if you can't say the words. Love is there within both of you—the man and the angel."

The sound of a horse galloping toward the farm broke the silent night. Joseph reined the horse. He jumped from the saddle and ran to be with the angels awaiting his return.

Colm was in the living room drinking whiskey and pacing, emulating Joseph's actions from two nights ago.

Joseph entered the living room with quiet urgency.

Colm's green eyes flashed silver light that diffused through his tears. "Ya children and their nanny are safe in Worcester."

Joseph breathed a sigh of relief. "Have the men returned?"

Colm's voice was thick with grief. "Aye, but Rufus Williams was killed. It's my fault for allowing him to go."

"No, it is my fault. I should have sent my children away weeks ago. What happened?"

"They were detained by a British patrol. The ensign in charge shot Rufus because Seamus wouldn't answer his questions. Seamus said the ensign, in turn, killed himself."

Joseph wanted to feel guilt for what had happened to Rufus, but Colm had already taken on that guilt for him.

Colm closed his eyes and rubbed his tense forehead. He opened his eyes and said, "Ian won't survive the night. I've failed him, and I've failed Liam."

Joseph looked Colm in the eyes. "You have failed no one."

He took the glass of whiskey from Colm's hand and set it on the fireplace mantel. They climbed the steps to above stairs.

Jeremiah and the angels were in the bedroom where Ian lay dying in Sidonie's arms. Emotional agony tainted the room. It reminded Joseph of the night his wife died.

Sidonie looked at Joseph and said, "Help our human souls move on, Dr. Warren. When they are gone, then all that will be left is Ian's spirit. Perhaps, it will survive."

Michael knew he couldn't endure what was about to happen. He left the room.

Jeremiah held out his hand to Joseph. "She wants it to be you."

Joseph looked at the dagger in Jeremiah's hand.

Jeremiah said, "This is Ian's dagger. She wants you to use it to kill their resurrected bodies."

Joseph realized what they expected of him was vastly harder than the battles he waged against King George III's tyranny. Yet, it was a merciful act of freedom that was no less liberating than everything he and his fellow patriots were fighting for. He took the dagger.

Wings rustled. Green, blue, yellow, and purple light filled the bedroom.

Joseph tried to gather the strength to do what needed to be done, but it seemed out of reach.

Then, Colm's golden radiance washed over the light of the angels' auras. He wrapped his hand around the hand in which Joseph held the dagger. Together, they ended Ian Keogh's and Sidonie Roux Denning's life on Earth. The angels' spirits ached as they felt the struggle the souls endured as their bodies died.

Colm summoned reapers to escort the human souls to their destiny. The gossamer draped reapers appeared. Colm made a decision normally left to God. He instructed the reapers to escort the souls to Heaven. The reapers looked at Joseph and Jeremiah with cold eyes, and then they moved in silence to the bed where the dead lay. A sorrowful wind gusted through the bedroom.

The angel was freed of the human soul. Its red aura darted and flashed in the bedroom like a firefly on a summer's night. A spark of red light infused Sidonie's soul. It was an eternal gift from the angel who loved her.

The reapers disappeared.

The colorful bright light in the bedroom went out. The angels lifted the dead bodies from the bed. Jeremiah accompanied them as they took the bodies downstairs.

Joseph watched them with a heavy heart.

"The time for grieving their physical loss has long since passed," Colm said to Joseph.

Joseph nodded. It was difficult for his human emotions to rationalize.

"The angel that possessed Ian's body will find another and will be back to fight with us. This time the angel will make sure the soul has been reaped before taking the vessel."

Joseph tried to smile.

"I need to soothe Michael," Colm said. "He's angry with me. He'll always be angry for one reason or another."

"Your burden is great, Colm. I wish to be someone you can lean on."

"Joseph, ya have already given me that—and more."

The archangel and the idolized patriot doctor left the bedroom. The angel once named Ian Keogh went to find a vessel in which his spirit could reside. Jeremiah and the angels buried the dead in the woods while Abe, Gordon, and Tatoson watched in silence.

The day after Ian's spirit was released, Tatoson returned to Concord. After they had both helped the angels, he and Samuel Prescott felt a need to renew their brotherly relationship and spend more time with Samuel's father, Abel.

Joseph lodged in Hastings House in Cambridge, close to the Provincial Congress and Committee of Safety meetings. Fergus moved to Dillaway House in Roxbury to oversee the fledgling provincial army stationed in Roxbury.

At Gordon's request, they both returned to the farm on the eerily quiet night of April 27. Everyone gathered around the large table in the farmhouse living room.

"I've already shown Colm this. I think we might be able to use it to combat Henry's lower demons." Gordon held his sketch of the Sigil of Lucifer up for everyone to see.

The angels looked at Colm in surprise.

Gordon tried to hand the sketch to Michael.

Michael shrunk from it. "We can't touch that! It belongs to Lucifer!"

"Did you agree to use this, Colm?" Patrick asked. He kept his eyes on the sketch as if it would come to life and strike him dead.

"Not yet."

"I've been thinking about how to use it," Gordon continued with no regard for Michael or Patrick's reaction. "Maybe, the sigil can be etched into a knife blade or a musket ball or any weapon that could be used to combat a demon. Maybe, we can have it tattooed on our bodies. Maybe, a blacksmith can forge the sigil so you can shove it up a demon's ass. I need your—"

"Did you not hear Michael?" Liam asked. "We cannot touch the sigil of a fallen angel."

"Oh Lord," Jeremiah interjected. "Do you hear yourself, Liam? You *is* a fallen angel."

Gordon grinned and huffed out a laugh. "Try touching the sketch, Liam."

"No!" Colm said. "No one touches it until I say so."

Gordon's grin faded. "That brings me to what I asked you about a few days ago, Colm. You said you could conjure spells. We might have to cast a spell over the sigil to release Lucifer's evil and counteract God's evil. I'm asking you again. What did you use spells for?"

Wings rustled and a breeze swept through the living room.

Jeremiah raised an eyebrow in surprise. He'd never heard the angels refer to using spells.

Colm's eyes traveled to each face around the table.

"Answer me, Colm!" Gordon demanded.

Michael stood up; his chair fell backward and clattered against the wood floor. He shouted at Gordon, "Leave him alone! He doesn't want to tell ya! And he doesn't *have* to tell ya!"

There was a time when Colm had refused to discuss his standing as an archangel with Gordon. He remembered Gordon saying Henry would kill Joseph and rape Michael. "No, Michael. It's alright."

Michael pointed at Gordon and said, "This fucker is doing this for himself, not for us!" Michael leaned over the table at Gordon. "Do ya have to kill demons to feel like a man?"

Colm folded his arms over his chest. "Sit down, Michael."

Michael sneered at Gordon. He fought the impulse to spit in his face.

Patrick said, "Stop it, Michael! We know you don't like Gordon, but give him a chance."

Abe looked nervously at Jeremiah. He remembered Michael had attacked Gordon in the woods near Lexington eight days ago. Jeremiah whispered to Abe, "Michael always acts like this. You'll git used ta it."

"You can think what you want, Michael. It makes no difference to me," Gordon replied.

Patrick got up and righted Michael's chair. "Michael, do what Colm said!"

"Stop coddlin' him, Brother," Seamus warned Patrick. Then he said to Michael, "Don't make me get up and sit you down."

Michael sat down, pressed his pouty lips together, and leered at Gordon.

"I used the spells to conjure divine visions," Colm said to Gordon.

"Don't tell him!" Michael snapped. "He doesn't deserve to know!"

Colm glanced at his brother and continued, "I'm the fifth archangel of seven. Most Judaic-Christian worshipers know little about my existence or my true divinity. Lore considered me the angel of death, because at one time, I escorted human souls to Heaven after they died. That was before Lucifer fell, and the archangels became God's warriors against Hell's demons."

Wings rustled.

"After Lucifer fell and God created reapers, my divinity changed. I summoned reapers and told them where God wanted them to take souls instead of doing it myself. Then, God assigned angels to me."

Gordon looked at the others. "That's when you became their commander?"

"Aye."

"I thought you shepherded the Grigori angels?"

"That was later."

"What's this got to do with conjuring spells?"

Colm got up and went to the china cupboard where he kept his whiskey. He poured a glass and then leaned against the fireplace. "I taught my men how to listen for God's command when a human was dying, take the soul to its egress, and summon a reaper."

Colm drained his glass of whiskey. He ran his fingers over the facets of cut crystal; Joseph had given him the elegant glass. He refilled it, and continued. "God gave me another assignment. I became the archangel of divine visions. This was at a time when the children of man were unaware of their creator. It was my task to make them aware of God's existence."

The angels' released their auras to comfort themselves.

"I had no idea how to conjure divine visions. It had never been done before. This was thousands and thousands of years before what the children of man consider *The Calling of Abraham*. I had no guidance and no example."

The horrible memories gave Colm the urge to unfurl his wings. He struggled with continuing his confession. He looked at Fergus.

Fergus spiritually reached for his archangel. The other angels responded to Fergus' attempt to soothe Colm. Their bright auras dimmed a bit and their wings quieted.

Colm went on. "I was afraid to fail, and in that fear, I looked too far back in time for answers. I recalled man's fear of everything that surrounded them because they didn't understand why they were alive."

Colm drained his glass and poured more whiskey.

"I conjured spells using the incantations ancient man used to ask spirits for protection. I invoked not only my power but also God's power when I cast those spells on the children of man. Those divine visions—those spells—killed them. It was too much power for them to endure spiritually or physically. I killed thousands of them before I realized what I was doing."

Colm's wings unfurled. The delicate plumes swept over Joseph, Gordon, and Jeremiah. Silver crystals rained on everything in the room. The crystal glass slipped from Colm's hand and shattered on the fireplace hearth.

Michael and Joseph both rushed to Colm's side.

"Don't say anymore!" Michael cried. Tears spilled down his cheeks.

Colm flapped his wings like an injured dragon trying to keep from spiraling toward the ground. Joseph became caught in their movement.

The other angels' wings involuntarily unfurled. Their auras beamed like the rays of the sun.

Jeremiah screamed at Abe, Gordon, and Joseph, "GIT OUTTA THE HOUSE NOW! THE ANGELS IS LOSING CONTROL!"

Abe and Gordon ran to the front door, threw it open, and hurled across the porch into the yard.

Jeremiah screamed, "GIT OUT, JOSEPH! THEY'LL ACCIDENTALLY KILL YOU!"

Joseph was engulfed in the realm of the angels' pain. His senses could not process the ancient angst. His mind could not comprehend what the sons of God were thinking. He knew that his fragile humanity would die if he did not get away from them.

Without warning, he was yanked away from the angels' emotional realm. He suddenly found himself standing on the road in front of the farmhouse. Jeremiah took him by the wrist and pulled him further down the road.

The horses in the barn whinnied and kicked wildly at their stalls.

Gordon and Abe ran up the road, which if they ran far enough, would take them to Menotomy.

The farmhouse trembled and groaned.

Jeremiah jerked Joseph's wrist and screamed, "COME ON!"

A part of Joseph wanted to let the angels' power do what it would with his life, but he thought of his children, and his unfinished crusade for liberty.

The horses broke free of their stalls and stampeded the barn door. They galloped to the road and the woods beyond.

The blinding angelic light went out. The trembling farmhouse stilled.

Joseph started for the house. Jeremiah pulled him back. "Don't go in there yet. Give 'em time ta calm down. Let's git Abe and Gordon and corral the horses."

Joseph gave Jeremiah a doubtful look, but he nodded. They walked the dark road toward Menotomy under a waning crescent moon that did little to illuminate their way.

"Did they do that often in Burkes Garden?" Joseph asked.

"Only twice in the twenty-five years I've known 'em. They'd warned me about it, so I knew ta run if it ever happened. I was eighteen the first time I seen one of their fits. Patrick fell four or five hundred feet inta a ravine. The fall shoulda killed his human body, but he used his wings ta break the fall. His legs and hips was broken bad. Colm sensed 'im fall and had a fit. 'Course, the other angels did the same."

"Gordon called it a *fit,* too. There must be a better word for it."

"What word wou'd you use?"

"I do not know," Joseph admitted. "What happened the second time?"

"Liam was out wanderin' alone, and he went missin' for three days. None of the angels cou'd sense him. After the first day, the angels got themselves worked up. By the third day, they was in a tizzy. I finally found Liam unconscious in the woods on the other side of Garden Mountain. We ain't sure what happened ta him. That uncertainty didn't sit well with Colm, and I doubt he's let go of it all these years later."

The horses trampled ground foliage in the woods. They snorted softly from time to time, shadowing the men as they walked the road.

"How did you meet the angels?" Joseph asked.

Jeremiah conjured the bittersweet memory. "I was five. It was the first time my daddy let me go huntin' with 'im and my two older brothers, Jebediah and Israel. When we come up on the ridge of the mountain, we seen Colm and Michael huntin'. I seen their auras right off." He glanced through the darkness at Joseph. "Colm said you seen his aura right off, too."

Joseph said nothing.

An owl hooted from somewhere in the woods. The horses snorted.

"'Course, I didn't know what I was seein' then," Jeremiah said. "When we crossed paths with 'em my daddy stopped and asked 'em who they was. I was scared of Colm, although he didn't look at me once."

"Colm told me that you are the only human friend they have ever had before he met me."

"My family weren't never friends with 'em. I didn't see the angels again for eleven years."

Jeremiah breathed deeply and waited until he was sure he wasn't going to cry like a child. An owl hooted again. He stopped walking. Joseph stopped, too.

"My daddy and momma moved ta Burkes Garden before I was born. 'Course, the valley weren't called that then. Daddy said he murdered a man, and they had ta run. He wou'dn't tell me or my brothers when or why or where. One thing I *did* know was my daddy had once been a gentleman. He didn't talk like one no more, but 'im and Momma could read. They had nice Sunday clothes. There weren't nowhere to wear 'em. Hell, there weren't hardly no white people in the valley."

A filly trotted out of the woods on the west side of the road and startled Jeremiah and Joseph. Jeremiah eased up to her and grasped her reins. The horse stood serenely while Jeremiah went on.

"It was April 1751. I was sixteen. I didn't mind my daddy that morning. He told me ta feed the chickens and chop wood. Instead, I sneaked off ta meet a Shawnee girl who let me fuck her sometimes. When I came home that afternoon, my family was hangin' from trees by their ankles. Blood dripped from the ends of their fingers and from their gouged-out eyes and open mouths. It was obvious that my momma'd been raped."

Jeremiah's breath caught in his throat. He coughed.

Joseph remained silent. He tried to push the images from his mind, but they refused to go.

"My family'd been livin' among the Shawnee in the valley for twenty years by then. I had a real hard time believin' that the Shawnee had murdered 'em." Jeremiah wiped at his eyes. "Anyway, I cut 'em down from the trees, and tried ta make 'em look like they was restin' instead of dead. I started diggin' their graves. I couldn't hardly see what I was doin' because I was cryin' so hard. Then, the angels came walkin' out of the woods. They let me grieve while they buried my family. They *became* my family."

Jeremiah cried. Joseph thought that the cover of the near-moonless night gave Jeremiah the courage to cry in the presence of another man. It did not occur to Joseph that he had given Jeremiah that courage by merely listening.

A gelding carefully made its way through the underbrush and trees until it was clear of the woods. It stopped near the patient filly.

Jeremiah worked for a minute to get his tears under control before he said, "Turned out my family was murdered by a rogue Shawnee tribe that also terrorized the Shawnee livin' in the valley." He tried to make out Joseph's facial features in the darkness. "I got me a Shawnee woman back home. Her name's Mkwa. She's carryin' my child. Colm said it's a boy. I ain't never gonna see her again. I ain't never gonna meet my own child."

Joseph's words were so quiet that Jeremiah barely made them out. "Do whatever you must to return to them. My wife died two years ago. I shall never stop feeling the pain of her loss. Do not let Mkwa feel the pain of *your* loss."

Voices approached. It was Gordon and Abe. Jeremiah dried his eyes and cheeks with his shirt sleeve. He was thankful for the darkness that hid his tear-reddened eyes. The four men met and turned to walk back to the farm. Two more horses wandered out of the woods and followed them.

As they walked, Abe asked, "What are we going to do from here?"

"Convince the angels to touch the Sigil of Lucifer, and figure out a way to use it against the demons," Gordon said with surety. "I will find the right spells, and I'm going to make sure Colm casts them."

"Why *are* you doing this?" Joseph asked Gordon. "Was Michael's observation correct?"

Gordon snorted a laugh. "Michael's not far off the mark. I kill demons from Hell for revenge, but killing any kind of demon will give me satisfaction."

"Revenge?" Joseph asked.

"Years ago, a demon from Hell possessed my father and killed my family right in front of my eyes," Gordon said. "Revenge is all I got now."

"That is all I have, too," Abe said. He looked up at the night sky. "My wife died birthing twin girls twenty years ago. I never remarried as I was expected to. Every battle I fought in the French and Indian War was an act of revenge for what God did to her and my babies. The best thing that has happened to me since is meeting all of you and the angels."

Jeremiah said, "I warned Joseph, and now I'm warnin' you, Abe. Damned angels will talk posey then act like jilts."

As they approached the farmhouse, Joseph started to ask Jeremiah if it was safe for them to return then thought better of it because it made no difference. He intended on going inside the house regardless of the circumstances.

સ

Colm's confession had been the equivalent of stripping the angels' spirits naked. They were huddled in the living room like baby birds abandoned by their mother and left to weather a storm in their fragile unprotected nest.

With the horses settled in the barn, Gordon was anxious to finish what they had begun earlier in the evening, despite the unsteady look about the angels.

He picked up his sketch of the Sigil of Lucifer and handed it to Colm. "You can't spend years trying to figure out if you and your men can touch this. Let's kill some demons—in the next few weeks."

"Gordon's right," Fergus said. "We need to get on with this. I will touch it." He crossed the living room and reached for the sketch.

Colm intercepted him. "NO!"

"You are no longer my commander."

Wings rustled.

Joseph tried to gage Colm's reaction.

Jeremiah said, "We ain't goin' through another one of your fits, Colm. Git outta the way!"

To everyone's surprise, Colm backed down.

Fergus took the sketch from Gordon. He traced the lines of the sigil with his forefinger. When his spirit had no negative reaction, he pressed the sketch against his cheek. "I feel nothing," he said, as he concentrated on the sensation of the paper against his skin.

Gordon smiled. "Good! Now, we need to determine if it will kill a demon."

"And if it won't?" Fergus asked.

"Like I said before you angels had your fit, we will find a spell that will release Lucifer's evil to counteract God's evil."

All eyes in the living room shifted to Colm.

The farmhouse door swung open. No one recognized the man who strolled in. Jeremiah reached for his skinning knife. Joseph pulled a pistol from the pocket of his coat and released the sear. Abe and Gordon got to their feet.

Seamus ran at the intruder, knocked him down, and fell on top of him.

The other angels ran and piled on Seamus.

Colm graced everyone with a rare display of ecstasy. He leaped on the pile of angels and shouted, "Ian!"

274

THIRTY

ROXBURY, MASSACHUSETTS
MAY 1775

Abigail Adams said an apprehensive goodbye to John as he departed for the Continental Congress on May 4. He was tired and suffered from a cough.

On that same morning, Liam and Michael sat behind the barn on the bank of the rocky stream. Michael couldn't come to terms with how close Ian had come to dying. He coped with his dread by remaining close to Liam as if that would comfort his unhappiness and prevent Liam's death.

Liam looked at Michael out of the corner of his eye. "You have to stop this, Michael."

"Stop what?"

"Overprotecting me."

Michael picked up a stone and tossed it into the stream. "Why?"

"Because it will not change things."

Michael tossed another stone into the water. "Are ya afraid?"

"Yes."

"What scares ya the most about dying?"

"Being alone."

"Me, too." Michael picked up another stone and turned it over in his palm. "Have ya asked Ian what scared him the most?"

"No."

"Neither have I." Michael tossed the stone in the water.

Liam watched the water ripple from the small splash. *When I am dead, I will forget the shimmer of rippling water.*

Michael jumped to his feet, held out his hand to Liam, and said, "Come on."

Liam looked up. "Where are we going?"

The breeze blew Michael's loose curly black hair in dark clouds around his head. "We're going to ask Colm about taking ya to see her."

"Colm does not want us to travel without him."

"Then, Jeremiah can go get her. Colm can't stop him."

Although Michael had not said her name, reference to her worried Liam. He desperately longed to gaze into her comforting brown eyes, but he knew it was ridiculous to believe Abigail Adams could save him from the evil that was killing him. But he *did* believe. He recalled unfurling his wings and releasing his green aura in the Adams' parlor. He remembered Abigail's words, *"I will plead with John to speak with Colm on your behalf. I will beg him to have mercy because you were tempted by my sin."*

Liam grasped Michael's hand and slowly stood up. The effort it took was more than he expected. A burning sensation flared in his tired leg muscles. He remembered that Ian's human vessel had begun to hurt not long before his aura went out.

"Colm *can* stop him," Liam said. "And even if he could not, Jeremiah's absence would worry him. Why would you distress your brother like that?"

Michael's palimpsest scratched at his emotions. The last thing Michael or his palimpsest wanted to do was worry Colm. Yet, Michael felt compelled to do this for Liam.

Ian opened the farmhouse back door and crossed the porch. He was relieved to see that Michael was still shadowing Liam's every move. Ian remembered everything about dying until the day his aura went out. It had been excruciating. His spirit ached for what lay ahead for Liam.

Liam and Michael stared at Ian. His physical body looked so different now.

Ian's straight graying brown hair was in a thin queue that ran down his back to just below his shoulder blades. Ian's former vessel had been lean. This one was a little thicker. His eyes were dark blue instead of pale blue. But Ian's red aura was bright and strong.

When Ian reached them, Michael asked, "Where'd ya get that vessel?"

"In Salem. He was a crew member on the HMS *Lively*."

"He was British?" Liam asked.

"No, he was Irish, like my other vessel. He wasn't in the navy. He was a civilian crew member."

"Why'd ya take an old vessel like Fergus did?" Michael asked, wrinkling his nose.

Ian frowned. "He's not *that* old. He's forty-one. And when he was dying, I heard women say he was handsome, and they were going to miss his favors."

Liam smiled and shook his head. Ian had definitely come back to them.

Michael laughed. "It sounds like those women were whores. Did he die in a whorehouse?"

"No. The women were standing on the docks near where the ship lay at anchor. I guess they knew he was dying."

"How'd he die?" Michael asked.

"A lung ailment. Why're you asking me so many questions?"

Michael shrugged. He turned to Liam and said, "Come on."

"Where are you going?" Ian asked.

"I'm going to do something about Liam seeing Abigail Adams."

Ian raised an eyebrow.

Michael and Liam walked to the house. Ian followed them.

In the living room, Colm, Gordon, Jeremiah, Abe, and Seamus leaned over the table where they sat and watched Paul Revere etch the Sigil of Lucifer into the blade of Jeremiah's skinning knife.

"Colm, I need to talk to ya," Michael said.

Colm glanced up at him.

Liam sat on a couch. Ian sat at the table.

Michael tried again, "Colm, I need to talk to ya."

Colm kept his eyes on the knife and said, "Be quiet and sit down."

Michael sighed and flopped into the last empty chair at the table.

Paul held the knife up by its haft and twisted his wrist back and forth to examine his work. "That is the best I can do without my own tools." He handed the knife to Jeremiah.

"Michael, give Paul your blade," Colm said.

Michael pulled his curved surgical blade from his coat pocket and slid it across the table toward Paul. Then he asked, "Colm, can Jeremiah take Liam to see Abigail Adams?"

Silver light flashed in Colm's eyes.

"Liam's already dying," Michael pointed out. "She can soothe him."

Paul furrowed his brow. "What does that mean—she can soothe him?"

"Her and Liam are friends," Michael said. He didn't understand Paul's implication.

"Michael, stop it," Liam said. "I do not think I can make the trip to Braintree anyway."

"And I never volunteered," Jeremiah added. "But Michael's got a point." He looked at Colm and said, "I'll take 'im if you'll let 'im go."

"I am still waiting for someone to tell me what Abigail Adams would do to soothe Liam," Paul demanded.

"Don't go gittin' yourself worked up," Jeremiah said. "The angels meanin' of soothin' ain't what you think."

Jeremiah's answer satisfied Paul. He set to etching the sigil in Michael's surgical blade.

"Maybe Michael and Jeremiah *shou'd* take Liam to Braintree. If they run across demons, they could test the sigil etched in their knives," Gordon suggested. "Once William gets here and tattoos the sigil on their necks, Michael and Jeremiah and Liam will be ready for the test."

"Fuck ya," Michael said to Gordon.

Gordon was used to Michael's hatred for him. In the beginning, he took it in stride, but now Gordon wanted to understand and fix whatever it was he had done to anger Michael.

Colm flashed his eyes at Michael.

Michael rolled his eyes at his brother.

Horses' hooves clattered toward the farmhouse.

"There is William now," Abe said.

William and Joseph tethered their horses and came in the house.

William went to the table.

Joseph sat on the couch beside Liam. He noted Liam's tired blue eyes and asked, "May I touch your wound?"

Liam nodded.

Joseph tentatively touched the unhealed gash on Liam's forehead. The tissue around the gash was dark and felt spongy under Joseph's fingertips. The wound exuded a noxious smell. Having seen the symptoms of Ian's near death experience, Joseph recognized them in Liam. He asked, "Does your body hurt?"

"Yes."

Jeremiah got up and walked to the couch. "You doctorin' angels now?"

"If only I could."

"Michael thinks I shou'd take Liam to see Abigail Adams. What do you think?"

"Is that what you want, Liam?" Joseph asked.

Liam's eyes watered. This odd sensation was the first time his human vessel had shed tears. He nodded.

"You told me not to let Colm bear the burden of Ian's death alone. Tell me what I should do about letting Colm bear the burden of your death?"

"My death makes no difference," Liam said. "What Paul and Gordon and William are doing today to help us combat the demons is much more important. I am but one spirit."

Colm got up and went to Liam.

"Why can you not infuse Liam with more of your aura?" Joseph asked.

"I've told ya why."

Joseph's eyes searched the archangel's face. "Tell me again. And this time tell me all of it."

Colm glared at Joseph. "Why are ya making me say it again?"

"Perhaps, I need to convince myself that it is acceptable to let someone die, no matter the risk, when the preventative is at hand."

"Joseph, I have asked you before not to interfere in what goes on between Colm and me," Liam said. "Let it go."

Joseph's eyes remained on Colm's face.

Colm crossed his arms over his chest. He sighed, then said, "I did it in an act of desperation. I have no idea what will happen if I try again."

"And?" Joseph asked.

Colm's eyes flashed. "I couldn't control it. I think it will kill us both."

"Why was that so difficult to admit?"

"Can the two of you put a period to it?" Paul asked. "Your imaginary duel is very distracting."

Joseph and Colm exchanged one last look, and then let the subject drop.

Paul finished etching the sigil in Michael's surgical blade. He slid it across the table to Michael, and then started working on Seamus' new butcher knife.

Gordon pointed to his sketch of the Sigil of Lucifer and said to William, "This is the sigil we want you to tattoo on our necks. Start with Michael, Jeremiah, and Liam."

"You must be Gordon Walker; you're the only black man in the room," William observed.

"Is that how Joseph described me?" Gordon asked.

"Yes."

Gordon smiled. "Well then. I have distinction. So, Mr. Dawes, can you tattoo the sigil?"

William was wary, but his fellow Sons of Liberty seemed undaunted by the sigil. Paul was etching it and Joseph didn't react to Gordon's request.

"We shall see. I was able to find a book with a description of how tattoos are done in Polynesia. I am a tanner by trade, and I can tool leather—I assume the techniques are similar. Like Paul, I had to borrow tools because I cannot return to Boston to fetch my own."

Ian got up so William could sit beside Michael at the table. William removed leather-tooling instruments, a bottle of ink, and a quill from the bag slung over his shoulder. He chose a tool with a sharp point.

Michael gathered his hair and tied it back into a ponytail. He tilted his head to the left and offered the right side of his exposed neck.

"Are you certain you want the tattoo on your neck?" William asked.

"Aye."

"You will have to be vigilant about wearing a cravat; otherwise you will scare every human who sees the tattoo."

"Will ya just do it?" Michael snapped.

William reached for the sketch and put it on the table where he could see it. He punched tiny holes in Michael's skin while delivering ink to the holes with the quill. It was a makeshift method, but it worked.

A day later, the seven angels and three men who lived on the farm had the Sigil of Lucifer tattooed on the right side of their neck. Every knife in the house, whether it was used in the kitchen or for self-defense, had the sigil etched on its blade.

They had yet to find out if it was worth the effort.

The Hudson-to-Champlain corridor was the most direct line between New York and Quebec; an adversary who controlled it could sever New England from the rest of the colonies.

The French had understood this. In the summer of 1757, they chose to take a defensive position at Fort Carillon at the southern end of Lake Champlain. This intensified the British efforts to capture the fort. The following year, the French blew up Fort Carillon rather than surrender it to the British. The British took control of the post, renamed it Ticonderoga, and rebuilt it.

By the spring of 1775, Fort Ticonderoga had fallen into a state of disrepair. It was also severely undermanned. The prize of the fort was not just its strategic location, but also dozens of aging heavy cannons, howitzers, and mortars. Given the meager resources among the Americans, the armaments would make a treasure-trove of rebel artillery.

Fort Ticonderoga was a topic Hereford and Gage had discussed regarding resources.

Thomas, Henry, Robert, Captain John Brown, and the newly demon-possessed dead Captain Anthony Jameson were relaxing in the Province House living room over dinner drinks when the subject of the fort came up.

John lit his clay pipe then said, "I have heard talk that the rebels have turned an eye toward Ticonderoga and the cannon housed there."

"Yes, John. We have all heard that talk," Thomas said. "I sent a letter to the fort's commander telling him to be especially on guard. He is sparsely manned, and I believe there are also a number of women and children living within the walls."

"Do not be so modest, Thomas," Henry said. "Tell John the rest."

Robert choked back a smirk. There was nothing impressive to tell John.

Thomas sipped his claret. "I have sent a missive to the governor of Quebec advising him to send troops to the fort in ready for a possible rebel attack. And I have ordered British troops stationed there to hold themselves in readiness for Boston, on the shortest notice."

Henry smiled. "Such forethought is the characteristic of a truly remarkable general, do you not agree, John?"

Robert swallowed hard to keep from laughing.

Thomas frowned. *Is Henry making sport of me?*

"Well, yes…of course," John stammered. He puffed on his pipe and wondered, *what does the general find remarkable about that?*

Henry's vessel was dead; his offensive body odor was gone. He was a confident demon, but now, his confidence as a *human* had increased two-fold. He smiled brightly.

Captain Anthony Jameson said little that evening. The demon that once possessed British Lieutenant William Sutherland was engaged in adjusting to its new thirty-year-old vessel.

≈

As the conversation continued in the Gage home on Beacon Hill, a young Connecticut militia commander named Benedict Arnold was regaling the Massachusetts Provincial Congress and its president, Dr. Joseph Warren, with tales of the treasures at Fort Ticonderoga.

281

Whether the fort was on land that belonged to New York or New Hampshire was a highly contested debate. As a result of Arnold's story, the Massachusetts Committee of Safety sent a missive to New York noting the importance of Ticonderoga and claiming they would not infringe on the rights of their sister colony.

But Joseph and his cohorts did just that. They gave Benedict Arnold a temporary commission as a colonel, authorized him to raise a force for the specific purpose of capturing the fort, and financially backed the mission. The commission he carried was ironically signed by one of the Committee of Safety's most trusted members—Dr. Benjamin Church.

It was also a decision of dire portent. The congress' financial backing included 200 pounds of rebel gunpowder.

Abigail Adams' distress over her husband's health abated. She received a letter from him assuring her that he was well and looking forward to the proceedings of the Second Continental Congress.

With John away, her hands were full managing a household and a stream of constant visitors. The day a forty-year-old, scruffy, blond-haired, bearded mountain man, and two angels of God came to her doorstep, her already evolving definition of religion changed forever.

Abigail was not in the habit of answering the door. That task belonged to her houseman, Philomon Morris. But on a brilliant sunny morning in May, Abigail hastened to throw open the door of her home to the sound of a knock she knew belonged to the knuckles of an angel she so much wished to see again—Liam Kavangh.

She vaguely recognized Jeremiah from the incident at the meetinghouse in March. The young angel with curly black hair and beautiful facial features raised such a vague memory that she could not place him.

Neither Jeremiah nor the young angel stirred her emotions. She only had eyes for Liam, and she knew something was terribly wrong with him.

"Liam!" she gasped. She delicately took his hand. "Please, come inside."

The two-hour journey on horseback from Roxbury to Braintree had punished his tired body. When Abigail touched him, Liam felt a relief that he had not thought possible. His palimpsest longed to call her Mother, fall into her arms, and lay his dying head upon her bosom.

Abigail was not the mother who had given birth to him and suckled him. She was not the mother who had grieved for him after he and his brothers-in-arms died battling the Normans in Wexford, Ireland. No—he had no mother. He only had a father he called God, and his father had ruthlessly slapped his face and banished him from his home in Heaven.

His confused dying thoughts led him to collapse on Abigail's door step. Michael and Jeremiah reached to lift him into a standing position.

Abigail opened her arms and embraced a dying angel who needed her comfort to face the chains of eternal darkness.

Jeremiah and Michael helped Liam into the Adams' living room and laid him on the couch.

Philomon came to answer the knock on the door. Seeing that Mrs. Adams had already done so, he observed her visitors from where he stood near the bottom of the steps leading to above stairs. He eyed Jeremiah's and Michael's dirty deerskin and homespun clothing.

He entered the living room with the intention of ridding the Adams' household of the filthy swains. "Mrs. Adams, who are these men?"

"They are friends. Please be tolerant."

Philomon cast his suspicious fifty-year-old eyes on Liam. "What is wrong with *him*?"

Abigail hated Philomon's question. "Get out!" she shouted.

Philomon turned on his heel and left the living room. He was angered by her uncharacteristic behavior. *I will see to it that she regrets her actions in front of those swains. I have been with this household far too long to be treated in such a manner.*

"Mrs. Adams, I'm Jeremiah Killam, and this is Michael Bohannon," Jeremiah said.

Abigail looked at Michael. "Are you Colm Bohannon's brother?"

Michael was dumbfounded by her beauty and manners, rendering him speechless. He nodded.

"It took us a lot of talkin' ta get Colm ta agree ta let Liam come here. He don't want the angels out of his sight, partly because Ian Keogh came real close ta dyin' a few weeks ago."

"Ian is the angel with lovely pale blue eyes."

Jeremiah didn't want to explain why and how Ian came to occupy an-other vessel. He said, "Yes."

She turned her attention to Liam. His blue eyes were tired and dull. She ran a hand over the top of his dark hair and down his cheek. "Are you hungry?" She asked him.

"No."

"Perhaps some rum?"

"Yes."

"Mr. Killam, there is rum in the cabinet," Abigail said pointing to a mahogany breakfront. "You will also find glasses. Do you mind pouring a drink for each of us?"

Jeremiah did as she asked.

Abigail looked down at Liam and asked, "Are you dying?"

Liam cried and reached for her.

Michael's wings rustled. They had just gone through this with Ian. Sidonie had been able to save Ian because she possessed a part of his spirit. Abigail Adams had nothing similar to give Liam.

Jeremiah shoved a glass of rum at Michael. "Drink this. All of it. Then I'm gonna pour you another, and you're gonna drink all of that too. You ain't gonna run from this like you did when Ian was dyin'."

Michael guzzled the rum. He thought about how he had begged Colm to let him bring Liam to Abigail, and now that they were here, he was afraid. He heard children laughing from somewhere in the house. Their happiness made him want to cry.

Liam sat up and took the glass of rum Jeremiah offered. He looked at Michael and Jeremiah, and hoped they would understand that he wanted them to leave him alone with Abigail.

Michael understood. He drank the rest of his rum. The liquor emboldened him enough to ask, "Mrs. Adams, is there an inn nearby?"

Abigail regarded Michael's beautiful face. *The Bohannon brothers look so different. Yet they both love with fierceness.* She touched Liam's cheek, and then she crossed the room to Michael.

"I will take care of him if at all possible," she said in an effort to reassure him. "I have four children who will ask a multitude of questions about Liam and his presence in our home. My servants will gossip. But I assure you, John will understand."

Michael didn't understand what she was saying; only that she was being kind.

"But I have not answered your question. Solomon's Inn is on the north side of town."

"Liam can stay only a few days; then we have to get him back to Colm," Michael said.

Abigail saw love and fear in Michael's green eyes. She realized that she understood something about the angels she did not think possible. That epiphany was the pivotal turn in her religious beliefs. "You are such delicate and loyal beings. Why does mankind not know that about you?"

Michael felt a strange heat in his face. He glanced at Liam. He bit his lip and looked at Jeremiah.

Jeremiah said, "We're gonna go on ta the inn, Mrs. Adams. We'll come back tomorrow. Cain we leave Liam's horse here for tendin'?"

"Of course."

"If you see any orange eyes lurkin', send someone ta fetch us right away."

"So, you have not found a way to rid us of the demons?"

"We're workin' on that."

"And what does that entail?" Abigail asked.

"Our friend, Gordon Walker, thinks we cain use this sigil."

"He's not my friend," Michael muttered under his breath.

Jeremiah unwound his neck scarf. He tilted his head to the left and brushed his hand over the sigil tattooed on the right side of his neck.

"I do not understand."

"It's the Sigil of Lucifer," Liam whispered.

Abigail shied away from Jeremiah. Her eyes fell on each face in the room, then back to Jeremiah's neck. "I remember now. God's demons are chasing you. You intend on fighting evil with evil."

Jeremiah replaced his neck scarf. "If Gordon's right, that's exactly what we're gonna do."

Abigail shivered and said, "We are in much greater peril than we realize. I think it is well there are only a small number of humans who are aware of our angels and their demons. John told me that Joseph and Colm are very close now. Is that true?"

Liam's words were weak and tired. "They have become like brothers."

"As it should be," Abigail said with a smile. "Joseph is very near to our own angel on Earth."

Jeremiah said, "We shou'd be goin'."

Michael went to Liam. "What's happening to ya isn't what happened to Ian. The soul who was Liam Kavangh is gone, but he left behind traces of who he was. Joseph calls it a palimpsest. It's not what's killing ya. God's wrath is killing ya. So, let ya palimpsest feel her comfort."

Michael put his hands on Liam's cheeks. "Is Mrs. Adams able to see ya aura?"

"Yes, if I release it."

"If ya can't see his aura anymore, send for us right away," Michael told Abigail.

Abigail's lips quivered. She nodded.

When Jeremiah and Michael were gone, Abigail sat beside Liam on the couch. She took the empty glass from his hand and set it on the floor. He laid his head in her lap. She stroked his dark hair. He cried.

Her children watched from the doorway. They saw Liam release his weak green aura and unfurl his silver wings to comfort himself. Silver crystals dusted their mother and everything in the room. The crystals drifted under furniture and against the walls.

Two days later, Abigail was compelled to write to her husband. John would soon arrive in Philadelphia, and enter the State House where the Continental Congress was to convene.

Braintree, May 6, 1775

My Dearest John,

I write this in distress and in need of your wise guidance. By the time you receive this, and I in turn, receive your reply, it may be too late. But I must try.

The archangel's brother, Michael Bohannon, and their human friend, Jeremiah Killam, have brought a dying angel to our doorstep. It has taken me a day to remember that Dr. Samuel Prescott and Michael were attacked at the meetinghouse the day of Joseph's Boston Massacre oration.

If you recall, Liam Kavangh is the dark-headed angel who sat among us and jumped upon the pulpit platform to protect our dear Joseph from the demon. He is the angel that came to call on me in Boston, when you were away on a family matter.

I long to have you here so that I may express the things I now understand about angels, whom we as human beings have wrongly understood. But I suppose that is the topic of another conversation.

After losing our darling Suky at just two years of age, I have mothered the dying. How do I mother a dying angel? Liam clings to me as if he is a child. He cries and his body hurts. He is afraid and in pain.

I realize you are burdened with so many important decisions that will decide the fate of not only our children, but all who live in America. Still, I ask for your guiding hand to steady me and comfort a dying son of God.

How did we come to face such a thing? It is unbelievable, is it not? Our lives will never be the same. I look forward to your wise words of encouragement. I hope that you are feeling well, my darling.

Fondly yours and with love,

Abby

THIRTY-ONE

ROXBURY, MASSACHUSETTS

O n the morning of May 11, Jeremiah and Michael rode through the crowded provincial army encampments in and around Roxbury on their way home from Braintree. The troops disrupted the community. They cut down trees and tore down buildings for firewood. They drank to excess and often fired at one another and volleyed with the British. The bloody flux and lice ran rampant. Most of the residents had fled to safer areas.

"I wou'da thought that Fergus wou'd have better control of his men," Jeremiah said. He tilted his head toward a loud group of dirty drunken soldiers. "Look at 'em. They're brawlin'."

Michael looked, but said nothing. His concerns lay with Liam.

Jeremiah was relieved that they were able to pass through the encampments without incident, considering the combative atmosphere among not only the drunken men but also among the militiamen from different colonies. One strike of the temperamental flint was all it would take to pull Michael into a fight, if he was provoked.

They arrived home as Colm, Brandon, and Patrick were crossing the road in front of the farm to hunt in the woods. Jeremiah and Michael dismounted and tethered the horses. Ian and Seamus came out of the house. They all converged on the road.

"Did you leave Liam in Braintree?" Brandon asked.

Michael nodded. "He wanted to stay with her."

"You got no problem with us leavin' 'im there?" Jeremiah asked Colm.

When did we become not enough for him? Colm thought. *Is this because of his palimpsest's need for his mother?*

Colm searched for answers in the faces of the angels and thought, *Brandon hasn't exhibited a palimpsest. Patrick had only one, frightening, experience with his palimpsest. Michael's palimpsest is very active, and he's sensitive to its existence and desires in the angels who possess one.*

"I don't think Fergus has a palimpsest," Colm mumbled.

"Colm, you with us?" Jeremiah asked.

"What?"

"I asked you if you're fine with us leavin' Liam with Mrs. Adams."

"Aye."

"Why did Liam choose her to soothe him instead of us?" Brandon asked Michael.

"He didn't. His palimpsest did." Michael studied Brandon's face. "Ya don't have one do ya?"

"What do you mean?"

"Traces of what used to be, showin' through what exists now," Patrick explained. "Traces of memories left behind by the souls of the men who occupied our vessels before they died. I felt mine once, and I never want to feel it again." He grimaced.

"I remember," Michael said. "Ya experience with ya palimpsest was so horrible that ya collapsed."

"I'm confused," Ian said.

"Didn't ya hear what Patrick said?" Michael said, exasperated. "It's a memory a soul leaves behind. Liam's palimpsest is the memory of his mother's comfort. Liam's sick, and he needs that comfort. He sees Abigail Adams as a mother."

"Liam Kavangh's mother lived another twenty years after he drowned in Wexford," Colm interjected. "I don't think his palimpsest knows she's dead."

Jeremiah began to ask Colm how he knew that, and then stopped himself. Colm knew that for the same reason he knew that Jeremiah's unborn child was a boy. Archangels were the closest beings to God, and God was omnipotent.

"Is that what was killing you, Ian?" Brandon asked.

"No. Ian Keogh's soul was killing me. His human emotions were so painful that I couldn't bear them."

Patrick's eyes widened. "His emotions were killin' you?"

Ian considered the question. "His grief over the death of his family was killing me. I've never felt anything so agonizing. The loneliness, the guilt, the hopelessness, and what those things did to his soul and body."

Patrick frowned.

"What's wrong, Brother?" Seamus asked.

"I'm afraid that's what's gonna happen to me. When my palimpsest took control of me, I saw somethin' horrible. Me and Michael and Brandon was only eleven years old. Well, not us, but them."

"Don't talk about it," Michael warned.

Patrick continued anyway. "We was out huntin', and when we came home, our village was burnin'. We were frantic. I didn't know who among my loved ones was dyin'. I thought Seamus had left years ago with Ian, to fight with Colm, but I wasn't sure."

"Patrick, stop it!" Michael shouted.

"Let him talk," Colm insisted.

"NO!" Michael screamed. "Didn't ya hear what Ian said? Human grief was killing him. Why wou'd ya let Patrick conjure human grief?"

"This is the last time I'm going to warn ya to be quiet."

Michael pouted.

Patrick focused on Seamus' face. "I needed you, but I didn't know where you was."

Seamus embraced Patrick.

Patrick rested his chin on Seamus' shoulder and wrapped his arms around his brother's waist. A tear rolled down Patrick's cheek, and wet Seamus' shirt. The sensation of shedding tears, and the feeling of them on his skin was foreign to Patrick. His vessel had never cried—until now.

"I think the Cullens' and the Bohannons' parents burned to death. So did Brandon O'Flynn's sister. The smell of all those people and animals burnin' was…"

Seamus put his hand on the back of Patrick's head and pulled him in closer. The Cullens' wings rustled.

"Why am I the only one with that memory?" Patrick sniffed into Seamus' neck. "You don't remember that the Cullens' parents died in a fire?"

Seamus and Brandon exchanged sorrowful glances.

"No, Brother, I don't."

Patrick tasted the salt of his tears. He wiped his eyes and lips with the back of his hand.

"But I had a flash of a memory involvin' you the night we was guardin' John and Samuel at Reverend Clarke's house. The memory didn't belong to my spirit."

Patrick untangled himself from Seamus' arms and stepped back so he could see his brother's face.

A strange foreign mist stung Seamus' eyes. He blinked hard and looked away.

Ian listened without comment. He had taken care to ensure the human soul that occupied his new vessel was gone before he took possession, but he thought he had been careful to do so in 1169. His spirit was heavy with dread that he might suffer the agony of a human soul again. Now, his uncertain understanding of a palimpsest brought more weight for his spirit to bear.

Brandon sensed Ian's uncertainty, and said, "I remember how Robert Percy took you away from me in the woods, and I couldn't do anything to stop him. Then, when we were in Concord, at the Barrett farm, I told Samuel the demon that tried to kill you got to your spirit, and that's why you were dying."

He looked into the faces of his brotherhood with the same uncertainty Ian felt. "I didn't know Ian *wasn't* dying from the wrath of God. I didn't know the wrath of God wasn't the only thing that could kill us." He ran unsteady fingers over the tattoo of the Sigil of Lucifer on his neck. "What if Gordon's wrong about this? What if we don't know—?"

"—the extent of your vulnerability? Let us find out. Shall we?"

Jeremiah and the angels broke their circle and turned around. Ten men, with simmering orange eyes and muskets at the ready, were standing in a line across the road. The brotherhood's closest neighbor, Abijah Cunningham, was among them. He was the only man they recognized.

Abijah leveled his musket at Colm. "You have taken the advice of a black man who thinks you can battle God's demons with Lucifer's evil. This is an interesting development that is worthy of General Hereford's attention."

Colm kept his eyes on Abijah, stepped between Jeremiah and the demons, and said, "Walk away, Jeremiah."

"If Jeremiah moves, shoot him," Abijah commanded the demons. "In fact, if anyone moves, shoot them."

Wings rustled, and a breeze swept over the men standing in the road. It ruffled their hair and coattails in a momentary distraction.

Colm slipped his hand in his coat pocket, gripped the haft of the paring knife there, and whipped the knife at Abijah.

Abijah fired. The musket ball hit the cartridge box slung across Colm's chest.

Colm's blade hit its mark. The demon's eye flared and sparked. The sigil etched in the knife's blade had no extraordinary effect on the demon.

Abijah extracted the blade from his eye. He tossed it to the ground and grinned. "It appears the angel you call Brandon was correct. The sigil is worthless. Now, what will you do, archangel?"

Colm aimed his rifle at Abijah's undamaged eye.

"You know the man I possess is not dead." He smiled and swept his arm outward. "None of these men are dead. But…you *did* try to kill me with that filthy sigil so I suppose you do not care to protect the children of man as you once did. Shall we see if that is true?" the demon challenged. "Shoot the angels with the curly black hair!" he ordered.

"RUN!" Colm screamed at Michael and Patrick.

The boys took the order and ran into the woods.

Jeremiah, Ian, and Seamus fired at the line of demon-possessed men. The men returned fire. Abe and Gordon had been watching the confrontation from the barn. They both picked up their muskets and ran to help Jeremiah and the angels.

Colm shot Abijah in the other eye.

Abijah screamed in agony as the demon possessing him erupted into flames. The flames licked the skin off Abijah's face. His hair and clothing caught fire. He fell into a blazing, screaming heap on the dirt road.

Colm dropped the rifle and stared in horror at what he had done. William Sutherland's death had been nothing like this. His death had been swift and its impact didn't settle in Colm's spirit. Abijah Cunningham was burning alive. Colm fell to his knees and unfurled his wings. Heaven's silver crystals rained down on Abijah and wet the flames.

Colm felt the struggle Abijah's soul endured as his body died. When Abijah died, Colm escorted his soul to its egress and summoned a reaper.

The gossamer draped reaper stared accusingly at the archangel. *If you embrace the Sigil of Lucifer and it becomes potent, we will no longer hear your summons. When you can no longer help the dying, what will you have left?*

Colm dumbly returned the reaper's stare.

How will we reap the soul of the human being you love so dearly and ensure his entrance into Heaven, if we can no longer hear your summons? The reaper continued on to fulfill its appointed task and left the archangel to contemplate its questions.

"Colm, they're gone! Colm!"

Silver light flashed in Colm's eyes when he blinked. He saw Jeremiah, but he couldn't focus on what Jeremiah was saying.

"The demons suddenly dispossessed them men. The men ran like they seen Lucifer. Colm, are you hearin' me?"

Colm watched Ian kneel beside a dead young man lying in the road with his arms and legs splayed. The man, possessed by a demon only a few moments ago, was shot in the throat. Ian escorted his soul to its egress and summoned a reaper.

Colm couldn't stand to face another reaper's pronouncement of his failures. In his distressed state, he cried out for Michael and Patrick, but he didn't see them return to the road or hear them answer. The silence he perceived terrified him.

The words spoken by the demon that possessed Abijah Cunningham came flooding back into his consciousness. *You have taken the advice of a black man who thinks you can battle God's demons with Lucifer's evil. This is an interesting development that is worthy of General Hereford's attention.*

A horrible epiphany raped Colm's spirit. *I've been purposely distracted! Robert's going to hurt Joseph!*

He screamed at his men, "Go in the house and don't leave until I get back!"

Michael watched his brother's frightening emotional struggle, but he couldn't just run away and leave Colm alone with his terror. He went to Colm and asked, "What's wrong?"

Colm seized Michael by the shoulders and shook him, "Take the order!"

Ian heard the hysteria in Colm's voice and saw it in his eyes. Fear knotted his spirit, but he got to his feet and went to help Michael. "You're scaring us!" Ian shouted. "Let Michael go!"

"TAKE THE ORDER!" Colm screamed at Michael. His attention shifted to Ian. He released Michael and seized Ian by the shoulders and shook him. "Tell me ya understand!"

Ian's dark blue eyes watered with fear. "I understand!"

"GO! NOW!" Colm thundered.

The brotherhood and the men fled for the shelter of the farmhouse.

Colm's rage caused his body to tremble uncontrollably. When his fury calmed enough that he was sure he wouldn't spook the horse, he picked up the paring knife Abijah had tossed to the road. Then, he mounted the filly Michael rode from Braintree, and spurred the horse into a gallop toward Worcester and the home of Dr. Elijah Dix, where Joseph was visiting his children.

꙳

"Stop it. Do you want the household to hear us?"

"I want you to show me how much you have missed me."

She kissed him and ran her hand down his smooth naked chest to just below his belly button.

A playful frown touched Joseph's lips when he looked into her brown eyes and asked, "That's the extent of which you have missed me?"

She feigned a pout.

He produced a villainous smile, and his radiant blue eyes lit up Mercy's world.

Joseph lifted his head from the pillow, wrapped a hand around the back of her neck, and kissed her hard on the lips. "Show me," he breathed.

She slid her hand between his legs.

He embraced her and pulled her on top of him.

She spread her legs and guided him to the warmth of her womanhood. She sat up and he slipped inside her.

His ambitions, perplexities, anger, and stalwartness in the face of a rebellion were forgotten. Angels, demons, rebels, and the British no longer existed. At that moment, he was only a man with urges.

Mercy bent to kiss his lips. His tongue found hers, and after a moment she pulled away and sat up. She prayed to God to give her Joseph's child. Her hips undulated to the rhythm of her lust until it was satisfied. Then, she changed her pace and pleased him.

He reached for her breasts and squeezed them hard. His hands moved to her cheeks. His fingers slid through her hair and entangled in the brown locks. Joseph's orgasm released the pungent odor of everything he had kept bottled up inside. Although the smell was odd, Mercy inhaled it deeply.

She relaxed and slipped her body over his; relishing the feel of her nipples as they brushed his chest. She kissed his neck and the curve of his shoulder. The result of his orgasm seeped from between her legs. It rolled slickly down her inner thighs and wet his hips. She sighed and burrowed into the warmth of his body.

He wrapped his arms around her. They drifted into sleep.

In the wispy fog of the early morning hours of May 11, Joseph gently urged Mercy off his chest. He had to return to his bedroom in Dr. Elijah Dix's home without arousing Dr. Dix or his wife, Dorothy's, suspicions.

Breakfast gave Joseph the opportunity to be with his children. When Joseph arrived at the Dix's home last night, his children were asleep. Now, the joy he and his children experienced at seeing one another reminded him of Michael, Brandon, and Patrick's reaction to Colm's initial arrival at the farm in Roxbury.

Elizabeth could not sit in her seat at the table. She wanted desperately to share with her father the rapture she felt when the angels came to rescue her and her siblings from Boston. At last, she got up and skipped around the table to where Joseph was sitting. He reached for her and enfolded her in his arms, much to the disapproval of Dorothy Dix.

In Dorothy's opinion, children should sit quietly during meals. Dr. Warren's indulgence for his children sparked a pang of jealousy in Dorothy's longing heart. Her husband had little interest in her. Their two young children were the result of the rare nights Elijah was able to get and keep an erection under the influence of rum.

Elijah Dix smiled at Joseph's lively interaction with his children at the table. Before dawn, he heard Mercy's and Joseph's moans of sexual satisfaction. The sounds were delightful. Elijah masturbated to the fantasy of their ecstasy while his wife slept beside him. For the first time in weeks, he was able to achieve an orgasm.

Joseph was aware of Elijah and Dorothy Dix's ruminations at breakfast. Their assumed discretionary glances at Mercy and he, satisfied Joseph's prodigious need for the shocking.

After breakfast, Joseph gathered his children around him. "I must go back to Cambridge."

"But, Father, you just got here," young Joseph whined. "I wanted you to play nine pins with me."

"Yes, Father, nine pins!" Richard exclaimed as he jumped up and down.

"It is a very long ride back to Cambridge," Joseph explained. "If I do not leave now, I may have to ride in the dark."

Mary plopped a thumb into her mouth and looked up at her father with adoring blue eyes. Joseph kissed the top of her blond head.

"Father, I wanted to talk to you about the angels," Elizabeth whispered.

Joseph smiled and said, "Betsey, we will talk about them the next time I see you. I promise." He kissed her on the cheek.

She returned his smile and nodded. She was afraid to ask how long it would be before he would return for a visit, for fear of his answer.

Joseph picked up his packed saddlebag from the floor. He looked at his children and Mercy for a moment before he said to Dr. Dix, "Thank you again for taking care of my family during this difficult time. I will send you more money next month."

Elijah clasped Joseph's hand and patted him on the back. "Take care, and Godspeed!"

Joseph remembered wishing William Dawes Godspeed the night he sent him to Lexington. So much had changed since then.

He glanced at Mercy one last time and walked out of the house. He mounted his horse and urged it eastward to Cambridge.

At three o'clock that afternoon, four hours into his journey, Joseph took a lonely horse trail north of the town of Newton. As he left Newton behind, he saw a single rider approaching from the east, and dressed in the brilliant scarlet coat of a British officer. Robert Percy slowed his horse and blocked Joseph's way on the trail.

Joseph recognized the demon right away. Fear rolled through Joseph's mind, but it didn't touch his heart. He spurred his horse and tried to go around him.

Robert's eyes flared. The flames rose like giants who held fireballs in their huge hands. They tossed the fireballs in front of Joseph's horse. The filly reared in fright and spilled Joseph from the saddle onto the dirt trail.

Joseph stood up and brushed the dirt from his coat. His fearless eyes exuded hate.

Robert saw his foolish bravado. "You cannot stop me any more than you can stop the British army. Yet, you stand there as if God has given you the power to do so."

Joseph attempted to mount his horse. Robert jumped from his saddle and intercepted him. They stood on the road facing one another. The heat from Robert's flaming eyes flushed Joseph's cheeks.

"You have been to visit your family. They *love* you, do they not?" Robert mused. He said the word love as if it left a vile taste in his mouth. "Does Mercy know that you have impregnated another woman?"

This was news to Joseph. He tried to control his reaction, but it got the better of him. He felt his heart quicken.

Robert doused his eyes. He stepped in closer to Joseph. "You do not know." He howled a laugh. "I am surprised the archangel has not told you because he knows."

Joseph closed his eyes for a moment. What he did with Margaret Gage was nothing more than an impulsive act. She came to him seeking a carnal need, and he was more than happy to fulfill it. They had been intimate. That was all. He opened his eyes.

"Why do you stand there speechless?" Robert asked. "From what I have heard, you are never at a loss for words."

"What do you want from me?"

"I want to see terror distort your handsome face. I want the people who idolize you to see your nasty flaws. Shall I call on Mercy so we can discuss the woman who carries your fifth child? That child is the child Mercy prayed you would give her this morning when you fucked her."

Joseph tried not to let doubt seep into his words. "Tell her what you want. It will make no difference because she will see through your lie just as I do."

"Is that so? Then, you are not seeing clearly."

"I will not stand here and listen to the words of an abomination like you."

Robert whipped out his right arm and wrapped one white-gloved hand around Joseph's throat. "I cannot kill you because Henry has forbidden it. But I can do *anything* else I please."

Joseph knocked Robert's hand away. He clinched his teeth and said, "You are a coward."

Robert leaned in closer to Joseph. "You assume you can speak to me like I am a human man, and I will cringe at your insults and challenges."

"Have you come here to harass me for the sport of it? Do you not have something better to do?"

Robert deflected the question. "Do you know that you have caught the attention of God's most powerful demon because you have befriended an archangel? Do you know that Henry despises you?"

Joseph ran a hand across his mouth, uncertain how to respond.

Robert pulled his saber from its scabbard and flipped the sharp tip to rest against Joseph's left eyelid. He let the saber tip travel down Joseph's cheek. It left a thin line of blood as it grazed the skin. The saber's tip dropped to Joseph's throat, and sliced his cravat.

"Henry despises a certain Scottish major as well. His name is John Pitcairn. I believe you have met him. It was his vanguard that fucked up and marched the wrong way across Lexington Green. Henry did not like Pitcairn's lack of humility."

"Why should I care?"

"Perhaps, I spoke too soon, and you should not care." The saber dropped to Joseph's chest.

Joseph punched Robert in the jaw.

Robert's head snapped back. He felt pain shoot through his neck and jaw. Henry's order not to kill Joseph Warren was forgotten. He flipped the saber and rammed it at Joseph's chest. The tip of the blade penetrated the breast of Joseph's coat and clothing and grazed his chest.

Despite the saber tip buried in his coat, Joseph turned to run for his horse.

Robert seized him by the upper arm. Joseph tried to get away, but the demon's grasp was bruising and debilitating.

Green light flooded the trail and the surrounding woods. A horse galloped toward them. Colm reined the horse and jumped from the saddle with the paring knife in his hand. The Sigil of Lucifer, etched in the blade, glowed in the green light.

Robert was taken by surprise, but he thought the archangel would not detonate his deadly golden radiance and risk disintegrating his pet. Still, Robert was afraid. He was unsure of the extent of the archangel's powers. He tightened his grip on Joseph's upper arm.

The demon's grasp was so painful that Joseph thought his humerus had fractured.

Colm charged Robert.

Robert jerked Joseph in close and shifted his arms so that one was locked around Joseph's neck. He splayed the fingers on his free hand, dug them into Joseph's cheeks and squeezed.

"I will break his neck, if you do not halt this minute!" Robert shouted at Colm.

Colm kept coming. He jumped Robert and knocked him to the ground. Joseph fell with Robert. Colm stabbed the knife, up to the hilt, into one of Robert's orange eyes.

Robert's eye flared. He howled in anger and lost his grip on Joseph's neck.

Joseph crawled away and got to his feet. He saw a halo of golden light surrounding Colm's body. The light flashed and brightened. He braced himself for death.

Then, Joseph heard shouts and saw men rush past him. They attempted to pull Colm off Robert. Amid the confusion and the shouting, Joseph tried to cope with the sudden shift in what was happening. He stood on the trail dumbfounded and wondering where the men had come from.

He realized Robert had pushed himself backward and out of Colm's reach. Joseph fell to his knees in front of Colm and put his hands on Colm's cheeks. "LOOK AT ME!" Joseph screamed. "REIN IN YOUR ANGER! I AM FINE!"

Colm saw and heard Joseph. His golden light dimmed. Then, he realized Robert was escaping. Colm scrambled to his feet.

As Robert hooked the toe of his boot into a stirrup and threw himself into the saddle, Colm seized the horse's reins. His eyes flashed silver light. "Tell Henry this ends now. Tell him I'm coming after him, and I *will* kill him no matter the destruction of human life."

Robert sneered. "Words, preceptor. That is all they are. You and your men are not capable of purposely killing the children of man, even if your human friends agree to die alongside you."

Joseph joined Colm. With Joseph so near to Robert, Colm felt his restraint slip. He tightened his jaw and forced his wings to stay furled. He released the horse's reins.

Robert smirked at Joseph. "We are not done yet, Warren."

He tugged on the reigns and turned the horse eastward. Then, he halted the horse and looked at Colm.

"By the way, the sigil etched in your knife is worthless because you are still bound to Heaven, even after God turned his back on you."

Robert spurred his horse toward Boston.

Colm looked at the bewildered men who had come to break up the fight. With stunning clarity, he realized, after millenniums of running, suddenly everything had changed. The angels were friends and allies with the children of man, and no longer merely soothers and beholders.

Joseph and Colm rode to Roxbury under the pink and blue sky of early evening. The happiness, safety, and future of those who depended on the archangel and the patriot doctor weighed heavily on them. And now, Joseph carried a new weight.

"Why did you not tell me?" he asked Colm. "Why did I have to hear it from a demon?"

"I failed to stop my flock of angels from creating God's forbidden children. I won't involve myself with ya forbidden child."

Joseph threw Colm a sideways glance. "So, she *is* carrying my child."

"Aye."

"Do you think I was irresponsible?"

"That's a human trait I don't understand."

"Then why—?" Joseph's voice faltered. "You did not tell me because you thought you were protecting me."

Colm saw the darkening bruises Robert's fingers had left on Joseph's cheeks and neck. The bruises stirred his simmering anger.

Joseph smiled. "What I did with Margaret is forbidden, but the British are not going to kill me for it. They have better reasons to kill me."

"That's not amusing. If Robert knows about ya child that means Henry knows. They might kill Margaret and ya child for the sport of it."

Joseph winced. If Henry told Thomas Gage, Joseph could only hope that Gage did not punish Margaret. He did not think that would happen because Gage had a reputation for adoring his wife. It was more likely Robert would kill her. Joseph was helpless to ensure the safety of his own child.

He felt Colm's scrutinizing eyes on him.

"I know what ya are thinking," Colm said. "I can't protect ya or ya children unless this is over. I told Robert that I intend on ending this demonic war, and I mean it."

"How do you intend on doing that?"

"I need to make us stronger. Gordon's right. I need to cast a spell over the Sigil of Lucifer to make it work against demons."

"Will he be able to find one for you?"

"No."

"Then what will you do?"

Colm struggled to say the words. Just the thought of them inflicted agony upon his angelic spirit. He wondered if his brother, Lucifer, had suffered in the same way before he fell and finally rejected Heaven.

Joseph saw the fear in Colm's eyes. "Whatever it is, I will not let you face it without me."

"I *can't* face it without ya. I don't know if my angels can face it at all. I don't know what it's going to do to us. It might weaken us. It could kill us. Or God might decide to kill us himself."

Colm's voice cracked. His jaw was so tight that he had to concentrate on relaxing it so he could continue. Finally, he said, "We must reject Heaven in favor of the children of man."

Joseph imagined being forced to turn his back on the patriots and side with the British under the threat of death. He would choose death. But what Colm intended on doing was the opposite. The angels would be choosing life without knowing the cost.

"Are you sure that is your only choice?"

"Aye. Robert knows Heaven is holding us back. I don't know why I didn't see that a long time ago."

"It seems Robert knows a great many things," Joseph sneered. "You should have killed him today. I was ready to die, but then those men came and I could not—"

"—let me kill them, too?" Colm gave Joseph a pained look.

"Yes."

"There's going to be human collateral damage if I'm to end this."

"That has become clear. Now, tell me, how will you reject Heaven?"

"We'll have to conjure a spell. The eight of us will have to do it together. Liam's in Braintree with Abigail Adams. He's real sick. I'm afraid if we take him from her, he won't survive. His palimpsest sees her as a mother, and he's clinging to her like a child."

"If you explain the importance of what you are doing, surely he could part from her for a few days."

"I don't know if he can."

"I do not mean to sound uncaring, but I must return to Cambridge. I need to write to Samuel and the Continental Congress, and insist that Massachusetts be allowed to form her own civil government. Furthermore, I must impress upon the congress that they have to appoint a general to take control of the provincial army. The men who make up the army come from towns throughout Massachusetts, Connecticut, and New Hampshire. They are clannish and suspicious of those they do not know. We need someone to establish order among those disjointed factions. We need someone the other generals, such as Fergus and Artemas Ward, can look to for colony-wide guidance."

Colm stared into the face of ludicrousness. She had dragged Joseph and him into her den of iniquity.

"When you are ready, send for me and I will come immediately," Joseph said.

"How much can ya bear before ya collapse?"

"I could ask you the same question."

"I was created to bear impossibly heavy burdens. Ya weren't."

"You cannot believe that, Colm. Not after everything we have faced together, and all that we have yet to face."

Thirty-Two

Colm's panicked orders and subsequent departure scared the angels. They huddled in the farmhouse confused and afraid for themselves and their archangel. Colm had given them no explanation, but they assumed it had something to do with Joseph's safety.

Jeremiah and Abe dragged the two dead men to the barn to keep them out of sight until they could be buried. When they returned to the road with Gordon to make sure they had not overlooked incriminating evidence, they saw several dozen volunteer soldiers from the provincial army camp walking toward the farm in response to the earlier sound of musket fire.

There was no denying muskets were fired. The smoke and the smell of gunpowder hung heavy in the stagnant air. The reason for it required lying; something the angels were incapable of doing.

"Why didn't Fergus stop them from coming out here?" Gordon asked Jeremiah.

"I got no idea. I ain't his nanny."

"Let me talk to them," Abe said. "Everyone knows they drink a bottle of rum a day and are usually rowdy. I think a similar story about what happened here will satisfy them."

The soldiers did, indeed, look drunk, except one young man who stepped forward and identified himself as Captain Amiel McCurdy; he seemed only marginally drunk.

Captain McCurdy assessed his surroundings. He saw nothing threatening—just an ordinary farm and three countrymen standing in the road. "What happened here?"

"A drunken friend of ours and his cohorts came by looking for a fight," Abe said. He jerked his head at Gordon. "Our friend does not like Gordon because he is a free black man. When he gets drunk, he rides over here and shoots at him."

A man standing near the front of the group pointed at the musket in Gordon's hand and said, "It appears that Gordon was shooting back."

There was scattered laughter among the soldiers.

Jeremiah's eyes darted from one man to another. They looked bored and restless, like a fight was just what they needed to break the tedium of sitting around all day waiting for action. Jeremiah reminded himself that these men where fellow rebels who posed no more threat than a drunken brawl.

"We were afraid the regulars were marching into Roxbury and killing Americans," Captain McCurdy said. He looked disappointed knowing that was not the case. "Do you belong to one of the companies come to join the army?"

"No," Abe said. "We live here, but if there is call to fight, we will answer it."

Jeremiah saw several men put a bottle to their lips.

"We thank you for coming out here, but we need to get back to the work we were doing before our friend arrived," Abe said to Captain McCurdy.

"I'm curious. Who is this man you consider to be your friend?"

The angels watched from the living room windows.

Gordon and Jeremiah exchanged glances.

Abe smiled broadly. "General Fergus Driscoll is a close friend of ours. He knows our unruly friend. Have you heard rumors about General Driscoll? Rumors about who he is?"

Ten men broke off from the group and walked away.

Captain McCurdy's stomach lurched. He willed his eyes to remain on Abe's face. "My company is from Hartford, Connecticut, but yes, we have heard the rumors."

"Those men who just walked away believe the rumors. You also believe the rumors."

Amiel McCurdy nodded.

The sound of hooves pounding the road grew closer. A cloud of dust surrounded the horse hurtling toward them from the west. Colm's hair was free of its queue, and it flowed in streamers away from his face. His unbuttoned coat billowed like a sail. His eyes were bright with urgency.

Abe saw, with satisfaction, Amiel McCurdy's eyes widen when he looked at the horse's rider.

Gordon and Jeremiah breathed a sigh of relief.

The thunderstruck Captain Amiel McCurdy and his eleven remaining men breathed, "Oh…my…God."

Colm slowed his horse and dismounted.

The soldiers from Connecticut sobered and fell to their knees.

Michael threw open the farmhouse door and ran to his brother. Without regard to the kneeling humans, he jumped on Colm and threw his arms around him. Colm hugged Michael tight. Michael sensed anxiety and fear in his brother's spirit. It scared him worse than Colm's panicked behavior earlier in the day.

The brothers let go of one another.

Colm considered the kneeling men. He looked at Gordon, Abe, and then Jeremiah. They smiled and shrugged.

"Get to ya feet," Colm said to the kneeling men.

The men shivered at the sound of Colm's voice.

The man closest to Colm began to cry.

Another man lowered his head, and begged, "Please, God, have mercy on us."

"I'm not God," Colm said. "Get to ya feet!"

"He emanates green light," Captain McCurdy murmured.

"Let's go inside," Colm said to his brotherhood. He nodded toward the soldiers from Connecticut. "I can't soothe them. They'll leave eventually."

Darkness wrapped her arms around the farm. Colm tried and failed to hide his anxiety and exhaustion while they ate dinner. His men had not eaten since the night before, and despite their archangel's spiritual state, they wolfed down their meal.

After dinner, Colm walked outside to make sure none of the humans were still kneeling in the road under the belief that he was God. The road was deserted. Captain Amiel McCurdy and his company from Connecticut left Roxbury that night, and never returned.

Everyone looked at Colm when he walked in the house. The living room was silent except for the sound of embers popping in the fireplace. They were waiting for him to explain why he had left them in a panic.

Patrick and Michael sat together on a couch, drinking excessive quantities of rum. The others were gathered around the big table, also consuming great quantities of alcohol.

"Robert attacked Joseph on the road just east of Newton," Colm said. He took the jug of rum Patrick was holding, poured a healthy drink into his tankard, and handed the jug back. "He sent those demons here to distract me so he could have his fun without interruption. I got there before he could do little more than leave bruises on Joseph's face."

"Robert touched Joseph?" Ian asked, appalled.

"Aye." Colm drained most of the rum in his tankard and shoved it toward Patrick for a refill.

Jeremiah got up and made eye contact with Colm. "You scared your angels ta death. Don't say it ain't none of my business, because it is. You didn't have ta make up a story ta satisfy them men who came here. Abe did. You didn't have ta worry about them same men maybe causin' a fight because they didn't like the color of Gordon's skin. I did. You didn't have ta bury Abijah Cunningham and the other dead man. Me and Gordon did."

Colm's jaw tightened.

"We expect you ta protect Joseph because he's one of us, but you could've said why and where you was goin'."

"Are ya done shaming me?" Colm asked.

"Damn archangel," Jeremiah spat. "Sometimes, talkin' ta you is like talkin' ta an infant. You're lookin' at me, but you ain't hearin' me."

Colm let Jeremiah finish, then said, "Gordon, ya are right. The sigil requires a spell."

"I thought so. We have to find one that will counteract God's wrath."

"How're we going to find a spell like that?" Brandon asked.

"I have a grimoire a witch living in Providence gave me ten years ago," Gordon said. His eyes lit up with thoughts of the past. "Her name was Phoebe. She was a young, black-skinned beauty who gave me a lot more than a grimoire. I would have stopped chasing demons and stayed with her forever if…"

Ian got up from the table and took the steps to above stairs. The ceiling in the living room creaked under his heavy footfalls. Then, they were silent.

"Was it something I said?" Gordon asked, surprised.

Seamus' eyes darted at the ceiling. "Sidonie's death is beginnin' to weigh on his spirit."

"Maybe, he didn't want to hear Gordon talking about fucking a woman and having to picture it in his mind," Michael retorted.

Rum spurted from Patrick's mouth, and he nearly choked laughing.

Brandon burst into laughter. Beer slopped out of his mug and soaked the front of his shirt.

Colm let the boys laugh and carry on. He was afraid that what he was about to say would silence their light-heartedness for a long time—if not forever. When the boys calmed down, he called for Ian.

Ian dragged himself down the steps and sat on the bottom riser.

"We can't use a witch's grimoire," Colm explained. "Those spells aren't for angels. Even if they were, we couldn't concoct one strong enough to accomplish what we need to do."

"Get on with it, Colm, before we all go crazy from watchin' you sulk over what's goin' on in your head," Jeremiah grumbled.

Colm sighed. His eyes flashed. "We must reject Heaven in favor of the children of man."

Wings rustled and a breeze swept through the living room. The angels released their auras. The human men squinted against the blinding light.

Seamus and Brandon knocked their chairs over backward as they jumped to their feet. Ian put his head in his hands. Michael and Patrick sat drunk and dumbfounded.

"Why would you even consider doin' that?" Seamus asked, incredulously. "You got no idea what that'll do to us!"

"Where did you get the notion that we need to reject Heaven?" Brandon demanded.

"I know it weren't Joseph's idea," Seamus growled. "He wou'dn't never say somethin' like that."

Colm didn't want to answer. His angels were already shaken, but he knew they'd continue to ask him where he got the notion, so he forced himself to respond. "I got the notion from Robert. He said the sigil would never work because we're still bound to Heaven."

"You listened to a demon?" Gordon was stunned.

"Robert's right," Colm said. "We can't fight God's wrath because we're still Heaven's messengers."

Tears rolled down Ian's cheeks. The spiritual burden he had begun to carry over Sidonie's death was heavy. Compounded with his fear of suffering a human soul again, he was certain he would never be able to shed those burdens if he rejected Heaven.

"What if we reject Heaven, and we ain't angels no more?" Patrick asked. He stumbled to his feet. His wings unfurled in response to his apprehension.

Michael grasped Patrick's arm and pulled himself up. He couldn't conjure a single rational thought in regard to what his brother had said.

"I know ya are scared," Colm said. He swallowed the dread rising in his throat. "We can't go on like this anymore. Our war with the demons must end. Otherwise, where will we go? Back to Burkes Garden? Or some other isolated place where we'll continue to hide from our fear?"

He looked at Jeremiah. "Ya told me when we moved to the farm that my boys were tired, and they *are* tired. I'm tired."

"You're suggestin' we kill ourselves," Patrick stated.

Michael's wings unfurled.

Colm was stunned by Patrick's clarity. He hadn't thought of it that way.

"What about Fergus and Liam. Don't they have a say in this?" Brandon asked Colm.

"We can't do it without them. It has to be a spell conjured and chanted by all eight of us. Maybe, if we reject Heaven, Liam won't die. Maybe, if we reject Heaven, we'll be able to throw off the chains that bind us, once and for all."

"What about Joseph and the other patriots we've formed a friendship with?" Seamus asked. "Are we gonna be able to protect them from Henry if we reject Heaven?"

"If we reject Heaven and counteract God's wrath, we may be so much stronger than we are now." Silver tears brimmed in Colm's eyes. "We have to have the courage to walk a different road because the road we've been walking hasn't gotten us anywhere. We're still scared and weak and unsettled. Do ya think I would purposely do anything to hurt any of ya? Ya are my family."

Ian's muffled sobs set off Michael. He laid his head on Patrick's shoulder and cried.

"Things have changed," Colm said. "Our family has changed. The children of man have joined our family. I know rebellion is a strange concept to angels, yet we've been participating in it with the children of man."

Seamus stroked his beard thoughtfully. His epiphany felt warm and strong within his spirit. "The patriots have rejected their motherland. Did that make them weaker? Did that make them someone they ain't? Did that take away their humanity? No, it didn't. In fact, I'd say it made them stronger."

Ian raised his head. He thought of the passion and fire he saw in Joseph's eyes when he delivered his oration commemorating the Boston Massacre. John Hancock and Samuel Adams had been hiding in Lexington the night of April 18, but their enthusiasm for the rebellion they were stirring resonated in their voices when they spoke.

"Seamus, you might be right," Ian said. He wiped the tears from his cheeks.

Wings rustled and the bright light dimmed.

Brandon saw the wisdom of Seamus' words. He said, "I'll fetch Fergus in the morning."

"Let's wait until we bring Liam back from Braintree," Colm said. "I'm going so I can speak to Mrs. Adams. The rest of ya can choose to go or not."

Michael wiped his wet cheeks on Patrick's shirtsleeve and said, "Me and Patrick are going."

Jeremiah watched Michael drying his cheeks, and was struck by Michael and Patrick's physical resemblance. It wasn't a new concept, but somehow, at that moment, it felt different.

He said, "I'll go."

Ian and Brandon chimed in at the same time, "Me, too."

"Me and Gordon do not need to go," Abe said to Colm. "Someone shou'd stay here. How long do you think you will be gone?"

"That depends on Liam's condition and how fast he can travel."

As the noose of the siege tightened around Boston, fresh provisions for its soldiers and citizens, as well as fodder for its livestock, became increasingly scarce. General Gage turned his attention to the many islands that dotted the reaches of Boston Harbor.

In the last week of May, Gage ordered four sloops to sail to tiny Grape Island near the town of Weymouth to pick up some recently harvested hay. The appearance of this little British fleet along the shores of Weymouth immediately created concern among the local inhabitants. Believing this a prelude to a full-scale invasion; people living along the coast south of Boston began to flee into the countryside.

The angels and Jeremiah found themselves caught up in this situation as they rode to Braintree. Alarm guns were firing in Weymouth and Braintree, causing several thousand militiamen to gather on the Weymouth shores. The angels and Jeremiah gathered with them.

Although they were out of musket range, the militia began firing on the British regulars as they gathered hay from Grape Island and loaded it on board the sloops. One of the sloops fired a few rounds from its swivel guns, but the balls flew over the rebels' heads.

The alarm and the sound of guns spurred Fergus to dispatch three companies from Roxbury to the Weymouth shore. When the companies arrived, Joseph was with them.

He saw Colm and his men sitting on horseback watching the skirmish and ready to participate, if the need arose. Joseph rode to meet the angels.

"I did not expect to see you here," Joseph said to Colm. He looked out across the sparkling water at the regulars loading hay. "We will put a stop to this and take care of Elijah Leavitt's audacity to sell his hay to Gage. Leavitt's done this before."

"I suppose that means ya will be burning his hay as soon as ya can get to the island," Colm quipped.

Joseph smiled. "Yes, it does!"

A sloop shot another round at the rebels. Again, the balls missed their target.

"Are you on your way to Braintree to get Liam?" Joseph asked.

"Aye."

A militia captain and several of his men approached Joseph. "Dr. Warren, there are a few lighters grounded near the shore. The tide's coming in. As soon as the lighters are floating we will row them to the island to chase off those rascals and show that loyalist, Leavitt, we are not standing for selling to the British."

"It appears we are not being invaded after all," Joseph replied. "I will ride to Braintree to spread the word and calm the panic." It was an excuse to go with the angels.

The militiamen left to join the others and board the lighters, which were now floating. Joseph and the angels watched them row to Grape Island and swarm onto the shore. The regulars hastily returned to their sloops. There was a brief exchange of British swivel guns and rebel muskets.

Joseph, Jeremiah, and the angels turned their horses west toward Braintree.

Joseph did not know if Colm had talked to his men about rejecting Heaven. He could not tell by the angels' demeanor. They were quiet, but they did not look downcast. Then, he realized their eyes kept darting to his face.

The fingertip-size bruises on Joseph's cheeks were black and painful. Hidden beneath his sleeve, his upper arm ached under a ring of heavy bruises from Robert's grasp. He said, "I am fine."

The angels gave him another solicitous glance.

309

"Really, I am fine."

"Robert Percy is the first demon I'm killing after we reject Heaven," Michael proclaimed. "He's not getting away with hurting ya, Joseph."

"That is the general reaction I have gotten when I am asked about the bruises."

"You're tellin' people Robert did that to you?" Patrick wondered.

"Of course not; but enough of that. Based on what you said, Michael, Colm has spoken to all of you about rejecting Heaven."

Michael nodded.

"Is that why you are going to get Liam? You have all agreed?"

Brandon said, "We still gotta get Liam and Fergus to agree."

Ian grimaced. "Can we talk about something else?" he asked.

It will take time to get accustomed to Ian's new vessel. Yet, there is no mistaking, his unhappiness with their choice to reject Heaven, Joseph thought.

Colm changed the conversation. "Joseph, did ya write ya missives to the Continental Congress?"

"Yes, and I have sent Benjamin to Philadelphia to deliver them."

Jeremiah saw the look on Joseph's face when he said Benjamin Church's name. "Paul told me he don't trust Church. You don't wanna admit it, but you're beginnin' not ta trust him either. Even I've heard Church has been ta Boston several times since Lexington and Concord."

"Benjamin is a member of our inner circle. I have known him most of my adult life." Joseph's eyes saddened. "I cannot admit it—not yet. He is one of the few who agree with my opinion that we should launch an assault on Boston before reinforcements arrive from Great Britain."

They entered Braintree in silence.

When the angels rode up to the Adams' house, Philomon Morris was in the front yard talking to several people who had fled Weymouth. Philomon recognized Jeremiah, Michael, and Joseph. A sneer tried to form on his lips. *How is Dr. Warren associated with these ruffians?*

"If you will excuse me," Philomon said to the people with whom he was conversing. "I need to inform Mrs. Adams that we have visitors."

Those standing in the yard eyed the approaching men. Some of them also recognized Joseph. They were surprised to see the man holding the patriotic cause together in Braintree.

The six angels and two men dismounted.

Abigail ran out of the house and into Joseph's arms. He hugged her tight.

She stepped back and looked into his young handsome face. A breath caught in her throat and her eyes opened wide. Her fingers fluttered near his cheeks. "Your face is badly bruised! Who did this to you?"

Joseph reached to calm her fluttering fingers. "We will talk about it later. The angels have come to take Liam home."

Abigail's eyes shifted from Joseph's face to search for the archangel she had spoken to at the meetinghouse nearly three months ago. He was there, tall and thin; he looked like a young fatherly king who would never dream of leaving his subjects desolate and afraid.

She went to him, "I must warn you that Liam is not doing well."

He nodded.

"Please, bring your men and come in, Mr. Bohannon. You will have to reacquaint me with them, except, of course, Jeremiah and Michael."

Abigail stepped aside as Colm, Jeremiah, Seamus, Michael, and Joseph filed into the house.

Brandon and Patrick lingered on the portico with downcast eyes.

Ian sat on the step, propped his elbows on his knees, and rested his chin in the palms of his hands.

"You and Michael look so much alike," Abigail said to Patrick.

He glanced at her.

"What is your name?"

"Patrick."

"I remember you. You shielded me from the demon in the meetinghouse."

Patrick nodded.

Sensing their shyness, she said, "Do not linger outside because you feel uncomfortable. Liam will want to see you."

Patrick and Brandon reluctantly entered the house. Ian remained on the step.

"Mrs. Adams, leave Ian," Colm said from where he stood near the door. "He'll come inside in his own time. Where's Liam?"

"Follow me," she said. "Quietly, please. My youngest children are napping."

The angels and the men followed Abigail up the steps. The Adams' saltbox farmhouse was modestly furnished. Colm was reminded of the furnishings in Joseph's house on Hanover Street.

Abigail led them to a bedroom near the end of the upstairs hallway. She knocked on the door and said, "Liam, your angels are here to see you. May we come in?"

311

There was no answer. She opened the door anyway.

Michael shrank from the door. Memories of Ian's pain and confusion at the Barrett farm paralyzed Brandon. He stood in the hall with Michael as the others entered the bedroom.

Liam was asleep. Light blankets covered his naked body from the waist down. His green aura flashed weakly just as Ian's aura had done before it went out. Colm sat on the bed beside him. He stroked Liam's dark hair and touched his cheeks. The gash on Liam's forehead had festered and grown to cover most of his forehead. The skin around it was black. The smell was noxious.

Abigail bit her lower lip, and then said, "He is in so much pain. Our physician here in Braintree, Dr. Abner Hall, has been attending to his wound, but the wound continues to worsen. Dr. Hall prescribed something to make Liam more comfortable and allow him to sleep. He eats very little."

She blushed. "He often pulls off his nightshirt. I do not think he realizes he is doing it."

"Dr. Hall cannot treat Liam like a human patient. Liam's human vessel is alive because of his angelic spirit. There is no way to balance his bodily humors," Joseph said. He examined Liam's rotting forehead. He touched Liam's bare chest, in several places, with his fingertips. Then, he touched Liam's arms and shoulders.

Colm saw the alarm in Joseph's eyes. "What's wrong?"

"This did not happen to Ian," Joseph said. He shook his head, as if in denial of what he discovered. "His muscle tissue is degenerating."

Colm stared at Joseph in disbelief.

"Wake him," Joseph said.

Colm didn't respond.

"Wake him."

Colm put his hands on Liam's cheeks and kissed the top of his head. His voice was soft and tender when he said, "Liam, wake up."

Liam moaned.

"Wake up." Colm stroked the top of Liam's head.

Liam's eyes fluttered. To the angels, it seemed an eternity before Liam succeeded in keeping his eyes open.

"Joseph?" Liam asked in a hoarse voice. He turned his head and shifted his eyes. "Colm?"

"We've come to take ya home," Colm said. He tried to smile, but the effort hurt his spirit.

Joseph saw that Liam's blue eyes were dull and cloudy.

Liam tried to focus on the others in the bedroom. It required an effort he could not put forth. He did not need his eyes to tell him his brotherhood and Abigail were there.

Joseph got up and went to Abigail. He whispered, "When did his eyes begin to show signs of cataracts?"

Abigail's lips quivered. "My daughter brings him breakfast. Afterward, she reads to him. It helps him concentrate on something other than his pain. Anyway, she saw the change in his eyes yesterday morning. It happened overnight."

In the hallway, Michael put his head in his hands.

On the step outside the Adams' front door, Ian did the same.

Brandon swallowed the lump in his throat. He stepped into the bedroom beside Patrick.

"Why are you taking me home?" Liam asked Colm.

Seamus sat on the bed beside Colm.

Liam reached for Seamus' hand.

Seamus grasped it. He looked to Colm for permission to answer Liam. Colm's eyes flashed hard and silver. He nodded.

"Colm may have found a way for us to beat Henry and the demons. It might…might…" Seamus wiped at the tears in his eyes. "…get you well. But we ain't doin' it unless all eight of us agree to it. Everyone's agreed except you and Fergus. We ain't told him yet."

Liam moaned. He raised his left hand. It traveled to the infected gash on his forehead—it looked more like a monster's decaying mouth than a wound. His forefinger brushed the black skin under the wound near his eyebrows. He cried out in pain.

Brandon and Patrick burst into tears. Joseph went to them. He opened his arms, and they fell into them. The angels' tears soaked the shoulders of Joseph's cloak. He stroked Patrick's curly black hair, and Brandon's broad shoulders.

Liam's hand moved to his chest. The fingers tried to tear away the nightshirt he thought was still there. He moaned. "Abigail, are you here?"

She sat on the bed beside Seamus and stilled Liam's groping hand. She said, "I am here, Liam."

Michael sobbed. Ian sobbed.

With the love and gentleness of the mother Liam's palimpsest longed for, Abigail asked, "Do you understand that Colm and your brotherhood are here to take you home?"

"Yes."

"Did you understand what Seamus said?"

"Colm wants me to agree to…something."

"Does this have to do with the Sigil of Lucifer?" Abigail asked Jeremiah.

"It does."

She released Liam's hand and looked at Colm. "Tell Liam what you want him to agree to before he cannot understand your words."

Wings rustled.

Joseph tightened his arms around Brandon and Patrick.

"Liam, do you hear me?" Colm asked.

"Yes."

I know he'll understand. He's always been the smart one, Colm thought. The thought stung his spirit. He said, "We have to reject Heaven to become strong enough to defeat the demons once and for all."

Liam's weak grasp squeezed Seamus' hand for reassurance. "I cannot think clearly." His left hand tried to travel to his forehead, but he was able to stop it. His hand dropped beside him on the bed. "You have my agreement, but whatever I must do, I cannot do it without Abigail."

Brandon's and Patrick's sobs abated. Joseph released them from his arms.

Michael and Ian continued to sob.

The angels and Jeremiah and Joseph looked at Abigail with expectance.

"I cannot leave my children and go to Roxbury," she said.

The momentary lucidity Liam had managed was slipping away. He reached for the last thread of it and said, "Abigail, if you do not help me, we may all die."

She looked at Colm and Seamus with an apology in her eyes.

The last thread of lucidity slipped from Liam's grasp. His palimpsest surfaced and said, "Mother, I am also your child. Why will you not help me?"

She touched her hand to her breast and breathed, "I…"

Michael's sobs, from where he stood in the hall, filtered into the silent bedroom.

Philomon Morris stood at the top of the steps and laughed while he watched Michael cry. He was tired of the dying man Mrs. Adams was caring for. Despite Dr. Warren's presence, Philomon was glad these men were grieving.

Michael heard Philomon and sensed his hateful thoughts. He wiped a hand across his blurry eyes, turned, and ran at Philomon. Michael was choking the servant before he realized what he was doing.

"Do ya think Liam's death is amusing?" Michael asked. The sneer on his lips and the hate in his eyes terrified Philomon. "Do ya know who I am? Do ya know who my brother is?"

Michael shook him.

Philomon gagged and his eyes bulged. His fingers clawed at the hand Michael had around his neck.

Michael's green eyes seared Philomon's soul with hatred. "We're done!" Michael screamed. "We won't have to bow to human filth like ya anymore! We won't have to bear the suffering and hatred and selfishness of the children of man. We'll finally be free!"

Philomon clawed at Michael's hand. The world turned gray.

Michael's angry words shocked Colm. He faltered before he dashed into the hall to pull his brother off. *That servant is a vile man,* Colm thought.

Abigail's two youngest children cried for their mother from behind closed doors.

Michael slammed Philomon against the wall. "LIAM'S DYING AND YA LAUGHED! YA LAUGHED, YA FUCKER!"

Just before his world went black, Philomon heard distant voices screaming Michael's name.

Seamus, Jeremiah, and Colm struggled to get Michael to let go of Philomon's throat.

"Ya are killing him!" Colm shouted. "Ya are gonna break his neck!"

Michael's body was numb, and his spirit was out of control. The hands that grasped him and pulled at his body seemed far away and unimportant. His palimpsest surfaced and spoke to him. *"I know ya are scared and angry, but ya aren't alone. I am here. Let Colm soothe us."*

Michael panted.

"Calm yaself."

Michael's breathing slowed, and he became aware of Colm's arms enfolding him.

"Let Colm soothe us."

Michael's palimpsest slipped below the surface of his memory and his hands slipped from Philomon's neck. The servant fell in a heap on the floor.

Jeremiah and Seamus let go of Michael and backed away without looking at the man on the floor.

Michael trembled in Colm's arms. His voice quivered. "He laughed at our grief."

315

Joseph stood in the hall. He made no move to help Philomon.

Abigail's joy at seeing Joseph and the angels folded in on itself. Her children were crying, the angels were upset, everything she had done to mother Liam seemed useless, and Philomon had revealed a callousness she did not know he was capable of.

Her three-year-old son, Thomas, came out of the bedroom crying. She picked him up and hugged him to her breast. Five-year-old Charles cautiously followed his brother. He was no longer crying, but upon seeing strangers crowding the hall, he clung to his mother's skirts.

"Joseph, are you not going to attend to Philomon?" Abigail asked. "What if he is—?" She did not want to say the word in front of her sons.

"He is not dead," Joseph said with disgust. "If he was, the angels would be tending to his soul despite what he did. What he is, however, is a contemptible human being. He deserved what he got."

A disconcerting silence settled in the hall.

"Let's leave Joseph and Mrs. Adams alone so they can say what they need to say to each other," Colm said to the angels and Jeremiah.

They filed into Liam's bedroom and closed the door.

Abigail set Thomas on his feet. He cried and threw himself on the floor in a fit of anger. She leaned into the stairwell and yelled down the stairs, "Nabby, John Quincy, come up here and get your brothers!"

Amid the little ones' crying and temper tantrums, ten-year-old Nabby and eight-year-old John Quincy managed to get their little brothers down the stairs.

Abigail knelt beside Philomon. His neck was bruised, but he was breathing. Satisfied, she stood up and faced Joseph. His eyes were somber and calm.

She sighed and said, "When Michael and Jeremiah brought Liam here, I realized the angels were delicate and loyal beings. I wondered aloud why mankind did not know that about them. I wrote to John asking for his guidance on how to mother a dying angel."

"Did John reply?"

She pressed her lips together to keep from crying and nodded.

Joseph waited for her to continue.

She sniffed. "John's advice astounded me. He told me I would have to turn my back on God if I hoped to help Liam. Not forever. Just until Liam either healed or…died."

"But now, you have chosen to turn your back on Liam."

"NO!" Abigail took a step toward Joseph. "I will not turn my back on Liam! I—love him."

"Then, why have you refused to help him and his brotherhood?"

She looked away.

Joseph put his hands on her shoulders. "Answer me."

"Liam has the Sigil of Lucifer tattooed on his neck. I know the other angels have the same tattoo. They want to reject Heaven because they are afraid and desperate. I am afraid of their desperation, Joseph!"

"Then help them!" Joseph resisted the urge to shake her. His hands dropped from her shoulders.

She studied his face. "You will do anything for them," she stated.

"Yes."

"Then, so shall I."

"Abigail, your devotion must be unselfish. The angels are incapable of offering apologies or expressing gratitude."

She gave him a small smile. "I am well aware of that."

On the floor, Philomon stirred.

"Despite your abhorrence for Philomon, I will not release him from our employment," Abigail said in an indignant tone, although Joseph had not suggested she release her servant. "He has been a part of our family since before I was born, and he shall stay."

Philomon blinked and ran a hand across his eyes. He struggled to his feet and touched his painful throat. "Mrs. Adams, what happened?" he asked in a hoarse whisper.

The bruises on Philomon's neck pleased Joseph, and he said, "You got what you deserved."

"Joseph!" Abigail hissed.

Philomon, in turn, noted the bruises on Joseph's cheeks. He tried, and failed, to raise his voice above a whisper when he hatefully asked, "Did you also get what you deserved, Dr. Warren?"

"That is enough!" Abigail warned. "Joseph, take care of our...friends. I will prepare for our journey. I am sure I can make arrangements for the children's care while I am gone. Philomon, come with me."

Abigail's shoes tapped on the wooden risers as she and Philomon went downstairs. When she crossed the living room, she saw, through the open front door, Ian sitting alone on the portico step.

"Philomon, rest. I will bring you some chamomile tea in a few minutes."

317

He feigned confusion and innocence. "Why are you choosing to help these strangers at the risk of endangering your children's well-being? What would Mr. Adams say about this?"

Abigail opened her mouth to retort his question, and then snapped it shut. *Joseph is right. Philomon does deserve what Michael did to him,* she thought. *I will not let him ensnare me in his hateful trap.* She did not look at him as she turned and walked through the open front door.

Ian's knees were pulled in close to his chest, and his arms were crossed over his knees. His forehead rested on his arms. He raised his head when he heard the swish of Abigail's skirts as she sat beside him.

"Are you Ian?"

He looked at her and nodded.

"Liam told me that Sidonie, your…friend…your female companion died recently. He told me that you almost died as well."

His gaze did not shift from her face. He said nothing.

Can I speak of these things to him? She wondered. *Yes, I think I can. Unlike Brandon and Patrick, he is not afraid to look at me.*

She asked, "Are those the reasons you will not see Liam?"

"You sound like Sidonie. She asked me questions I couldn't answer."

Abigail smiled. "I think you *can* answer my question; you chose not to."

Ian considered her delicate features. Except for her brown eyes, Abigail's facial features were not much different from Sidonie's. He asked, "Did Liam tell you what me and Michael and Seamus did to get us banished from Heaven?"

"Yes. He said you are the one who still has trouble controlling your… urges."

"I'd satisfy my urges with you if it wasn't forbidden."

Why do I find his words sensual instead of inappropriate? Stupid woman. You know very well why. It is because he is an angel who occupies a handsome body.

Ian stood up. He looked out over the tiny front yard and the coastal road to the shoreline beyond, and squinted to see the blurry thoughts in his spirit. He cocked his head. "We strayed too far in favor of copulation with human women, and now, we have strayed too far in favor of the children of man," he said. His eyes shined bright with what he saw in his spirit.

He turned and ran into the house. His boots thundered up the steps to above stairs and down the hall to Liam's bedroom. Despite, the oppressive weight of the angels' anxiety, and the melancholy sight of Liam asleep in Patrick's arms, he shouted, "I know some of the words to conjure the spell!"

THIRTY-THREE

K ing George III dispatched three major generals to America. On the afternoon of May 24, the generals, accompanied by their servants, sailed into Boston Harbor on the man-of-war *Cerberus*. The irony was not lost on Henry. Cerberus was the name of the three-headed dog of Greek and Roman mythology said to guard the gates of Hell.

It was obvious to Henry, as well as most of the high ranking British officers, that the generals were sent as a solution to the errant colonies' behavior because of the King's tarnished confidence in General Gage. This development was worth a celebration in Henry's view.

When, General Henry Hereford was alive and living in London, he was acquainted with the three major generals. With luscious perversion Henry thought, *they would be mortified if they knew Henry was dead, and a demon occupies his body.*

Sir William Howe was the ranking member of the trio. Swarthy and good-looking, Howe was Henry's favorite of the three major generals. He had a penchant for high living, gambling, and women. His sister, Caroline, threw parties in her London home for her brother and his friends. It was at one such party that Henry had met General Howe, and an older American gentleman—Benjamin Franklin. Henry and William had, both, served in the British Parliament.

Next in order of rank was the small, fair-haired, Henry Clinton, who grew up in New York where his father served as governor. Clinton was sensitive to criticism and stoic, but unlike Howe, he was not distracted by indulgences. Henry found Clinton to be brilliant but boring.

The junior member of the triumvirate, John Burgoyne, was the oldest in age. When he was given the order to sail to the colonies, Burgoyne tried to convince King George III, and other politicians, that his skills were a waste of time in Boston. Henry appreciated Burgoyne's skills: witty charm and passionate writing. Charm and passion were traits Henry believed he himself possessed.

Thomas confided in Henry that he knew the arrival of the three major generals marked the beginning of the end of his days as commander-in-chief of the Massachusetts Bay Colony. What Thomas did not admit was the relief he would feel when he could leave Henry and his menacing aide-de-camp far behind.

On the evening of May 25, Henry, Robert, Captain John Brown, Major John Pitcairn, Captain Anthony Jameson, and the trio of generals gathered in Gage's living room for after dinner drinks. They were discussing besieged Boston and what should be done about it.

"You should have seized Samuel Adams and John Hancock when you had the chance," General John Burgoyne declared to Thomas.

"That would have been possible long *before* you received Lord Dartmouth's order for their arrest in April," General William Howe added.

Captain John Brown lit his clay pipe and puffed serenely.

John Pitcairn shifted uncomfortably in his chair.

Henry, Robert, and Anthony masked their amusement.

"Someone who knew of our plans to march to Concord took that information to Joseph Warren. Warren sent riders to Lexington to warn Hancock and Adams. They managed to elude us," Thomas said. He sounded neither shameful nor apologetic. However, Joseph Warren's name lingered like a bad taste in his mouth.

General Henry Clinton said, "Tell me, Thomas, who do you suspect betrayed that information to Warren?"

Thomas sighed wearily and thought, *I have done my due diligence to carry out all of my orders from Lord Dartmouth, including the seizure of rebel armaments and ammunition from Concord. I have kept the best interests of our parliament in mind with each action I have taken. Now, these haughty generals, who know nothing about the tribulations I have faced, dare question me as if I were a fool.*

Thomas said indignantly, "I have no idea." As far as Thomas knew, only his trusted secretary, who was also his brother-in-law, Samuel Kemble, and Colonel Francis Smith were privy to the campaign beforehand.

John Pitcairn was sympathetic to General Gage's position. He stepped out of bounds and said to General Clinton, "Bloody Hell! You cannot expect to assemble that type of campaign in complete secrecy! Eight hundred men assembled on Back Bay is cause enough for suspicion!"

Thomas did not look at Pitcairn. He neither welcomed nor needed a champion on the matter.

Henry despised Pitcairn, but he couldn't dispute his point.

General Clinton raised an eyebrow but said nothing.

A servant entered the room to refill empty glasses with claret.

William Howe motioned to the servant to fill his glass, and asked Thomas, "Do you have any idea where Hancock, Adams, and Warren are now? They are responsible for the siege Boston is suffering under."

"My intelligence has reported that Adams and Hancock are in Philadelphia attending the Continental Congress," Thomas said. "Warren spends most of his time in Cambridge. He is president of the illegal Provincial Congress."

John Burgoyne became distracted by Henry's disconcerting yellow-green eyes. John remembered that Henry Hereford had brown eyes. He wondered how a man's eye color could change so dramatically. He ventured to ask, "Henry, do you believe a rebel attack from Cambridge is imminent under Warren's command?"

An imminent rebel attack was exactly what Henry hoped for. An attack from either one of the opposing forces would do, and if an imminent battle was not brewing, he would provoke one. That had occupied his treacherous thoughts since the archangel told Robert he intended to put an end to the angels' demonic pursuit, regardless of the cost to the children of man.

John Burgoyne's question provided Henry a chance to begin that provocation. "I not only believe an attack is imminent, I am certain the offensive will be led by one of Warren's new military handmaidens, General Artemas Ward or Colonel Israel Putnam."

John Brown puffed his pipe and made eye contact with Thomas. The non-verbal exchange between the two friends asked the question, *where did Henry get that information?*

Henry drained his glass of claret and rose from his chair. "Please excuse us gentlemen. Robert, Anthony, and I must leave to attend a small private party."

Robert and Anthony rose. Both demons were happy with Henry's announcement. The after-dinner discussion was tedious and boring.

"William, would you consider joining us?" Henry asked with a grin. "I am sure you would enjoy…the guests."

❧

Flickering candlelight haunted the parlor where Henry sat alone at a table. He was very drunk. Sloppy drunkenness was something he tempered at parties, but tonight, he intended to indulge.

William Howe was standing near a door that entered into a first-floor bedroom. A petite young woman stood in front of him. She brushed his face, chest, and hips with her fingers as she spoke. William smiled down into her sweet face and touched the neat curls of dark hair that fell down her back.

Robert and Anthony were nowhere in sight.

Henry supposed their entertainment was already in progress. It was time for him to do the same.

A server brought a refilled tankard of rum to Henry and set it on the table. The man had been watching General Hereford all evening. The general's eerie yellow-green eyes and rough masculinity were alluring. "Is there anything else I can do for you, General?"

Henry's eyes swept the shadowed room. Everyone was engaged in some type of foreplay. He shifted his eyes to the server. He was, perhaps, eighteen-years-old with thick black hair and effeminate facial features. Perversely, the young man reminded Henry of the archangel's brother. His eyes slid down the young man's chest to his crotch. He flipped his eyes back up to the young man's face and smiled broadly.

This is an unexpected pleasure, Henry thought. "What is your name?"

"Jared." A smile played at the corners of his mouth.

Henry's awakening erection raised its head. He took a long drink of rum and then rose from his chair.

"I am not without a price," Jared said softly.

Henry's erection insisted on attention. He nodded.

The young man took Henry's hand and led him above stairs to a small but lavishly appointed bedroom. Exclamations of carnal pleasure filtered through the walls and into the bedroom.

Jared brushed his fingers over the shadow of beard on Henry's cheeks.

Henry had little patience for foreplay. He allowed it from Constance, Margaret's personal maid, because he enjoyed her perverse sexual brutality. Jared cupped Henry's cheeks and moved to kiss him.

Henry seized Jared's wrists. "Strip me of my clothing. My boots and breeches first; then you will suck me. You will remove one piece of my clothing and suck me. And you will do it again and again until I am naked."

"I wish so much to kiss you," Jared ventured with a longing look, but he did as he was asked.

Once he was stripped of his boots, breeches, and stockings, Henry rose from the edge of the bed. Jared got to his knees and sucked Henry's erection with his warm wet mouth.

He tastes strange, almost like death, Jared thought. *Yet it is erotic.* He tilted his head just enough to look up into the general's yellow-green eyes. Jared felt his own erection rise, and he stroked himself without interrupting the general's pleasure.

Henry smelled Jared's sexual aroma. He closed his eyes and imagined that Jared was the archangel's brother. The fantasy brought him to the brink of an orgasm sooner than he wanted.

General, you are so beautiful, Jared thought still gazing up at Henry's face. His own orgasm threatened to explode.

Henry sensed Jared's thoughts. His eyes flew open. He pulled away from Jared's mouth and jerked him to his feet. He shouted into Jared's surprised face. "Demons are not beautiful! That is a disgusting analogy for angels!"

Jared's neck snapped when Henry slapped his face.

Henry dressed. On leaving the bedroom, he took a last look at the dead young man on the floor, and smiled. "I believe your broken neck completes my fantasy about the archangel's brother."

To the east of Charlestown were two contiguous islands, Hog, and the much larger Noodle's Island, which together formed a peninsula that reached from the town of Chelsea toward Boston to the southwest with the town of Winnisimmet on the opposite shore directly north. Hundreds of sheep, cattle, and horses grazed on both Hog and Noodle's Islands.

After the incident at Grape Island, the Committee of Safety ordered the removal of all livestock and hay from the islands. Knee-deep creeks separated the islands from one another and the mainland; therefore, boats were not required. General Artemas Ward deployed Colonel John Stark and his regiment out of New Hampshire to carry out the mission.

As Jeremiah, Colm, Michael, Seamus, and Ian neared Boston Neck on their journey home from Braintree, they saw black smoke rising from Noodle's Island. Coupled with the sound of cannon and musket fire, they surmised that the fire had something to do with livestock and hay. Colm suspected Joseph of having a hand in the situation, and that he was probably in the thick of things.

They reined their horses and tried to assess what seemed to be a skirmish.

"We're too far away," Colm said as he raised a hand to shield his eyes from the early evening sun. His hand dropped to the cartridge box slung across his chest in an unconscious gesture of verifying his ammunition. Now days, they never traveled unarmed. "Let's go see what's happening," he said.

When they arrived at the town of Winnisimmet, they saw the British sloop, *Britannia,* anchored off shore in the deeper waters. A British schooner was sailing north up Chelsea Creek, the narrow waterway that lay between the islands and the mainland. A large force of Major Pitcairn's Royal Navy marines was rowing longboats toward both islands and the mainland shore.

Jeremiah and the angels could clearly see that a burning barn was the source of the smoke from Noodle's Island. About 30 rebels were on the island corralling livestock. A small number of no more than 40 Royal Navy marines stationed on the island were advancing on the rebels.

Michael pointed eastward. "It looks like they're driving sheep from Hog Island across—"

The schooner, *Diana,* suddenly fired her swivel guns and six-pound cannons at John Stark's regiment of rebels on Noodle's Island. The men exchanged fire with their muskets. More rebels congregated on the mainland shoreline near Jeremiah and the angels. They, too, fired at *Diana.*

"Looks like we might wanna take part in this," Jeremiah said as he dismounted.

The angels also dismounted.

Diana glided further north into the shallow waters near Hog Island in an attempt to trap the rebels there until high tide made the creek harder to forge. The schooner exchanged fire with the rebels on Hog Island.

Jeremiah moved northeastward. He and other rebels volleyed with the marines swarming out of the longboats.

The angels waited for Colm's order. The sound of exploding gunpowder, shouting men, booming cannons, and the smell of smoke rushed through Colm's spirit. He had seen men kill one another for a loyal cause countless times over thousands of years. This time, however, he wasn't just an observer. He had promised his brotherhood's loyalty to the patriotic cause without truly understanding the price of that loyalty.

We aren't supposed to kill the children of man, he thought. *Yet, since we've come here, we have killed them anyway. If we do reject God, will we be able to fulfill our pledge of loyalty without regret?*

Colm's spirit struggled under the weight of his indecision and doubts. *Jeremiah warned ya about losing control. He told ya that's what Henry wants,* his conscience admonished.

"I didn't lose control," Colm whispered.

No? Then why are ya forcing ya angels to reject Heaven?

"I'm not forcing them."

Do ya really believe that?

"I—"

Are ya exchanging ya vows to ya angels for vows to Joseph Warren and the patriots?

"No. I'm protecting them—all of them."

Ya aren't strong enough.

"I have to make us *all* stronger. They have to be able to take care of themselves if I'm dead."

Henry's going to make ya choose no matter what ya do. Will ya choose Michael or Joseph?

"I'll kill Henry before that happens!"

Then, ya had better kill him soon, because time's running out.

"I realize that!"

Ya told Joseph there wou'd be human collateral damage when ya and Henry finally clashed. Can ya stand up under that and stay strong? If ya can, prove it now.

"Colm? Colm? Colm!"

Colm blinked.

Seamus studied his archangel with concern. "We know you're strugglin' with our destiny. We ain't gonna let you struggle alone."

Ian and Michael surprised Colm by smiling. Their faith and love for him made his spirit ache. If he made the wrong decisions, he would be sentencing them to death.

Under heavy provincial rebel fire and with an outgoing tide threatening to ground his schooner, *Diana*, the commanding officer, Lieutenant Thomas Graves, sought the aid of a dozen longboats to tow him back down the creek in the dying breeze.

In hopes of ambushing *Diana* before she reached the safety of the harbor, the rebels rushed down the north shore of Chelsea Creek toward Winnisimmet. By 9:00 p.m., the sun was setting. Colonel Israel Putman and Joseph arrived at Newgate Landing with two field pieces and more men.

Putnam directed his cannon fire at *Diana* that was now slowly drifting south along the shore.

The Royal Navy marines had transported several cannons to a hill on Noddle's Island. Out of the deepening darkness, cannonballs whistled down at the rebels as they waded into the creek and fired at the longboats towing *Diana* past the Winnisimmet shore.

The rebel cannons returned fire with such effectiveness that the British longboat crews were forced to abandon *Diana*. The schooner soon drifted toward shore and grounded on the wooden rails extending from the ferry dock.

Lieutenant Graves and his men attempted to use their anchor to drag the schooner to deeper water, but as the tide ebbed, the schooner began to roll onto her side. They had no choice but to abandon her for the sloop *Britannia*.

Jeremiah drifted along the shore with the movement of *Diana* and the rebels who dogged her. He encountered Joseph when the rebels moved north to Newgate Landing.

Joseph was surprised to see him. "If you are here, the angels must be here."

"They're here somewhere. I left 'em. I finally realized that I don't wanna live every minute of their struggle over killin' humans and rejectin' God. They were so much calmer in Burkes Garden where they were protected, for the most part, from constant human turmoil."

Powder flashed in the darkness and Putnam's cannons boomed. British musket fire responded. "They do not deserve what is happening to them," Joseph lamented.

"No, they don't." Jeremiah paused. "We might end up dyin' for 'em, and we've both accepted that."

"Take them home, Jeremiah. Tell Colm that we spoke, and not to worry—if that is possible."

Putnam's cannons thundered. Powder smoke choked the cool night air.

Jeremiah turned to leave, then stopped. "I don't give a damn what's happenin' with your buddin' war or your responsibilities ta your cause. You gotta be with 'em when they reject Heaven."

Joseph smiled. "They have my love, faith, and loyalty just as they have yours."

༈

Later that night, the rebels plundered *Diana* of her guns, rigging, and equipment, and then, with some strategically placed hay, set her on fire. The flames reached the vessel's powder magazine, and *Diana* exploded.

That same night, Israel Putnam and Joseph returned to Cambridge to report the outcome of the battle to General Artemas Ward.

"I wish we could have something of this kind to do every day," Putnam crowed.

General Ward was aware of Putnam's reputation as a firebrand. However, the general was more cautious. He frowned and said, "I am afraid that what happened tonight might provoke the British to launch a sortie from Boston that we may come to regret."

Putnam was undaunted by the general's worry. "We shall have no peace until we gain it by the sword."

Joseph said, "I admire your spirit, Colonel Putnam, and I respect General Ward's prudence. Both will be necessary for us, and one must temper the other."

The skirmish at Chelsea Creek was a clear rebel victory. It also consumed a large amount of gunpowder. That consumption, along with the 200 pounds of gunpowder the Provincial Congress had sent with Colonel Benedict Arnold on his mission to Ft. Ticonderoga, worried Joseph. Since the battles of Lexington and Concord, he had favored an assault on Boston. Now, he had a more realistic view of his army's preparedness for a major offensive against the British. In his opinion, they were prepared in spirit and desire, but not in armaments.

His concerns prompted him to write to Samuel Adams seeking guidance on the matter.

THIRTY-FOUR

The angels and Jeremiah returned home from the Battle of Chelsea Creek long after midnight. An unfamiliar carriage was parked in front of the farmhouse. The carriage meant Liam was home.

The angels were anxious to see him despite their physical exhaustion, but Colm ordered them to their beds instead of allowing them to huddle around Liam. When he was certain they were settled, Colm went to the tiny hidden alcove that served as his bedroom above stairs in the farmhouse.

He was surprised to see Abigail lying on the narrow bed beside Liam with her arms wrapped around him, just as Sidonie had done the night she sacrificed herself for Ian. Liam's green aura blinked once. It was enough to reassure Colm and coax him into resting his own drained body and spirit. He went to sleep in the barn with Gordon and Abe.

When the first rays of the morning sun brightened the eastern horizon, Colm rose and walked to the stream behind the barn. The urge to baptize his body and spirit couldn't be ignored. He stripped off his clothes and sat cross-legged in the shallow rocky stream. The cold water bubbled and flowed over his legs and hips while he bathed and washed his hair and clothes. He rose from the stream and shivered in the light morning breeze. He hung his wet clothes in the low branches of a tree. Then, he walked naked through the woods to the place where Ian Keogh, Sidonie Roux Denning, Abijah Cunningham, and an unknown man were buried.

He knelt before the graves. The muscles in his thin strong body tensed, and he tried to remember the freedom of existing without physical restraints. He released his green aura and slowly unfurled his imperial silver wings. Silver crystals showered the graves and drifted into the surrounding woods. Golden radiance shined from his spirit.

"I don't remember the name God gave me," Colm said, looking down upon the graves. "I don't remember the names of my six brothers. Only Lucifer's name remains in my memory."

He sat down and folded his legs. Perhaps, if he strained to hear the ancient melody of Heaven, he could remember. Or perhaps, if he released himself from his Earthbound vessel he would encounter their energy in the cosmos, and their names would be unimportant because he would not have to pray to them.

Silver tears seeped from Colm's eyes and rolled down his cheeks. "Brothers, can ya hear me?"

The late May sun rose a little higher above the eastern horizon. It caught a glimpse of the shivering archangel and heard his pleas. It murmured, *my energy and your energy are God's celestial creations; therefore, we are bound. You were born on the fifth day after God created the Heavens and the Earth. It was a day of much joy for your older brothers, Michael, Raphael, Gabriel, and Uriel; as it was for me.*

Colm's wings fluttered and he looked into the comforting rays of the sun. "Did ya once love me, Brothers? If ya did, help me! What do I have to do to save my angels and the children of man I love?"

Silence.

"I haven't asked ya for anything since our banishment!"

You have no right to ask anything of us—Brother.

"Three of my angels created Nephilim, but their intentions weren't heinous! They did nothing out of malice!" Colm cried. "Four of my angels were innocent of disobedience, yet still they were punished! Why did ya blindly take our father's side against them?"

Colm put his forehead in his hands. Drops of silver tears seared the ground. "They were my responsibility. I shou'd have been punished, not them! They're still my responsibility. I'll sacrifice myself if that's what I must do to protect them."

A startled flock of swallows took flight from the trees. Colm raised his head and watched them soar skyward. Amid the flurry of their snapping wings, he heard—*you deserve to dwell in the chains of eternal darkness, Brother, as do your angels. Perhaps, if you throw yourself upon Henry's sword, Father may let them live, but you are detestable; and Father may not be that merciful.*

With the warm sun shining on his back, Colm realized for the first time that their ability to escort a soul to its egress, and pass the soul's God-given fate to a reaper, was a cruel joke designed to keep the banished angels in Heaven's grasp until the demons finally killed them.

"Then we have no choice. We must reject Heaven," Colm whispered. "And I have to kill Henry before he forces me to choose between Michael and Joseph."

Then, the archangel, who had spent millenniums protecting seven banished angels, cried for everything they had lost and everything they had yet to lose.

Joseph was asleep in Hastings House in Cambridge when Colm fell to his knees in front of the graves. He was awakened by the macabre sound of an archangel crying. Joseph dressed and rode to the farm in Roxbury.

Fergus sensed his archangel's attempt at baptism. He rose from his bed in Dillaway House in Roxbury and got dressed. He told Captain Enos Woodbury that he was needed at the farm, and he was uncertain when he would return.

There were many mouths to feed at the farm. Gordon, Ian, Patrick, and Abe left before dawn to go hunting. When they left, Colm was asleep in the barn. When they returned with the spoils of their hunt, Colm was gone.

Jeremiah's skinning table was just off the back porch. It wasn't much different than his skinning table in front of his rough cabin in Burkes Garden. As he skinned and dressed the rabbits from the hunt, he thought of Mkwa. He missed her laughing, yet shaming brown eyes, the intoxicating smell of her shiny long black hair, and the feel of her warm silky skin against his naked body. He missed their conversations and her wisdom.

He gathered the rabbit carcasses and skins and walked to the stream. The stream's flowing water rinsed the blood and pollution from them. The reddening water reminded Jeremiah of the cycle of birth and death. Mkwa's time was growing near. He hoped Colm would sense when that time came. The thought brought a smile to his lips.

What Jeremiah heard coming from the woods on the other side of the stream, wiped the smile away. *Oh Lord*, Jeremiah thought. He shivered as he stood up. *Colm, what're you afraid of?*

He looked back at the farmhouse. The angels were standing on the back porch looking into the woods beyond the stream. Their faces were calm. Their wings were furled and silent. Their auras were doused. Brandon and Ian were supporting Liam so he could stand. Abigail was beside Ian. The angels' calm quietude unnerved Jeremiah worse than their violent show of emotions.

Gordon and Abe crossed the porch and approached Jeremiah.

"It has to be tonight," Gordon said. "They won't be able to endure another day of uncertainty."

"That ain't our decision," Jeremiah said. "It's Colm's decision." He glanced at the angels. "Colm's doing somethin' in the woods that's upsettin' 'em, but they look calm."

Gordon heard the archangel weeping. Gooseflesh formed on his skin. "Whatever Colm's doing can't be revoked."

A chill ran up Abe's spine. "What makes you say that?"

"They came here to finish their war with the demons. I think that time is very near, and—"

"—and besides rejectin' Heaven, he's tryin' ta figure a way ta end it without them all dyin' in the battle," Jeremiah interjected. He shivered at the thought of all that celestial power exploding on a battlefield—angels and demons warring on Earth.

Horse hooves thundered on the road. Fergus and Joseph arrived at the farm concurrently. They dismounted and ran, side by side, beyond the barn to the stream.

"Stop!" Jeremiah shouted at them. He reached out and hooked a hand around Fergus' wrist to keep him from splashing into the stream.

Joseph came to a stop beside Abe.

Fergus tried to pull away from Jeremiah.

"Slow down, Fergus!" Jeremiah shouted. He lowered his voice. "See 'em standin' on the porch?"

Fear burned Fergus' spirit. Liam needed help to stand. He knew Liam was sick, but he didn't realize how close he was to dying. And he saw something in the angels' demeanor he didn't understand.

"They're scared of what Colm's doin' out there in the woods, but they got the sense ta let him do what he needs ta do," Jeremiah said, calmly. "Act like the second ta an archangel is supposed ta act and take care of 'em until Colm comes back. I don't give a damn if he released you from his command. Do it anyway."

Jeremiah let go of Fergus' wrist.

Seamus stepped off the porch and approached Fergus. He said, "We were gonna fetch you back to the farm today anyway."

A new flame of fear seared Fergus' spirit. His boyish face tensed with shame and grief. "Liam's going to die soon, and I didn't sense it. Seamus, how did I move so far away from our brotherhood?"

Seamus said nothing. Fergus would have to struggle with the answer on his own.

"Something else is terribly wrong," Fergus observed.

"We ain't sure if it's terrible or not, but it scares us real bad. We think that's what Colm's strugglin' with as we speak."

Fergus and Seamus forced themselves to remain focused on one another in deference to the woods beyond the stream.

"He ain't here so I'm gonna tell you myself," Seamus said. "Colm thinks we need to reject Heaven to get strong enough to beat Henry and his demons. Ian and Patrick already conjured the words to the spell we're gonna cast."

Fergus' tense expression intensified.

"Damn it!" Gordon exclaimed. "We have to fetch William! Fergus doesn't have the tattoo. He has to have it before they can cast the spell!"

"I will fetch William," Abe volunteered. There was no need to discuss the importance of the tattoo. He was mounted on Fergus' horse and riding to Watertown before anyone could say otherwise.

"What tattoo?" Fergus asked Seamus.

Seamus unwound the cravat around his neck and tilted his head.

The Sigil of Lucifer. Fergus recalled his bravado the night he touched it against Colm's will. The sigil had not harmed him at the time, but the idea of having it tattooed on him was daunting. His emotions from everything his brotherhood had been through and what they had yet to face beset him. He struggled not to splash across the stream and run until he found comfort in the arms of his archangel.

Patrick jumped off the porch and ran to comfort Fergus. He pressed his palms against Fergus' cheeks. "Colm said the road we've been walkin' ain't got us nowhere and he's right. We gotta do this, and we cain't do it without you. The spell has to be cast by all of us. Liam don't have much time left. Maybe, if we reject Heaven, he won't die. We gotta try."

Fergus shifted his eyes to Liam's pale drawn face. He saw Abigail Adams standing beside Ian. "Why is Mrs. Adams here?"

The last thing Patrick wanted to do, at that moment, was explain a palimpsest. Michael could explain it later. Uncertain how to answer Fergus, Patrick let his hands drop from his cheeks. He took a step back.

Seamus saw his little brother's quandary and said to Fergus, "Her and Liam has formed a close friendship, and she offered to take care of him."

Fergus sensed there was more to it than that, but he didn't ask anymore questions. He was already overwhelmed with the idea of rejecting Heaven, Liam's impending death, and his archangel's tears. He walked to the porch and looked into the calm, but distressed, faces of his brotherhood. Their existence was about to change forever—if they continued to exist at all.

He jumped onto the porch and went to Liam. Brandon and Ian each had an arm around Liam's waist and an arm around his shoulders. Liam was sweating and trembling. His dissipating green aura blinked once. Fergus pulled him into his arms. The rotting gash on Liam's forehead made his spirit ache.

"I will not leave you again," Fergus whispered. The foreign sensation of tears dropped from his eyes and wet Liam's cheeks. "I didn't realize how close to death you are. If I had, I wou'd have come back to stay with you."

Michael winced and emitted a low grievous grunt.

Liam wanted to tell Fergus that commanding a budding provincial army unit was more important than a dying angel, but he could not gather the right words in his mind, let alone speak them.

Joseph was worried about Colm, and he could not endure the angels' tension another minute. He turned to wade across the stream. Jeremiah stopped him with a curt, "Joseph, I'm gonna tell you the same thing I told Fergus. Stay here and leave Colm alone."

"Do not tell me what to do," Joseph snapped, "and if you dare to try to stop me, we will come to blows."

He quickly crossed the stream. When he stepped onto the far bank, Joseph saw Colm's clothing draped over low hanging tree branches. He took the damp breeches and walked into the woods.

Colm heard Joseph approach. Without looking up, he said, "I can't remember the name God gave me."

"Does it matter now, after you have chosen to reject Heaven?" Joseph asked.

"My archangel brothers spoke to me for the first time since we were banished. Their hatred for me is—" He wiped a hand down his face. "They see me as an abomination like—"

"—God saw the Nephilim?" Joseph asked. He sat beside Colm.

Colm's eyes flashed when he looked at Joseph. "Aye."

"That is not the way I see you."

333

A fresh stream of silent tears coursed down Colm's cheeks. "We've been alone since we fell, but until today, I didn't understand the finality of our banishment. We've been blinded by fear and desperation and exhaustion."

"You are not alone, Colm."

Colm wiped his face and eyes with the back of his hand. "I understood that with clarity today, and I know that our power doesn't lie in God's hands or Heaven's shelter. It lies in our loyalty, faith, and love for one another and the brotherhood we have formed with the children of man. Ya are my brother now. Jeremiah, Gordon, Abe, Abigail, Paul, William, John, Samuel—all of ya are our brothers now."

Concern and kindness mingled in Joseph's tone. "You are terrified of something. What is it?"

Colm knew what Joseph was asking, and he had no intention of *ever* answering the question.

"Answer me," Joseph insisted.

Colm remained silent.

"You do not intend to tell me." Joseph observed. He handed Colm the breeches. "Put these on. Your men are nervous and unhappy because they do not know what you are doing or what you are thinking. Fergus is here. Abe has gone to get Paul and William. Ian and Patrick have conjured the words to your spell. It is time to take care of what needs tending."

THIRTY-FIVE

ROXBURY, MASSACHUSETTS

JUNE 1775

On the afternoon of June 1, William Dawes tattooed the Sigil of Lucifer on Fergus' neck while Paul Revere etched the sigil into Fergus' dagger.

Just before sunset, seven children of man and seven angels ate a dinner of rabbit stew that Abe and Brandon prepared. Colm tried and failed to get Liam to eat. It was 10:00 p.m. when Gordon began to draw an octagon on the top of the round table in the dimly lit living room.

Liam slept on a couch with his head in Abigail's lap. She hummed softly and gently stroked his cheek.

Michael, Brandon, and Patrick hovered near Liam while they watched Gordon draw the octagon. The three boys were trying to get drunk, but their anxiety absorbed the alcohol before it had a chance to affect their vessels.

Joseph, Paul, William, Jeremiah, and Abe were also attempting to get drunk. They, however, were succeeding.

Seamus, Ian, and Fergus sat at the table and copied the words to the spell on pieces of linen—one for each angel.

Colm stared at the forming octagon. In the number symbolism of Medieval Europe, eight was seen as representing cosmic balance and eternal life. It was a cruel oxymoron.

Gordon drew the last line of the octagon and threw tiny remains of the piece of graphite into the dead fireplace. He unfolded his sketch of the Sigil of Lucifer and laid it in the center of the octagon.

Colm shelved his tankard of rum on the fireplace mantel and went to Liam. "Wake up. It's time to cast the spell," Colm said gently. "We need ya to cast this spell so ya have a chance to survive."

Liam's eyes fluttered open. He tried to absorb the comfort of his archangel, but it felt out of reach.

"I think I prolonged ya death by infusing some of my spirit with ya spirit. I didn't know." Colm looked into Liam's half-open eyes for a moment. Then, he took Liam from Abigail's arms, lifted him, and set him on his feet. Brandon and Patrick reached to help steady Liam so he could stand somewhat on his own.

"Liam, do ya know what we're doing?" Michael asked tenderly.

Liam remembered that Michael was his archangel's brother, but he remembered little else about the beautiful angel standing before him.

"He can't do this!" Ian protested. "Colm, we have to cast the spell without him. He's too sick!"

Michael turned to run from the room. Paul and William hooked their arms around him so he could not escape. Michael struggled with them for a moment and then gave up the effort.

"Wait a moment!" Abigail said, jumping to her feet. "Liam can do this, but you must let me speak for him. If some of you can keep him on his feet, and ensure he holds the words to the spell in his hands, I can be his proxy." She looked at Gordon. "Will that work?"

"I don't know, but it appears we have no choice."

Seamus and Fergus handed the pieces of linen to each angel and Abigail. Paul and William released Michael.

The angels gathered in a circle around the table. Brandon and Patrick supported Liam. Michael ensured that the linen with the words to the spell stayed in Liam's hands even as he held his own copy of the spell.

Colm stood across the table from Liam so he could keep a close eye on him. His eyes flashed silver light as bright as stars in the darkest night sky when he looked at each member of his brotherhood. They were outwardly calmer than he expected, but he sensed their strong inner apprehension.

Joseph came to Colm's side. Colm resisted the urge to fall into Joseph's arms and sob.

Joseph said, "You can do this. All of you can do this. No matter what happens tonight, you will find the strength to go on, knowing you did what you thought was best."

William, Paul, Gordon, Abe, and Jeremiah gathered amongst Abigail and the angels.

"Let's begin," Colm breathed.

With trepidation, the angels spiritually touched one another. Their wings rustled. A breeze swept through the room and blew out the candles. They were plunged into a frightening darkness that reminded them of Liam's impending death—*chained in eternal darkness forever*. The angels released their auras, and with Abigail, began to chant in unison.

"Hear now the words of the Angels.
The secrets we once hid from the Children of Man

Joseph and Jeremiah exchanged worried glances.

The oldest of God's creations invoke their power
The melody of the ancient tune of Heaven is deafened."

The Sigil of Lucifer began to glow green, purple, blue, yellow, and red.

"In this night and in this hour
The Love of our God is discarded
In favor of the devotion of the Children of Man
Devotion God forgot thousands of years ago when he punished
His Sons with a wrath unworthy of a loving Being.

Liam moaned. The angels quivered. They clung to the strength of their brotherhood.

We finally and completely turn our backs on our Home and our Father
Knowing that We have strayed too far."

The last ounce of physical strength Liam possessed drained away. His knees unlocked, and he slipped toward the floor. Brandon and Patrick tightened their grasp on him. Terror propelled Colm to vault over the table and land on his feet beside Abigail.

She backed away to give the angels room to tend to Liam. Dread settled in her soul. William wrapped an arm around her trembling shoulders.

The light from the angels' auras intensified. Paul ludicrously thought that the angels' bodies would explode if their auras continued to intensify. Jeremiah thought of the time, in Burkes Garden, when Liam went missing for three days, and how the angels had nearly self-destructed as their stress over Liam's absence escalated.

They ain't gonna survive this, Jeremiah thought. Tears daggered his eyes.

Colm cradled Liam in his arms. He sat on the floor and held Liam's body tight against his chest. Colm's wings unfurled and a faint golden light surrounded him. Joseph kneeled beside him. The other angels fell to their knees around Colm and Liam. Their wings unfurled in a shower of silver crystals, and blocked Colm, Liam, and Joseph from the view of the others in the room.

Silver tears dropped from Colm's eyes and soaked Liam Kavangh's handsome face and dark hair. Colm shook so badly that his right arm slipped; Liam's right arm flopped backward, and his limp hand slapped the floor.

The angels' spirits clung to their archangel to keep from being washed away in an emotional flood of hysteria.

Abigail sobbed. William held her tighter. Hot tears burned his cheeks.

Gordon and Abe hardly noticed the tears that spilled from their eyes and blurred their sight.

Paul stood beside Abe, dry-eyed and stoic. The last bastions of his unquestioning faith in God had been destroyed. An angel had died and no one, not even an archangel, had been able to stop it. What was worse was the knowledge that God *let* it happen.

Colm looked at Joseph through bleary eyes. "I killed him."

"No, you did not," Joseph said in a strong yet trembling voice.

"I punished him for his disobedience. I didn't protect him."

"This is my fault!" Abigail cried out. "I asked him to show me his heavenly beauty!"

"No, Abigail," William whispered. "It is not your fault." He stroked her dark tumbled hair. "They will never see it that way. You know that."

Joseph touched Liam's wrist to check for a pulse. There was none. Liam's vessel was dead.

Michael fluttered his wings. They brushed Joseph's face with the delicacy of a mother stroking her newborn infant's cheek.

Joseph waited until he could speak in a controlled manner. Then, he asked Colm, "What did I say to you just before you cast the spell?"

A river of tears streamed down Colm's cheeks. His throat constricted, and he struggled to draw in a breath. "No matter what happens, I…will find the strength…to…" He gulped in another breath. "to go on… knowing I did…what I thought was best."

Colm's gold radiance flashed.

Joseph said, "Stay in control. You cannot let your men become hysterical. You cannot—"

Colm looked at Joseph. "I can't sense him."

"What do you mean?"

"I can't sense him."

"What do you mean by that?"

Lines formed on Colm's forehead, and his eyes exuded confusion. Salty tears ran over his quivering lips and into his mouth.

Joseph looked into the faces of the other angels for an inkling of clarification. He saw nothing but the same confusion and angelic grief.

"I can't sense him," Colm repeated.

Michael wiped his wet cheeks and eyes. He edged in closer to Liam and reached to close Liam's blue eyes so he looked as if he was asleep instead of dead. Then, he looked at his brother and said, "He's gone. Just gone."

Colm studied Michael's face while the realization of what had happened to Liam settled in his spirit. Michael was sensitive to everything. That was why his behavior was often volatile and explosive. Colm knew it was also the reason Michael understood what had happened to Liam before the others in the brotherhood.

The question and the answer terrified Brandon, but he asked it of Colm anyway. "Liam's not dead?"

"Michael's right," Colm said. "Liam's just gone. I don't sense him suffering in the chains of eternal darkness. He didn't die an angel's death."

Patrick exhaled a loud frightening cry. "Maybe you cain't sense him because we ain't angels no more!"

"I don't feel different," Brandon said.

"I don't feel different either," Seamus said. "Do you feel different, Brother?"

Patrick sniffed and shook his head.

Ian remembered little of his own miserable spiral toward death, but he had been pulled from the precipice of eternal darkness before he had chance to look over the edge. Had Liam been aware that the edge of death was the rim of the black pit of nothingness? His wings fluttered.

The brotherhood unconsciously fluttered their wings in sympathy.

Fergus was trembling as badly as Colm. "I don't feel different, but… when I think…about Liam…I feel like I'm falling." His fluttering wings flapped, and a feathery whisper stirred the air.

"So do I," Michael cried. He crawled in closer to Colm.

The angels' wings flapped in concert with Fergus' wings. Then, they sped up.

Gordon slapped the palm of his hand on the sketch of the Sigil of Lucifer to keep it from blowing off the table.

As the angels dwelled on Liam's fate, their wings threshed in a horrible attempt to steel themselves against a nothingness they didn't understand—a place that was beyond their senses. Their wings swept the ceiling and the floor in a flurry that stirred a wind storm of silver crystals.

Abe, Gordon, Jeremiah, Paul, William, and Abigail dashed out of the reach of the angels' frenzied wings.

Abigail's motherly instincts tempted her to offer comfort to this cataclysm outpouring of emotions. She glimpsed, through the threshing wings, the inner circle of the grieving celestial beings. It was all bright light and emotion. It blinded her and overwhelmed her soul.

Joseph was inside that circle. She wondered when and how he had found the strength to withstand the grief of the sons of God. Abigail heard Joseph speak in a gentle tone she had heard him use often.

"Colm, settle them down. They cannot go through this again if another of you—" Joseph swallowed and started again. "You are at war and have been for thousands of years. Do you realize how fortunate you are to have come this far and to have lost only one of you?"

Michael sidled closer to Colm.

"Look at me, Colm," Joseph said.

Colm's eyes shifted to Joseph's face.

"I understand what you have done tonight is unprecedented, and that Liam did not die the way you expected him to die."

Colm's wings quieted.

Joseph continued, "You told me once that you are the closest being to God, and that you are a warrior. Your fear and exhaustion has dimmed that warrior. Find him again. If you find him, they will find theirs as well."

Colm heeded Joseph's comforting words. He closed his eyes and let the last of his tears seep away. His wings stilled.

The angels' wings stilled. Their auras dimmed.

The glowing sigil dimmed in response.

Gordon reached to pick up the drawing of the sigil and thought better of it. The octagon, in which the drawing lay, had shifted to a heptagon, and it was seared into the table top. He nudged Abe and pointed at the heptagon.

At forty-five, and before he met the angels, Abe would have said he had seen almost everything. What he witnessed tonight convinced him that he would never fully understand anything again.

"It changed," he said, surprised.

"The spell worked," Gordon said.

Jeremiah and Paul looked over Abe's shoulder to see what Gordon had pointed out.

There had been eight. Now, there were seven. The notion hit Jeremiah like a thunderbolt. He left the house to grieve under the cover of the moonless night.

Colm calmed his grief and guilt to the point that a new emotion crept in on him—rage. Liam wasn't chained in eternal darkness because they had succeeded in rejecting Heaven, but Henry had ultimately erased Liam's existence. Colm's gold radiance brightened with his rage. He backed it down. The pledge he made to himself when he was alone in the woods burned brightly in his spirit. He felt strong enough to stop Henry from making him choose.

At first, the angels thought they should bury Liam Kavangh's body in a different place than the little graveyard beyond the stream. But Liam Kavangh and Ian Keogh had died as human brothers-in-arms in Wexford, Ireland in May 1169, and their bodies deserved to rest side by side.

Joseph took Abigail home to Braintree two days after Liam's loss. She spent the last days at the farm weeping and trying to come to terms with the notion that the angel who occupied Liam Kavangh's body no longer existed.

In fact, all the children of man who had been with the angels that night found it difficult to cope with the knowledge that even an angel's existence could end at any time. Furthermore, the human regret that Liam had not had a chance to say goodbye saddened them.

The heptagon seared in the table in the living room was a constant reminder of their loss. Michael, Patrick, and Brandon chopped the table into firewood and burned it in the fireplace.

Colm sent Fergus back to Dillaway House.

"Ya succeeded in becoming a general by learning to understand the children of man," Colm said on the morning Fergus left the farm. "I have a long way to go, but I'm learning, too. Ya fight the British, we'll fight the demons, and we'll all end this thing."

Fergus' boyish face had aged just a little. "I thought I was strong enough to leave our brotherhood. Now, I'm unsure."

Colm thought of Joseph's words the night Liam died. *Do you realize how fortunate you are to have come this far and to have lost only one of you?*

"When we first arrived in Boston, and Michael and Brandon encountered those demons in that tavern on Beacon Hill, I shamed them for being cowardly. I've been cowardly, too, and that ends now," Colm said. "Joseph's right. I…we have to find the warriors within us again."

"There's something else weighing on you. What is it?"

Colm realized that he had to confide in someone before the weight crushed him. "Henry's going to try to make me choose between Michael's life and Joseph's life."

"How? When?"

"I don't know, but I have to kill him before he has the chance."

"The children of man will die just like they did in 1318 when you and Henry had your first confrontation."

"Aye."

"What do you want me to do?"

"If I don't survive, take care of them—if they survive."

Fergus supposed he should have faced the fact that another showdown between Henry and Colm would be their last. That *was* the fundamental reason they had come to Boston, yet somehow, the stark reality of it had escaped him and the other angels. "I will take care of them," he promised. "What about the sigil? Gordon said the spell worked."

"It's still just an assumption on his part."

"We will find out soon enough."

"Aye. Now go on, Fergus, and stay as far away from the brotherhood as ya can until this is all over."

Fergus mounted his horse. He smiled and gave his archangel a curt nod.

THIRTY-SIX

Joseph's thirty-fourth birthday was on Sunday, June 11. His friend and junior colleague, Elbridge Gerry, planned a surprise celebration at Hastings House in Cambridge.

A lively debate concerning the party was held on the back porch of the farmhouse in Roxbury.

"I am not going," Abe announced the day before the party. "I do not fit in with the lawyers, doctors, merchants, and army officers who are Joseph's friends."

"That's stupid, Abe," Michael said. "Ya are Joseph's friend, too."

Gordon quipped, "Do you think I fit in? There won't be another black man or woman there except the servants."

"How're we supposed to know who fits in where?" Seamus pointed out. "We don't know a damn thing about human celebrations."

"You've seen Shawnee celebration rituals in Burkes Garden," Jeremiah said.

"That cain't be the same as white colonist celebration rituals."

Abe eyed the angels and said, "Your clothes are improper attire for a doctor's birthday party. The only one of you who has proper clothing is Fergus, and he is not attending."

The angels glanced down at their grubby clothing with sheer unconcern. Michael stuck out his lower lip, looked at Patrick, and shrugged.

"Liam had proper clothes, but we buried his vessel in them," Ian said.

Seamus frowned. "That ain't helpful, Ian"

Jeremiah and Gordon snorted a laugh.

"Neither one of you look any better," Abe scoffed.

"Our clothes didn't seem to matter to John Hancock, John Adams, or Samuel Adams," Colm said, thinking about their initial meeting with the patriots. That meeting in the Green Dragon Tavern basement seemed so long ago even in the scheme of an archangel's existence.

Abe sighed and rolled his eyes. "This is a *party*. There will be ladies there." He paused. "At least bathe. Do you want the ladies to be repulsed by your presence?"

"Will they be pretty ladies?" Michael asked enthusiastically.

"I wou'd say there is a good chance, but they will find your filthy hands and face disgusting."

Gordon had given up hope that he and Michael could be civil. Poking the angel was at least entertaining. "What difference does it make, Michael? You can't do anything with them anyway."

"Fuck ya!" Michael shoved Gordon; he went sprawling off the porch edge. Michael leaned over and spit on him.

Gordon jumped to his feet and onto the porch. He snatched Michael by the hair and yelled in his face. "I've had enough of your nasty behavior!"

Michael jammed his palm into Gordon's face and kicked him in the shin.

Brandon ignored Michael and Gordon. The thought of having to speak to a lady gave him the urge to rustle his wings. He said, "Colm, maybe I can stay behind with Abe."

Patrick fidgeted with the hilt of the blade he held in his hand. "We ain't got no idea what to do at a party."

"Put a period to it," Colm said, sternly. "Michael and Gordon, stop it." They reluctantly separated.

"We've *all* been invited to the party, and we're *all* going," Colm ordered.

"Do not tell me what to do, Colm," Abe grumbled.

Colm flashed his eyes at Abe. Then he said, "All of ya bathe like Abe said. We'll leave for Cambridge in the morning."

☙

Large, public, and elaborate birthday celebrations were generally reserved for royalty. The party held for Joseph was large and public, but not particularly elaborate.

Colm and his men arrived at Hastings House at three o'clock in the afternoon; well after the party started. Lilting voices, bursts of laughter, tinkling crystal, and melodious violins escaped from the house's windows. A number of party-goers had spilled out onto the front and side lawns.

The nine newly arrived guests reined their horses to an uneasy stop in front of the house. Parked, departing, and arriving carriages and chaises clogged the road and the yard.

"Let's leave," Brandon said, fretfully. "Joseph's not going to miss us. Look at all the people here!"

Colm was anxious, too.

What're we supposed to do with the horses if we stay? Patrick wondered.

"Brandon O'Flynn? Damn! It *is* you!"

Brandon recognized the man with the outstretched hand and alcohol-flushed face—Dr. Samuel Prescott.

"It is good to see you!" Samuel exclaimed.

Brandon's anxiety evaporated. He dismounted and met Samuel with outstretched arms. They embraced. After much back patting and muttering their pleasure at seeing one another, they stepped apart. Brandon smelled rum on Samuel's breath and said, "Where do I get a cup of what you're drinking?"

Samuel's initial euphoria dulled as he looked among the faces of the slowly dismounting angels. "Where is Ian? Do not tell me he is dead."

Brandon tilted his head in Ian's direction. "That's him. He was forced to find a new vessel."

Samuel's eyebrows shot up. He frowned at the man Brandon indicated. This man was at least seven years older than the vessel Ian had previously occupied. His eyes were dark blue instead of pale blue. His graying brown hair fell in a long queue down his back instead of the neat black-haired ponytail Ian used to wear.

Samuel stared at Ian and said awkwardly, "It will take me time to get accustomed to your new body."

Ian laughed at Samuel's perplexed expression and flashed his red aura for Samuel's benefit.

"Mrs. Barrett told me that Sidonie went back to Charles Town. Why?" Samuel asked Ian.

Ian grimaced.

"Let's talk over full tankards of rum," Brandon suggested.

Samuel's eyes fell on Michael. He went to embrace the angel with whom he shared a different bond. The day Michael and he were assaulted outside the meetinghouse would remain a clear memory.

Michael's wings rustled in response to his joy at seeing Samuel. The sound astonished the angels, but Colm was clearly unsettled by Michael's reaction.

A man with graying brown hair much like Ian's approached with long hurried strides. He shouted, "I'll be damned! Abe Rowlinson! I have not seen you since we fought at Fort Beauséjour! I had no idea you were acquainted with Dr. Warren!"

"William Prescott?" Abe went to meet him. They engaged in back slapping and shoulder patting then strode toward the house in a flurry of conversation.

Four adolescent boys, two black and two white, raced across the lawn and stopped in front of Colm. Their young eyes widened when they looked up into Colm's pleasant face.

"Are you God?" asked a white freckled-face boy.

"Ya didn't come to ask me if I was God. What do ya want?"

"Dr. Warren sent us to take care of your horses, and he asks that you go inside to join his celebration," said a black boy who wore a worn out bicorn hat.

The young boys led the horses away.

Colm wondered, *how was Joseph able to see us arrive with the constant flux of arriving and departing vehicles and horses and hundreds of people inside?* He surveyed the windows, the yard, and the tangle of parked carriages and chaises. Among that tangle, he saw a nondescript black coach with blue curtains over the windows. The driver's seat was vacant.

"Go join the party," Colm ordered his men. "Jeremiah and Gordon, go with the boys."

The angels took the order.

Colm turned and walked away from the Hastings House festivities. He had to clear his mind and think about the implications of Michael rustling his wings in joy. And he'd heard Joseph and Margaret Gage speaking. He felt their emotions as they sat together in the nondescript coach. Colm wanted to block those things from his spirit.

"I wanted…needed to see you," Margaret breathed as she stroked Joseph's cheek. The bruises there had faded to yellow ghosts.

He leaned in and kissed her passionately. She forgot the ghostly bruises.

She returned his hungry kiss, and then pulled away from him. Her eyes savored every speck of his being. She longed to feel him between her legs. But that act was what had driven her, in dangerous secrecy, to Cambridge to tell him that she was with child.

"I realize I have only confused you by telling you of my pregnancy, and that I am unsure whether you or Thomas is the father," Margaret admitted.

Joseph was afraid to speak lest he blurt out that he knew the child was his because an archangel had told him.

Margaret misunderstood Joseph's paralysis. She pushed him away. "This has been a mistake," she hissed. "How could I have been so foolish? I have risked everything to see you, yet you sit there as if my words mean nothing!"

"No! That is the furthest thing from the truth!"

She wanted to believe him. She wanted to believe that she was not an easily fooled woman. She thought of the general with the yellow-green eyes, who had been quartering in her home since February. She shuddered. *Why did I think of him when I am with Joseph? It's a disgusting intrusion on my desire for this beautiful man who sits here beside me.*

Joseph reached for her. She let him touch her cheeks and shoulders. He slid his hands into the tight bodice of her dress and past the stays. Her nipples hardened and she moaned.

"If I told you I know the babe in your womb is mine, would you promise to believe me?" His hands slid from her breasts and traveled to search the complication of her long skirts for an entrance to what he wanted to touch.

Margaret relaxed her thighs and spread them wide so Joseph's hands did not have to search hard for entrance. She sighed as he pulled his body in closer to her and found a pathway to what he was searching for.

"Tell me," she whispered.

Joseph's desire blurred his thoughts. He pushed her skirts and petticoat up to her waist, unbuttoned his breeches, and slipped between her thighs.

Margaret moaned. He was inside her before she had a chance to take another breath. He took her with quiet elegance. Margaret did not realize that she had been holding her breath until he reached orgasm.

Joseph lay pressed against her, waiting for his breathing to settle.

She ran her hand over the top of his sandy blond hair, and said, "Tell me how you know this baby is yours."

He lifted his head and looked into her eyes. *I heard it from a demon first,* he thought. He killed the thought and kissed her. In earnest, he said, "An archangel told me."

She tried to push him away. "Why would you say something...?" She saw honesty in his eyes. "You *are* telling the truth."

The sound of a carriage and six horses approaching Hastings House startled Margaret and Joseph. They quickly arranged their clothing and hair. Joseph slipped open a curtain. The newcomers were party guests and not a threat. Beyond the arriving guests, he saw Colm walking along the road away from the house.

Joseph closed the curtain, and grasped Margaret's hand. "It is time you return to Boston before the length of your absence is questioned." He thought of her return home and the demons quartered there. If Henry or Robert wished to harm Margaret and his unborn child, he was powerless to stop it. "Take care, Margaret." His hand traveled to caress her belly where an indication of her condition was becoming visible.

He softly knocked on the coach door to indicate to Margaret's driver that it was time to take her home. The coach rocked as the man climbed into the driver's seat.

"I do not know when we will see one another again," Margaret said.

Joseph heard what sounded like regret in her voice. He reached to open the coach door, and then stopped. "There is a tall thin man with long curly brown hair. His queue is secured with a silver ribbon. You will pass him on the road just after you leave here. Look at him closely, and believe what your heart tells you about him."

She saw gentle love in Joseph's eyes and knew that love was for the man he spoke of—his archangel.

He kissed her one last time and got out of the coach.

The driver urged the horses to turn the coach toward Boston.

Margaret pulled back the curtains. The man Joseph described stood at the edge of the road as the coach passed by. She swore she saw silver light flash in his eyes when he looked at her. Soft words slid through her mind. *Ya child is a girl. Tell her about her father. Tell her he has great courage.*

Colm walked back to Hastings House. Joseph stood in the road with his arms crossed over his chest, waiting for him. They crossed the lawn and entered the house without speaking.

A young servant handed glasses of claret to Colm and Joseph. The flurry of people who suddenly surrounded them overwhelmed Colm, but he stayed by Joseph's side. Colm was introduced to Elbridge Gerry, Colonel Israel Putnam, Colonel William Prescott, General John Thomas, General Artemas Ward, the chairman of the Committee of Supplies, Moses Gill, and James Otis.

"General Ward, Mr. Gill, and I have sent a plea to New York to send us as much gunpowder as they can spare," Joseph explained to Colm. "Our gunpowder is in critically short supply due to the skirmishes we have been fighting."

"We have asked that they send it by land in a manner that will not alert the enemy of our lacking," General Ward interjected.

"Does New York have the supply ya need?" Colm asked.

"We do not know. We have asked them to beseech the other colonies for help on our behalf."

Joseph saw Abe, Gordon, and Jeremiah standing on the perimeter of the clutch of men surrounding Colm and him. Joseph motioned for them to step in closer that he may conduct the same introductions for them as he had done for Colm.

"I did not realize you were already acquainted with Colonel Prescott," Joseph said to Abe.

"Old fighting comrades is all," Abe said, embarrassed. He felt out of place among the likes of Colonel Putnam and General Ward.

"The Provincial Congress will soon vote by ballet on whether or not to bestow the rank of major general on our dear friend, Joseph," Elbridge Gerry explained with a hearty smile. "Of course, even if he is given the rank, the Continental Congress must approve the commission."

"I see no problem in securing the commission," General Artemas Ward said. "John Hancock, John Adams, and Samuel Adams maintain a high degree of clout at the Congress in Philadelphia."

"Why, Joseph will outrank us all!" Colonel Israel Putnam crowed in delight.

General John Thomas was not as enthusiastic as the others over the prospect of Joseph outranking him. The Committee of Safety had already nudged him out of what he considered to be his hometown right by appointing General Fergus Driscoll in command of the provincial army stationed in Roxbury. The rumors that Driscoll was an actual angel of God were ridiculous, only to be believed by the ignorant and the Godless. It galled Thomas even further that General Driscoll's swain friends were among the guests at Warren's birthday party.

Thomas tried to hide his contempt. "It is well known that Hancock and the Adams cousins are close friends with Joseph. I've no doubt they are already aware of his desire and will act accordingly to fulfill his ambition."

Jeremiah leaned in toward Gordon and said, "I'd say Thomas is jealous."

Joseph's attention was drawn to a small group of men standing on the other side of the room. Michael and Patrick were conversing with his younger brother, twenty-seven-year old Eben Warren, and his youngest brother, twenty-two-year old, Dr. John Warren, whom Joseph called Jack. A foreboding shadow scudded like a storm cloud across the knot of the four little brothers. Joseph shook his head to chase away the discomforting mirage.

"Joseph, are you alright?" James Otis, inquired.

"I am fine, James. Please excuse me." He crossed the large living room to the front door, paused, and caught Colm's eye.

Colm issued a slight nod in response, and then regarded the group of four little brothers. *Something has unnerved Joseph.* He quickly searched the room for Ian, Brandon, and Seamus. Ian was in a shadowed corner with a pretty, dark-haired woman. She brushed a lock of hair away from her forehead with delicately boned fingers that made Colm think of Sidonie.

Seamus and Brandon were lounging on a couch with Samuel Prescott. Rum sloshed from the tankards they held when a man Colm didn't recognize said something that made them laugh.

With his angels accounted for and Jeremiah, Gordon, and Abe in sight, Colm waited for Joseph's cue. Joseph opened the front door and walked outside without closing the door behind him. Colm followed.

The lawn was considerably more crowded than it had been when Colm and his men had arrived. Joseph was unable to walk more than a few feet before someone called his name or reached to touch his arm or hand.

A woman, finely dressed in a sophisticated blue silk gown, advanced on Joseph from behind. Her blond hair was curled and pulled away from her young attractive face. She clenched the collar of Joseph's coat and whirled him round to face her.

Her orange eyes flamed and sparks stung his cheeks. She let go of his coat collar and slapped him with unmerciful strength. Joseph's jaw dislocated. His ears rang and his vision blurred. The demon viciously jerked the ponytail at the nape of his neck so his head was wretched to the side.

Colm seized the back of her dress near her shoulders and pulled her away from Joseph. She screeched and kicked and tried to propel herself toward Joseph to wreak further damage. Her dress ripped, and she slipped from Colm's grasp.

The young lady's behavior was so shocking that the nearby party guests stopped and gasped.

William Prescott shouted, "Get her away from Dr. Warren!"

A flurry of men ran to help Joseph. Colm lost sight of him. Gordon and Jeremiah barged into the flurry.

Gordon quickly closed the gap between him and the demon that now had Joseph on the ground and was crawling on top of him. Gordon snatched her hair and dragged her backward until she was lying on the ground face up. The Sigil of Lucifer flashed on Gordon's blade when he cut off his cravat to expose the tattoo on his neck.

The demon scrambled to her feet, gripped his wrist, and screamed, "I'm going to strangle you first!"

Her hand flew to his neck. When her splayed fingers brushed the tattoo of the sigil, Gordon heard a loud hiss. The demon recoiled. Gordon jammed his blade into one of her eyes. The demon that possessed the woman screeched. Orange flames shot skyward. The men who were trying to help Joseph scattered. Embers sparked and popped. Wisps of smoke snaked through the air.

Gordon put his palms on his knees and panted.

The demon had possessed a corpse. The dead woman lay face up on top of Joseph with hollow smoldering eyes. The hair around her face was burned away. Her forehead and cheeks were striated with strips of pink raw and black charred skin. Gordon's blade protruded from one incinerated eye.

The human onlookers' nonplussed faces ranged from grimaces to complete horror. Colonel Prescott and Colonel Putnam, on the other hand, appeared pleased at the outcome of the unexpected battle waged on the lawn of Hastings House. Prescott and Putnam had heard the rumors that the Sons of Liberty were allied with an archangel and his men. They had also heard rumors of the demons the angels came to fight. The two colonels were looking forward to participating in the alliance they now knew was not a rumor.

Colm seized the dead woman by the neck and flung her body aside. James Otis, Elbridge Gerry, and Moses Gill gathered around her. She was not someone they recognized.

Joseph tried to gather his wits, but he was dizzy, and his world was revolving as if it had suddenly been catapulted out of its orbit. He heard Michael say, "Ya gonna be alright!" Then, Joseph felt Michael's arms tighten around him.

A shy frightened girl exhaled an inaudible cry when Michael lifted Joseph into his arms. Michael heard her muted fear. He glanced at her, and for the first time in a very long time, he allowed himself to breathe deeply of her enticing scent.

Michael carried Joseph inside the house. He lay him on the couch that the intoxicated Seamus, Brandon, and Samuel had occupied before the demon attack drew them into the yard.

Colm came to Joseph's side. His wings unfurled in distress when he saw that Joseph's forehead and the tip of his nose were skinned. The angels gathered around their archangel. They released their auras and their wings unfurled in a shower of silver crystals.

Joseph's brothers looked on. Their first physical exposure to the angels and demons should have been unspeakable confusion, but the recollection of the hour spent in conversation with the beautiful angels with effeminate countenances, soothed the Warren brothers.

John Warren waded through the silver crystals and angel wings to his brother's side.

Colm still had no idea what Joseph had seen that made him abruptly leave the house. He vowed to never leave Joseph alone again.

None of the three major generals King George III sent to the colonies on the *Cerberus* were particularly pleased about sailing into the cauldron of occupied Boston. General Henry Clinton, the least social and most detail-oriented of the three, could not believe that so little was known about the countryside beyond Boston, despite a number of marches into the territory. This discussion began at ten o'clock in the morning at the home where the generals were quartered on Beacon Hill—the home of John Hancock.

General William Howe was hungover from another private party he had attended the night before with General Hereford, Captain Percy, and Captain Jameson. William's cock was raw from the hours he managed to keep an erection and fuck more women than he thought possible in one night. He was slumped in his chair, drinking rum. He hoped that he would get drunk before one of the generals in the room demanded he have a coherent opinion.

Henry and Robert sat across the room from William. From over the rim of his glass, William eyed Henry. Not only did Henry look as if he had not had a drop of alcohol and a good night's sleep, his impeccable dress was sweat and wrinkle-free. His unsettling yellow-green eyes were alert and smiling. Robert appeared to be in the same condition.

Henry Clinton made a point to look at Thomas Gage when he said, "I recommend we take immediate action to secure the surrounding environs."

Thomas slipped a glance at Henry Hereford. Despite their somewhat uncomfortable relationship, they had shared a home for almost five months. That domestic familiarity was what Thomas held on to now.

Henry flashed Thomas a smile, but it was not born out of the familiarity Thomas clung to. Henry realized that the three major generals would not sit idly by and watch Boston implode. They were about to construct the opportunity Henry needed to force the archangel to choose between his little brother, Michael, and his pet, Joseph Warren. It was so close that Henry could feel it in his God-given wrath.

"On Sunday, June 18, when most of the provincial army in Roxbury is attending religious services, John will begin cannonading Roxbury from Boston Neck," Henry Clinton explained. "In the meantime, William can lead a detachment to Dorchester Heights, build two redoubts, and attack General Driscoll's army in Roxbury."

William felt the urge to touch his raw cock in an effort to soothe it. *Can Clinton be any more tiresome with his drivel about cannonading Roxbury and attacking from Dorchester?*

To William's surprise, Henry Clinton said something that made him forget his discomforts.

"We need to focus on the heights at Charlestown, to the north across the Charles River, as well," Henry said. He sipped a cup of one of Boston's precious commodities—tea. "These areas are essential to the safety of Boston, and an attack would shake those rebel wretches and possibly disperse them for a time."

"I am in agreement," General John Burgoyne replied. He sipped his own cup of precious tea.

Despite John's acquiescence, it made no difference to him. He was more than content to take quill to paper and write any dramatization the five generals in the room cared to announce. Therefore, on June 12, he turned his quill to crafting a proclamation for Thomas, stating there would be no British compromise with the patriots. Any persons after the date of the proclamation, who took up arms or otherwise aided and abetted the rebel cause in any way, even if only by a single secret correspondence, were to be judged rebels and traitors and treated as such.

Then, Thomas decided to institute martial law in Massachusetts.

A few days later, he asked John to offer clemency to all patriot leaders who promptly surrendered, with the exception of John Hancock and Samuel

Adams. John Burgoyne wrote with an overblown, pompous tone that did nothing more than drive a wedge deeper between the rebels and loyalists.

Thomas had finally sealed his fate. The man who was to replace Lord Dartmouth as Secretary of State to the Colonies, Lord George Germaine, lamented to his peers that General Gage was in a situation of too great importance for his talents.

THIRTY-SEVEN

As the leader of the Provincial Congress and the Committee of Safety, Joseph was the one to whom prospective officers appealed when they were angling for a commission in the provincial army. John Adams, still in attendance at the Continental Congress in Philadelphia, read and reread the letter Joseph had written:

> *I had never, till now, any idea or suspicion of the selfishness of this people, or their impatient eagerness for commissions. In the British army, an officer comes from the English upper class and has to purchase his commission. In our new American army, no such social and financial qualifications exist. Instead of paying for a commission, an officer is expected to earn it by recruiting the sufficient number of men. The lowest can aspire as freely as the highest. There are no people on Earth so ambitious as the people of America.*

Similarly, Samuel Adams received a letter from Joseph concerning his disappointment in discovering that a close colleague, Dr. John Jeffries, harbored English loyalist ambitions to elevate his social status, and like the former Royal Governor of Massachusetts, Thomas Hutchinson, Dr. Jeffries was willing to step on anyone who impeded his way. Joseph wrote:

> *The English ambition to rise to a higher social station requires the need to sacrifice people. What is needed in America is a government in which the only road to promotion may be through the affection of the people instead of attaining membership in a group that exists above the people. This being the case, the interest of the governor and the governed would be the same.*

As the Adams cousins, received, read, and took to heart Joseph's concerns and observations, Joseph was recovering from a demon attack. His forehead and the tip of his nose were skinned. His body was sore from his uncontrolled fall to the ground, and his thoughts were unclear. Colm forced Joseph to drink excessive quantities of rum before John Warren painfully reset Joseph's dislocated jaw.

In a drunken, uncharacteristically tearful state within earshot of his brother, Joseph told Colm about his encounter with Margaret and his regret that he would never be a father to his own child. Joseph also bared his soul regarding Mercy, and the things he had done to lead her to believe that they might have their own children.

"How can I possibly live a normal life knowing what I know now?" Joseph lamented as he touched his painful jaw. He slowly swallowed a mouthful of rum.

Colm listened in silence. Human regret was a horrible burden that his rejection of Heaven had not lessened. Or maybe, it was his devotion to Joseph that had not lessened the burden.

Joseph finally fell asleep.

There was an insistent knock on Joseph's bedroom door. John went to answer the knock. Colm heard John say, "He needs rest." Then, "Yes, yes, I will relay the message to him."

John quietly shut the door. "They never let him rest," he whispered to Colm. "They act like children who cannot make a decision without him."

The following day, a discussion took place in Hastings House in regard to securing the highlands in Cambridge and Charlestown. Although Israel Putnam and his men had established redoubts on some of the smaller hills, the redoubts recommended on the larger hills had not been built.

William Prescott and Israel Putnam were in favor of constructing those redoubts to provoke the British into coming out of Boston and fighting rather than wait for a possible siege.

"I think building redoubts and breastworks in the face of the British is a rash decision at this time," Joseph advised Israel.

"I am in agreement with Dr. Warren," General Artemas Ward said. He addressed William and Israel. "An offensive action on our part should be forestalled."

"Forestalled until when?" William demanded.

Artemas looked at William as if he were daft. "Until the provincial army is better organized and supplied. You know very well that we are in short supply of gunpowder."

"Mr. Bohannon, your experience far outweighs ours," Israel said. He was delighted at the chance to speak to the archangel concerning matters of war. "What is your opinion?"

Colm was leaning against the meeting room back wall with his arms crossed over his chest. This type of strategy planning wasn't what he was used to. He was used to conferring with Fergus and Seamus, if at all, and making the final decision on his own. As Heaven's warriors, the archangels never conferred.

Colm's palimpsest surfaced and whispered, *the man Colm Bohannon once belonged to a larger army in Ireland.*

Those memories are with his soul, Colm argued.

But ya remember what happened that night in Wexford when he and his men ran out of ammunition, don't ya?

Colm uncrossed his arms and stood up straight. "Have ya ever run out of ammunition during a battle, Colonel Putnam?"

"Of course not."

"What do ya think will happen if ya run out of ammunition during a battle?"

Israel shot an uncomfortable look at Artemas.

"Ya don't need my opinion. Ya need to answer the question," Colm insisted.

"I do not think that will happen. The battle would have to go on—"

"Ya will die if ya run out of ammunition," Colm said. "Is that so hard to understand?" His eyes flashed and Israel took a step back.

A drawn-out silence ensued, but it did not dim the individual convictions among the men in the meeting room.

There was another topic that needed to be discussed.

Artemas glanced at Joseph's bruised jaw before he said, "Mr. Bohannon, we have heard rumors of the demons that pursue you and your angels. We know the woman who attacked Dr. Warren yesterday was possessed by a demon. Your men refuse to speak of it. Even, Dr. Prescott stays silent. Do you intend on telling us what else we may be facing besides the British army?"

Joseph and Colm exchanged a long look.

Then, Joseph told them the angels' story.

❧

By June 15, it was clear that the British were about to make a preemptive strike on Roxbury, Dorchester, and Charlestown. Joseph and the Committee of Safety decided that the provincial army must make a preemptive move of their own despite the shortage of supplies.

After determining that Fergus Driscoll's army in Roxbury was not strong enough to take and hold nearby Dorchester Heights, the committee decided to implement a plan proposed by Israel Putnam. In the early morning hours of June 17, the provincial army, under the command of William Prescott, would seize the currently unoccupied high ground above Charlestown.

Joseph begged Colm to take his men and accompany William.

"I told ya, I'm not leaving ya without my protection," Colm said, exasperated.

Joseph's jaw was still painful, especially when he spoke. "If you do not go with William, there will be no one to protect," he retorted. "This is the hour in which we must present our strength or all may be lost going forward."

Colm said nothing. The hollow place where Liam's spirit once resided would never heal. His fear of that place growing larger with every new loss wanted to control him.

Joseph grew impatient with Colm. "ARE YOU, OR ARE YOU NOT, GOING TO BE THE WARRIOR YOU ARE SUPPOSED TO BE? IF NOT, THEN WE NEED TO END THIS RIDICULOUS CAROUSEL RIDE!"

Colm looked down into his tankard of rum. The liquid rippled in his shaking hands.

Joseph covered his mouth with the splayed fingers of his left hand and sighed. The effort of yelling at Colm hurt his jaw, but that was the least of his discomfort. His hand slid from his mouth. "I feel the void Liam left in your spirit, in all your spirits, because I feel it in mine as well. Abigail told me she will never recover from his loss. Still, I cannot imagine losing someone who was a part of my life for millenniums."

What Joseph did not say was—*I cannot imagine losing you.*

Colm drank the rest of the rum and set the tankard on the floor. He rose from his chair and pulled Joseph into his arms. He tried not to hurt Joseph's sore body in his desperation to hold on to the human he should never have loved. Colm remembered the day Robert had threatened Joseph in the meetinghouse, and he thought of what he had told Joseph afterward. *Archangels are merely beholders and preceptors. We don't invest in the human condition.*

He released Joseph. "We'll do what ya want, but ya have to stay away if there's a battle."

"I cannot promise that."

"Ya are needed by the people to lead the patriotic movement. Ya political position doesn't warrant getting killed on the battlefield."

"I will do what I must, even if that means going into battle only to offer care for the wounded and dying."

Colm was unable to steady his shaking hands. "And what of ya major general's commission? It's what ya wanted, which tells me ya want to be more than a doctor on the battlefield."

"Yes, I do."

"Do ya understand that the next time there's a battle, it may be a real battle with the demons not just possessed men sprinkled among the troops?"

Joseph said nothing.

"DAMN IT! Every time ya ask me to do something like this is another time I don't go after Henry! I need to do it before…before the rebels are faced with an all-out demonic battle! I CAN'T KEEP DOING THIS, JOSEPH!"

"Colm—"

"I need to be with my men," Colm said. He walked out of the room and stormed up the stairs.

The angels, Gordon, Abe, and Jeremiah were in a cramped bedroom. The three men and Seamus shared the two small beds in the room. The windless June night was warm. Crickets chirped from somewhere in the darkness beyond the open windows. Ian, Brandon, Patrick, and Michael were lying on the floor atop the blankets stripped from the bed.

Colm sat beside Michael.

Michael sat up. "We're all awake," he said.

Gordon exhaled a loud snore.

He goads me even when he's asleep, Michael thought.

"Then ya know what we're going to do tomorrow," Colm said.

"We do," Seamus whispered.

"If a battle breaks out and something happens to me, ya will let Fergus take care of ya. I told him to stay away from us. I think it's safer."

Patrick was lying beside Michael. A cry of sorrow escaped him. He rolled over on his side.

Colm's eyes stirred toward the sound, then to his brother's face. He said, "Michael, I want ya to stay beside me, no matter what. Do ya understand me?"

Strangely, Michael thought about the girl whose scent had distracted him when he picked Joseph up from the ground after the demon attack. He had never had a second thought about a girl in his existence, not even after he created Nephilim.

He looked at his brother long and hard. "I understand," Michael finally said. He understood the order, but he didn't understand the reason behind it.

Colm put a hand on the back of Michael's head and kissed Michael's forehead. Then he said, "Abe and Jeremiah, ya don't have to go with us. Neither does Gordon."

A bed creaked as Seamus and Abe sat up. Gordon continued to snore.

Abe said, bitterly, "Colm, you cannot believe any of us would walk away. Not after everything we have been through together."

"It ain't just that," Jeremiah interjected. "We're patriots as much as Joseph Warren or William Prescott. This is our cause, too."

"Indeed, it is," Gordon murmured.

Michael squelched the urge to say something hateful now that Gordon was awake. But it was time to let go of his hatred. After all, Gordon had killed the demon that attacked Joseph and proven the validity of the Sigil of Lucifer's power.

There was soft shuffling. Brandon sat up. His voice quivered, "I miss Liam. I can't stop thinking about him. I can't accept that he doesn't exist anymore."

Seamus sighed. "None, of us cain. We ain't never gonna stop missin' him and wonderin' about him."

Patrick rolled on to his stomach and buried his face in the blanket beneath him to muffle his sobs. Seamus slid off the bed and wedged into a sitting position between Brandon and Patrick. He tried to soothe his brother while his own tears wet his graying beard.

"It's not…just Liam," Ian said. "I miss Sidonie. I didn't think I would. She wanted to teach me how to express love like men and women do. I didn't understand the purpose. I still don't." He sighed. "She's in Heaven, and I'm never going back there. Our spirits will never dwell in the same place." He rustled his wings to comfort himself, and his red aura lit up the bedroom.

The doleful atmosphere reminded Gordon of what the master of the tobacco plantation, where his family lived, worked, and died, had told him the day he was given his freedom—the day Gordon's demon-possessed father killed his wife and children. The bit of wisdom sounded silky as Gordon spoke the words. "Some things are not really gone if you look at it the right way."

Colm closed his eyes and listened to the echoes of grief and regret in the room. His hand was still on the back of Michael's head. He gently pressed Michael's face against his chest and rested his chin on the top of Michael's head.

Brandon released his yellow aura, and he huffed out a frightened laugh. "Patrick was afraid we wouldn't be angels anymore if we rejected Heaven. Yet, I feel more like an angel than I have since we were banished. I feel stronger… less scared somehow." He mumbled, "It has to be because we're connected to Lucifer, because of the sigil. We're disconnected from Heaven just like he is."

Abe absently touched the sigil tattooed on his neck.

Patrick's sobs quieted. He sniffed and sat up.

"Brandon has a point, Colm," Seamus said. He studied his archangel's face in the bright light of Ian's and Brandon's auras.

"We heard you and Joseph shoutin' at each other. We heard you sayin' somethin' about not bein' able to go after Henry because—" Seamus stopped himself from saying because of Joseph's wishes. It wasn't his place to question Colm's decisions. "We're better armed now, so when are we gonna have an all-out battle with the demons?"

Colm looked at Seamus.

"That's what this is about, ain't it, Colm? You think we might be walkin' into a battle with Henry. That's what all that talk about Fergus lookin' after us is about."

"And you don't want Joseph to know," Gordon added.

Jeremiah got up and crawled across both beds until he was able to sit on the edge of the bed beside Abe. "Why do you want Michael to stay near you?" he asked.

"That's enough!" Colm ordered. "Ya have freewill, Jeremiah, but it's not ya place to question me."

Jeremiah met Colm's stare. "It ain't my place ta stand by you because you're like a brother ta me? It ain't my place ta be scared ta death for what's gonna happen ta all of us? It ain't my place ta mourn for Liam just like you do?" He ran a hand over his dark-blond beard. "I'm willin' ta die for you. My unborn son won't never know me because I'll die for you. Michael was right. You chose Joseph over us."

The moment he said those last words, Jeremiah regretted them, but an apology would be lost on Colm. Of deeper concern was the agonized look in Colm's eyes.

Colm's grip on Michael's head intensified. His palimpsest tried to surface in order to entice him to break down and cry. He mentally spit at it, like Michael's habit of spitting at his opponent when confronted. The muscles in Colm's arm flexed harder and pressed Michael's face tight against his chest.

Michael struggled against Colm's grip. "I can't breathe, Colm!" His wings rustled, and he pulled at Colm's arm. "Let go!"

"Let go of him, Colm!" Abe shouted. "You are smothering him!" He hesitated to become physical with the archangel. It was something he had never done.

Blue light burst forth as Michael released his aura in distress.

Patrick scrambled to his knees and without thinking, he screamed, "LET GO OF MICHAEL!" and slapped Colm's face.

Colm looked at Patrick through bleary eyes. His arm relaxed. Michael squirmed away and drank in gulps of air.

Colm and Patrick considered one another in a haze of intense emotion.

Then, Colm cupped Patrick's cheeks and said, "Stay away from Henry. If I say run, ya run. Do ya understand me?"

Patrick's gray eyes misted, but he didn't cry. "I understand."

Colm patted Patrick's cheeks and smiled.

"Brandon said he feels stronger," Patrick said. "I do, too."

Michael's palimpsest barged in, and like Colm, he shoved it away before it could overwhelm him with emotion. He said to his brother, "I feel stronger, too."

Colm let his hands slide from Patrick's cheeks. He looked at the three boys—Michael, Patrick, and Brandon. "I hope ya *are* stronger. I hope we're all stronger. But what I said stands. That includes ya, Brandon. If I say run, ya run."

At 9:00 p.m. on Friday, June 16, 1775, nearly one thousand provincial soldiers under the command of Colonel William Prescott assembled on the common in Cambridge opposite Hastings House. Another two hundred men from Connecticut, under the command of Captain Thomas Knowlton, waited near Willis Creek to join them.

Dressed in homespun clothing with sweat-stained hats on their disheveled heads, the men were less an army than a ragtag group of patriots. They looked just like the militiamen who had fought at Lexington and Concord. They shouldered their own muskets. Some of the weapons dated from before the French and Indian War. Almost no one had bayonets. Many had picks,

362

shovels, and other entrenching tools. Most had blankets and little more than a day's provisions.

Abe Rowlinson, Gordon Walker, Jeremiah Killam, Michael Bohannon, Seamus Cullen, Patrick Cullen, Brandon O'Flynn, Ian Keogh, and Colm Bohannon were among the lot. Joseph Warren, Elbridge Gerry, Artemas Ward, and James Otis looked on from the lawn of Hastings House as Reverend Samuel Langdon said prayers in the deepening darkness. The prayers were meant to encourage and soothe the men who, unknown to them, were about to face one of the bloodiest battles of the American Revolution.

Under the cover of darkness, Prescott and two sergeants carrying lanterns led the column east out of town. After crossing several wooden bridges, they met up with Captain Knowlton and his company. The word spread like wildfire that angels of God were marching among them, and those angels were known to Colonel William Prescott and Dr. Joseph Warren.

Colonel Israel Putnam and Lieutenant Colonel Richard Gridley, a noted engineer and commander of the artillery regiment, joined Prescott just before they reached Charlestown Neck. The combined column moved onward until they came to the crossroads at Charlestown Neck and followed the right-hand fork. Their destination suddenly became clear; they were marching toward Bunker Hill.

The Charlestown peninsula was almost a small-scale mirror of Boston, but with a narrower neck, low rolling hills, and a widening land mass southeast from the neck to the point where the Charles River separated the peninsula from Boston. The ground rose in a series of hills that peaked and then stepped downhill toward Boston. The first of these was a hill 110 feet in height that sloped steeply toward the waters of the Mystic River to the northeast and the Charles River to the southwest. This was Bunker Hill, and there was no question about its name.

From Bunker Hill, a ridge descended down to a lower, broader hill. There was no common name affixed to it. The fields on this hill were partitioned by stone walls and rail fences. The easterly portions of the hill were used mainly for hay fields and pasturing; the westerly portions contained orchards and gardens.

Copp's Hill, in northern Boston, was about twelve hundred feet away across the Charles River. British cannons placed among the gravestones of Copp's Burial Grounds stared at what would later be known as Breed's Hill. A quarter mile to the south laid the wharves of Boston.

As General Henry Clinton had noted, whoever controlled the heights of the Charlestown peninsula controlled much of Boston.

The waning gibbous moon, rose in the east and began to shed light on the hills above Charlestown.

It was 10:00 p.m. with dawn set to arrive at 4:00 a.m. In six hours, they were to build a fort before the morning light revealed their efforts to the British in Boston. There was much debate between Prescott, Putnam, and Gridley over where to build the fort.

"If we place the redoubt here, and equip it with cannons, we can rake British shipping and the British waterfront," Putnam insisted.

"I'm in command of this mission," Prescott retorted. "The breastworks and redoubt are to be built on Bunker Hill. To place a fort in the face of the British is an entirely different undertaking than my orders from the Committee of Safety."

"I say we invite General Gage to come out and fight!" Putnam crowed.

As the colonels argued over the redoubt's position, Colm and his men stood anonymously within the dark abyss of 1,200 provincial soldiers. The soldiers could not hear what Putnam said to Prescott, but they saw Lieutenant Colonel Richard Gridley begin to lay out gridlines for a redoubt.

Prescott ordered his men to dig the small fort that was to be 10 rods long on all four sides. The V-shaped front faced Copp's Hill and did not take into account the defense of the open slopes on the left, which dropped gently toward the Mystic River.

As his troops dug, Colonel Prescott was afraid they would be heard so he sent a group of sixty men down into the empty village of Charlestown. He also feared that sentries on board the Royal Navy ships in the Charles River would raise a cry of alarm. Near dawn, he heard a routine call from the watch aboard the twenty-gun sloop the HMS *Lively* report "all is well."

Colm and his brotherhood also heard the call from where they were building the breastwork above the redoubt that Prescott's men were still digging.

But the rebels' activity *had* been heard.

General Henry Clinton awoke in the bedroom, where John Hancock once slept, with the feeling that something ungodly was about to happen. He rose, dressed, and went for a walk along the streets of Beacon Hill. The absence of wind in that early morning hour amplified the sounds of shovels and pickaxes banging against rocks. The sharp noises bounced across the smooth waters of the Charles River. He returned to Hancock's house to retrieve his spyglass, and then hurried to the wharfs. He held his spyglass to his eye and, thanks to the bright gibbous moon, saw the rebels at work.

"Despicable wretched rebels!" he grumbled. He returned to Hancock's house to rouse William Howe and John Burgoyne from their beds.

"What is this about?" Howe demanded as Henry jerked open the curtains that enclosed the canopy bed where he slept.

"Get your ass out of bed, William! The rebels are up to something on the heights over Charlestown!"

The three major generals hurried to Province House and roused the entire household by banging on the door and calling Thomas Gage's name. After some time, a sleepy-eyed black servant, holding one small flickering candle, opened the door. The generals pushed past the servant before he could inquire about the nature of their 4:00 a.m. visit.

Heavy footsteps thundered down the steps from above stairs. Thomas, Henry, Robert, and Anthony joined the three major generals in the living room.

Clinton described what he had seen, and then said, "I recommend a landing in two divisions at daybreak to squelch the rebel offensive."

Thomas remained calm. "Let us see what the light of day reveals before we throw ourselves headlong into a panic."

William Howe looked at Henry Hereford. Henry's eerie yellow-green eyes glowed with an enticing anticipation of what was to come. He grinned at William.

William would think later that he should have run from Gage's house like a scared boy before the events that played out broke his sanity.

Margaret and her personal maid, Constance, stood undetected on the stairs and listened carefully to the men in the living room discussing the rebels' activities and their counterattack. As the five generals and two captains in her living room conferred over how to beat the wretched rebels into the ground, Margaret felt a shiver run down her spine.

Constance turned and ran up the stairs to her bedroom. She dashed across the room and snatched the porcelain wash bowl from the top of the dresser. Vomit spewed from her mouth before she was able to position the bowl to catch it. Locks of blond hair clung to her cheeks and neck in ropy vomit-coated strands. The bowl slid from her hands and shattered on the floor. She sat on the edge of her bed and cried.

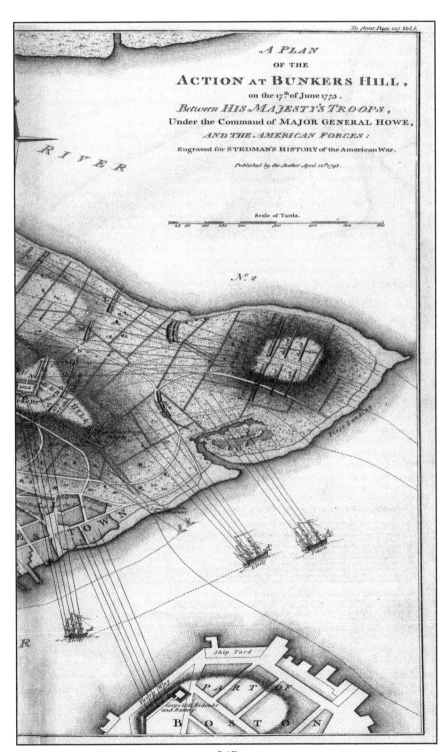

A PLAN

OF THE

ACTION AT BUNKERS HILL,

on the 17th of June 1775.

Between HIS MAJESTY'S TROOPS,

Under the Command of MAJOR GENERAL HOWE,

AND THE AMERICAN FORCES:

Engraved for STEDMAN'S HISTORY of the American War.

Published by the Author April 12th 1793.

Scale of Yards.

N.º 2

RIVER

First Landing

Lively

Falcon

Lively

Ship Yard

PART OF

Copps Hill Redoubt
and Battery

Ferry Way

BOSTON

367

THIRTY-EIGHT

BREED'S HILL, MASSACHUSETTS

It came gradually—the brightening of the sky in the east toward the islands of Boston Harbor, and the fading of the stars overhead into a gray, increasingly blue sky. A lookout on the HMS *Lively* heard sounds coming from the heights about half a mile away, and he saw the rebels throwing up a redoubt on a hill at the back of Charlestown.

As the morning brightened, the provincial soldiers realized that instead of being set back in the height of Bunker Hill, they were on a little knoll overlooking Charlestown. There was nothing to prevent an army of British regulars from landing at the tip of the peninsula and attacking the rebels from their unprotected left. They were alone, already exhausted and sleep-deprived.

They heard the soul-shattering roar of the HMS *Lively's* first nine-pound cannon and knew for certain they had been discovered. The black dot of the cannonball mesmerized the soldiers as it arced through the cloudless sky and then smacked in the nearby ground. Dirt clods flew several yards into the air followed by clouds of brown dust.

In addition to the *Lively's* guns, cannon fire began to pour down upon the rebels from Copp's Hill. The Breed's Hill position was every bit as exposed as William Prescott had feared. He saw not only exhaustion in his men's eyes, but also terror. Israel Putnam had retreated to Bunker Hill with his men, leaving William and his men alone to defend their little redoubt.

"Colonel, I think it is time we request reinforcements," Captain Jothan Bond said as the cannonading from Copp's Hill increased. "After building a fort, we cannot be expected to defend it. We are tired and hungry and have had little else to drink but rum."

Prescott's pride formed his answer. "We are the ones who built these walls, and we are the ones who should have the honor of defending them."

Despite Prescott's optimistic bravado, many men began to desert the appalling ensnarement they found themselves in. His eyes swept over the dirty, tired, and thirsty expanse of his men and thought, *if we were where we were supposed to be on Bunker Hill, there would be no need for reinforcements. Damn Putnam for his intervention in my decision making! And now, he languishes on Bunker Hill as if he has nothing to do with our predicament!*

He remembered the conversation he had just two months before with his loyalist brother-in-law, Abijah Willard.

"Your life and estate will be forfeited for treason if you take up arms against Britain," Abijah had warned.

Prescott recollected his response, "I have made up my mind on the subject. I think it is probable I may be found in arms, but I will never be taken alive."

From his reverie, Prescott saw Colm emerge from the soldiers building and reinforcing breastworks. The angels, Gordon, Jeremiah, and Abe followed Colm like the apostles of Jesus Christ. Seven hundred men suddenly stopped their work to watch the archangel approach Colonel Prescott.

The simple country folk, who had come to stand up to the British on this little hill, were inspired, not only by the archangel, but also, by Dr. Joseph Warren's belief in the archangel. Yet, it wasn't Colm presence alone that inspired them. It was also Prescott's determined bravery.

Colm and William stood face to face while cannon balls whizzed through the hot June morning air.

"Admit ya need reinforcements, Colonel Prescott," Colm said.

Prescott was unafraid of the battle to come, but at that moment, with the archangel's eyes upon him, he realized the soldiers watching them might feel differently. He swallowed his pride and nodded in agreement.

"Major Brooks!" Prescott called.

John Brooks, a twenty-three-year-old doctor from Medford, separated from the dark abyss of clustered soldiers. He slowed his pace the closer he got to Colm. Colm simultaneously frightened and awed him. John trembled as Colonel Prescott disseminated his orders to walk to Cambridge and relay their situation to the Committee of Safety and ask for reinforcements.

General Henry Clinton wrote in his journal that his advice was not heeded. General William Howe's far less risky plan, in General Gage's opinion, was to be carried out. Envelope the rebel redoubt and attack it from several sides simultaneously.

"As soon as the troops and boats are readied and gathered at Long Wharf, we can transport them across the harbor to Morton's Point where the water is shallow. We need to be ready to land with the next high tide," Howe said with an authority that angered Clinton.

Clinton, however, kept his anger to himself.

"The next high tide is not until two or three o'clock this afternoon," Robert pointed out. He had remained subdued since the arrival of the three generals. It was a sham that he would maintain until Henry gave him permission to do otherwise. Robert was certain that permission was about to be granted. He caught Anthony's attention and exchanged a conspiratorial orange eye-flare with him.

Howe did not look at Robert. *Perhaps the weasel will shut his mouth if I ignore him.*

"I will send word to Major Pitcairn to ready his marines," Thomas said.

There was a brief knock at the closed living room door. Without waiting for an invitation to come in, two kitchen maids entered with tea, coffee, beer, and meat pies. Despite the siege Boston was under, the generals were enjoying pies while some of the poorer citizens were literally starving to death. After setting up breakfast, the kitchen maids discreetly exited the room.

Thomas also left the room then returned after a short time. "Word has been sent to Major Pitcairn, Brigadier General Pigot, and Admiral Graves. The cannons on Copp's Hill belong to Graves and the Royal Navy. I will meet with him in regard to what kind of protection we can expect."

Henry, Robert, and Anthony helped themselves to generous portions of pie and beer. John Burgoyne also indulged in breakfast. William Howe drank beer, while Henry Clinton poured a cup of tea.

Thomas neither ate nor drank. He sat in a chair and thought about Margaret's pregnancy, and what he was sure was Joseph Warren's involvement in the foray playing out on the Charlestown peninsula. *What do I have to lose by letting Howe have his way and do what he pleases with the insurgents? Nothing at all.*

Henry not only saw the look of resignation on Thomas' face, he sensed Thomas' fear that Margaret was pregnant with Joseph Warren's child. It was a delightful discovery on Henry's part, but it also stirred the realization that the moment to force the archangel to choose between his brother and his pet was at hand.

"William, my captains and I will accompany you on your mission to defeat the rebels," Henry proclaimed.

William Howe glanced at Henry and drank of his beer. Henry seemed much changed since the last time they had met in London. Howe did not care for the change.

"Of course, we will attend in the capacity of soldiers under your command," Henry acquiesced.

Fergus heard the rider thundering toward his headquarters at Dillaway House in Roxbury. He shivered. The news the rider was bringing could not be good.

Word that the British were planning a preemptive strike on Roxbury and Dorchester had arrived a week prior via Paul Revere from the Committee of Safety. Each day since, Fergus and his officers huddled in long strategic meetings. They had two major obstacles to face: supplies and ammunition. Those obstacles shifted from General Fergus Driscoll to Colonel William Prescott as British General William Howe turned his attention to Charlestown and Bunker Hill instead.

Fergus and his officers stood on the lawn of Dillaway House and watched Revere rein his horse and jump from the saddle.

"Fergus..." Paul glanced at the officers. "I mean...General Driscoll, General Ward dispatched me to tell you that Prescott and Putnam were sent to build a redoubt on Bunker Hill." Paul paused to catch his breath. "Prescott disobeyed orders, and the redoubt was built on the rise east of Charlestown. They are being fired upon from British sloops and cannon from Copp's Hill Burial Ground, according to Major John Brooks."

Captain Enos Woodbury asked, "Does this mean the British have lost focus on attacking Roxbury?"

"I cannot say for sure," Paul said.

Fergus tried to sense Colm, but he couldn't make the connection and that scared him. "Is Colm with them?" he asked Paul.

Paul nodded grimly.

"And Joseph? Where is he?"

"I do not know," Paul admitted. "He did not deploy with Putnam and Prescott last night."

"What are General Ward's orders for us?" Fergus asked.

"For now, he wants you to be aware of the situation, and that it may quickly turn. You may need to deploy on a moment's notice." Paul studied

Fergus. "You know something that perhaps I should know as well. What is it?"

Fergus thought of what Colm told him the last time they were together. *"Henry's going to try to make me choose between Michael's life and Joseph's life. The children of man will die."*

"I do," Fergus admitted. "But I can't tell you, Paul. Colm confided in me, and I can't betray that confidence."

Paul gave Fergus a rare smile. "I understand." He looked at the other officers. "I will try to keep you abreast of developments on the Charlestown peninsula, if it all possible."

Then, he was off, galloping the road back toward Cambridge.

Fergus wondered who of his brotherhood and human friends he would ever see again.

Paul had assured Fergus that Joseph did not deploy with Prescott and Putnam the night before, but Joseph had frightened many of his colleagues with wild words about joining Prescott and his men on Bunker Hill. And now, Joseph was nowhere to be found. With Joseph out of commission, no one seemed willing to act. Finally, General Ward reluctantly sent all of the New Hampshire regiments stationed in Cambridge to the Charlestown peninsula.

By noon, Prescott felt satisfied the redoubt and breastworks were completed. Israel Putnam tried to cajole him into sending men back to Bunker Hill to dig entrenchments in case of the need to retreat.

"I have already lost a significant number of men to desertion," William replied. "If I send any of the men away with tools, not one of them will return."

At that moment, a cannonball flew passed them. The shockwave narrowly missed the head of Captain Ebenezer Bancroft, one of Prescott's fellow French and Indian War veterans. Bancroft clapped a hand to one eye and collapsed. Several men ran to attend to their downed comrade.

At this, Putnam left with the tools and a considerable number of soldiers—none of whom would ever return to Breed's Hill.

"FUCKER!" Prescott screamed at Putnam's retreating back.

Bancroft and those attending him were bathed in blue light, when Michael and Patrick arrived to offer comfort to the war veteran suffering from the shock of losing sight in one eye.

Prescott stalked off after Putnam. Colm intercepted him. Cannonballs rained from the sky and landed thickly in the ground around them.

"General William Howe is coordinating a strike against us," Colm said.

Prescott opened his mouth to ask Colm how he knew, but realized it was better to listen to what the archangel had to say than to wonder.

"They'll land at high tide," Colm said. "That leaves us scant time to be certain we're ready."

The noise of an artillery captain and his men arriving with several field pieces distracted them. The redoubt Colonel Gridley had laid out made no provision for cannons. There were no openings in the walls, and Putnam had taken the digging tools back to Bunker Hill.

"Can you disintegrate Putnam?" Prescott seethed.

Colm realized then that William was a strong warrior by his own right. Still, his frustration over Putnam's behavior was not to be taken lightly.

Generals Gage, Clinton, and Burgoyne positioned themselves at the battery on Copp's Hill. Except for the distraction of the British sloops and warships, *Lively, Glasgow, Symmetry, Falcon*, and *Spitfire*, their eyes traveled across the harbor. The water shimmered under the boiling June sun; each small ripple flashed points of glaring diamond light.

Now, they saw the first wave of British boats, twenty-eight of them, rowing across the harbor with forty regulars in each, their muskets glittering in the sun. In the forward-most boats, brass field pieces glistened. Two raft-like gondolas, each equipped with a twelve-pound cannon, brought up the rear of the flotilla.

The fighting at Lexington and Concord was only visible to Bostonians as a distant cloud of dust and powder smoke moving across the countryside. This morning, the big guns of the warships and the battery on Copp's Hill were already filling the air surrounding Boston with booming noise and gray smoke, but that was just a prelude.

The people were witnessing what was going to be a true battle, unfolding with painstaking deliberation before their very eyes as Howe's red-coated army rowed across the sparkling harbor toward a green hill where the provincials were entrenched.

Howe's order of battle included two regiments and ten senior companies of grenadiers and light infantry to depart from Long Wharf. Two more regiments were to march to the North Battery and embark from there. The regulars were alert and ready to make a good landing and march to action the moment their boots hit the ground.

Three additional regiments, Major John Pitcairn's First Battalion of Marines and several more companies were held in reserve and ready to embark if needed.

Colm, Prescott, Jeremiah, Abe, Captain Thomas Knowlton of Connecticut, and an artillery officer, Captain Samuel Trevett, stood atop the redoubt walls and watched the British long boats grow closer to Morton's Point. The rebels had become accustomed to the onslaught of British cannonballs and learned how to avoid them for the most part. The earthen walls of the redoubt and the breastworks absorbed the impact of the cannonballs as well.

Colm ordered his men to remain within the protection of the redoubt and stay near him. He turned and looked into the redoubt for reassurance. The angels were there with their muskets at the ready, alongside the other rebels. Seamus motioned for Colm to come closer.

Colm squatted so he could hear Seamus. "We cain't control our auras, and the men cain see them," Seamus said. "Some of them said the light is distractin' them."

An elderly grizzled man standing beside Ian shoved his thumb in Ian's direction and grumbled to Colm, "His wings unfurled twice and got in my face. How's I supposed to shoot accurate if I suddenly got feathers and silver snow on me?"

Prescott squatted beside Colm and said, "I heard what Seamus said. Do not think of leaving. When this thing begins, light from six angels' auras is going to be the least of their distractions. I'm going to see if some of these artillery officers actually know how to fire their own field pieces."

He stood up in time to see three companies deserting the redoubt and running toward Bunker Hill. *"Damn!"* He and artillery captain, Samuel Trevett, climbed down the redoubt wall toward the cannons that protruded through the earthen walls. With their tools on Bunker Hill with Putnam, the artillery officers had blasted the openings using those same cannons.

"Where's Gordon?" Colm asked Seamus.

"I got no idea. He muttered somethin' about rebel demons and stalked off."

"Are you the archangel?" a young black man, standing beside Michael, asked.

"Who are ya?" Colm asked.

The man's wide brown eyes shifted to Michael.

"Why're ya looking at me?" Michael asked. "Colm asked ya a question."

"I'm Peter Salem," the man said as his eyes slowly moved to behold Colm.

"We can't protect ya, Peter. Do ya understand me?"

Peter nodded. "I do. Michael said there is real life demons coming to fight this battle with the redcoats, and if'in I see orange eyes, I'm supposed to shoot them in both eyes."

Colm swallowed hard. Michael's propensity to befriend humans and offer them kindness when he saw fit hadn't changed. They had rejected Heaven, lost control of their auras, lost control of their wings, but they *were still* angels.

"Ya will do well to listen to Michael," Colm said to Peter, and stood up. "And, Peter, I am indeed the archangel."

Prescott returned to the redoubt wall alone. He addressed Colm and Captain Thomas Knowlton. "I ordered Captain Trevett to move two of his field pieces in the direction of Morton's Point and fire on the British when they disembark from the boats. Captain Knowlton, I want you to take your men and provide Trevett with whatever protection he might need when he opens up on the regulars."

"Yes, sir," Knowlton said. He jumped from the redoubt wall and gathered his company of 200 men from Connecticut. Along the way, they came across a ditch. Just ahead of the ditch was a fence made of stone at the bottom and rails of wood at the top. It ran parallel to the ditch as it extended across the width of the peninsula to the Mystic River. With a few modifications, the fence could at least *look* like a sturdy defensive structure.

Prescott then sent a detachment of men into Charlestown to join the sharpshooters he had sent earlier. If the British landed or moved troops in that area, the rebels were to fire on them.

❧

The first wave of regulars landed at Morton's Point. Colm, Abe, and Jeremiah saw hundreds of sets of simmering orange eyes among them. Henry had infused Howe's army with his demons. Colm was sure there were hundreds, perhaps thousands, more, including Henry himself, in the second wave of longboats that rowed across Boston Harbor toward Morton's Point.

Gordon had run some distance back toward Bunker Hill and climbed a tree to get a better view of the surrounding farmlands and pastures. He was sure that Colm and the angels had forgotten the possibility of rebel demon possession because Henry and Robert were entrenched with the British.

He watched the longboats come ashore and the British regulars, dressed in heavy woolen clothing and burdened with full haversacks, disembark with ordered confidence. Grenadiers unloaded the glistening brass field pieces and ammunition from the boats. There was no mistaking the number of orange eyes that swept the shore and hills above them.

"What are you doing?"

Gordon looked down from his perch. William Dawes stood with his neck craned and a hand shading his eyes from the bright afternoon sun.

"Is that you, Gordon?" Dawes asked.

Gordon climbed down from the tree. "William! I had no idea you were a soldier."

"I am not," Dawes quipped. He brandished his pistol. "I am stubborn. At least that is what my wife, May, says."

"They've landed," Gordon said. "Henry has sent an army of demons with them."

Dawes thought of his wife and four children trapped in Boston. Like Paul, he had no idea how his family was faring because communication was cut off. He supposed if he died today, he would die trying to free them. He and Gordon walked toward the pathetic little fort on the wrong hill.

"You are about to face demons and your sigil is not visible," Dawes derided. "I did not spend all that time crafting a tattoo on your neck so that it would never be seen."

Gordon huffed a laugh. He untied his cravat, slipped it off his neck, and dropped it. "Better?"

They entered the redoubt and joined the angels. William Dawes' appearance was bittersweet. At William's urging, Jeremiah, Abe and the angels cut their cravats and neck scarves away to reveal the Sigil of Lucifer.

As this reunion of men and angels reinforced the strengths they had so desperately reached to build together, the second wave of Howe's troops came ashore.

Colm leaped onto the redoubt wall. He saw what he knew he would see eventually—Henry was disembarking at Morton's Point with his minions by his side. The only comfort Colm could muster was that Joseph wasn't among the provincial army on the Charlestown peninsula.

❧

William Howe's regulars landed on the Mystic River side of the Charlestown peninsula unopposed. This eastern side was not visible from Boston.

Howe and his temporary aide-de-camp, Captain Richard Seton, walked up the hill with Henry. Anthony lagged behind the two generals with Robert. From the top of the hill, they saw the rebels had been successful in building a redoubt and breastworks. Past the rebel fort, on Bunker Hill, was a line of provincial soldiers. This, along with the rail fence that Howe misinterpreted as an earthwork, moved him to send a request for reinforcements to General Gage. He and his aide-de-camp left without a word and walked back to Morton's Point.

Henry, on the other hand, was not distracted with the rebel position or movement. His eyes swept the area near the redoubt and found what he was looking for—the archangel standing atop the redoubt wall. Behind the archangel, five glowing auras emanated from the angels standing in the redoubt. Henry frowned. Two of the angels were not there.

He looked at Robert questioningly. "The angel they call Liam is not there. He could not have died of his wound. I do not sense him chained in eternal darkness."

"The second they call Fergus is also not there," Robert added. He glared across the fields at the rebel line.

Henry produced a spyglass and held it to one eye and squinted with the other. After several minutes of surveillance, he lowered the glass and handed it to Robert. "I see the angels' human friend, Jeremiah Killam, standing on the redoubt wall, but I do not see Joseph Warren."

Robert took the spyglass and commenced his own surveillance. Just as Henry didn't need a spyglass to see Colm and his men, Colm didn't need a spyglass to see Henry or Robert, but the demons needed a spyglass to get a clear view of the rebel humans. When Robert's magnified view fell on Colm atop the redoubt wall, Robert sensed something was amiss—no it was more than that—something was *different* about the archangel.

Colm looked at Robert.

Robert saw a phenomenon never seen in all the millenniums the demons had pursued the angels. Gold light glimmered in Colm's green eyes. An angel's aura was not visible in their eyes, nor was the gold radiance God had bestowed to the archangels. Robert dropped the spyglass as if it had burned his hand.

Irked by Robert's behavior, Henry snatched him by his coat lapel and jerked him in close. Anthony, who thus far had not uttered a word, flinched and took a step back.

"I do not care what you think you sense or what you think you saw," Henry fumed. "You WILL carry out your orders to the letter. If you do not, I will kill you myself without hesitation, and I promise you that my execution will be so much more painful than death by disintegration from an archangel."

Henry shook Robert then shoved him away. He snapped his fingers at Anthony.

Anthony came to the general's attention.

"You have been my third in command for quite some time; therefore, I am not sure why your possession of Captain Anthony Jameson has not gone well in contrast with the satisfying officer I had in the possessed Lieutenant William Sutherland. Nevertheless, I give you the same warning I gave Robert. Is that clear?"

"Aye, sir." Anthony now realized that his possession had somehow been tainted. *That arrow-wielding hag, Serepatice, is responsible for what I have become*, he thought; unaware that angels had witnessed his possession ceremony on the shore of Back Bay while they rescued Joseph Warren's children.

The three demons' attention was redirected to the sound and sight of British reinforcements landing on the beach southwest of Morton's Hill near Charlestown. Brigadier General Robert Pigot and Major John Pitcairn, along with 700 troops, had arrived.

THIRTY-NINE

Ascrappy spirit of backwoods New Hampshire, and the man who General Ward had sent to Chelsea Creek, forty-six-year-old John Stark, had the largest regiment in the provincial army with 400 men. His major, Andrew McClary, six foot six and of athletic build, marched proudly alongside a scowling Stark toward Charlestown Neck.

Warships had clustered gunfire around Mill Pond Road and had turned Charlestown Neck into a war zone. Cannonballs flew across the narrow strip of land and ripped the earth into ragged furrows. The ships fired bar shot: evil-looking dumbbells of metal designed to take down the rigging of a sailing vessel, but which also did devastating things to a human body. The smoke, dust, deafening roar, and bloody chunks of torn flesh had paralyzed a crowd of provincial soldiers on the approach to the Neck.

Major McClary boomed at the soldiers, "Step aside so that Colonel Stark and his regiments may march across to Bunker Hill!"

Stark was not impressed by what he found on Bunker Hill. Israel Putnam sat atop his white horse sans the long-sleeved coat an officer was expected to wear. A thousand mostly idle soldiers were assembled around the peak of Bunker Hill. To Stark, it seemed as if Putnam was unable to focus.

Later, Stark would say, "Had Putnam done his duty, he would have decided the fate of his country in the first action."

Stark led his regiment south. The British directed their artillery fire toward the swarm of rebels on Bunker Hill, and as a consequence, the march south proved to be almost as hot as what they had encountered on the Neck. Up ahead and to his right, Stark saw the redoubt and the breastwork; directly in front, he saw Thomas Knowlton and his men fortifying the rail fence; to the left was the Mystic River. Beyond, about a half mile to the south, were more than two thousand British regulars.

Colonel Stark's eyes followed the rail fence. It did not extend all the way to the water's edge, where a steep bank went down to a narrow beach. If General Howe sent a column of soldiers along the beach, he would render useless the rebels' efforts with the breastwork and rail fence.

Stark's men began to build a stone breastwork that would fill in the gap between the beach and the rail fence. They were soon aided by the arrival of a New Hampshire regiment of 300 men led by Colonel James Reed.

⌘

Captain John Chester of Connecticut had just finished his mid-day dinner in his quarters in Cambridge when beating drums, ringing bells, and shouting commenced. He dashed outside. Israel Putnam's son Israel, Jr., rode up in a full gallop. Captain Chester was immediately apprehensive of this messenger. "What is the matter?" he asked.

"The regulars are landing in Charlestown, and Father says you must all meet and march immediately to Bunker Hill!"

Without question, Captain Chester ran to his quarters and retrieved his musket and ammunition. Then, he went to the Anglican Church, which served as a barracks for his men, and ordered them to ready and march.

In Roxbury, Fergus received a desperate message from the Committee of Safety. "The troops are now landing at Charlestown from Boston. You are to judge whether this is designed to deceive or not. In haste, we leave you to judge of the necessity of your movements."

⌘

To the right of the redoubt and breastworks, William Howe was arranging his command.

"You will fall into two horizontal lines consisting of 300 men each!" he ordered his officers in command of their perspective companies of light infantry and grenadiers.

Howe considered the rebel company stacking stones into a barricade near the beach. He wiped one white-gloved hand across his sweating brow. It did not occur to him that donning gloves on a windless, stifling June day was ludicrous, because no self-respecting British officer would do otherwise.

"Colonel Abercrombie! Captain Osborn!" Howe shouted.

The officers immediately attended—high on adrenaline after months of doing little more than drilling in the mud on Boston Common.

"Form columns of your infantrymen and march them to the beach to-ward the rebels building that stone barricade. You are to execute a bayonet

380

attack unless forced to do otherwise," he ordered Osborn.

"Colonel Abercrombie, form columns of grenadiers to attack the rebels in the right flank. I want to form the right side of a pincer that will enclose the rebels in our claws. Is that clear?"

"Aye, sir!" they responded, enthusiastically.

Artillery led the way with cannons blasting as Howe's regulars began their march toward the beach of the Mystic River and what was the right side of the redoubt from where the regulars marched. There were unanticipated complications. Most of the cannon had been provided with the wrong size cannonballs, and the artillery men had to fire alternative projectiles called grapeshot. This stalled the initial momentum.

Further, most of the hay on the hillside had not been harvested, forcing the regulars to wade through waist-high hay where rocks, holes, and other obstacles lurked under the soldiers' feet. When they encountered a rail fence, the column had to stop to take down the rails.

After landing on the beach near Charlestown, General Robert Pigot and Major John Pitcairn prepared to lead their men against the left and center of the redoubt and breastwork to form the left pincer of the British claw.

The detachment of men Colonel Prescott sent into Charlestown hid inside unoccupied buildings. They watched while Pigot's regulars and Pitcairn's marines fell into the same formation as Howe's troops. Then, the rebels opened fire.

Major Pitcairn was reminded of the ambush the British had suffered as they retreated from Concord to Boston two months before. He urged his marines to make haste toward the rebel's redoubt.

The British had yet to load their muskets.

It was three o'clock in the afternoon when one of Joseph's former medical apprentices, twenty-two-year-old Dr. David Townsend, arrived at Hastings House. David learned that the British were firing heavy on the provincial soldiers on Bunker Hill, so he hurried to Cambridge to assist Dr. Warren with the wounded if needed.

When Townsend arrived, the town of Cambridge was silent and deserted. The troops were gone and Hastings House was empty. He sat in a chair in the living room to rest after his two-hour walk from Brighton. The sound of footsteps approaching from behind startled him. He jumped up and whirled around.

"Dr. Warren!" he exclaimed. He saw that the doctor's blue eyes were strained and tired. He knew immediately that his former master physician was suffering from one of his oppressive nervous headaches. "Were you resting?" he asked.

Joseph had done well to hide his sick headaches, which often drove him to lie down in a dark quiet room until they passed, from acquaintances and more importantly, Colm. But like William Eustis, Townsend had lived in the Warren household for two years, and it was difficult for Joseph to hide his affliction from a member of his household.

"Yes, I was resting," Joseph admitted.

David was sympathetic to his mentor's pain, but stress compelled him to blurt out, "Then perhaps you have not heard that the men on Bunker Hill are being fired upon by the British?"

Joseph's head pounded, his eyes hurt, and his stomach was queasy. He could not allow this appalling news to make his symptoms worse and debilitate him. His mind raced, and his adrenaline spiked, but he had to force himself to settle down and take relief.

"I have not heard. We will make haste to Bunker Hill to offer our services. First, I must have a cup of chamomile tea to calm my headache. Will you join me?"

After they shared a cup of tea, Joseph rose and went above stairs to his bedroom.

He wrapped the curls above his ears around his index finger to neaten them, and adjusted the fashionable pins that held the horizontal curls in place. The clean elegant shirt, vest, and coat he wore when he wedded Elizabeth Hooten in 1764, hung on pegs in the shallow closet in his bedroom. He washed his face and hands before removing his clothing in favor of his wedding suit. The small scarred mirror on the wall over the wash basin reflected the physical beauty of a man with smooth skin, sandy blond hair, blue eyes, a straight nose, rounded chin and fine stature. The beauty that resided in Joseph's mind, heart, and spirit needed no mirror to be seen by others.

Joseph descended the stairs to the living room.

"Your eyes look brighter and color has returned to your cheeks," David observed as if Joseph was his patient. "Are you feeling better?"

"I am. Shall we go?"

Joseph and David walked toward Charlestown Neck. As they approached, several provincial soldiers recognized the two doctors and stopped them.

"We just took five wounded men to that house," one said, and pointed to a house just up the road.

"David, please stay and administer care to them," Joseph said. Without waiting for a response, he turned to continue on toward Bunker Hill.

"Dr. Warren," a soldier called.

Joseph stopped.

The soldier held his musket in one hand and his cartridge box in the other. "Take these, Dr. Warren. You cannot go into battle unarmed."

હ

Dark smoke and deafening noise engulfed the Charlestown peninsula. The spectators on hills, rooftops, and steeples in Boston watched the encroaching death and destruction.

On Copp's Hill, Generals Henry Clinton, John Burgoyne, and Thomas Gage watched William Howe's troop formations and maneuvers with discerning eyes.

Henry said to John and Thomas, "Howe's advance is exceedingly soldier-like. Whatever misgivings I may have had were unfounded. His troop disposition is perfect."

"It needs to be," John said sourly. "A defeat here will be the final loss to the British Empire in America."

Thomas raised his spyglass and focused on Howe's troops. He could have cared less about Howe's disposition. What worried him was General Henry Hereford's presence among the troops. Thomas was certain Henry would be the cause of something horrible, as if the coming battle was not horrible enough.

હ

Aware of their short supply of gunpowder, Colonel William Prescott ordered the rebels to hold their fire until they could see the whites of the regulars' eyes. Colonel John Stark issued the same order to his men along the rail fence and behind the stone wall near the beach.

The men standing on top of the redoubt walls had diminished to Colm, Abe, and William Prescott. Private Peter Brown was now at the ready in the redoubt beside Jeremiah, Gordon, William Dawes, Peter Salem, and the angels. Captain Benjamin Ames' and his company, under the command of Colonel James Frye's regiment, had recently joined the provincials in the redoubt.

The angels were trying desperately to control their wayward auras and wings, but to no avail. Ian's rebellious wings irritated the elderly grizzled man beside him, as they continued to intermittently unfurl and flap in the man's face. With the British regulars advancing and the shifting atmosphere of bra-

383

vado, determination, and trepidation, the elderly man began to soften toward the angel. There was a human quality about the angel, which the elderly man had not recognized until then.

The man said to Ian, "Degory Bennett's me name."

Ian didn't look at the man. The angels were distressed, overwhelmed, and unable to focus on much of anything but their archangel's emotions. Their loss of control over their auras and wings was impossible to comprehend, and although they reached for one another spiritually, and succeeded in making and maintaining that connection, they were tormented and afraid.

"You got a name?" Degory asked Ian.

Michael could no longer contain his anxiety. He released some of it by yelling at the old man, "Leave Ian alone! He can't help it! None of us can help it!"

Degory thought he had offered an olive branch to the angel with the red aura, therefore, Michael's angry words surprised him. Then, the seventy-seven-year-old man saw the sigil on Ian's neck and experienced a revelation that he knew had not come from God. The revelation had come from within his heart.

He dodged Ian's rogue wings and went to confront Michael. Never in his life had he seen such a beautiful young man as he saw in Michael, and the angel with the blue aura who stood beside him. Both had the same sigil tattooed on their neck. "What are ya names, boys?" Degory asked.

"I'm Patrick," Patrick tilted his head. "He's Michael."

"Ya boys come here to die today?"

Neither angel was sure of the answer. Cannons boomed and arcing balls whistled past them, then slammed into the redoubt dirt floor. No one flinched. Finally, Patrick shook his head and said, "No."

"Tell me, then. Why are angels marred with the Sigil of Lucifer?"

"It's demons," Peter Salem interjected.

Degory asked Peter, "Is that so?" but he kept his eyes on Michael.

"Leave them alone, old man," Gordon warned. Degory's eyes slipped from Michael's face. Gordon tilted his head to the left and ran his index finger over his tattoo. "It's demons, alright, but if you distract us from killing them, they will kill us all."

Salem Poor, a young free black man enlisted in Captain Ames' company, listened without comment although he was somewhat surprised that the black man with the tattoo on his neck knew the angels.

"'Tis no way for me to kill demons, then?" Degory asked.

"You gotta stab them or shoot them in both eyes, but your chances of gettin' away with that and survivin' ain't good," Seamus interjected. His wings threatened to unfurl.

Private Peter Brown found this bit of information exciting. "I shall do so!" he exclaimed.

Seamus lost control of his wings. They unfurled in a bright shower of silver crystals, causing several men to complain.

Barnabus Miller, a blue-eyed, thirty-year-old father of six from Menotomy, sniped, "You are getting me wet with your silver rain."

Seamus thought of Ian's original human vessel when he looked at Barnabus, which led to remembrances of Liam. Seamus shoved those thoughts away as hard as his spirit would allow.

Above the noise of cannon fire, a cheer of "Huzza! Huzza!" rose from the ranks of the anxious provincial soldiers.

Jeremiah, Gordon, William Dawes, and the angels turned to see Joseph walking through the open space in the back of the redoubt. He was dressed impeccably, carrying a musket, and smiling. Colm, Abe, and William Prescott didn't immediately hear the cheering from where they stood on the redoubt wall.

"Oh Lord," Jeremiah said to himself. "This is exactly what Colm was afraid of when I accused him of choosin' Joseph over us. He *is* gonna have ta choose." He looked wildly at Gordon. They both ran toward Joseph.

"Go back ta Cambridge now!" Jeremiah shouted at Joseph.

"I cannot walk away while you, my friends, are facing Hell on Earth. I must not act cowardly and leave my fellow rebels to fight what I would not."

"Your responsibility for these rebels ain't fightin' demons and the British in a filthy little redoubt," Jeremiah said. He hoped that his words had come out sounding strong instead of quivering with the dread he felt inside.

William Prescott realized that Joseph was in the redoubt. He jumped off the wall and strode, with a brave heart to meet him.

Prescott's sudden departure brought Joseph's presence to Colm's attention. He leaped onto the floor of the redoubt with the intention of running to Joseph's side, but he saw Michael and froze in his tracks.

"General Warren, I relinquish my command to you," Colonel Prescott said, bowing.

"No, William. My commission is not official yet. I am here to fight as a volunteer under your command."

The angels looked on from the place where they stood by the redoubt wall. Their millennia-long discipline and order in a battle situation held them firm. Their out of control auras and wings were a horrible intrusion that felt akin to their emotions running blindly through a fog bank filled with creatures they couldn't see or imagine.

Yet, the spirit of Colm and his men was made of love, devotion, and bravery; those qualities returned to the forefront of their spirits. They would realize a victory for their fallen brother, Liam. Fergus was absent, but he wasn't dead. In fact, his safe place in Roxbury gave them an anchor to hold them steady in the roar of a tempest.

The angels huddled together. For a short while, they were who they used to be before they fell from Heaven—a brotherhood devoted to comforting humans and escorting souls to their egress. A brotherhood devoted to one another no matter the atrocities others benevolently committed.

Colm looked at the faces of the loyal angels whose intentions were never heinous. Despite their lustful transgressions, they were honorable and trustworthy. Then, he looked at Joseph—a man who was just as honorable and trustworthy. Colm loved them all and knew if he didn't make a move soon, he would lose them all.

Colonel Prescott walked past Colm and returned to his position on the redoubt wall. Howe's regulars were almost upon them.

Joseph joined the angels and the others at the redoubt wall. He felt Colm's eyes on him as he loaded his musket. When he finished, Joseph went to stand beside Colm. He saw gold light flash in the archangel's eyes. The sight should have alarmed Joseph. Instead, it served as a sign that the warrior in the archangel had returned.

"I have to do this, Colm," Joseph said with determination. "It is better to die honorably in the field of battle than ignominiously hang upon the gallows. You must understand and accept that."

Joseph's words tormented his spirit, but Colm nodded mutely.

Prescott suddenly shouted, "AT THE READY!"

The men in the redoubt positioned themselves into a three-man-deep line across the front and left flank walls and stood at the ready.

"FIRE!" Prescott yelled.

The rebel line exploded with a roar of thunder and a profusion of gun smoke. British Colonel James Abercrombie's grenadiers brandished bayonets and tried to scale the small fort's walls. As one rebel reloaded his musket, another stepped forward and shot at the grenadiers.

"FIRE LOW!" Prescott shouted. "SHOOT THEM IN THE LEGS!"

The rebels adjusted their aim.

The grenadiers fell like sacrificial lambs. They screamed and dropped from the redoubt walls. Their excruciating wounds, imbedded with musket balls, were aggravated further by their fall to the ground. Leg wounds almost always resulted in amputation. William Prescott knew that suffering trumped death.

Salem Poor finished reloading his musket in time to see Colonel James Abercrombie scramble over the redoubt wall. Salem had no idea who the soldier was, only that he was a British officer. He fired his musket and shot James Abercrombie in the heart. Prescott turned in time to see Abercrombie's body drop from the wall onto the redoubt floor.

Michael and Joseph stayed close to Colm. Colm struggled with their proximity to one another, as the last men in the initial line of grenadiers and infantry were shot down. If Michael and Joseph stayed near him, he could watch over them and protect them. On the other hand, they were vulnerable to being captured or killed in one fell swoop. Although, there were no orange eyes among the first line of regulars the rebels shot down, Colm knew for certain they would come, and he didn't want to leave Michael and Joseph to pursue Henry.

FORTY

As they marched from Charlestown to the redoubt, Major John Pitcairn and his marines, and General Robert Pigot and his regulars heard the deafening rebel volley and saw black smoke roil from the redoubt.

John Pitcairn thought, *At least I am facing this with my own marines, instead of with companies of unfamiliar men that General Gage forced me to command at Lexington.* He resisted the urge to turn and look for his twenty-three-year-old son and second lieutenant, William, among the 300 Royal Marines marching behind him.

At the beach, Colonel John Stark, Captain Thomas Knowlton, and their men, were positioned along the rail fence and behind the stone wall. The approaching column of light infantry, led by Captain James Osborn, had yet to load their muskets.

With a loud "Huzza!" the rebels fired on them. With nowhere to run and hide in the open fields, and steep banks sloping down to the Mystic River, the front lines of the British were slaughtered.

A second line of infantrymen stepped over the dead bodies of their comrades to attempt a bayonet assault. Colonel Stark, Captain Knowlton, and their men faced a column of flaming orange eyes.

Captain John Chester, the man who had just finished his mid-day dinner in Cambridge when Israel Putnam's son Israel, Jr, rode up to tell him of the news on Bunker Hill, led his company across Charlestown Neck. All around them, provincial soldiers were hiding behind boulders and haystacks and trees. Twenty men gathered around a wounded man who did not need twenty men to assist him, and then retreated through the Neck. Others were retreating without any explanation or excuse.

Israel Putnam was still on Bunker Hill when Captain Chester and his company arrived. Chester's eyebrows knitted together in doubt and disgust when he asked Colonel Putnam why he and his men were not amongst the fighting.

"The artillery is gone, and they stand no chance for their lives in those circumstances," Putnam whined. He thought of Dr. Warren stopping to ask him where the fighting was the hottest. Even to a battle-worn, rough and tumble soldier like Israel Putnam, Joseph's handsome face seemed to glow with angelic light in anticipation of the answer.

"Are you taking command?" Israel had asked Joseph. "They have no officers to lead them."

"My major general commission has not been finalized. I have come to fight as a volunteer."

Captain John Chester watched Colonel Israel Putnam reflect on something that he hoped would haunt Putnam forever. He called for his company to move on.

As they marched toward Breed's Hill, they came under heavy cannon fire from the HMS *Glasgow* and HMS *Symmetry* anchored off the peninsula in the Charles River. Dead rebels lay in the surrounding fields. A middle-aged farmer died in sight of Captain Chester and his men when a cannonball separated his head from his body.

Still, the company from Connecticut kept marching toward Breed's Hill.

The new line of British grenadiers approaching the redoubt decided to switch from a bayonet assault to a firearms assault. They halted to load their muskets. This sudden stop caused the second line of grenadiers to stumble into the first. Then, some of the men disobeyed General Howe's orders and fired at the redoubt. This confused jumble of soldiers became an excellent target for the rebel soldiers.

They also provided a clear view of their simmering orange eyes.

"Oh Lord!" Jeremiah muttered as Howe's demon-possessed men reorganized their lines. He leaned in toward Gordon and asked, "Are you seein' what I'm seein'?"

"Yes, and we've got to tell Colonel Prescott to change his firing orders."

They waded through the lines of rebels until they found William Prescott.

"Colonel, we need ta talk ta you," Jeremiah said, calmly.

Prescott was aware of possible demonic possession among the soldiers on both sides of the conflict. He had warned Colonel John Stark and Captain Thomas Knowlton of the danger before he sent them on their separate missions near the beach. Prescott couldn't remember if he had warned the artillery officer, Captain Samuel Trevett, who was near the beach with his cannons.

"If you have come to tell me about the swarms of demons possessing the regulars, you are too late. I see them."

Prescott's attitude frustrated Gordon. "You have to tell the men to fire at their eyes!" he demanded. "Shooting them anywhere else isn't going to stop them. We will be overrun by hundreds of demon-possessed regulars!"

The renewed sound of cannon booming and musket fire was heard from the beach on the Mystic River, and the HMS *Falcon* anchored in the waters south of Morton's Point.

"What are you waiting for?" Gordon demanded. "These men have accepted the angels! They'll accept the existence of demons, too. If they don't, they will die!"

"The archangel needs to tell them," Prescott said more to himself than to Gordon.

"*You* have to issue the order!" Gordon insisted.

Prescott considered Gordon's genuine concern then said, "I will speak to Colm."

The angels' bright auras blinked on and off in the hazy redoubt. As Prescott walked toward them, he imagined being enveloped in a colorful shifting mist. When he reached the angels' position, he saw Colm standing on the redoubt wall surveying the peninsula. With a clear view of Howe's possessed grenadiers and infantrymen, Colm was unable to locate Henry or Robert among the British army.

Prescott shouted for Colm to come down.

Colm jumped to the redoubt floor beside Joseph. Joseph cast a sideways glance at him.

"I have been advised to change my firing orders," Prescott said to Colm.

Gordon and Jeremiah rejoined the group. Gordon said to Colm, "I've been trying to tell him, but he won't listen to me."

Colm's eyes flashed. "Colonel Prescott, if my men or Gordon Walker or William Dawes or Joseph Warren give ya advice about demons, ya will want to listen. If ya don't, they'll disobey ya in favor of what they know to be true. Do ya understand me?"

For the first time since they met, William Prescott was afraid of Colm. He nodded.

"Then, give the order," Colm said.

Prescott shouted, "ATTENTION! THE FIRING ORDERS HAVE CHANGED!" The rebels quieted down enough to hear their commander. "Demons are among us, and they have possessed quite a number of men fighting here today." He glanced at Colm, and then continued. "They are recognizable by their orange eyes. If you see them, shoot both eyes out."

The men silently looked at the angels.

"The angels made that clear before the first shot was fired," Private Peter Brown ventured.

"You have the order," Prescott shouted. "Now, you will follow it!"

Satisfied, Colm turned to jump onto the redoubt wall, but the angels became unhappy and insecure with his movement. Their wings rustled loudly and a breeze swept through the redoubt. The haze of lingering smoke swirled and blew away.

"Where're you goin'?" Patrick asked Colm. "You ain't leavin' us, are you?"

Colm touched Patrick's cheek. "Didn't ya tell me at Hastings House that ya felt stronger?"

Patrick frowned and nodded. That strength seemed to have drained away.

Colm looked at the angels and the men gathered around them. "I have to find Henry and Robert and keep them away from ya—from all of ya."

Michael's blue aura blinked and then went out. He tried to release it to comfort himself, but he couldn't control it.

The voices of British officers shouting orders at Howe's grenadiers and infantrymen filtered through the stifling afternoon. Cannons boomed incessantly from the beach. Howe's field pieces resumed their assault as his regulars began their march toward the redoubt. A cannon ball arched over the wall and smacked the redoubt floor less than a rod from Degory Bennett and Salem Poor.

Colm suddenly experienced a contraction of physical pain. He tried to let go of it, but the pain insisted. A woman cried out. Colm recognized her tone and emotions. Mkwa was giving birth to Jeremiah's son while men were dying on Breed's Hill at the hands of one another.

"Jeremiah, your son is being born," Colm said breathlessly. He winced, and tried again to release the pain of Mkwa's labor.

The mountain man ran a hand over his forehead and swept his blond hair away from his rugged face as if the action would clear his thoughts. His green eyes stayed focused on Colm's obvious struggle to rid himself of the foreign sensation of physical pain.

Abe thought of his dead wife and infant daughters. Life went on no matter how hideous man, God, or Lucifer were to one another.

Colm finally succeeded in releasing Mkwa's labor from his spirit and body. He said, "Jeremiah, it's time for ya to go home to Burkes Garden."

"I cain't just walk away!"

"Ya have sacrificed enough for us. Go home to ya family."

"You're my family." Jeremiah's eyes traveled to the angels' faces, then William Dawes, Abe, Gordon, and Joseph. He remembered Joseph's words the night Colm confessed his failures as an archangel. *My wife died two years ago. I shall never stop feeling the pain of her loss. Do not let Mkwa feel the pain of your loss.*

"Brandon, can ya still cloak ya aura?" Colm asked.

"Yes, but I'm not sure how long I can keep it cloaked."

"Take Jeremiah to Cambridge to get one of our horses. Then, ride to the farm. Let him have all the ammunition we got left, if any. When he leaves, go into Roxbury, find Fergus, and stay with him until I come to get ya."

"I ain't leavin'," Jeremiah insisted.

Joseph said, "Your son deserves to know his father."

"What about your children?" Jeremiah asked. "Did we rescue 'em from Boston so they cou'd become orphans while you die in this filthy little fort at the hands of the British?"

Joseph thought of the baby Margaret was carrying, and his children in Worcester with Mercy. He had no intention of dying today.

"Put a period to it, Jeremiah," Colm said. "Ya are making it harder on all of us by refusing to go."

"Time's runnin' out!" Seamus warned Jeremiah. "The regulars are comin' as we speak. Get out while you cain!"

A cannon ball smashed into the redoubt's left outer wall. Dirt sprayed and avalanched from the point of impact.

The fear of never seeing his family again paralyzed Jeremiah. His eyes betrayed that fear. It compelled Ian to say, "If Henry's here, this battle will decide our fate. You can't change what's going to happen, Jeremiah. That's in our hands."

Jeremiah knew Ian was right.

William Prescott growled, "If that fucker Putnam or anyone else tries to stop you at the Neck, tell them they will have to answer to me."

He climbed the redoubt wall and walked eastward along the top. Howe's line of regulars had stopped to dismantle a rail fence that blocked their way. Once they passed the fence, it would be only a matter of minutes before they would be within firing range.

"Go on," Colm urged Jeremiah.

Tears blurred Jeremiah's vision. He offered his hand to Colm. The archangel grasped it. Jeremiah pulled Colm into an embrace and said, "Come home soon. I want my son ta grow up with his family." He and Colm tightened their arms around each other for a moment then released one another.

Brandon wrapped his arms around Colm's shoulders and buried his face in Colm's neck where the Sigil of Lucifer was tattooed. He bravely fought off the need to cry.

Colm sighed, kissed the top of Brandon's head, and whispered, "Stay safe, and do what I told ya."

Brandon nodded into Colm's neck.

Jeremiah pulled his skinning knife from the pocket Mkwa had sewn on the thigh of his deer skin breeches. He handed it to Joseph. "Kill as many of them fuckers as you cain."

Joseph stared at the skinning knife. The sigil etched in the blade winked in the bright June sunshine. He thought of the night Jeremiah had handed him Ian's dagger. That night seemed like an eternity ago. Joseph took the knife. He met Jeremiah's expectant gaze and nodded.

"Take care of them," Jeremiah said to Abe and Gordon. They glanced at the angels.

In their distressed state, Michael's and Patrick's wings flapped like baby birds desperately trying to fly away from the beak of a hawk that was about to rip the flesh from their bones.

Jeremiah turned and walked toward the open back of the redoubt. Brandon cloaked his aura and fell in beside him. "Don't look back no matter how much you want to," Brandon whispered.

The men in the redoubt stood at the ready and waited for Colonel Prescott's command to fire. The line of regulars was almost upon them. The regulars' flaming orange eyes made it impossible for the rebels to follow the colonel's previous order to hold their fire until they saw the whites of their eyes.

Colm leaped onto the redoubt wall. Gun smoke from the breastworks and the beach on the Mystic River hung in shrouds of thick gray clouds over the peninsula. Cannon thundered and cannon balls whistled through the air as Captain Trevett's artillery company fired on the column of advancing British infantrymen and Welsh Fusiliers. British cannons answered in kind from the field pieces that moved with the British column, and from the HMS *Falcon* in waters off the southern tip of the peninsula.

It seemed strange to Colm that he heard very few men screaming with mortal wounds. The lack of verbal human suffering told Colm that men were dying quickly, or few men were actually dying at all because they were possessed. Perhaps, it was both.

But his immediate concern was: *Where are Henry and Robert?* It was difficult to see clearly through the disparate mix of hazy sunshine to the west and the gray smoke shrouding most of the lower peninsula. The confusion of the battle was interfering with his senses.

Colm saw British regulars advancing from the west near Charlestown where the shroud of smoke was translucent. Colonel Prescott also saw this movement because Colm heard him shouting orders to reposition the rebels so some of them were firing westward. Captain Nutting of the Massachusetts Ninth Regiment and his 100 men were scrambling to position six field pieces north of Charlestown. Behind General Pigot's grenadiers and infantrymen, and Major Pitcairn's marines, the archangel found Henry, Robert, and another demon Colm didn't recognize; they were bringing up the rear guard. The demons had moved their position to confuse the archangel.

In the back of his mind, Colm heard Colonel Prescott shout, "FIRE!" as Howe's line of regulars reached the redoubt.

Colm gave it no thought. The Sigil of Lucifer tattooed on Colm's neck throbbed in time with his human beating heart. He let the same evil he and his archangel brothers had fought strip him down to the raw warrior he had been when they had battled Lucifer.

He unfurled his wings and leapt from the redoubt wall. General Pigot, Major Pitcairn, and their troops—more than 700 men—became deranged at the sight of the archangel bathed in green and gold light, bounding toward them, with his imperial silver wings spread wide like a powerful mythical creature. Some of the regulars shot at Colm. Others fell to their knees and bowed their heads. Nearly 300 demon-possessed regulars and marines turned and ran west toward the shelter of their leader and his second.

Major John Pitcairn felt as if he was reliving the disaster on Lexington Green, but this time, he could not make sense of what was happening.

General Pigot was no longer in his sight. What he *could* see through the gathering powder smoke overwhelmed him. *Am I seeing an angel?* Pitcairn wondered stupidly as Colm neared the front line of the British soldiers.

Musket fire abruptly ceased among Pigot's and Pitcairn's ranks.

"Oh God," Pitcairn breathed. The angel was running directly at him. "I am going to die." He feared for his son, William, who was among the marines. As the resplendent angel slowed to a stop in front of him, Pitcairn knew his death would not be at the hands of the angel. He fell to his knees with his eyes downcast.

Colm's eyes darted over the rank and file of 400 kneeling soldiers. He looked down on the frightened major. The urge to soothe the children of man overcame him. His wings fluttered and stirred a breeze in the hot June air. The kneeling soldiers exhaled cries of fear and reverence in response to the movement of the archangel's wings.

Colm bent to touch John's wet cheek. Before his fingers brushed the skin, John looked up at him with watering blue eyes.

The trembling major sputtered, "Your angels…were in Lexington." He inhaled and then exhaled slowly. "Am I…going to die…today?"

Gold light flashed in Colm's eyes when he said, "Aye."

Major John Pitcairn uttered a cry and vomited. He wiped his mouth with the back of one gloved hand and looked up. The archangel was gone. He got to his feet.

The sunny June afternoon suddenly exploded with golden light that was so bright he had to close his eyes to keep from being blinded. Electrical currents of gold lightning incited the surrounding air. Hundreds of men screamed in agony and terror. Some pleaded for their lives. Static electricity raised the hairs on the back of his neck. He staggered and turned to search for his son, even if that meant he had to grope each face like a blind man until he found William.

The 400 men on their knees were now on their feet. Some had the sense not to run impetuously. Others stampeded the field only to stumble and fall over rail fences, boulders and into ditches.

Men running past Pitcairn caused him to sprawl face first into the grass. His arms and legs were trampled under heavy booted feet. *I cannot die like this!* He felt the bones in his left wrist break.

Cannons boomed. The gold light faded. Hands slid beneath him and lifted him from the ground. The screaming tapered off.

"Father!"

John Pitcairn blinked and opened his eyes. Lieutenant William Pitcairn, General Robert Pigot, Captain Andrew Hay, and Captain James Murray surrounded him with concern.

"Father, are you alright?" William asked.

John glanced down at himself to make sure he *was* alright. "I am fine," he said. He raised his hands to brush the dirt and grass from the front of his brilliant scarlet coat. His broken wrist protested, but he continued through the pain.

"What happened?" John asked. The stampeding regulars had come to a stop. The dazed expressions on their faces told him that he had not had a terrible hallucination.

General Robert Pigot shook his head. Blood dripped from a cut over his right eye and streaked his dirty, fifty-five-year-old freckled cheeks. He did not want to be the first man to say it, but he was the senior officer and someone *had* to say it. "Orange flames ignited in the eyes of at least 300 of our men when they saw the…archangel." He swallowed hard. "They turned and ran as if Lucifer himself had appeared."

Robert Pigot faltered. When it was evident he was not able to continue, Lieutenant William Pitcairn said in a steadier voice, "The archangel ran past our lines, then gold and green light shot out from his body in all directions. The men with the orange eyes, men we all know and have served with, disintegrated."

Captain James Murray wondered why William Pitcairn sounded calm as he spoke. They had just witnessed the mass murder of friends and comrades by one of Heaven's most powerful beings. James had a wife and three children quartered in Boston. His family and he were devoted Christians. What he witnessed today redefined the meaning of God-fearing.

Captain Murray was close to tears. "Why did God send an archangel to kill us?"

The other four men stared at him in disbelief.

Captain Andrew Hay, a tall, middle-aged man with a shock of red hair pulled into a ponytail beneath his tricorn hat said, "James, our friends and comrades were possessed by demons. How could you not see that?"

"What?"

"There is another war being fought here that we have no knowledge of," Captain Hay said. His eyes shifted to the redoubt. "I think the patriots know exactly what that war is."

꙳

The Battle of Bunker Hill paused as Colm Bohannon lit up the already bright June afternoon with blinding golden light. The retreating possessed regulars and their subsequent shrieking as their bodies were disintegrated, shook the British and caused them to pause. Not only Pigot's and Pitcairn's troops marching from the west, but also Howe's light infantry and fusiliers near the beach and the breastworks, and his ragged line of grenadiers, attempting a frontal attack on the redoubt stood still.

The rebels in the redoubt were less overcome with Colm's show of power than the British. Still, it caused them to reconsider their mortality and what they believed to be their own strengths. Colonel Prescott and his men contemplated the part of the rebels' front line formed by the angels, William Dawes, Joseph, Abe, and Gordon, as Colm's gold radiance faded from the western sky. Peter Brown, Degory Bennett, Peter Salem, Barnabus Miller, and Salem Poor stepped up to solidify that line and reinforce their alliance.

The pause in the hostilities was short-lived.

From behind their makeshift wall of stones and rail fence, Colonel John Stark and his men volleyed at the column of British Captain James Osborn's light infantry. Captain Thomas Knowlton's company had hastily constructed fleches between the redoubt breastworks and the rail fence. Now they, along with the provincials behind the breastworks, assaulted Osborn's column of infantrymen with continuous musket fire. As the front men were shot down, the next line stepped forward, only to be shot to death. Captain Samuel Trevett's cannons thundered.

In the face of this concentrated fire, the British assaulting the redoubt's flank near the beach were slaughtered. The regulars who had not fallen turned and fled back toward Morton's Hill.

The confrontation on the redoubt was going no better for Howe's grenadiers.

Captain John Chester and his company joined the rebels in the redoubt and fell into ranks with them. The men standing behind the fort's earthen walls fired incessantly as the regulars advanced. The grenadiers dropped like tin soldiers as their lines stepped up to the redoubt walls only to be shot to death by the rebels. Those who were demon-possessed and had not been shot in the eyes attempted to overwhelm the redoubt.

Abe raised his musket at a demon standing on the redoubt wall. Before he could pull the trigger, the demon leaped on him and knocked him down.

The demon wrapped its hands around Abe's throat. The moment its fingers brushed the Sigil of Lucifer tattooed on Abe's neck, the demon's human vessel burst into flames. The living possessed man screamed in agony.

Abe shoved his boot heels into the dirt and pushed backward until he was able to get to his feet without catching on fire himself. The smell of burning flesh and the sight of a man's body engulfed in flames mortified the rebels and the British alike.

Joseph was horrified. He tried to rationalize the reason the poor man was dying in agony. Colm's voice interfered. *"There's going to be human collateral damage if I'm to end this."*

Gordon searched for and found William Dawes. "We need to draw the sigil on every man in this redoubt starting with you!"

ॐ

General Pigot's and Major Pitcairn's human army marched toward the rebel redoubt and left the demons and archangel behind them. It was easier to go forward in denial than look back into the face of reality.

Henry, Robert, and Anthony had seen the archangel leave the redoubt in a flurry of wings, silver crystals, gold and green light, and rage. Colm's angelic urge to touch the frightened human, John Pitcairn, was exactly what Henry had expected. It slowed the archangel down, if only for a few moments.

Henry watched Colm disintegrate the 300 demon-possessed regulars and marines. As far as Henry was concerned, those demons were nothing more than rats scurrying about and waiting for his orders. As Colm approached, Henry wondered how much power the archangel possessed and, more importantly, how far reaching was it. It was difficult to protect your nest when vermin swarmed it.

Anthony and Robert stood close to Henry. Both demons feared that Colm would aim his destructive power at them. When Anthony was suddenly disintegrated, Robert darted for the shelter of his leader.

Henry threw his arms wide open as if he was waiting to embrace Colm.

Colm's eyes were wild. He fisted his hands and spread his arms out in front him. When he opened his hands, golden lightning bolts shot from them. The bolts sizzled with green light as they raced through the air toward Henry.

Henry dodged the currents. A bolt grazed his left arm and disintegrated the fabric of his coat and shirt sleeves. The magnetic field created by the electrical currents threw Robert against Henry. Henry shoved Robert away.

The demon leader gathered his wits immediately and took advantage of the pause in Colm's offensive. He asked with venomous pleasure, "Shall we begin, archangel?"

Henry's yellow-green eyes sparkled. He reached into the air as if he was picking an apple from a tree—and then another and another.

At first, Colm didn't understand what Henry was doing. It had been so long since the angels were disembodied spirits that Colm forgot there were thousands of disembodied demons. Henry was plucking their flames from the ether.

Henry held his fists up and smiled at Colm. Then, he threw his outstretched arms behind his head and opened his fists. Fireballs rocketed toward Charlestown where Colonel Prescott had sent 60 sharpshooters to snipe the British regulars as they landed nearby. The fireballs exploded and caught the wooden buildings on fire.

Charlestown's sudden ignition made the generals on Copp's Hill smile with smug satisfaction. The people of Boston viewed it with uncertainty. They were uncertain of who was defending the Charlestown peninsula just yards from the wharfs of Boston. If they had known, perhaps they would not have watched with morbid curiosity as men they knew and loved were dying.

Henry sneered, "You and I both know that this is the final chapter of God's enactment. Angels versus demons. It is such an old tale to tell is it not?"

Colm's failures as an archangel, his inability to protect the humans he loved, and Liam's loss seemed to come together to tell the horrible presaged tale. *Is God capable of distracting me even after we have rejected Heaven?* He shook the delusion off, furled his wings, and unconsciously brushed strands of loose hair away from his neck.

"What is that filthy thing on your neck, archangel?" Henry asked and took a step toward Colm. "Have you and your angels rejected Heaven?"

Colm saw orange flames of uncertainty flicker in Henry's yellow-green eyes. The unanticipated sight of doubt should have provided a welcome weakness to Colm, but instead, it was disconcerting. *Is he afraid of the sigil? Or do I see something I don't understand?*

Colm whipped the blade from his coat pocket and threw the knife at Henry's eyes. Henry caught the knife by its hilt before it could damage his eyes. He tossed it to the ground. *It is time to redirect the archangel's energy away from that sordid sigil.*

"Listen and feel, archangel," Henry instructed.

Heat from the crackling, exploding fires in Charlestown coupled with the late afternoon sun, baked the peninsula. As they waged war, the colonial rebels were also fighting intense thirst and fatigue. From the east, cannons thundered like Greek gods clashing on Mount Olympus. Incessant musket and cannon fire, and men shouting and screaming played a constant din.

"Where do you suppose Robert has gotten off to, preceptor?" Henry asked. His eyes shined brightly.

At that moment, Colm made a horrible mistake. He turned and ran for the rebel redoubt.

What a pleasure this will be! Henry thought.

FORTY-ONE

The grenadiers' futile attack on the redoubt fell apart at the sight of one of their own soldiers burning to death. Possessed or not, Colonel James Abercrombie's line of grenadiers broke apart. Like Howe's infantrymen on the beach, the men fled back toward Morton's Hill. Their sudden retreat halted General Pigot's and Major Pitcairn's advance on the redoubt's left flank.

Joseph, Ian, and Abe extinguished the burning body of the demon-possessed man. Joseph stared down at the putrid body. He wondered if an angel came to guide this soul to its egress, although the man had been possessed by a demon when he died.

Colonel Prescott approached Joseph. "This man needs to be buried. I cannot have this morbid sight among us."

Abe somberly volunteered. "I will do it."

"Thank you, Abe," Joseph said, quietly.

Peter Salem and Ian helped Abe remove the corpse from the redoubt to bury it.

William Dawes handed his pistol and ammunition to Barnabus Miller. "How am I to draw the sigil on hundreds of men before the British regroup and attack us again?" William asked Gordon.

The answer became more complicated as the sharpshooters Colonel Prescott had sent to Charlestown entered the redoubt. There were 60 of them when Henry caught Charlestown on fire. Ten had been trapped in buildings and burned to death. Many of the survivors were burned and wounded. Joseph went to care for them.

Seamus sat with his back against the front redoubt wall. Michael and Patrick sat beside him. The boys were able to release their blue auras to comfort themselves. Seamus, on the other hand, couldn't control his purple aura. He struggled with it for a while and then realized it was hopeless.

I'm supposed to be in command of the brotherhood with Colm and Fergus gone, but everythin's fallen apart and there ain't nothin' to be in charge of, Seamus thought.

⁂

General William Howe stood alone on a rise near the rail fence. He felt the devastating brunt of what had just transpired in the hills overlooking the raging flames of Charlestown. Every member of his staff was either dead or wounded.

Both the colonial rebels and Howe's regulars looked on in astonishment as he stood there, oblivious, resplendent in his scarlet uniform; a sure target for the rebels.

Surrounded by the dead and the dying, having learned that the light infantry, who were to have assured him of a victory, had been repulsed; Howe experienced a life-altering sensation. Staggered by grief, shock, anger, and embarrassment, he turned and started down the rise. He picked his way through the fallen bodies and considered what to do next. *Do I withdraw my troops and avoid more bloodshed?*

Howe's next act was preordained. With generals Clinton, Burgoyne, and Gage watching his every move from Copp's Hill, he had no choice short of shame other than to regroup and try to thwart the rebels once again. *I'll direct my energies toward the redoubt and the breastworks.* But he had to act quickly before the provincials had a chance to reinforce their numbers.

He sent a request for reinforcements to General Gage.

Remarkably, despite all they had been through, his surviving troops expressed enthusiasm when he ordered a fresh assault. Dispensed of packs and other unnecessary equipment, they cried, "Push on! Push on!" the British soldiers advanced toward the breastworks and the redoubt in a column of eight men across instead of exposed lines of hundreds of men across.

⁂

The colonists in Prescott's redoubt could not afford even the hint of a victory celebration. They had lost few men and had broken the British advance, but they had done so with repeated firings. Their gunpowder supply was nearly as exhausted as they were after a sleepless night of digging and a hot day under frequent bombardment with no food and little to drink but rum.

Furthermore, Henry's demons were infiltrating the British soldiers in large numbers, and Colm wasn't there to soothe the angels and the rebels who depended on his protection. The provincial reinforcements, trickling in

402

through the back of the redoubt, were little comfort to those who knew the battle was inhuman.

Captain John Stark's troops abandoned the stone wall and the breastworks and tried to flee to the redoubt, but the British began cannonading them. They were forced to prepare and defend the redoubt from outside its walls.

Many of Colonel Prescott's troops had withdrawn or deserted. Less than 150 men remained in the redoubt.

Joseph finished caring for the injured sharpshooters and returned to the angels. He sat down beside Seamus. "Can you sense Colm?" he asked as he reloaded his musket with one of the last cartridges in his box.

Seamus shook his head.

Patrick fought the urge to crawl into his brother's lap like a confused and terrified infant. Peter Salem, Ian, and Abe returned from burying the burned British soldier. Their return provided enough solace to stifle Patrick's urge.

Michael reloaded. With his musket in one hand and his curved surgical blade in the other, he scooted in closer to Joseph. William Dawes and Gordon Walker approached them. William kneeled and asked Joseph, "I have been carving the sigil into the skin of those who wish it. Do you want me to do the same for you?"

"No, William. Prepare yourself for the coming assault."

"Joseph, I think you shou'd let me do this."

Colonel Prescott shouted, "FALL IN!"

Joseph stood in response to Prescott's order. "Come, William. We have orders to carry out."

"Joseph, I really think you—" William's words were lost in the flurry of men falling in. An odd unwelcome feeling crept into the pit of his stomach.

The sharpshooters formed the first line of rebel defense along the redoubt wall. Seamus, Patrick, Michael, and Joseph fell into ranks with Abe, Ian, Degory Bennet, Peter Salem, Peter Brown, Barnabus Miller, Gordon, William Dawes, Salem Poor, and the few men left under Colonel Prescott's command. They formed a line behind the sharpshooters.

The cannon fire from Captain Samuel Trevett's artillery company near the beach ceased.

The men in the little fort on the wrong hill listened to General Howe's regulars chant "Conquer or die!" as they marched toward them from the south. General Pigot's regulars and Major Pitcairn's marines had also rallied; they approached the redoubt from the west.

With the retreat of Captain John Stark's company, and the silence of provincial cannons, some of Howe's infantrymen were able to reach the beach and begin flanking the redoubt.

Colonel Prescott and Captain Chester leaped on to the top of the redoubt wall and ran along its length, knocking up the muzzles of the men's muskets to prevent them from firing too early. From his vantage point, William Prescott saw Colm and a teenage boy run through the back of the redoubt; they fell into lines with the waiting rebels.

The angels overreacted to Colm's arrival. Their wings unfurled and interfered with many of the men's ability to see what was happening.

Colonel Prescott pointed at the angels and shouted at Colm, "Get them under control!"

Colm eased into the line between Michael and Patrick. The boys looked at Colm, relieved. He stroked their cheeks and said, "Furl ya wings if ya can. It's going to be alright." Then, he soothed Seamus and Ian in the same way.

"Don't leave us again," Seamus said to Colm. "We ain't doin' so well."

"I can see that."

Joseph asked Colm, "Did you find Henry?"

Colm couldn't tell Joseph that he had lost track of Henry and Robert because he had panicked.

Joseph looked at Colm carefully.

Gold light flashed in Colm's eyes.

"Colm, where is Henry?" Joseph asked.

Michael and Patrick released a cry of distress.

A shiver ran up Ian's spine. He and Seamus looked at one another. Seamus' gray eyes, bearded face, and narrow-brimmed beaver felt hat were familiar to Ian. Ian's new vessel, with its dark blue eyes and graying brown hair that fell below his shoulders in a long queue, was finally beginning to seem unsurprising to Seamus. Their purple and red auras lit up bright and strong; it was who they truly were and how they truly saw one another.

Colm met Joseph's stare and said, "I want ya and Michael to stay beside me."

"You do not know where Henry is, do you?" Joseph demanded.

Patrick could no longer contain his distress. He shouted, "Answer Joseph, Colm!"

The current of the angels' apprehension pulled Abe and Gordon in closer to them.

Then, Colonel Prescott yelled, "AT THE READY FOR AN ASSAULT!"

Captain John Chester ordered some of the men, including Patrick, Peter Salem, and Gordon to man the west wall against General Pigot's regulars and Major Pitcairn's marines.

The fifteen-year-old boy who had entered the redoubt with Colm, wielded a bayonet with careless abandon. Patrick snatched it from the boy before he could hurt anyone in the redoubt, then followed Captain Chester.

The boy fell in beside Patrick.

"Who are you?" Patrick asked him.

"John Greenwood. I'm a fifer with Captain Bliss' company out of Massachusetts," the boy explained proudly. He considered Patrick's blue aura. "You must be one of them angels I heard about. Can I have my bayonet back?"

When they were positioned at the west wall, Patrick gave John back his bayonet.

Suddenly, British field pieces thundered and grapeshot showered the redoubt. The British were within three rods of the redoubt's west and south walls.

Colonel Prescott shouted, "FIRE!"

The redoubt erupted with gunfire. They shot unmercifully at the bright scarlet coats of the British officers' first, and then took aim at the regulars and a sea of orange eyes.

At the west wall, Major John Pitcairn's marines were heavily assaulted and their lines broke, but they didn't retreat. Confusion ensued and John Pitcairn tried to locate his adjutant, Lieutenant John Waller. Waller and a large number of marines were pinned down by provincial fire behind a stone wall and some trees. Pitcairn saw simmering orange eyes among them. He thought he'd left his demon-possessed troops behind and that the archangel had destroyed them.

John Pitcairn shook off the morbidity of seeing those eyes. What was much worse were the growing numbers of dead and dying British soldiers surrounding him. From the redoubt, he heard Colonel Prescott shout the order for a short pause in the firing.

Lieutenant Waller and Major Pitcairn took the opportunity to get the marines in order. Then, they rushed the redoubt. One hundred marines jumped a dry ditch and landed at the base of the redoubt wall. Major Pitcairn waved his bayonet at the rebels and yelled, "Now, for the glory of the Marines!"

Peter Salem, Patrick, Gordon, and the other rebels at the west wall opened fire.

Andrew Hay, the marine captain who suspected there were two wars being waged, was shot in the throat. He collapsed into the dusty ditch. In the distance, he heard someone shout, "Captain Hay has been hit!" Captain James Murray and two ensigns ran to Hay's side and attended him as he died.

John Pitcairn's son, William, watched in horror as Peter Salem aimed his musket at his father. "NO!" William screamed. He reached to shove his father out of the musket's site. Peter fired and hit John Pitcairn in the chest.

John collapsed into William's arms. While the marines charged forward in the final assault, William carried his wounded father out of the line of fire. Soaked in his father's blood, William laid him on the ground, and cried, "You will be fine, Father! You will be fine!"

John Pitcairn was an experienced veteran. He knew his chance for survival was poor. Despite the searing pain in his chest, John whispered to William, "Go on and finish this."

With Major Pitcairn down and two of his captains, Hay and Forsyth, dead, Lieutenant Waller ordered the marines to stop firing their muskets and execute a bayonet assault. Hundreds of marines, as well as General Pigot's regulars, climbed the redoubt wall.

The first demon-possessed marine that clambered over the top jumped Patrick and snatched him by the hair. With a vicious yank, the demon screeched, "You *will* die angel!"

The demon suddenly fell backward. Patrick fell with his hair tangled in the demon's hands. Patrick heard a grunt. Orange light flared. Then, someone was untangling his hair. He looked up at his rescuer and saw Gordon holding a bloody butcher knife with the Sigil of Lucifer etched in the blade.

"STAND UP!" Gordon shouted at Patrick.

Patrick scrambled to his feet.

The man within the demon-possessed body emitted an ungodly scream when he caught fire. His screeching pleas for help went unanswered.

There was neither time nor inclination to help the burning marine. Demons and humans armed with bayonets and muskets were swarming over the wall. The rebels defending the west wall had no more gunpowder. Gordon and Patrick wielded their sigil-etched butcher knives. It took as little as one touch of the blade on human skin to ignite the destruction of a demon and the vessel it possessed.

A demon snatched the back of Peter Salem's shirt and whipped his bay-onet up to Peter's throat. Peter threw his sigil-carved forearm backward and dragged it over the top of his attacker's head. The demon, and the man it possessed, shrieked when the body they shared caught fire. Peter's back and neck were burned as he twisted away from the demon's grasp.

A young rebel screamed in pain when a British regular stabbed him in the knee with a bayonet. The young man fell to the redoubt floor where a bayonet-wielding marine attacked him. "God help me! God help me!" the young rebel pleaded as the marine stabbed him to death. Blood flowed from the young man's filleted abdomen and spurted from his jugular vein.

Patrick felt the struggle the man's soul endured as his body died, but he could do nothing about it. He could no longer hear God's instructions, nor could he summon a reaper. He felt sorry for what was no longer a part of him.

A short stocky redheaded marine tried to run his bayonet through John Greenwood. Greenwood jumped back, wheeled around, and punched the marine in the mouth. Blood slid from the corners of the marine's mouth. He bent over and spit out four teeth.

Gordon lost the tip of his middle finger on his right hand to a musket ball. He stared dumbly at it for a moment—long enough for a regular to jump him and knock him to the ground. Gordon's head smacked the blood-soaked dirt. His vision blurred, and he readied himself for death.

Peter Salem slammed the butt of his musket into the regular's head and killed him. Then, he offered his hand to Gordon and yelled, "Get up!" Gordon grasped Peter's hand with a grunt, and Peter hauled him to his feet.

Captain John Chester ordered the men at the west wall to retreat to the redoubt's south wall where Howe's grenadiers and light infantry were over-whelming the rebel defenders. Most of the men did indeed retreat, but not to the south wall. They fled the redoubt. Some were killed by grapeshot fired from British field pieces. Others were mildly injured, losing a finger or an eye.

Still, what was ending the rebel resistance was neither lack of courage nor unstoppable British resolve. It was the depleted supply of rebel gunpowder.

As they ran to help the men at the south wall, Patrick, Peter Salem, and Gordon saw Degory Bennett, Ian, Peter Brown, Barnabus Miller, and Salem Poor grab the barrel end of their empty muskets and swing the butts at the grenadiers pouring over the south wall. Some of the rebels picked up stones and threw them at their assailants. Others turned and ran.

Colm, Joseph, Michael, and Seamus were together. Michael swung his curved surgical blade in a wide arc over and over again. He cut off the heads of four demons and two human infantrymen in rapid succession. Colm and Seamus were defending themselves with the sigil-etched butcher knives Gordon had given them before Jeremiah and Brandon left the redoubt. Joseph wielded Jeremiah's skinning knife.

Patrick ran to fight by Seamus' side.

Barnabus Miller dropped his musket and began punching and kicking his way through the throngs of regulars until he was able to escape the redoubt.

A regular ran Degory Bennett through with a bayonet. Peter Brown tried to keep the old man from falling where his body would be trampled, but the effort was impossible. Peter fled with the rest of the terrified provincials.

Colm backed away from the wall in step with Michael and Joseph, who were to his left. To his right, someone cried for help. *It's a trick,* Colm thought. *Robert and Henry are here, and they're trying to distract me.* What he saw stumbling toward made him feel ashamed.

John Greenwood was supporting a twelve-year-old-boy whose face was so battered and bloody that he was unrecognizable. The boy was clutching his stomach. He had been eviscerated. His intestines and blood spilled through his splayed fingers.

The boy's knees unbuckled and he slipped from John's grasp. Colm caught him before he fell into a pool filled with the blood of so many other men. The boy looked up into the archangel's eyes and sighed. Colm felt the struggle the boy's soul endured as his body died. Like Patrick, Colm could no longer hear God's instructions nor could he summon a reaper.

A musket ball gouged Michael's forehead. He fell onto the bloody, gut-slicked floor, hitting the back of his head on the stony surface. Dizzy and disoriented, he labored to get to his knees. As he pushed his upper body up, someone clutched his hair and dragged him backward. Suddenly, he was jerked to his feet. His hair was pulled so hard that the back of his head nearly touch his shoulder blades. Robert Percy wound Michael's loose wild hair tight around his hand, and breathed in Michael's ear, "Will he choose you or will he choose Warren?"

Michael tried to wrench away, but the position his head was in thwarted his movements. His wings rustled.

Robert laughed and said, "It is over angel. We have won."

Michael raised his arms, bent them backward over his shoulders, and groped for a hold on Robert. In response, Robert broke Michael's wrists in two smooth movements of his right hand. The contact with Michael's skin burned Robert's hand badly. He shoved the angel away in surprise and disgust.

Joseph saw Michael stumble. With bruising strength, a British officer stepped in and wrapped his arms around Michael like a perverted lover. It took Joseph a moment to realize that the British officer was Henry.

Michael's spirit and human vessel writhed in agony under Henry's vicious grip. The physical pain was worse than anything Michael had ever imagined.

Henry turned Michael around so Michael's back was touching his chest. "Keep squirming," Henry crooned. "The feeling of your body against mine is luscious."

From behind him, Joseph heard a familiar voice say, "I cannot touch the angel, but I can touch you," Robert purred as he slid his arms around Joseph's waist and chest and pulled him into a backward embrace. Joseph struggled and tried to pull away, but Robert was almost as strong as Henry. Robert plucked the skinning knife from Joseph's hand and threw it over the redoubt wall. It was the last bastion of Jeremiah's place in the battle.

Robert turned Joseph around and shoved him into the redoubt wall. He splayed his fingers and dug them into Joseph's cheeks. "The bruises I left on your face less than a month ago are faded. Perhaps, I should blacken them." Robert squeezed Joseph's cheeks so hard that Joseph's teeth cut the inside of his mouth. Blood drained down his throat.

Despite the pain that erupted in his jaw, Joseph rammed a knee into Robert's groin and pulled Robert's punishing fingers from his cheeks. He darted sideways.

Robert exhaled a grunt, but the blow only served to anger him. He snatched Joseph's coattails, jerked Joseph back into his embrace, and slammed him against the redoubt wall. Robert doused his eyes and jammed the palms of his hands into Joseph's chest. "Did you really believe that you could slip from my grasp that easily?"

Their eyes met.

"If you intend on killing me, then do so," Joseph spat. He tried to pull Robert's hands away from his chest. The deed was impossible.

"The time has come for the archangel to choose," Robert said. His fingers returned to punish Joseph's cheeks. "If the archangel chooses his brother, I will relish in killing you." He let go of Joseph's cheeks and stepped in so close that their bodies touched. "In fact, I may kill you anyway."

Joseph did something he learned from Michael. He spit in Robert Percy's face.

❧

As the last of the provincials retreated from the filthy little fort on the wrong hill, Colm realized that his little brother was in the hands of Henry Hereford.

"There you are, archangel!" Henry exclaimed. "I must tell you that if you insist on making any kind of movement, I will rape your brother and then kill him."

"Fuck Henry!" Michael shouted at his brother. "Let him do whatever he wants, but get the rest of us out—"

"No, Michael! Don't speak!" Colm ordered.

Henry mocked Colm. "No, Michael. Don't speak!" He ripped Michael's shirt off and threw it into a muddy pool of blood. "I have imagined myself raping this beautiful angel so many times. Whores just do not quite fulfill my fantasy as they should."

Terror and mania threatened to ignite Colm's spirit. He couldn't let his eyes or mind wander from Michael and what Henry would do to him, and he didn't know where Joseph was.

"Now that you have rejected Heaven, my fond name for you—*preceptor*—no longer seems appropriate," Henry gloated. "But I suppose it makes no difference because you will die today."

Colm saw Ian and Seamus creeping up on Henry from behind. He tried to spiritually warn them away, but Henry's presence was blocking their ability to communicate.

Seamus signaled for Patrick to stand down. Patrick's aura brightened as his brother stepped closer to Henry. He tried in a panic to dim it.

Seamus and Ian exchanged glances. They both knew they couldn't kill Henry, but they could distract him. They nodded at one another and continued to move in on Henry.

Colm had no idea what to say to make Henry let go of Michael. *Joseph would know, and he would do it with a calm demeanor*, Colm thought. He became agitated as he watched Ian and Seamus inch closer to Henry.

Henry barely flinched when he whipped a hand behind him and broke Seamus' neck. Seamus crumpled to the ground like a rag doll.

"SEAMUS!" Patrick screamed. His wings unfurled, and his aura blinked out.

Ian buried his sigil-etched dagger to the hilt in Henry's spine between the shoulder blades.

Henry snapped Ian's neck without a backward glance.

410

Patrick's spirit became irrational. He heard Colm scream, "RUN, PATRICK!"

The sight of his dead brother was enough for him to understand that he had to take Colm's order. Patrick ran.

Colm was hobbled by his love for Joseph. After seeing Seamus and Ian die, he couldn't let Joseph become a victim of the collateral damage he had promised would occur if he was to defeat Henry.

Trapped in Henry's cruel embrace, Michael could neither see nor understand what had just happened. He spiritually tried to draw Colm's attention, but something was terribly wrong, and Colm wasn't responding.

Henry's hand snaked down Michael's smooth bare chest. "You will want to pay attention, archangel." His hand traveled to the waistband of Michael's breeches and ripped the front of them open. "It is time for you to choose—your brother or your pet."

Colm heard Joseph whisper, "I love you, Colm."

"Joseph, where are ya?" Colm's green eyes flashed with unimaginable dread.

"He is here, archangel."

Robert shoved Joseph at Colm, then he shot Joseph in the face with a pistol. The ball entered just below Joseph's left eye and exited through the back of his head. The handsome young widower with four children; the gentle physician; the situational leader of the patriotic cause; the man adored by the people of a nation yet to be born; the human an archangel loved beyond reason, died before his body hit the ground.

The heavy haze of gun smoke cloaking the Charlestown peninsula dissolved, replaced by the haze of imminent grief.

The Sigil of Lucifer, which Paul Revere had etched into the blade of the butcher knife, winked when Gordon stabbed Robert in the throat. Robert ignited into an inferno of flaming death throes.

Colm's human vessel dropped dead onto the ground beside Joseph. Abe Rowlinson, William Dawes, and William Prescott ran to them. They fell to their knees beside the bodies.

Michael was still unable to see or understand what had happened. His fear, confusion, and physical pain weakened him. He couldn't summon what comforted him much less remember how to leave his broken human vessel. Blood from the wound on his forehead ran into his eyes and down his cheek like scarlet tears.

Robert's death made no difference to Henry. He slid his hand down the front of Michael's torn breeches and reveled in stroking the treasure within.

"I so wish to have my way with you, but I suppose it is time for me to pursue the archangel," Henry purred. "I do not think I will kill you. When I destroy the archangel, you will die a miserable death, and then blink out of existence just as the angel you call Liam did. But before that happens, I will return to have my way with you."

He squeezed Michael's crotch so hard that Michael squirmed and emitted a squeal of pain. Then, he threw Michael face first into the filthy redoubt floor and disappeared.

Michael's inability to sense Colm or any of the angels scared him. He used his elbows to push himself to his knees. He couldn't stand, and he fell forward onto his broken wrists. Agony made his ears ring with his brother's words—*"If I say run, ya run. Do ya understand me?"*

Saliva dripped from Michael's mouth when he said, "I understand ya."

At that moment, Michael sensed that Ian and Seamus were gone. If they were gone, and Colm was impossible to sense, where was the rest of their brotherhood? And where was Joseph?

Many arms surrounded Michael and set him on his feet. Through a blur of caustic tears, Michael saw Abe, William Dawes, Gordon, and William Prescott standing beside him. But it was his brother's words that propelled him forward.

Michael ran without stopping to look at the dead because that was what Colm wanted. He ran through Charlestown Neck toward Prospect Hill, but grief overwhelmed him, and he sprawled face first into the grass.

FORTY-TWO

The people watching the Battle of Bunker Hill from the rooftops, steeples, and hills of Boston saw the bright June day darken. Generals Henry Clinton, Thomas Gage, and John Burgoyne, watching from Copp's Hill, were sure that General William Howe had succeeded in crushing the American rebellion. Then, the skies turned gray and thick black clouds scudded in like harbingers of what the next eight years of an American revolution would bring.

Except for the crackling roar of fire burning Charlestown, Breed's Hill was nearly silent when General William Howe and General Robert Pigot saw General Henry Hereford slide his hand down the front of a beautiful young man's breeches. The generals, their officers, and the nearby regulars stared in disbelief while Henry stroked and squeezed the young man. They saw the general throw the young man down, and then vanish.

When the regulars moved to capture the young man and his rescuers, General Howe stopped them. He watched the young man run wildly through the back of the redoubt. Then, he looked at the bodies of Joseph, Colm, Seamus, and Ian. Nearby, he noticed a pile of ash topped with a nearly melted pistol. Finally, his dark eyes shifted to Colonel William Prescott and the three men with him.

The sound of marines moving Major John Pitcairn onto a chaise to transport him to a boat at Morton's Point distracted Howe for a moment. He had been told that Pitcairn suffered a terrible wound.

"I am not sure of what happened here," Howe said to Prescott. "This was no ordinary battle." Howe regarded Joseph's and Colm's bodies. Colm had fallen so that he was lying beside Joseph with one arm draped across Joseph's chest. "They are not ordinary men." He pointed at Colm's body. "In fact, General Pigot claims that he is an archangel."

General Pigot shivered in the stifling heat of the late afternoon. The thick black clouds overhead signaled something much more ominous than a brewing thunderstorm.

"You are not surprised by that statement?" Howe asked Prescott.

Prescott said nothing.

"Well, then, I suggest you start running before I change my mind."

Gold lightning bolts lacerated the sky.

The rebels ran.

Hundreds of British and American men lay dead and dying on the blood-soaked earth.

The sky sizzled with gold light and thundered with unearthly ire.

Howe knew that many more men were about to die. It would not be until the next day that he would realize the man who lay dead beside the archangel was Dr. Joseph Warren.

No longer fettered by a human vessel, Colm's power had no bounds. His gold radiance was free. It raced with unleashed fury through the skies over the northern hemisphere and into the heavens.

He sensed Henry leave his human vessel.

Henry's army of demons—disembodied or not—remained on the Charlestown peninsula under the impression that the archangel would not strike them dead if they were among the children of man.

Colm unfurled his wings. Silver crystals pelted the earth with deadly apocalyptic hailstones that built horrible mountains of anguish. He reined in his power and redirected it. Gold radiance swept the sky over Charlestown like a plague of locusts. The disembodied demons exploded all at once in a firestorm just above the surface of the earth on the lower Charlestown peninsula.

Hundreds of terrified British marines and regulars caught fire. They ran screaming toward the waters of the Charles and Mystic Rivers only to accelerate the flames that melted their clothing and charred their bodies. Fire and sparks ignited gunpowder. Regulars were maimed or killed when the muskets and cartridge boxes they were carrying exploded. Loaded field pieces fired cannon balls and grapeshot as if ghosts had lit the touch holes. The cannons on the deck of the HMS *Falcon* and HMS *Lively* fired wildly, in kind.

Stupefied and appalled, General Howe and General Pigot tried to control the panicked troops by shouting orders, but it was a ridiculous effort in the face of what was happening. The generals were caught up in the maelstrom and stampeded, alongside their men, toward Morton's Point and the boats waiting on the shores of the Mystic River.

A tempest of embers whirled and rushed across the Charles River and Boston Harbor, and were extinguished in the waters.

The people watching the battle from Boston ran for shelter from the lightning, hail, and sudden explosions. Generals Henry Clinton and John Burgoyne, and their aides, fled Copp's Hill and made a mad dash for the sanctuary of nearby Christ's Church.

General Thomas Gage paused among the cannons and tombstones to watch the bank of heavy smoke roll over the Charlestown peninsula. The hailstones pelting him were what he deserved. Through his spyglass, he had witnessed General Henry Hereford's perverse acts with a frightened young man.

"I have been a blind fool, but no more," Thomas declared. "I will not allow that filthy general near Margaret and my children ever again. I will send my family to England, or to the ends of the Earth, if that is what it takes to keep them away from him."

What Thomas Gage had not seen was Joseph Warren die at the hands of Captain Robert Percy. There had been a time when Thomas would have been happy to hear the situational leader of the rebellion was dead. But when he learned of Warren's fate the next day, he told General Howe that Joseph Warren's death was as damaging as the loss of 500 men.

In Braintree, Abigail Adams and her children, Nabby and John Quincy, stood on Penn's Hill and watched the smoke and fire, and listened to the cannonading from the Charlestown peninsula.

Abigail hurried the children out of the storm and into the house. Before she followed them inside, she paused and studied the sky. Gold lightning flashed and static electricity raised the hairs on the back of her neck. In her heart, she knew that the angels were in the battle and if they were there, Joseph was with them.

If the storm was the result of an archangel's grief and anger, Abigail also knew that not all of them had survived. She sat on the portico step and let the silver crystalline hail pelt her while she cried.

Eight-year-old John Quincy came out onto the portico and wrapped his small arms around his mother's quivering shoulders. He would become the sixth president of the United States, and he would never recover from the death of the Adams' gentle family physician, Dr. Joseph Warren. Dr. Warren had repaired young John Quincy's badly injured finger so that he was able to write again. Dr. Warren was his hero.

❧

Every member of the provincial army stationed in Roxbury was perched in trees, sat on rooftops, or stood outside with their necks craned and their eyes on the sky. Fergus and his officers watched and listened to the battle from the roof of Dillaway House.

His wings rustled uncontrollably throughout the battle, and his purple aura shined so brightly that some of his officers complained. He lost spiritual contact with his brotherhood. Fergus knew things had gone terribly wrong, not only for the angels, but also for the rebels.

When gold lightning raced through the black clouds over the skies of New England, Fergus knew Colm had left his human vessel. He climbed down from the roof of Dillaway House and walked the road to the farm. Tears flowed down his dimpled cheeks and soaked the front of his vest and shirt. He tried desperately to establish contact with his brotherhood. Then, he saw Brandon running toward him. Fergus caught Brandon in his arms.

❧

Patrick fell at the crossroads on Charlestown Neck. He lay on the dirt, curled up into a tight ball and cried. His spirit was in agony, and he had no way to soothe his pain. All he could see in his mind was Henry snapping Seamus' neck and his brother's human vessel lying dead on the filthy redoubt floor.

When his body began to shake uncontrollably, Patrick rolled over and threw up.

He felt wet silver crystals hail down upon him. The energy from those silver crystals was familiar and soothing. Patrick pulled his knees up under his stomach and cried harder. Something had happened to cause Colm to leave his human vessel and unfurl his wings in the sky over New England.

Patrick had never felt so afraid and so alone. He spiritually reached out for his brotherhood, but no one responded. He threw up again. His body curled into a tighter ball in the pool of his vomit.

Static electricity filled the air around him.

Then, beyond the noise of his cries, the thundering skies, and running and screaming men passing him by, Patrick sensed Michael's physical and spiritual agony. He got to his feet, wiped the tears from his eyes, and pushed his hair away from his filthy vomit-coated face. On shaking legs, Patrick followed his senses until he found Michael lying face-down in the front yard of a vacant house.

Patrick collapsed beside Michael. Gold lightning raced through the thick black clouds overhead when Patrick kissed the top of Michael's blood and dirt-caked head.

"Michael!" Patrick cried.

Michael responded and rolled on to his back. The angels curled up together like baby birds trapped in a nest, to which their mother would never return.

෨

Jeremiah was riding through Dorchester, south of Boston, when black storm clouds rolled in from the north. The lack of wind associated with the moving bank of clouds was his first clue that it was no ordinary thunderstorm. He tried not to look skyward again, but gold lightning, static electricity, and silver crystalline hail were signs he couldn't ignore. Colm had left his human vessel, and the final showdown with Henry was about to commence.

Thoughts of his son were the only thing that kept Jeremiah from turning the horse around and riding to Charlestown. He slowly stroked his beard in a symbolic act of self-control meant to keep him sane when he knew insanity had prevailed in the little fort on the wrong hill. His hand traveled to the empty pocket on the thigh of his deerskin breeches.

"Joseph, I hope you put my skinnin' knife ta good use," Jeremiah whispered. "I know if you had the choice, you tried, but I got a feelin' you didn't have that choice." He resisted the sobs forming in his throat.

He looked skyward and wondered why he had let Colm, Joseph, and Ian talk him into leaving the battle. *Ian was probably right. My stake in the battle with the demons wou'dn't make no difference ta the outcome. But it ain't that, not really. It's the fact that I ain't got no idea what's happened ta them. If Colm's rage is causin' that storm—*

Jeremiah shuddered and tried to leave his thoughts alone. It was a wasted effort.

Gold lightning streaked across the sky in all directions.

He reined his horse and turned around in the saddle for one last look at Boston. A wall of fire exploded over the lower Charlestown peninsula.

෨

William Dawes, William Prescott, Abe Rowlinson, and Gordon Walker heard the explosion and felt the heat just as they crossed Charlestown Neck. The men kept running toward Prospect Hill. Abe got a stitch in his side and slowed to a walk. Then, he stopped and bent over to catch his breath.

417

Gordon realized that Abe was no longer with them and shouted, "STOP!"

Both William Dawes and William Prescott stopped. They went with Gordon to join Abe. Abe straightened up and gave them a reassuring nod.

Prescott said, "I have to report to General Ward." He cast a nervous glance toward Charlestown. "I wish you—" He frowned. "I nearly said I wish you Godspeed. Life looks different now. I think I shall forget the disdain I have for Israel Putnam if I ever see the old scoundrel again. I hope Colm succeeds in destroying Henry. I hope we, as humans, recover from this horrible tragedy."

He turned and walked toward Cambridge before his intense sorrow paralyzed him.

Abe, Gordon, and Dawes watched him go.

"We shou'd go home to the farm," Abe said. "Someone shou'd be there if any of them…come home."

Gordon tried to swallow the heartbreak he felt, but it choked him. His chest hitched in a sob.

William Dawes turned his eyes to the sky. He had lost one of his oldest and closest friends, and the angels he had grown to consider his brothers. If he did not concentrate on his breathing, he was sure to break down and cry. Without a word, he began walking toward Watertown to take the news to Paul Revere.

Abe shut his eyes and drew in a deep breath to steady his own desolation. When he opened his eyes, he saw Colm's grief streak through the sky. Abe's heart begged for the return of a family he knew had been blown apart.

FORTY-THREE

Colm soared above the churning black clouds of his horrible grief. He couldn't cope with the suffocating flood of his emotions. He considered letting his gold radiance escape him completely. Perhaps in doing so, he would incinerate everything in a world where there was very little worth saving. If he destroyed the surviving angels' human vessels, they would be free to join him in the cosmos where they belonged. If Jeremiah, Gordon, Abe, Paul, and William died, their souls would rest in Heaven with Joseph.

He told himself that he was through with the children of man and the pain that came from loving and protecting them.

He suddenly yearned for the millenniums the brotherhood had spent running from God's demons. Everything they cherished lived in those centuries— family, love, and devotion. They were whole.

They would never be whole again. Liam, Seamus, and Ian were gone.

With their brotherhood in pieces, Colm understood that if he carried through with his promise to sacrifice himself to protect his angels, the survivors would suffer more than if they had died at Henry's hands. He had to disconnect his spirit from his angels to protect them if Henry *did* kill him.

Colm reached to soothe their spirits. Michael, Patrick, Brandon, and Fergus fell into unconsciousness. Then, he tried to dam the flood of his emotions, but he had no inkling where to place the first stone to build the dam.

With Jeremiah gone and Joseph dead, he had nothing and no one to turn to for guidance. Henry had taken that away from him. The churning black clouds of his grief intensified. Funnel clouds formed in the violent rotating wind of his anger.

"FACE ME, DEMON!"

Thunder rumbled.

"WHY ARE YA HIDING FROM ME?"

He isn't hiding from me, Colm thought. *He's planning his attack while he basks in the black clouds of my grief. I have to let them go.*

The archangel susurrated his imperial silver wings and the resulting breeze cleared the skies above New England. The sun's rays baked the earth once again. Colm looked down onto the Charlestown peninsula. Henry's demons still possessed General Howe's regulars and Major Pitcairn's marines, even after the battle was over. Colm's gold radiance bolted through the sky and blew the demons and the humans they possessed apart.

"ANSWER ME, DEMON!"

Henry's voice slid through the atmosphere. "I am here, archangel. I see you no longer have qualms about killing the children of man." Henry's brief laugh rumbled like distant thunder. "It makes no difference. Your human toy is dead."

"Toy?" Colm asked in disbelief and anger. "If ya believed Joseph was nothing more than a toy to me, why did ya murder him?"

"Me? I did not murder your toy…I mean your pet. Robert did. But I suppose it is all the same to you."

Colm's wings rustled as he tried to keep the rage of his grief at bay. He needed to convince himself that Joseph's death wasn't his fault. "Answer me! Why did ya murder him?"

"It was a mistake. Robert was overzealous. I intended to make you choose between Warren's life and your brother's life so you would suffer the torment of your decision for the rest of your existence." Henry saw Colm's gold radiance flicker in distress. He smiled, and cooed, "But you already knew that, archangel."

Colm's control slipped a little.

"You should have masked your love for your pet," Henry advised. "An angel's love is bright and ardent, and easy to take advantage of."

"Shut ya mouth, demon! Ya know nothing about an angel's love!" Colm spread his wings wide. Silver crystals glittered in the sun as they fell to earth. His spirit flew at Henry, and he screamed, "WHERE ARE MY ANGELS?"

Henry's energy blinked in surprise at Colm's sudden voraciousness. "I do not know. Perhaps, you should ask God what happens to angels who reject Heaven, and then die. It makes no difference. The rest will follow quickly once you are dead."

Colm suddenly understood that Henry, in his rapacity, had never considered that victory would only bring about his own destruction. God would have no use for him once the angels were dead.

Like flickering ghosts, Henry's ragged army of demons began to rise from the earth's surface in answer to their leader's silent beckon call.

"What is left of your army is useless," Colm said.

"Perhaps, but they are no longer needed. It is just you and I now, as it should be." Henry laughed as though he had delighted himself by solving a riddle. "Did you turn your back on the children of man in order to serve your brother, Lucifer? It is not surprising now that I contemplate it. You are a pariah. Your brothers despise you. Even the man the Christians worship had the sense to say 'Get thee behind me Satan'."

Colm threshed his wings in response. He soared above Henry and the army of demons like a hawk seeking prey. Green light and gold radiance spun in a centrifuge of vehement violence. Stray electrical currents of gold lightning incited the sky.

Henry sensed the thrust of Colm's energy. It was not the basis of power he fought in 1318, when Colm and he had clashed at the Battle of Faughart. Colm's energy was charged with human emotions. The weaknesses of that power were endless. The strengths of that power depended on the depths from which it was drawn.

For Colm, his capacity for human emotion was an unexpected end to a journey that had taken him to a place of enlightenment he didn't know existed. He let the flood of his emotions sweep him away.

Henry wielded Colm's enlightenment like a sword. He anticipated Colm's reaction with glee when he said, "You failed to choose between your brother and your pet. Since your pet is dead, I will satisfy myself with your brother. Then, I will kill him, too."

"*I* failed? Robert took him from me!" Colm's rage detonated with the roar of thunder. The last of Henry's army exploded. Fire rained from the late afternoon sky.

The electrically charged particles from his energy collided with gaseous particles in the Earth's atmosphere, and the northern hemisphere lit up with the green lights of the Aurora Borealis. Colm redirected his tempestuous fury away from Earth. It raced through space and dimmed the sun.

Henry escaped and returned to the Charlestown peninsula to repossess his vessel.

Colm's grotesque grief flared. He pictured Liam dropping dead the moment the angels rejected Heaven. He saw Henry snap Ian's and Seamus' necks. He heard Joseph say, 'I love you, Colm.' He smelled gunpowder and saw Robert shoot Joseph in the face. The tempestuous fury Colm had directed away from Earth came flooding back into his spirit.

Then, Colm's palimpsest, the last remnants of Colm Bohannon's human soul that had been a part of the archangel's spirit for 600 years, spoke to him. *"It will hurt ya spirit, but ya must let Henry's intentions play out."*

Colm went after Henry.

Major John Pitcairn was taken by boat back to Boston and put to bed in a house on Prince Street. General Gage sent a loyalist town physician, Dr. Thomas Kast, to tend to Pitcairn.

"Where are you hurt?" Dr. Kast asked as he sat in a chair at John's bedside.

Pitcairn's hand hovered over the wound to his chest. "Here."

"Let me have a look. The wound may not be fatal."

"No. I know that I am bleeding internally and will die soon."

"Major, you must let me—"

"Please, do not touch me until I set my affairs in order."

The young doctor agreed to Pitcairn's request.

Several hours later, after his affairs had been settled, he agreed to submit to Dr. Kast's examination. When Kast pulled Pitcairn's waistcoat away from his chest, blood gushed out. It splashed the doctor's face, soaked the bed linens, and stained the wooden floor.

Major John Pitcairn hemorrhaged to death while his son, William, looked on in a state of shocked horror.

Henry repossessed his strong, virile thirty-nine-year-old human vessel. He stood over Michael and Patrick's sleeping bodies and looked down upon them. Patrick lay on top of Michael as if he were protecting him. Henry found the angels' position particularly erotic.

His breeches tightened as his erection swelled. The palm of his right hand tingled as he recalled squeezing Michael's crotch, and the sound Michael made in painful response. He kneeled, rolled Patrick off Michael and onto his back, and thought, *He is as beautiful as the archangel's brother. Perhaps I will enjoy them both.*

"I know you are here, archangel, and you are watching. Your presence pleases me," Henry said as he straddled Michael's naked hips. He gazed down at Michael's sleeping face and said to Colm, "We have both finally learned what we value in the children of man. It is a shame that you will not exist long enough to enjoy your lessons."

The heat from Colm's vehemence shimmered as he hovered above Charlestown peninsula. It took every ounce of willpower he had to heed his palimpsest and remain a spectator. He thought of Joseph's last sexual encounter. It had been with Margaret Gage on Joseph's birthday. *It was a part of Joseph's being, and I tried to block it out of my mind,* Colm thought in shame. *I did the same thing to Ian when Sidonie came with him to Boston. I was blinded by my need to overprotect them.*

Henry slid his hands over Michael's bare bruised chest. *I caused those bruises,* he thought with elation. He traced the edges of the darkening bruises with an index finger. His erection throbbed. His hands slid over Michael's filthy cheeks and his fingers entangled in Michael's dirty hair. Henry's heart and erection throbbed in an orchestrated rhythm. One hand untangled from Michael's locks. Henry ripped open the front of his breeches and freed his erection.

God's wrath thundered. His demons were forbidden to copulate with angels.

Deaf to God's warning, Henry bent to kiss Michael cheeks. Blinded by lust, his mouth moved to the angel's neck. His lips lingered on the Sigil of Lucifer tattooed there.

God's ire shook the universe. His demons were banned from the Gates of Hell and forbidden to worship Lucifer. Not only was the demon leader disobeying his commandments, the demon had failed to destroy the archangel and all of his brotherhood.

Colm sensed the black hole of God's wrath open. He had wrongly assumed by rejecting Heaven, his spirit could no longer sense God. What Colm sensed at that moment made his spirit burn with dread. He was about to die because Henry had disobeyed God just as Ian, Michael, and Seamus had done. Colm tried to harness his gold radiance. His palimpsest warned him one last time to remain a spectator to Henry's disobedience. It whispered, *"Ya will have to sacrifice yaself after all."*

Henry's lips parted and the tip of his tongue tasted Michael's neck. He moaned as his tongue roamed down Michael's chest and abdomen and hips. Henry stroked his erection with one hand while his other slid over Michael's crotch and slipped beneath the torn fabric. He viciously ripped Michael's breeches.

Colm lost control of any restraint he had ever possessed. His unleashed spirit flew at Henry.

Henry tried to roll Michael over onto his stomach.

The black hole of God's fury opened wide and unleashed a tempest that pulled the demon leader and the archangel into the dark pit of purgatory.

FORTY-FOUR

Michael woke in confusion. His body hurt so bad that he exhaled a cry of pain. The sun's rays blinded him, and his eyes watered. He lifted his hands to wipe his eyes. Agony exploded in his broken wrists. It knocked the wind out of him, and for a moment, he couldn't breathe. He thought, *I need to leave this vessel, but I can't remember how.*

He heard a woman ask, "What is your name? Were you in the battle?"

Michael's hand dropped to his chest with a renewed burst of pain. He blinked. A young woman was looking down at him. Her face was blurred by the early morning sun that shined like a halo around her head.

"Go away," Michael groaned.

The woman repeated her questions.

"Patrick, where are ya?" Michael rolled onto his stomach. Pain roared in his ears when he tried to get to his hands and knees. "PATRICK! WHERE ARE YA? PATRICK!" He tried in vain to sense Colm.

"He is badly wounded," a man observed.

"PATRICK!"

"Patrick must be the man lying beside him," another man said.

Michael's roaring pain quieted enough for him to hear a familiar voice speak to the people surrounding him. He tried again to get to his knees, only to collapse into the damp grass. He shouted, "John Warren? Is that ya, John?"

"Yes, it is me." John kneeled beside the angel. His eyes traveled over Michael's bruised shoulders and back. He took note of Michael's swollen, bruised, and deformed broken wrists.

"Can you get up?" John asked.

"No. Where's Patrick?"

"Look to your left. He is there beside you." John glanced at Patrick who, unbeknownst to him, still slept under the spell of his archangel.

425

Michael turned his head and saw Patrick sprawled face up on the ground. "Is he dead?"

John moved to examine Patrick. He pressed a finger against the inside of one of Patrick's wrists and detected a pulse. "He is unconscious."

"Dr. Warren," the woman looking down at Michael, said. "Please, let us help. The man who is awake looks badly hurt, and he will not tell us his name."

John looked up. He recognized twenty-two-year old Ann Schotts. She had enticing bright blue eyes and midnight black hair like the rest of the Schotts family. The Schotts and the Warrens were long-time acquaintances. Although the Schotts lived just down the road in Somerville, Joseph Warren was their family physician.

"His name is Michael Bohannon, and yes, I will need your help, Ann." John tilted his head. "He is Patrick Cullen."

"We don't need their help," Michael snapped. His wings rustled. He had an urge to cleanse his cheeks and neck. A handful of dirt ground into his skin or a hard slap would suffice. Anything to change the way his cheeks and neck felt.

John ignored Michael's protest. "If we get you to your feet do you think you can stand?"

Michael nodded. Grass rubbed against his right cheek. He turned his head and laid his left cheek in the grass. He nodded again. His cheeks felt a little better.

Ann's older brothers, Elbert and Duncan, and her father, Simon, helped John lift Michael and set him on his feet.

Michael wobbled then steadied himself. The extent of his injuries became shockingly clear to the people surrounding him. His shoulders, back, arms, chest, abdomen, hands, and cheeks were covered in blackening bruises and streaks of dried bloody mud and gunpowder. Blades of grass stuck to his filthy cheeks. There was a gash on his forehead.

Ann averted her eyes from Michael's torn breeches.

"Those are not just battle wounds, Michael. Someone beat you. Who?" John asked.

"He didn't beat me." What Henry had done to him in the redoubt was a terrifying blur of pain for which he had no words.

"You are in physical pain, which I know is impossible for an angel. Who hurt you?"

Michael shivered in the hot June morning. He managed to release his aura to comfort himself. "Henry did."

"You are one of the angels?" Duncan asked Michael with wide-eyed reverence.

In response, Michael edged away from Duncan and toward John.

"Tend to Patrick," Simon said to John. "We will look after Michael so he does not collapse." Simon noted John's shaking hands. "What is it, John?"

John looked at Michael, then down at Patrick. They were all little brothers whose big brothers were missing. His voice quivered so intensely that the Schotts had difficulty understanding him.

"Has…anyone…seen…Joseph?"

"Do not say he was in the battle!" Ann blurted out. She covered her mouth with one hand to keep from saying anything more, lest she reveal the secret sexual desire she had for Dr. Joseph Warren.

"I have only arrived from Salem," John said. He calmed himself as he knew Joseph would want him to do when faced with something so horrible. "I have heard reports that my brother is missing as is Michael's brother, Colm, and Patrick's brother, Seamus."

Michael suffered under a new wave of pain that coursed through every inch of his human vessel. His knees buckled, and he collapsed. The Schotts men caught him and kept him upright.

"We have not seen Joseph," Elbert said. "We are unfamiliar with—Oh! Colm is the archangel!"

John turned and kneeled beside Patrick. He was able to hide his tears while he tried to rouse the sleeping angel.

Patrick woke in the same state of confusion in which Michael had awakened. The sun glared in Patrick's eyes as he looked up. "John Warren?"

John nodded. "Are you able to stand?"

"Aye." Patrick's spirit was drained of energy. He struggled for a moment before he was able to get to his feet. A vision of what Henry had done to Seamus and Ian nearly knocked him back down.

John grasped him by the shoulders to steady him.

Tears rolled down Patrick's cheeks. "I saw Henry break Seamus' and Ian's neck. I can't sense them anymore."

A sob hitched in John's throat. He asked, "What of Joseph and Colm?"

"I don't know."

Michael shed the Schotts' helping hands then huddled beside Patrick.

"I cain't sense Colm cain you?" Patrick asked Michael.

Michael's pouty lips quivered. His blue aura blinked brightly then went out. "I can't sense any of us."

Patrick's wings unfurled. Silver crystals showered the ground and drifted against the Schotts' legs. He tried to furl them, but he couldn't control them. He glanced at Michael, and said to John, "I'm dyin' of thirst. I know Michael is, too."

"Go fetch water, Ann," Simon Schotts said. When Ann had gone, he asked, "When was the last time you boys ate?"

The angels shrugged.

"Come home with us so you can eat and rest for a while," Simon offered.

The angels looked at John and huddled closer together.

John had learned a great deal about the angels from Joseph. He understood their apprehension. "That is kind of you Simon, but I want them to come with me so we can look for our missing brothers together."

Ann returned with a pitcher of water. She offered it to Patrick. After he helped Michael to drink from it, he quenched his thirst and tried to hand the pitcher back to her. Instead of taking it from him, she stared at him.

Patrick was reminded of the day the angels stood around the fire pit in the backyard of the Greystoke Inn. Jane Greystoke had poised a pitcher of rum in mid-air and stared at Brandon with passion. The memory saddened Patrick. His wings furled.

"Your eyes are gray," Ann said. She had not meant to say the words out loud, but the angel was so beautiful that she had not been able to restrain herself. "I have never seen gray eyes. They are enchanting. *You* are enchanting."

"Ann, mind yourself," Elbert warned.

Patrick's instinct was to cast his eyes downward and shrink from her, but he inadvertently offered a shy smile. Ann returned the smile and took the pitcher from his outstretched hand.

"Shall we go?" John asked the angels.

"Wait," Simon Schotts said. He pulled his tunic over his head and held it out to Michael. "Do not go half-naked. The British will jeer at you. Do not allow them that opportunity."

Patrick took the tunic from Simon and slipped it over Michael's head. Michael gave Patrick a miserable look before he slid his wrists through the sleeve holes. The tunic was long enough that it covered Michael's badly torn breeches.

"Please. Wait. I must know," Simon begged the angels. "My wife, Priscilla, died giving birth to Ann. Does her soul rest in Heaven?"

"We cain't answer that," Patrick said. "God don't talk to us no more."

The three little brothers turned their backs on the Schotts and walked the short distance to Charlestown Neck.

Fergus and Brandon were almost to the farm when Colm put them to sleep. Abe and Gordon found them lying on the road and carried them home. When the late morning sun's rays filtered through the windows, both angels woke from where they slept on the living room floor.

Brandon lay awake and stared at the ceiling until Fergus stirred and sat up. "I can sense Michael and Patrick, but Colm, Seamus, and Ian are a void," Brandon said quietly.

Fergus stood up. His ponytail had come loose from its ribbon. He ran his hands through his thick blond hair.

Brandon wiped his dirty face with his dirty shirt sleeve and got to his feet.

A sudden banging on the farmhouse door startled the angels.

"General Driscoll, are you in there?"

Fergus wiped a hand across his eyes. "I can't sense Colm, Seamus or Ian, either."

"General Driscoll! Please, open up if you are there!"

The angels gave one another a long look, then Fergus opened the front door.

Captain Enos Woodbury and three provincial soldiers stood on the front porch. Relief shined on their young faces.

"General!" Enos exclaimed. "Are you alright?"

"Yes."

"The word has spread that we lost many men during the battle yesterday. Some are saying that Dr. Joseph Warren and your archangel, Colm Bohannon, died at Bunker Hill."

"That's why I can't sense him," Fergus whispered.

"Sir?"

Fergus' eyes shifted and focused on the men approaching from behind Captain Woodbury. Gordon and Abe were returning from a hunt. They mounted the porch and walked past the soldiers.

Before he went in the house, Abe stopped and said to Fergus, "We need to talk."

Fergus motioned for Captain Woodbury and the other provincials to come inside. Abe dropped his bag containing the spoils from the hunt. Brandon sat on a couch. His spirit was churning with dread. Fergus shut the door.

Abe looked at each man in the room before he said, "Joseph is dead."

Joseph Warren had become America's first martyr. His death would inspire the patriots to keep fighting a war they had tried to avoid.

Brandon put his head in his hands.

"Then, the rumors *are* true," Captain Woodbury exclaimed. "How?"

"Robert Percy shot…shot him in the face," Abe said. "In turn, Gordon killed Robert."

Brandon raised his head. *The despicable demon is finally dead.*

Captain Woodbury and the soldiers were aware of what Henry and Robert were. Fergus had spoken the truth weeks ago.

"Brandon and I can't sense Colm, Seamus, or Ian," Fergus said. His cheeks dimpled in misery.

"Their human vessels are lying in the redoubt," Gordon said quietly. "Abe and I have no way of knowing what happened to their spirits."

"I promised Colm that I would take care of us if he didn't…survive. Michael and Patrick are alive. Brandon and I need to find them."

"We would like to stay and wait for your return, if that is alright with you and your family, General Driscoll," Captain Woodbury said.

Abe spoke for Fergus, "It would please us more than you know. We have plenty of beer and rum." He reached for his bag of rabbit and quail from the hunt. "And we have supper."

∼

Beyond the crossroads on the western end of Charlestown Neck, a British blockade surprised John, Patrick, and Michael. A sentry aggressively stepped toward them and shouted, "You cannot pass!"

"Please, I have come to find my brother," John said humbly.

The sentry looked at the bedraggled angels and curled his lip in disgust. "Perhaps, if you had not brought these swains with you I would have allowed you to pass." He swept his bayonet up and pressed the sharp tip into John's breast. "Leave!"

"I will not leave! You must let us pass to find our fallen brothers!"

The sentry shoved his bayonet into John's chest.

Blood bloomed on John's waistcoat, and he grimaced in pain.

"YA STABBED HIM?" Michael screamed in disbelief. "I'LL KILL YA!" He ran at the sentry and threw his arms around the sentry's waist. They both fell hard onto the ground.

"No, Michael! Get off him!" Patrick yelled.

He and John tried to pull Michael off before the other sentries got to him. They lost their grip and stumbled backward when he threw his torso upward and tightened his thighs around the sentry's hips and waist. Michael slammed his elbow into the sentry's nose.

The sentry screamed and tried to push Michael off by jamming the palms of his hands into Michael's chest.

Two sentries seized Michael by the arms, but his hysteria was stronger than the sentries' will to restrain him. He jerked his arms away then slammed his elbow into the sentry's cheekbone. The bone shattered and blood spurted from the sentry's eye. The skin on Michael's elbow split open. Drops of blood spattered the sentry's already bloody face. The sentry blacked out.

A sentry tried to restrain Michael's arms again. Patrick kicked the sentry under the chin. The man's head snapped up. He fell backward and sprawled onto the ground.

John saw the third sentry release the sear on his pistol and aim it at Michael's face. He screamed, "NO!"

At that moment, Michael's wings unfurled. Patrick's wings unfurled in response.

The stunned sentry dropped his pistol. He and the sentry, who was still standing, made eye contact then they turned and ran.

Michael raised his elbow. Patrick blocked it before Michael could pummel the unconscious sentry again.

"Michael, stop it!" Patrick yelled.

John clasped Michael's wrists, hoping the pain would get his attention. "Michael, look at me! LOOK AT ME!"

Michael's green eyes focused on John's face.

"Let it go," John said. "They have gone to get reinforcements. We cannot help our brothers if we are dead."

Pain flooded Michael's body and spirit. John's blue eyes looked so much like Joseph's eyes. Michael looked down at the bloodied and broken face of the sentry and spit on him.

Michael refused Patrick's and John's offer to help him stand. He furled his wings and struggled to his feet. Patrick's wings furled in response.

431

The three little brothers left Charlestown Neck. The young men stopped at the crossroads.

John's eyes misted over and betrayed his self-control. "I cannot tell my brothers and my mother that Joseph is dead unless I see his body." John's breath caught in his throat. "If he *is* dead, his children are orphans."

The angels didn't know what to say in response. Their wings rustled.

John heard the rustling just as Joseph had heard it when he first met Colm and Fergus in the basement of the Green Dragon Tavern. "Joseph loved all of you with an intensity I did not know existed," John said. He blinked hard to stave off his tears. "What are you going to do now?"

"Go back to the farm and try to find Brandon and Fergus," Patrick said.

John smiled at the beautiful angels. "What our brothers had together was a miracle. I will never forget you." He turned and walked toward Cambridge before the weight of what had happened on Breed's Hill collapsed in on him.

Michael stumbled and fell on the walk to Roxbury. Patrick did his best to support Michael so they could continue their journey, but both boys began to tire from hunger, anguish, and desperation. A mile from the farm, Michael fell for the last time.

He fell near the spot where the boys had passed out the night they had gotten drunk with William Dawes and Paul Revere at the Green Dragon, while Liam disobeyed his archangel and revealed his wings and aura to Abigail Adams. Like Liam had done that night in February, Patrick sat on the road and guarded Colm's little brother.

On this long June day, the sun took its time arching across the sky toward the western horizon. There was still so much sadness and misery to illuminate before the Earth turned another rotation to plunge the people of New England into a disconsolate night.

"Go on to the farm, Patrick," Michael said from where he lay on the dusty road. "Maybe, Brandon or Fergus is there."

"I ain't leavin' you."

Michael finally understood human suffering, and it was so much worse than he had ever imagined. "Do ya remember how to leave ya vessel?" he asked.

Patrick shook his head.

"Me either. I wish Henry had killed me."

Patrick shut his eyes and wished that Henry had killed both of them.

A warm breeze fluttered the angels' curly black hair. Patrick sensed Fergus and Brandon before they touched him. He opened his eyes. Fergus hooked his hands behind Patrick's head, pulled him close, and rocked him like a mother who had discovered her abandoned infant naked and cold.

Brandon knelt beside Michael, stroked his filthy cheeks, and kissed his bloodied forehead.

Fergus urged Patrick to his feet.

"Michael's vessel is in pain," Patrick said. "Robert and Henry got to him."

Michael bit his lips to keep from screaming when Fergus and Brandon lifted him into their arms. Mercifully, he blacked out.

FORTY-FIVE

Two days passed before Michael awakened in the bed where Colm used to sleep. His body was stiff, sore, filthy, and stripped of clothes. He felt exhausted and incapable of getting out of bed. The smell of urine didn't deter the fact that, above all, he was starving.

"Colm, where are ya?" he whispered. His eyes swept the alcove that served as Colm's bedroom above stairs in the farmhouse. The steps from the living room creaked and groaned. Michael turned his head toward the sound.

Patrick came into view. He sat on the bed with a jug of rum in his hands. "Drink as much as you cain," he said to Michael. "We're gonna tend to you. Before we do that, I wanna talk to you."

Michael let Patrick tip the jug to his lips, and he drank. He laid his head back on the bed and waited for Patrick to speak.

Thanks to the rum, Fergus, Brandon, Patrick, and Gordon got Michael downstairs, bathed, and into clean clothing without hurting him too much. When he was settled on a couch in the living room, they gathered around and ate the supper Abe had prepared. Patrick fed Michael then he ate his own supper.

Fergus drank from the jug of rum and held it out to Patrick. Patrick didn't acknowledge the offered jug.

"What is it?" Fergus asked.

Patrick's downcast eyes regarded Michael before he looked at Fergus and said, "Me and Michael is goin' back to Burkes Garden."

"NO! THE FOUR OF US IS ALL THAT'S LEFT!" Brandon shouted. "And you can't possibly take care of Michael on a journey that long!"

Fergus winced as if someone had slapped his face.

Abe and Gordon exchanged grievous looks.

Patrick sat beside Michael on the couch. "Do you think we wanna leave you?" Patrick cried. The pain in his spirit was almost debilitating.

Brandon did something angels had never done—he begged. "Don't do this! I can't go with you! I can't go back to the place where we lived so happily for all those years. How can you do this?"

"Do you think this is what Colm would want?" Fergus asked.

"Colm's dead," Michael said. "I feel empty without him. Patrick and I can't go on without our brothers. We need to be in the place where we felt safe."

"Don't go!" Brandon pleaded. He looked at Fergus for support, but he saw only sorrow in Fergus' eyes. "You're gonna let them go? Why?"

"They need to heal. I can't soothe them the way Colm cou'd," Fergus said. "Let them go, Brandon. It's the only way we can help them."

Brandon wiped a hand across his watering eyes, and asked Patrick, "How are you gonna take care of Michael? He can't even ride a horse."

Abe set his plate aside. "I will go with you. I have nothing keeping me here. My farm can go back to the land."

"You'd do that for us?" Patrick asked, shocked.

Abe shrugged. "Why not? Jeremiah's there. I assume you have a place to live, and if you do not, then we will build one." The truth was he, too, needed to leave Massachusetts to find a place where he could live in peace. The idea of carving out a new life was comforting.

Fergus thought of the rundown three-room cabin the angels had lived in in Burkes Garden. It was a far cry from what he had become accustomed to living in Dillaway House. He would give anything to live in that cabin with his brotherhood again, but the brotherhood was gone. He had fulfilled his aspiration to become the general of a human army because Colm had allowed it. Somehow, he felt that Colm would be disappointed if he turned his back on his achievement to return to a place he no longer belonged.

"Brandon, the Committee of Safety made you a lieutenant last March," Abe said. "Why not take advantage of it? You cou'd stay here under Fergus' command."

Brandon wrinkled his nose as if the suggestion stank.

"We ain't dyin'," Patrick reminded him. "We're just goin' to Burkes Garden. Maybe, when we feel stronger, we'll come back to Roxbury."

Brandon nodded, although he was uncertain of what he was in agreement with.

"Gordon, wou'd you consider coming with us?" Abe asked.

Gordon hated himself for allowing Robert Percy to live long enough to kill Joseph. He hated that the family he had come to love was in shambles. He hated everything that happened on Breed's Hill despite the Sigil of Lucifer. The only way he could make something good from all that hatred was to return to what he was doing before he met Colm Bohannon.

He said, "I have the business of revenge to get back to."

"Killing demons from Hell?" Fergus asked.

"Yes."

"Is there a chance that I can get you to join the provincial army and stay with me and Brandon?"

"Maybe, but not now. I have to be on my own for a while before I lay my heart and soul out for a cause or a—" Gordon's laugh sounded like a man who was trying to stifle a sob. "—or a family."

Paul Revere and William Dawes came to the farm to quietly mourn Joseph and the lost angels, and to say goodbye to those who were leaving.

Paul was surprised at the depth of the loss he felt for Colm, Seamus, and Ian. He did not realize what an integral part of the patriotic cause they had become. In their innocent manner, the angels had taught him that life held secrets unimagined and that men had choices beyond what society taught. Above all, he realized that they had become loyal friends he would dearly miss.

And there was an opportunity Paul seized upon with fatherly satisfaction. As a silversmith, he occasionally fashioned teething rings and pacifiers for children of the very wealthy. Thanks to a colleague in Dorchester, who had the materials available in his silversmith shop, Paul had crafted a pacifier from silver and adorned it with red coral. The smooth coral satisfied the baby's urge to suck. The bells and whistles attached to the end of the pacifier satisfied the baby's urge to scream.

Paul entrusted the delivery of the gift for Jeremiah's son to Abe.

William Dawes was much more open and unsurprised about his melancholy mood. He thought of Joseph as he watched Gordon and Fergus lift Michael up until he was able to slide the toe of his left boot into the stirrup. From where he sat in the saddle, Abe slipped his hands under Michael's arms. Michael pushed himself up while Abe pulled him into the saddle to sit in front of him.

Brandon tethered the horse, which he hoped Michael would eventually be able to ride, to Patrick's saddle horn.

Fergus double checked the saddlebags on all three horses for food, rum, water, and ammunition. Patrick, Michael, and Abe had muskets strapped over their backs. Colm had told Brandon to let Jeremiah take all the ammunition left at the farm, but Jeremiah had refused to take something so precious from his angels.

Everything that could possibly be said, every tear that could possibly be shed, and every sentiment that could possibly be conveyed was exhausted. There was nothing to do now but let them go. Fergus, Brandon, Gordon, William, and Paul stood in the road and watched until they were out of sight. It was the last day they would spend on the farm.

The Gage's stood on Long Wharf under a stunningly clear late June sky. The *Charming Nancy* tugged at her moorings. The ship swayed on the continuous swell of wakes and the outgoing tide.

"I am sorry, Margaret."

"There is nothing to apologize for, Thomas. I know you are looking out for us by sending us away from the misery of smallpox and food shortages that the people of this besieged town are suffering. I suppose we have both grown weary of Boston."

There were so many people dying in Boston that Thomas had ordered the city's death bells silenced.

Three Gage children followed their nanny and boarded the ship. Constance McCaskey, lingered near the Gage's for a moment, then she too boarded. Margaret had promised to keep Constance's pregnancy a secret for as long as possible. Constance had confirmed what Margaret already suspected—General Henry Hereford was the father.

And General Hereford and his aide-de-camp were listed as missing after the Battle of Bunker Hill.

"I'm looking forward to seeing our daughters again," Margaret said. "I received a letter from Maria only yesterday. She writes that they are doing well. She and several other girls from school traveled to London to see *Romeo and Juliet.*"

She forced a smile and offered the letter to Thomas.

Thomas took the folded letter from Margaret's hands. Sweat bloomed on his forehead and under his arms. His courage to send his pregnant wife back to England without him seemed to be dwindling. He had not been able to gather an ounce of courage to tell Margaret that Joseph Warren had died at Bunker Hill because he feared her reaction to the news.

Margaret and the children were eating breakfast in the garden at Province House when she received the news of Joseph's death. A brief note had been delivered to her by an unknown messenger.

From where he stood at his office window, Thomas had watched her unfold the small unsigned piece of paper. She gently laid a hand on her swelling belly and read the note. Her eyes widened, and her mouth dropped open. The note slipped from her hand and fluttered to the ground. Thomas heard her agonized lament. Tears coursed down her cheeks and trickled into her open mouth. She aspirated the salty tears and choked on them. The memory would never fade from his mind.

Thomas held his daughter's letter in his sweating hands. *I should care about Maria's letter. But after everything that has happened, I cannot concentrate on nor validate anything that does not serve to soothe what Margaret and I have been through.*

Margaret stroked Thomas' long cheek. It was uncharacteristically rough with beard stubble. She looked into his droopy brown eyes. Those eyes were the reason she had admitted to him that the child she carried could be Joseph Warren's child. She had to be able to look Thomas in the eye and know she had nothing to hide.

"I expect you to be a kind man." She briefly touched her belly. "This child is without sin. She deserves your love just as our other children do."

Margaret is right. The child is innocent, Thomas thought. "I will join you in England as soon as I can. And I promise I will be a good father—"

Margaret kissed him on the lips to silence his words. He returned her kiss. She turned and boarded *The Charming Nancy.*

≈

Mercy Scollay disbelieved the initial news that Joseph and Colm were dead. The message, from Elbridge Gerry, read that neither Joseph nor Colm had attended the Committee of Safety meeting in Watertown on the afternoon of June 19.

"Joseph was probably not feeling well," she told herself on the morning of June 20 as she held the message in her damp, shaking hand. "He is prone to headaches. Yes, that must be the reason he did not attend the meeting."

When news arrived that they were indeed dead, Mercy took to her bed. Dorothy Dix was left to care for her two children and Joseph's children.

A recurring nightmare haunted Mercy. She dreamed that she was with Joseph visiting the places they often went together. When she turned to speak to him, he was not by her side. Her eyes searched every face. She screamed his name. He was just gone.

The dream upset her to the point that she fought off sleep until she was so exhausted that sleep easily got its way. As the insufferable hours turned to days, she became more and more numb—incapable of drawing on a single emotion except grief.

A new dream intruded in on her sleep. The angels came to rescue her and the children from the Dix house and take them back to Boston and the house on Hanover Street. On the journey, the angel named Seamus collapsed and died. Joseph and Colm appeared to escort Seamus to Heaven. Mercy tried to speak to them but they did not acknowledge her. She reached to touch Joseph's cheek. When her fingers brushed his skin, he burst into flames.

She began to fear for his afterlife. *Has Joseph been granted entry into Heaven despite his loyalty to the banished angels whom he loved so much?*

Five days after Mercy took to her bed, Dorothy Dix entered her bedroom uninvited. She sat on the edge of the bed and grasped Mercy's thin hand. "You must tell the children that their father is dead," Dorothy said gently. "It is not my place. They are asking questions: Elizabeth and Joseph, in particular. They are frightened because your behavior is out of the ordinary."

Tears flooded Mercy's eyes, and she wished she could drown in them.

Dorothy swept loose locks of hair away from Mercy's wet cheeks, and said, "Elizabeth is also asking about the angels. Mercy, you must pull yourself together and take care of his children as he would expect you to do."

Mercy threw her arms around Dorothy's shoulders and sobbed into her neck. "How am I to live without him?"

Dorothy gathered her in her arms. The women cried in their miserable embrace.

FORTY-SIX

CONCORD, MASSACHUSETTS
JULY 1775

D r. Samuel Prescott looked up from his account book. Tatoson was standing in the study doorway.

"Come in," Samuel said. He closed the book and stood up.

Tatoson remained where he was. "My grandmother has died. I am leaving Massachusetts."

Samuel folded his arms over his chest and frowned, "You are running away," he stated.

"I am to be wed. I am following her people, the Nantucket."

The truth was that the death of Joseph Warren and the angels was more than he could bear. He knew he was not hiding it well because Samuel was studying him with mournful eyes that reflected Tatoson's inner feelings. They were both suffering from an inability to cope. It would ease with time, but in the meanwhile, time stretched out before them.

"I suppose I should propose to Lydia," Samuel said. There were often stretches of months, sometimes years, when Tatoson and he did not see one another. Yet, Tatoson's announcement saddened him. Samuel was losing a brother, just as Michael and Patrick had lost their brothers.

Tatoson said nothing.

"Where is the Nantucket migrating to?" Samuel asked.

"West of the English man's war. We will not make the same mistake as our ancestors did during King Philip's war."

"What is her name? The woman you are to wed."

440

"Assawetoug. I have already given her a child."

The ensuing silence between Samuel and Tatoson stretched out heavily. Then, they were embracing one another with no memory of crossing the room to do so.

≈

Word of the Battle of Bunker Hill reached the Second Continental Congress on July 2. Abigail Adams' letter to John arrived two days later.

As Patrick Henry and Thomas Jefferson, delegates from Virginia, debated about tactics the southern colonies should take in response to what had happened in Massachusetts, John Adams opened the letter from Abigail. The paper on which it was written was tear-stained. Her handwriting appeared to be uncharacteristically untidy, and the paper was blotched with ink here and there. A numbing dread spread in John's heart.

"Now, that we have dispatched George Washington to Cambridge to set up headquarters and form a cohesive provincial army…"

Thomas Jefferson's voice faded from John's mind as he read his wife's despairing words:

> *The Day: perhaps the decisive day is come on which the fate of America depends. My bursting heart must find vent at my pen. I have just heard that our dear friend Dr. Warren is no more but fell gloriously fighting for his country-saying better to die honourably in the field than ignominiously hang upon the gallows. The angels Colm, Seamus, and Ian have fallen with him. Great is our loss…and the tears of multitudes pay tribute to their memory…*

John did not realize he had exhaled a cry of anguished grief even after Samuel Adams and John Hancock attended him with distress. He crumpled the letter into a ball and tightened his hand around it like it was a noxious animal that deserved to die because of its mere existence.

Samuel's voice quivered. He found he was unable to raise it above a whisper when he asked, "What is it, John?"

John released the crumpled paper and the horrible words written upon it.

John Hancock, the ever conceited, extremely wealthy merchant, and loyal patriot watched the balled-up letter drop to the table. The paper was heavy with sweat and grief from John Adams' hand and heart.

John Adams rose and stormed from the room. The delegates of the

Continental Congress silenced. Samuel and John Hancock looked at one another with anticipated horror. Then, Samuel scooped the letter from the table and smoothed the paper so he could read it. John looked on and silently read the words with Samuel.

"What news?" Thomas Jefferson tentatively asked Samuel.

Samuel crumpled the letter into a ball and threw it blindly away. Then, he, too, stormed from the room.

There was no mistaking among the delegates that the news John Adams received was greatly afflicting. The men had heard rumors of angels fighting with the patriots in Massachusetts. They had heard whispers of Dr. Joseph Warren's affiliation with those angels. Whether or not they doubted the rumors made no difference. Abigail Adams' letter had confirmed the existence of Warren's angels.

"Please, John, what news?" Thomas Jefferson asked with thoughtful tentativeness and respect.

John Hancock rose from his chair. He swallowed hard against the tide of grief that wanted to wash his sensibilities away. The self-control he called upon to allow him to say the words without sobbing was something he did not know he possessed. "We have lost our dear friend, Dr. Joseph Warren, and three of his angels."

FORTY-SEVEN

BURKES GARDEN, VIRGINIA

SEPTEMBER 1775

The first autumn chill arrived on September 27. The wood pile was nearly as high as the cabin's outside walls. Jeremiah had chopped wood all day. As the sun dropped lower in the western sky, his chore was done. White smoke curled from the cabin's chimney and snaked into the pink and orange cloud-streaked sky.

Inside the cabin, Mkwa prepared supper. She kept one eye on her task and the other eye on the fussing three-month-old baby lying on a blanket on the floor near the fireplace. He was practicing his new ability to roll from his back to his stomach with great impatience.

Jeremiah cleaned the axe blade then turned to go inside the cabin. The sound of horses picking their way through the dense white oak and hickory forest surrounding the cabin was cause for alarm. Since Bunker Hill, some colonists were moving west, out of the reach of King George III's long arm and the horrors of war. Not all those who passed through Burkes Garden were friendly.

He tightened his grip on the axe and rested it against his shoulder.

Unsteady soft words floated from the edge of the woods that fronted the cabin.

"I can do it myself."

"No, you cain't."

"Stop treating me like a baby."

"You're gonna fall like you did last time and hurt yourself—again."

"I'm going to fall *on* ya if ya don't move."

"I ain't movin'."

Jeremiah recognized the listless voices. He leaned the axe against the cabin wall and ran across the dirt yard to the edge of the woods. He saw Michael sitting astride a horse and looking down at Patrick with dull dissatisfaction. Patrick stood beside Michael's horse with his arms stretched up in a gesture that was meant to say, *I'll catch you if you fall.* Jeremiah had seen the boys go for months without bathing or covered in gunpowder, dirt, and blood from a battle, but they were beyond unwashed or battlefield dirty.

A third horse picked its way through the underbrush. Jeremiah saw that the horse's rider was Abe.

Abe reined his horse and slowly dismounted. It had been days since he and the angels had eaten. They were on the verge of becoming trapped in a vicious circle of starvation and what starvation did to weaken their capacity to feed themselves.

The boys gotta know they've arrived at my cabin. They cain see it if they turn their heads, Jeremiah thought as he approached them with caution.

The boys stopped arguing and looked his way with lackluster eyes. Patrick focused on Jeremiah, but he didn't move or smile.

"Don't you recognize me?" Jeremiah asked.

Patrick and Michael made lifeless eye contact. Despondency had been slowly killing them for months. Soon, it would have its way.

Abe wondered if he should do something to stir the boys' memories, but he could not muster the mental strength to figure it out. He watched in a dumb stupor.

Jeremiah was hesitant to move toward the angels for fear of their reaction. He asked again, "Patrick, don't you recognize me?"

Patrick stared at Jeremiah for a moment. Finally, recognition sparked in his eyes. "Jeremiah?"

"It's me."

Patrick ran to him. Jeremiah caught Patrick in an embrace. He clasped the back of Patrick's head and buried his face in Patrick's matted hair.

Patrick wrapped his arms around Jeremiah's waist. His emotions erupted and he cried out, "Joseph, Seamus, Ian, and Colm is dead!" His shoulders shook with thick sobs.

Jeremiah stroked Patrick's hair and murmured, "Shhhh." He glanced up. Michael was solemnly watching them.

Patrick tried to get a hold on himself. He wiped his wet face on the front of Jeremiah's shirt.

Michael dismounted, stumbled, and sprawled headlong onto the ground.

Jeremiah unwound Patrick's arms from his waist and went to help Michael. He asked Michael, "Are you hurt?"

"You have no idea what you are asking," Abe said to Jeremiah in a tone as dull as the angels' eyes.

Together, they hauled Michael to his feet. Jeremiah grasped Abe's hand and pulled him into a brief embrace. "It's good ta see you." He paused and a small smile skimmed his lips. "You've been tryin' ta take care of 'em ain't you?"

"I do not need to tell you that taking care of angels is an almost impossible task," Abe said wearily.

Jeremiah turned his attention to Michael.

Michael didn't move or speak.

Jeremiah studied Michael's dirty wan face. There were dark circles under his eyes and dark bruises were visible through the layer of gray dirt on his cheeks. Jeremiah's eyes roamed Michael's thin, frail vessel then returned to his face. "You're in physical pain, ain't you?"

Michael looked away.

"Oh Lord," Jeremiah muttered.

Mkwa opened the cabin door and stepped into the yard with her infant son in her arms. The angels' terrible physical and spiritual condition was heartrendingly obvious. She looked past them and into the woods beyond.

"We are starving," Abe said in quiet desperation.

Jeremiah turned and looked at Mkwa. She lifted her chin in the direction of the woods behind the angels and nodded.

"Let's git you fed and warmed up," Jeremiah said. Abe and he took hold of the horses' reins and led them out of the woods.

Patrick and Michael huddled together at the edge of the clearing. Jeremiah's offer of food and shelter went unnoticed. Michael's stomach cramped. He clenched his teeth and issued an involuntary grunt. His filthy face contorted with pain. He stepped back into the woods. Patrick moved with him.

Abe and Jeremiah stopped and watched them withdraw into the last remnants of their spiritual comfort—one another. Abe moved closer to Jeremiah and whispered, "Can you not see that the angels are dying? I do not know what to do to help them. I cannot give them what they need."

"Come on, Abe," Jeremiah said firmly.

With a last backward glance at the boys, Abe followed Jeremiah inside the warm cabin.

The sun dropped below the western horizon and plunged Burkes Garden into cold stark darkness.

"I hope it's over soon," Michael whispered.

"So do I," Patrick breathed.

"Do ya regret leaving Fergus and Brandon?"

"No."

"I don't either," Michael said. He pulled Patrick in closer to him. "I can't sense them anymore. I hope they didn't die."

"If we cou'd remember how to leave our vessels, wou'd you feel different about what's comin'?" Patrick asked.

Michael shook his head. "Our spirits aren't whole without our archangel."

Patrick looked up through the dwindling canopy of tree leaves. The waxing crescent moon was no competition for the brilliant starlight overhead. "We ain't been whole since Liam died."

"At least our palimpsests don't know their brothers are dead." Michael's eyes followed Patrick's gaze skyward. He knew what Patrick was wondering. They had finally stopped asking the question out loud. Only their death would provide the answer.

Michael groaned, pressed a hand on his stomach, and bent over. He reached for a low tree limb to steady himself until the pain subsided.

With grim resignation, Patrick thought, *Michael's vessel is gonna die in horrible pain. I'm gonna have to watch unless I die first.*

The boys experienced a shared illusion when the forest was suddenly bathed in green light. They heard Colm say, "I won't let either one of ya die."

Michael and Patrick couldn't comprehend the illusion of Colm's presence. They wrapped their arms around one another in deference to the death that awaited them.

"I'm here," Colm whispered to the boys. "*We* are here. Reach for our spiritual strength. I know ya haven't forgotten how."

"I hear Colm speakin' to us," Patrick sobbed. "I'm finally dyin'."

Colm unfurled his resplendent wings and enfolded his disconsolate angels in his healing spirit. "Ya aren't dying, Patrick. Calm yaself."

Michael's eyes were closed, and his forehead was pressed against the Sigil of Lucifer tattooed on Patrick's neck. He experienced the sensation of hands caressing Patrick's cheeks just before Patrick's body was pulled out of his arms.

In horror, Michael closed his eyes tighter. Then, he realized he could no longer sense Patrick. With wild terror, his eyes flew open. The illusory green light still illuminated the dark forest, but now, Michael saw purple light as well. He put his head in his shaking hands and cried.

Fingers slid under his quivering chin. They forced Michael's head out of his hands. "Look at me, Michael. I'm not an illusion."

Michael refused to believe what he was seeing. His eyes shifted toward the purple light. He saw Seamus' wings unfurl and shower the cold forest floor with silver crystals. Michael's eyes moved back to look at the angel who stood before him. He saw Colm, but he couldn't sense him.

"Ya lost contact with Patrick, didn't ya?"

Michael stared at Colm.

"Answer me, Michael."

Michael's lips quivered.

"Seamus has Patrick in the cradle of his spirit. Ya will feel him once ya both accept that we're real."

"Ian, too?" Michael asked dumbly.

"Ian's here. Let go of ya grief and ya will sense all of us. Do ya understand me?"

"Colm?"

"It's me."

Michael blinked. The sensation of Patrick's spirit came flooding back into Michael's spirit. He suddenly felt like he was falling, plummeting from one existence to another.

Colm's wings threshed. Gold radiance caught Michael's spirit, and Colm's arms caught his body. Michael succumbed, and sobbed, "I can sense ya."

They are both sick and exhausted, Colm thought. Then, he lulled the boys to sleep.

ॐ

As dawn approached, the sun peaked over the Appalachian Mountains to find the dense forest of Garden Mountain awash in green, purple, blue, and red light. In that forest, five angels slept huddled together and blanketed by their resplendent silver wings.

Colm woke first. He looked at his angels for a long time before he roused them. They had survived Henry and his demons, but at what cost?

And Michael and Patrick would have so many questions. He was ready to answer all of them—except one.

When the angels were awake, Colm sent Ian and Seamus to Jeremiah's cabin to fetch breakfast from Mkwa. Then, he turned his attention to Patrick and Michael. They were so dirty that it was impossible to assess their physical condition. Colm needed to see the damage Henry had inflicted on Michael's vessel.

He said, "Come on. Ya both need a bath."

Patrick and Michael surprised Colm by complying with his order without argument. They walked in silence through the dense forest. There was a sudden break in the tree line through which a wide shallow stream ran. The water reflected the lightening morning sky in shimmering mirages as it splashed over boulders and stones.

Michael's stomach cramped when he removed his coat. The coat, stiff and heavy with months of dirt, dried sweat, and dried mud, slipped from his hands. He grimaced and pressed the palm of his hand against his stomach.

Colm thought, *Henry has done something much worse than rape. He has somehow connected Michael's vessel and spirit. If I had known that was possible, I wou'd have forced the angels to leave their vessels two hundred years ago, when we first arrived in Burkes Garden. Now, it's too late.*

Colm washed the boys' clothes while they bathed. Clouds of swirling gray and brown dirt formed in the water; then they were swept downstream only to be replaced with new clouds as the filth of a three-month journey was washed away.

The boys' silence concerned Colm almost as much as Michael's pain.

Finally, Patrick asked, "How'd you kill Henry?"

It was the question Colm had never answered.

"We've been waitin' for months ta hear the answer," Jeremiah said.

Colm and the boys looked up.

Jeremiah stood on the bank of the stream with his son in his arms. Mkwa, Abe, Seamus, and Ian were gathered beside him.

Seamus said, "You cain't hide it no more, Colm. The damage is there for all of us to see."

All eyes shifted to Michael. Stripped of his clothes, Michael's injuries were apparent.

Colm imagined he heard Joseph say, *"You must be strong for them. Without shame or regret, tell them what happened."*

Colm nodded as if Joseph was standing beside him waiting for an acknowledgment. He said, "I didn't kill Henry. He incurred the wrath of God, and we were both thrown into purgatory."

Jeremiah shifted his son in his arms, and asked, "What did Henry do ta incur God's wrath?"

Colm avoided looking at his little brother.

"Look at Michael when you confess, Colm."

"I can't, Joseph."

"Yes, you can."

Colm's jaw was so tight that he had to work to relax it enough to speak. He looked at Michael and said, "Henry tried to copulate with an angel."

Patrick and Michael exchanged dismal glances. Then, Patrick jumped up and splashed through the water toward Colm.

Colm felt absurd relief to see that Patrick's thin and undernourished vessel was unhurt.

"DID YOU LET HENRY DO THAT TO MICHAEL?" Patrick screamed.

"NO! My palimpsest warned me to let Henry's intentions play out. I wou'd have stopped Henry if it had gotten to that point!"

Michael focused on the water flowing over his legs, and summoned a long-forgotten memory—the sensation of copulating with a human woman. His act had been consensual. Michael understood enough to realize that Henry had tried to rape him in every way possible.

"Stand down, Brother," Seamus warned. "You ain't helpin' by screamin' at Colm."

Patrick knew that Seamus was right. He forced himself to stay calm when he asked Seamus, "Where did you and Ian go when Henry killed your vessels?"

"We was thrown into purgatory, too."

Colm intervened, "It had to have something to do with the Sigil of Lucifer. Whatever it was, angels don't belong in purgatory. We were released."

"Where's Liam?" Michael asked without taking his eyes from the mesmerizing flow of the stream.

"We don't know," Seamus admitted.

"Do Brandon and Fergus know you're alive?" Abe asked.

"They know," Seamus said. "Me, Colm, and Ian went back to the farm. No one was there. We found Fergus and Brandon at Dillaway House."

Patrick's calm erupted and anger flushed his cheeks. "But you got here before we did! It took us three months to get here because we was so tired! Why didn't you look for us?"

"We spent days backtracking through the Appalachian Mountains looking for you!" Ian exclaimed. "We were racked with worry and grief! The only thing that gave us comfort was knowing Abe was with you."

Seamus recalled the walk from Breed's Hill back to Roxbury after he and Ian and Colm repossessed their dead and buried vessels. The countryside was eerily quiet that night. They experienced a haunting emptiness as they stood in the living room of the abandoned farmhouse. At that moment, Seamus had been sure Patrick was dead.

Jeremiah saw that Colm's consciousness had left the conversation. He handed his son to Mkwa, waded through the stream and garnered Colm's attention.

"Me and Joseph saw the struggles you all endured aligning with the children of man. You cried for the first time. You clung ta one another seeking comfort from confusion, doubt, and fear. Liam died. It was like watching the Romans throw innocent lambs ta the lions, yet all of you stood up under the weight of constant exposure ta human emotions."

Colm's eyes flashed hard golden light.

Jeremiah continued, "I know Joseph's death is inflicting agony on your spirit. It hurts all of us, but don't shy away from the children of man because you're afraid of the pain of lovin' 'em."

Colm said nothing.

It was what Jeremiah expected.

Mkwa noticed that Patrick was shivering. She removed the blanket draped over her shoulders and handed it to him.

Her son began to fuss in her arms. A silken thread of drool slid from the baby's mouth.

Abe fished in the inside pocket of his coat where he kept a gift, that was until now, forgotten. It was a pacifier crafted from red coral and silver. He scooped it out of his pocket and offered it to Mkwa. "This is a gift for your son from a friend—Paul Revere."

Mkwa had never seen red coral, but she had seen silver many times within the angels' wings and the crystals that rained from them. She was surprised to see that silver could become tarnished as it had on the pacifier.

"Jeremiah has spoken of Paul Revere," she said.

The baby cried out in frustration.

"May I give him the pacifier?" Abe asked Mkwa.

She nodded.

The baby took the pacifier and sucked on the red coral with contentment.

Colm remembered the first time he had seen the baby. He had asked Mkwa, "What's ya son's name?"

"I think you know his name," Mkwa had said, smiling.

Colm had nodded. *Joseph.*

FORTY-EIGHT

PORTLAND PLACE, LONDON
DECEMBER 25, 1775

Margaret's labor began in the early hours of Christmas morning. She called for her personal maid, Constance McCaskey. Constance was heavy with child. She would soon give birth to her own babe.

A few hours later, with Thomas pacing the living room, Margaret gave birth to her eighth child—a blond-haired, blue-eyed baby girl. She kissed her baby's soft cheek and sighed, "Your father was a man of great courage."

ABOUT THE AUTHOR

Salina is an avid student of Colonial America and the American Revolution. Her lifelong passion for history and all things supernatural led her to write historical fantasy. Reading, extensive traveling and graveyard prowling with her husband keep that passion alive. She has three forthcoming novels in the works for 2017. Salina lives in Austin, Texas and is a member of The Writers' League of Texas.

CPSIA information can be obtained
at www.ICGtesting.com
Printed in the USA
LVHW092027170720
660992LV00003B/330

9 780998 755809